THE HERMIT KINGDOM

SHANE RILEY ADVENTURES

BOOK 1

NICK THACKER

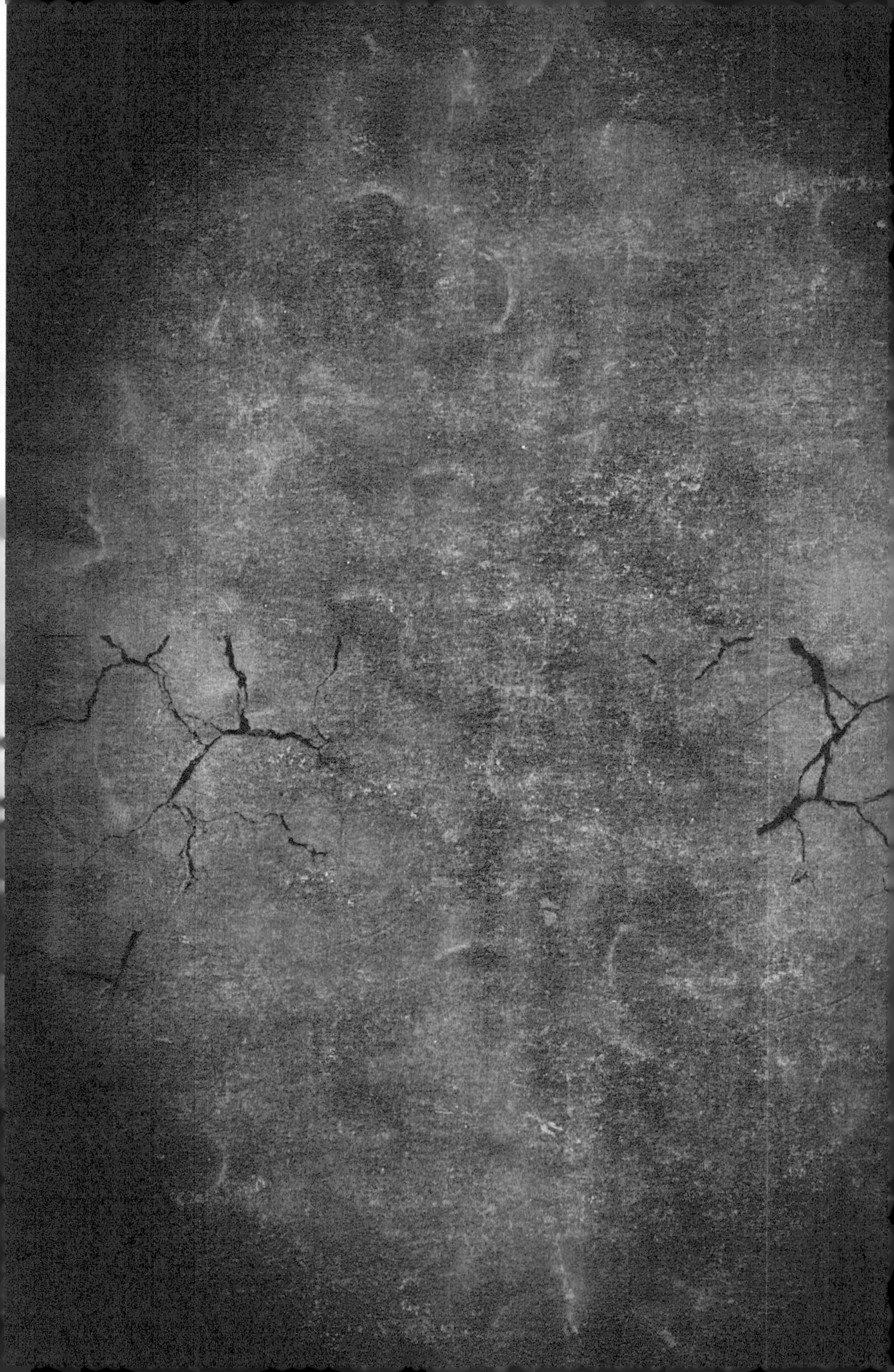

1
SHANE

SHANE RILEY'S wife was dead on the bottom of the ocean floor inside her Subaru Outback.

He dove straight down, checking his regulator and gauging his numbers as he descended. It was about a 60-foot drop, and while the shallower waters boasted vibrant, massive displays of color at the edge of the reef, the floor farther out was more barren, save for piles of large rocks and a few corals that preferred the deeper waters.

He was not alone down here. Thousands of fish swimming in schools pecked at his hands and arms as he moved through them, curious and testing to see if he was food.

In a sense, he was. He knew it was true that everything in the ocean wanted to kill him, but here off the eastern coast of Australia, it was actually quite possible. Here, everything wanted to kill him, and much of it was large enough to actually do so.

Though he was armed with a spear, it would do little damage against the beasts that roamed these waters. The great white shark was a constant threat, and there were saltwater crocodiles to worry about as well.

A few large groupers swam near enough for him to attempt to snag one, but the spear was sitting on its mount on his back, next to his dive tank. He was not here to fish.

He was here to find *her*.

Shane Riley, a former member of the Australian 2nd Commando Regiment, had long since given up the life of killing humans for his government and had chosen to settle down into a new career.

Now, he was a finder.

He found objects, artifacts, and art – whatever the person paying him wanted to find. Typically, the person paying him even knew where to look, so in those instances, Shane was more of a retriever.

He was basically a private investigator — but hunted down objects rather than people.

Never people.

His mission today reminded him why. His wife of two years had been kidnapped, strapped into the seat of her own car, then shot point-blank. Everything — car and all – had been carried out to sea and dumped into the waters off the coast of Australia.

His stomach turned just thinking about it. It had taken him another year to get to the point where he could even process the onslaught of emotions. There was still grief, a severe pain ripping through him whenever he thought her name.

Kate, I'm coming, he thought.

He never found people in his line of work because they always ended in situations like this. Death, destruction of human life, grief.

He had closed that chapter in the book of his own history, and he was far more content dealing with objects of antiquity and things of value.

And yet he knew he needed to find her.

There was more closure he needed, more work to be done. He would find his wife, see her for one last time – knowing full well what she would look like after a year in the ocean – and say goodbye.

And then he would find the people who did this to her, and he would kill them.

They had been looking for him, trying to use her as leverage. It would have worked, if Shane had even been around to notice. He had fallen off the grid, a mission gone awry, one of the last work-for-hire jobs he had taken for the government. He had not been employed by the military at the time, so he had not had time to fix this.

While he was away, they grabbed her, waited with her for three days, then a week.

Shane had eventually returned to civilization and was able to receive messages.

But by then it was too late.

He reached the ocean floor, then turned to the north and prepared to swim the underwater mile lined by the huge piles of rocks and boulders that formed the edge of a shallow shelf. The vehicle could be anywhere below him, and of course, it could have fallen off to his right, to the slightly deeper waters at the foot of the shelf.

That would be the outward boundary of where the GPS signal was lost. The Subaru's tracking system had worked up until the car was fully submerged for a minute, and he knew a sinking vehicle would not find a straight path to the ocean floor.

Still, it would not deviate much, maybe 100 feet in each direction. That put Ground Zero right beneath him. He swam upright for a moment, floating, suspended above the boulders, and looked out in every direction. He saw plenty of lumps that were the size and shape of a car, but none that matched the profile perfectly. It wasn't quite a needle in a haystack search, but it wasn't far off. This would take him days, potentially weeks.

But he had the time.

He didn't need the money, not right now. He worked when he needed to, when he wanted to. There were always rich and wealthy collectors who wanted to add another piece to their collection, and oligarchs who wanted to track down something of value they could use as leverage against another. Even zealous museum curators who did not care for following proper procedure and simply wanted something to appear on the black market so they could snatch it up and claim it for themselves.

He helped these people, and they paid him very well for it.

But he had no current plans for work and would not until he found his wife. If he needed to dive here every day for the next year, he would. Whenever the weather permitted, the trickling columns of light strong enough to make their way down to the ocean floor, he would be out here looking. He would do it at night if need be, using his powerful underwater lantern.

He had purchased a cheap bungalow on the coast, just outside of Brisbane. There, he had set up shop as he prepared for this phase of the search. It was nice enough, falling apart in some ways from the battering of the sea breeze and maritime weather. It was enough for him. He had nothing more, so what did it matter to him that his house wasn't fancy?

Seeing nothing he wanted to investigate further, he began his slow crawl along the curving line of boulders of the short cliff, generally heading north-northeast. He knew the GPS unit would be accurate up until it had gone offline, and though he had been surprised it had been able to triangulate its position even underwater for a minute, he was not surprised his wife's murderers had not disabled it. She was already dead – they had sent him the pictures confirming it. What could he do?

There had been no other message, no warning beforehand. The threat was neutralized. They had no more use for him — or his wife. They had obviously wanted him for something, for a job, and they would do anything to get it.

They *had* done everything they could to get in touch with him, and he had missed the opportunity. They were done with him now, too, and therefore had no need to send any message other than the pictures.

His fists tightened, and his jaw clenched as memories washed over him. He had stared at the pictures in disbelief, actual shock coming over him. He was numb, unable to comprehend how drastically he had failed her.

If only I had gotten out of the jungle a day early, he thought. *An hour, even.*

He had done what he always did — found a burner phone and checked his virtual remote mailbox. It was a habit that allowed him to feel connected to civilization after a long trek through uncharted and uninhabited territory. Every mission had ended the same way, with him checking his voicemail box to see what was going on in the world of his clientele.

But the messages he had heard that time had been different — threatening and impending. He had listened to half of the first message before quickly dialing the return number. It rang and rang, but no one ever answered.

He had checked the rest of the messages while in the back of a taxi, finally getting to an airport large enough to bring him home. He had purchased the first flight out, as well as a Wi-Fi package, and upgraded his cheap flip phone to an unlocked smartphone that would allow him to browse the web and make plans while flying.

But all of it had only led to more failure. He had been too late, and he had paid dearly. Kate had paid the ultimate price.

He would never forgive himself for it, nor did he want to.

But he would find her, he would see his wife one last time.

And then he would avenge her.

2
SHANE

SHANE WAS ABOUT 50 meters into his dive when he sensed movement above his head. He stopped, jerking his head around and peering toward the surface. A long shape appeared far above him, leading with a dark shadow. It was a boat, and he heard the high-pitched whine of its motor as it passed directly above him.

He turned again, checking his dive watch and realizing his bearings. The boat was headed straight toward his own boat, a small single-engine outboard he had anchored on the rocks. He swam upward a bit more, trying to trail the V-shaped and dark shadow ahead of it. The boat was small, larger than his, but certainly not a yacht or sailboat. He saw the wake begin to ripple as the boat slowed, and he saw the shadow of his own hull grow larger as he continued his ascent. He needed to check how deep he was to avoid the bends.

He unlatched the spear from his back and held it in his right hand. He pulled himself upward with his left, kicking to increase his speed.

The boat stopped next to his, and for a moment everything above and below was still. Shane didn't want to give away his own position in the water in case whoever these people happened to be were hostile and happened to glance down into the water.

He waited there for a minute, trying to listen for any sounds that might clue him in as to who these people were and what they were doing on his boat. Theft wasn't common, but it wasn't unheard of, either. Sometimes young idiots who liked to fancy themselves pirates looked for single-operation dive boats like his and waited for a while, ensuring the diver was well into whatever excursion they had planned down below. Then they would sneak onto the boat and take whatever things of value there were. Pawn shops up and down the coast were littered with dive gear, fishing equipment, and any number of ocean-related treasures that had been snatched from unsuspecting victims.

Shane would not be one of those victims. He kicked again, increasing his speed to rapidly ascend so that he would pop out of the water and halfway over the edge of his own boat. He aimed for the far edge, away from the new boat, putting his own craft between him and the intruders. In case they were armed, this would allow him to reassess, diving straight back down and letting them have their way with his gear.

He didn't take too kindly to thieves, but he also didn't want to be shot for something as petty as a couple of twerps hoping for a prize. He launched himself out of the water as planned, leaving his mask over his face but letting his eyes quickly adjust to his new surroundings.

He saw two figures, still blurry as his eyes shifted, but also noticed they weren't imposing or threatening. In fact, they were sitting down, calmly parked next to his anchored boat.

He frowned, then pulled the regulator out of his mouth and the mask up and onto his head. He wiped his eyes with the back of his free hand, letting the spear be seen in clear detail as he hoisted it up and over the edge of his small fishing boat.

"And you are?"

There were two men, both seated, one at the pilot console and the other in the passenger chair next to it. It was a speedboat, the type often rented to tourists for day trips out on the water.

The man farthest away from him – the one driving the boat – spoke first.

"Shane Riley?"

"Who's asking?"

"Sorry to interrupt your day, sir, but we are here with a job offer. An opportunity."

"I'm not interested in opportunity. I don't need a job, either. Sorry to disappoint, but I've got work to do," he said as he pulled the mask down over his eyes and reached to shove the gag back in his mouth.

The second man spoke. "Mr. Riley, this is an extremely important request."

"Depends on whose definition you go by, I suppose." He let his thick Australian drawl ring clear over the water. In other parts of the world, he downplayed it, sometimes even hid it altogether, taking up an accent of a local dialect.

That life was mostly behind him now. He didn't have to fake anything, didn't have to operate as if everyone was trying to kill him at all times, didn't need to blend in. Now, he was who he was, and that was that. He wasn't interested in these guys or their "important" mission.

"If you don't mind, we've been charged with asking you to come with us."

"I do mind."

He waited then, feeling out the situation. If these men were going to be hostile, now was the time for a show of power – perhaps a not-so-subtle wave of a pistol that had been previously hiding on one of the men's laps or even standing up and pulling out a weapon from a concealed holster. Kneeling, neither option transpired. Instead, the second man looked at the driver and then back at Shane.

"Look, we're not here to threaten you or hurt you. We've been told that would be a bad idea. But this is a matter of importance to our boss, which means it could very well be a matter of importance to our nation."

Shane squinted through the bright strands of afternoon sunlight. A matter of national importance. "What nation?"

He knew these guys were hired guns, and trying to judge their background and nation of origin would be challenging at best. And it wouldn't tell him anything – they could be working for any number of governments who needed to hire someone with a matter of plausible deniability.

"Mr. Riley, if you could just –"

"Gotta say, I expected a little more persuasive tactics. I'm in the middle of something here, and it really can't wait."

"Looking for your wife can't wait?" the boat's pilot asked.

Shane narrowed his eyes further, pulled himself up the side of his boat, feeling it rock against him as he did. He chewed his lip for a moment. That information was not something most people were privy to. It wasn't exactly classified that he had lost his wife a year ago, but it did imply that these men were telling the truth. They were working for a government entity of some sort.

More than that, though, it intrigued him. Who was the person behind these men? Who was pulling the strings? And why had they opted to collect leverage on Shane? Most people wanting to hire him simply told him how much they would pay and what they needed found. There was little reason to coerce him.

"Mr. Riley," the second man said, "we are prepared to pay you $10,000 — US currency — just for coming with us, on our boat. It's not a trap. Our boss is just willing to pay you well for your time."

The first man spoke again. "Hear us out. Our boss wants to have a conversation with you to convince you to help him. You don't even have to say yes."

Ten thousand dollars was an absurd amount of money for 'just a conversation.' He didn't trust these men, but they didn't seem like soldiers or mercenaries. They genuinely appeared to be some sort of assistants, lackeys who could be sent on an errand without threatening whoever they were meeting with. Either the boss had deep pockets or had a very big prize he wanted to acquire. It didn't matter.

Shane wasn't exactly looking for work, but it seemed like easy money. He had a decent stash of cash back at the small bungalow and even more in a safety deposit box, but cash always seemed to find a way to run down to a trickle.

And the first man's implication wasn't far off. His wife was down there, somewhere. But she wasn't going anywhere. She had already waited a year. Eventually, her bones would settle, the car and body reclaimed by the ocean. Algae and dirt sediment would set in. A new coral system would form, animals would move in, and the circle of life happening beneath the waves would be in full effect.

But he had time. At least another six months, possibly even a year before the car became unrecognizable and his wife drifted away to dust. Even then, he could still visit her. Her body might not be there anymore, but the car would be a shrine to her memory. Once he marked the location, he could visit her resting place whenever he wanted.

Most of all, though, he was intrigued. He dropped back down into the water, thinking for a moment. He had left the spear lying between the two plank seats. It would be a final test of their hostility. If they reached for it, or even looked at it suspiciously, he would have his answer.

He bobbed in the water near his motor for another few seconds. They waited calmly, watching him.

Finally, he swam around the stern of his small craft and grasped the handles of their ladder. He popped his flippers off and tossed them back onto his own boat. Next, he rolled the tank off his back and let one of the men help him out of the water with it. He stood there on the back end of their boat, dripping wet and eyeing each man as they watched him.

"I'm just supposed to leave my boat here?" he asked.

The pilot smiled. "I'm thinking ten thousand dollars will be enough to replace that little guy."

3
SHANE

THE MEN KNEW where they were going, but they didn't care to clue him in on where exactly that was.

They did, however, give him their names: Smith and Donovan. The pilot of the boat had been Donovan, his reddish auburn hair giving away his nationality, while Smith was of the more generic middle-aged white guy type.

He assumed both names were aliases, but as he had suspected, neither of the men seemed to be operatives. Smith was thin, with a pockmarked face and skittish personality. Donovan was a bit beefier and stoic, but Shane suspected it was not muscle from years of fieldwork and combat.

Both seemed harmless, and treated Shane well enough. They had obviously been told not to give away any crucial information like where they were going or who they were meeting with, but they were otherwise amicable. They reached the marina and got into a black SUV.

Donovan once again got behind the wheel, and they twisted and turned through the streets of Shane's small town, even passing his bungalow before reaching a private airport to the west of the city.

Shane had been surprised to see that they were just going to cart him away immediately, without so much as stopping for supplies.

Smith seemed to sense his hesitation. "There's a packed bag for you in the back of the SUV," he explained. "A couple of changes of clothes in your size, enough cash to buy some snacks, and a phone. I wish we had more time, but our boss is under a lot of pressure."

Shane nodded, taking in the information, but looking out the window nonchalantly as he did. It was more gear than he was given for some missions, so that was good.

But this wasn't a special operations mission — whoever was behind all of this was scared. Using these tactics was not normal. Usually someone who wanted him to find something was greedy and wanted it as soon as possible, but they would understand not to rush Shane or his work.

This person either didn't care about Shane's comfort or feelings, or they were terrified and reacting as such. They parked and walked him through the airport, then veered right and headed toward the offset, single-building terminal used mostly for postal and cargo delivery. Shane's eyebrows raised as he saw what they would be flying.

An expensive private jet.

So this guy isn't sparing any expense. Whatever they were after, it must be worth a fortune.

"You do have time to grab a quick bite if you want it," Smith continued, "but the in-flight meals are actually quite good. If possible, we request you wait until we take off, and we'll have the in-flight crew whip something up for you if you're hungry."

Shane nodded again, not interested in any of the crappy, sugar-laden snack food in the small airport anyway. He boarded the plane and found a seat on the port side of the craft, about halfway back. It was luxuriously appointed – clearly a plane owned by a businessman or woman interested in impressing guests and acquaintances. He was greeted warmly by a female attendant, and the pilot and copilot waived in greeting as he sat.

Smith and Donovan sat near the front of the plane, giving him space. He placed the packed duffel bag on the seat next to him, not bothering to look inside just yet. This was all mysterious, and he had to admit — even a bit fun. He was going to meet the person behind all of it soon, and he wanted to build a good estimate of their persona before he did so. Within minutes, they were taxiing around the single airstrip airport and eventually were airborne.

Shane suddenly felt tired, the toll from his brief dive apparently enough to fatigue his arms and legs. He was about to close his eyes, yawning, when the flight attendant walked back up the aisle and offered him a small menu. She offered him a drink as well, but he declined. He chose a sandwich and she informed him it would be about 30 minutes.

He smiled, thanked her, then closed his eyes and laid his head back.

He knew Kate was waiting for him, knew that he felt the longing growing in him again. He pushed it back. *I'll be there, Kate,* he thought as the sound of the engine lulled himself to sleep. *I'm coming to find you. Just hang tight for a bit longer.*

It was not an adventure he had expected, but it was an adventure none-theless.

And Shane Riley loved adventure.

4
SEONG

SEONG PARK WAS SCARED out of her mind. In fact, she had never been as scared as she was right now. She had watched her mother die a slow, miserable death from cancer, scared to see the light of their lives snuffed out.

That fear had been nothing compared to this.

They had grabbed her in the middle of the night, somehow sneaking into her apartment and creeping into her room, up to the edge of her bed while she slept. She had sensed it, felt their presence. They didn't even shake her awake; for all she knew, they could have been standing there for hours.

Watching her sleep. Watching her breathe soundlessly, nothing but her own dreams to keep her company.

And then when she trusted her subconscious to wake up, to respond to the danger it sensed, it was too late.

A hand slid over her mouth, the cold steel of a pistol barrel on her forehead.

Her eyes widened, her mouth curled into a scream, one that was snuffed out by the hand—cold and clammy—that had nearly strangled her.

She writhed on the bed, trying to break free of the man's grasp but never losing sight of the weapon aimed directly at her. Another man, another shadow, was there as well, appearing from the darker recesses of her room. It gripped her legs, held them down, forced her to lie still.

Then they had slid a gag over her mouth, a dark cloth bag over her head. She felt herself forcibly lifted from the bed, their strength incredible, as if she were a mere child.

They had marched her out of her room, out of her own apartment, then stuffed her into some vehicle.

Seong had cried the entire time, whimpering in fear. She heard no voices, no clues or signs as to who these people were and where she was going.

And that still had not been the most scared she had ever been.

No, she was now far more scared than that. Far more scared than she had been to learn that she was going to lose both parents in a six-month span.

This new fear was unbelievable. Palpable. Fear that sat over her like a cloud, thick and heavy, and holding her down like the man who had taken her had done.

She cried, knowing that the moisture in her eyes was all but exhausted. There was nothing left.

Now, she was strapped to a metal table. Her arms above her head, the gag still on. She couldn't scream, couldn't call for help. Her feet had been crossed and bound together, then they, too, had been somehow tied down to the table.

She could see only a single bulb above her head, brighter than the sun, piercing into her eyes. She knew nothing else about the room she was in, couldn't see anything but the light above her, darkness around that.

But the shadows moved. She knew she was not alone in the room. She lay, back on the table, arms above her head, as the shadows moved and danced and turned around her.

For hours the shadows had moved. She had been here at least that long, though it could be far longer. She didn't remember passing out, only that she had awoken like this.

Every now and then she heard a low chuckle, a laugh, and the fear would ratchet up the tension inside her once more.

Twice now, someone—just a hand, an invisible figure in the dark—had touched her when the light would dim and go dark completely. She would blink, seeing the greenish globe behind her eyelids, though there was no light beyond them. There, in pitch black, they would touch her.

She first felt a single finger, slowly sliding up her leg.

She was in some sort of gown, like a hospital gown that hung only to her thighs. It was thin and did nothing to keep out the cold table and the cold air from the room. It was split—two pieces, the shirt barely covering her breasts, her tummy exposed.

The finger slid all the way up her leg, slowly, menacingly. Over her calf, then past her knee, then up her thigh. And then... It had stopped.

She yelled, crying empty tears and hearing hardly any noise escape the sides of her gagged mouth, then eventually lay still once more. After a few more minutes of darkness, the light turned back on, and she tried looking around, still seeing nothing but the huge orb of light clouding her vision.

The second time the light had shut off, they had touched her tummy. A whole hand, warmer but still eerie. Disgusting. It felt her, stroked her. She was 34 years old and in great shape, and the hand that was touching her seemed to want *more* of her. It stayed around her exposed parts, never grasping, never threatening to squeeze or choke her. But it moved, tickling her.

The third time, she thought she even heard the sickening groan of a man's voice, obviously pleasured by the feeling of her body.

It was pure torture. She had no information, no knowledge of what was happening, and yet whoever had done this was groping her, asserting dominance over her.

Then the hand had stopped, falling away once more, and the light had returned. The blistering, excruciating light.

And there she had lain, for another indeterminate amount of time, silent and scared, closing her eyes to fight away the brightness and trying to forget the incredible fear and trepidation that racked her entire body.

5
SEONG

SEONG PARK HEARD the door open. As usual, she sensed no change in the air as someone entered. She heard soft and light footsteps, indicating the presence of a person next to her.

Suddenly, she heard a voice. It was the first she had heard in hours, besides the ominous chuckle of laughter from the person who had caressed her. She waited, listening to the words.

"We need information," the voice said. It was Korean and had the tinge of dialect to it she recognized from the North. "We need information on what you have been working on. What you have stolen and sold."

Tears returned, and Seong felt goosebumps all over her body. She didn't recognize the voice, but she suddenly realized what it was asking for as the voice's owner ripped the gag out of her mouth.

Her work. Her life's work. She had sensed this might be the case — sensed this might be what they had taken her for. She had not wanted to believe it, wanting to assume that the people who had taken her in the night were just criminals, people who would kill her and discard her body.

That would have been better than this.

She would have much preferred that.

Now, as she felt prickliness in her arms that had long since fallen asleep, she knew this was far worse. They didn't just want her body, they weren't just after lust.

This was torture. This was all planned, strategic. They wanted information — specifically information about what she had been researching for the last year. Research she had thought she had kept hidden, research she thought would go unnoticed by her government.

Now, they would torture answers out of her. There was no one who knew what she knew, and somehow they had discovered that.

"I know you have this information, Ms. Park," the deep voice said. "And I know you are uncomfortable here. Tell me what you found and this will all be over."

She squeezed her eyes shut, biting back more sobs. "You will just kill me," she said.

"This is true," the man's voice said immediately. "You must understand, this is a matter of national defense now. We cannot let you live. But I hope you understand the situation clearly, Ms. Park. My soldiers here are not well-trained interrogators. They don't understand the finer nuances of extracting information from a victim."

She waited as the man explained, unable to argue or fight back. "My men are untrained, but they are hungry. They have little here for entertainment. As such, I thought it would be prudent to allow them a bit of... exploration. For now, I will keep them gentle, keep them from harming you. I'm sure it will be torturous enough to be strapped here all alone, but I've allowed each of them to come in every hour for a few minutes, for a little of this exploration."

She listened, horrified. She had been correct — this was a form of torture, one far more damaging than simple pain. Physical harm would certainly not be fun, but the mental and emotional damage these men would do to her if left to their own devices...

"Of course, eventually we will have to make you talk if you refuse to cooperate. Though they are not well-trained in interrogation techniques, there are plenty well-trained at removing skin, fingernails, entire fingers, perhaps."

"What do you want from me?" she asked.

He smiled, gesturing in the light. "I believe you know, Ms. Park. But in case you're considering leaving something out, how about we just start with everything you know regarding the research project on bio-weapons? How it came to be, how you got involved, and, of course, all of your known associates."

She jutted her chin forward. "You can try all you want, you will never get what you want."

"You have no idea what I want."

They eyed each other for another long moment, and finally, the man spoke once more. "Have it your way, Ms. Park. You're not the only leverage I'm holding. You, of all people, should know that. We can make this last as long as you'd like, and we can make it as painful as you prefer. Yes, you will die here.

The speed, swiftness, and amount of pain you feel before that death, however, is entirely up to you."

He began walking away, and her startled eyes tracked him as he left the room. For the first time, now that the light had dimmed enough for her to see something besides the light itself, she could make out more of the space she was in. It was white, with subway tiles lining every wall. The space was dingy and dirty. It did not look like it had been cleaned recently, if ever. Dust collected in one corner, and a greasy line of rust fell from a crack in the wall.

The man stopped at the door, opening it but turning to face her. "Ms. Park, I am a very busy man. There is much I have left to do. I don't want to extend our little interaction any longer than it must be required. Please, for your sake and mine, start talking soon."

With that, he turned and left the room.

Seong was left alone in the dimly lit room, her heart pounding in her chest. She knew that she had a choice to make: to give in and divulge the information they sought or to hold onto her secrets and endure the torture that would inevitably come. As fear and determination wrestled within her, she knew that no matter the outcome, her life would never be the same.

6
SHANE

SHANE LOOKED out of the wide windows of the apartment and took in the panorama of the city outside — Seoul, South Korea. He frowned and crossed his arms, realizing he had slept for quite some time. They had only traveled a few time zones away from where they had taken off, and he hadn't realized how long the trip had been.

"I purchased this suite for the view," a man's voice said from behind him. Shane turned around quickly, noticing a small Korean man entering the room from next door. The two assistants, Donovan and Smith, sat lazily on a couch up against the far wall, out of the way of the main area of business.

The apartment was every bit as Korean as he would have expected, with the man describing a stereotypical Korean house. It was clear this man had wealth. Art hung from the walls, and he recognized a statue in the corner.

"Please, make yourself comfortable," the man said.

Shane stood, his arms still crossed.

The man made a face and shrugged, then walked over and sat on another couch, facing two comfortable-looking chairs on either side of Shane. The couch itself faced the broad, floor-to-ceiling windows, and he imagined this man sitting at night sipping a scotch or Japanese whiskey while looking out at the city, or perhaps a nice view of the skyline.

"I appreciate you coming here," the man said in impeccable English.

"Did I have a choice?" Shane asked.

The man smiled, but it didn't reach his eyes. He had a sadness about him, a hesitation. "There is always a choice, Mr. Riley."

"I was told that if I said no, even if I said no, I get paid for my time," Shane said, making it clear he wasn't asking a question but stating a fact.

The man nodded slowly, bowing deeply. "I hope it will not come to that. I hope I can convince you to help me."

"You seem to know a lot about me," Shane said. "About what I do."

"I am a man of means, as you can see. But I'm also one with connections, both good and bad. There are favors I have called in, but it will likely not fix all of this. So, your reputation precedes you. I am told you are the person to ask for when there's something to be found... something of great value."

Shane studied the man for a moment, squinting through one eye. He knew narrowing his eyes this way looked hostile, looked too scrutinizing. But it was a tic he'd had all his life, a physical manifestation of his mind working, trying to piece things together.

"You've offered me $10,000 in US currency just to be standing here right now. At the risk I say no, not interested. Either you're bluffing, and your two dudes over there are willing to kill me in order to get me to say yes, or you *actually* lost something near and dear to your heart."

"Yes," the man said, suddenly snapping his eyes up and boring holes through Shane. Shane was surprised at the intensity, surprised at the suddenness of it. This man was not just wealthy, he was quick, sharp-witted.

Shane's squint deepened.

"What they took cannot be replaced," the man continued. "But we will get into that. I am waiting on friends and a few more acquaintances. Can I bring you tea while we wait?"

Shane shook his head. "We can probably save a lot of time if you just tell me what's going on, what you want me to get and where. I can be out of your hair in a minute, on my way. Obviously, you're strapped for time, so —"

The man held up a hand, palm out. Shane stopped talking. "I am as anxious to get started as you," he said slowly. "But the others coming, they need to hear this as well. And I do not like to repeat myself."

Shane curled his bottom lip. *Can't argue with that,* he thought.

They stared at one another for another minute, neither man offering any ground. Finally, there was a slight knock at the door. Donovan was on his feet in an instant, marching over to the door. Shane eyed the Irishman, not noticing any telltale bulge of a weapon under his pants or jacket. For whatever reason, the wealthy Korean whose house he was now in was not a fan of armed bodyguards. He wondered if he had other means of security — something hidden, to force people like Shane to keep their guard down.

The door opened and Donovan invited three more men inside.

In an instant, Shane knew that these men were, in fact, trained. Military or mercenary, these men had seen combat. The way they carried themselves, the way they looked at every corner of every space they could see as they entered, before even making eye contact with Shane and the wealthy Korean man told him everything. He noticed one of them brushing his palm against his pants, another telltale sign that Shane shared. Checking to see if the weapon was still there, knowing full well it was but wanting to feel the weight of it.

These men weren't immediately threatening, but they were certainly on their guard.

Shane sized them up. He would have a hell of a time getting through them, if it came to that. He hoped it wouldn't, hoped he had not been duped. These guys were operatives of some sort, and they knew and he knew they were sizing him up as well.

"Please, take a seat," the older man said. There was a pause, and finally the leader of the newcomers, a man who seemed to be in his mid-40s, strode forward. The other two followed suit.

They all eyed Shane as if he were the only threat in the room. Perhaps he was. He still didn't know why he was here. They walked over to the couch and chairs, two of them sitting in a chair and one of them opposite the couch from the wealthy individual.

"If any of you would like anything, please let me know," the man continued. "Otherwise, I am interested in getting started, looking to begin as soon as possible."

7

DR. YUN

DR. CHUL YUN squeezed the skin around his temples. Nothing he could do could ease the frustration. Nothing would make the anxiety go away.

He sat behind his desk, an ugly, sinister-looking thing. All metal, rusting on the edges of the feet. It had been here since this facility had been first built in 1939, and it had belonged to all of the directors before him, going all the way back to Kim Il-Sung himself. He glanced over at the picture of Kim Il-Sung on the wall, mounted right next to the picture of Kim Jong-Il, a requirement for any public or private place throughout the kingdom.

He glared at the picture of the supreme leader. He hadn't disliked the man – he had only met him a couple of times – but he was as incompetent as any other politician. Sure, he had the world's greatest, most advanced Army to order around, to protect the nation. And he had achieved some impressive feats during his reign.

But Yun was no idiot – most of the claims made about the supreme commander were fictitious or falsified, or even outright lies. Claims that he flew on the back of a dragon, among other tales of North Korean lore, were almost comical.

And yet the man had built and shaped a nation so closed off to the rest of the world that its citizens truly believed their leader was a god.

Which only left people like Dr. Yun to have to carry the mantle, to do the actual work that allowed their leader to take all of the credit.

He was truly good at his work. He had already made strides far beyond what was possible in the Western world — because he was not afraid to take risks like the rest of the Western world.

He was not afraid of the downsides of experimentation, of truly studying the human form.

And he was close, closer than anyone had ever gotten. Ever since this place had been established in 1939, its two dozen researchers and scientists had worked toward one supreme goal: to find or build a virus that could wipe out an entire race in one fell swoop.

The ultimate designer virus – one that would totally and utterly affect one slice of the population while leaving the rest of the world's population alone.

He smiled as he rubbed his temples. *Focus on the goal,* he told himself. *Ignore the anxiety. Ignore the naysayers.*

Lately, those in his own government — the ones paying him — had been questioning his methods. *This is North Korea,* they would say, *where we have always performed such experiments. But we are waking up as a nation – we are starting to learn humanity and ethics from the rest of the world.*

He swallowed, smacking his fist down near the pad of paper on his desk.

No, he reasoned. *This is North Korea – and for that reason, we must continue forward. We cannot become like the rest of the world – weak-willed and meek. We cannot bow to their demands.*

He knew that what he was building here was just the sort of thing the world needed. It was just the sort of thing North Korea needed, to finally gain the recognition it had long been building.

But there were issues. Both inside and out. Some officials in his own government were trying to stop him, trying to persuade him not to continue down the path he had been traveling. But his biggest threat currently was the girl.

Seong Park, the young woman downstairs, still had not cracked. She still had not revealed her secrets to him.

And he *needed* those secrets. He could get them otherwise – through painstaking trial and error, years of research and experimentation – but she had them in her head, right this moment.

It frustrated him to no end. Couldn't she see that by helping him it would end all of her suffering? Couldn't she see that all he wanted was knowledge, information?

He had tried explaining as much to her.

And the longer she lived — the longer she was in his care — the greater the threat she became.

Her father was a somebody. He had power in South Korea, which meant he had pull and influence in North Korea. He had not known precisely what that sort of pull and influence might look like, but he did now.

Seong Park's father, Chung-Hee Park, had tried calling his bluff. He had warned the man that there was no way to retrieve Seong before he got what he wanted, at which point he would kill her. He had not asked for money, he had not asked for power.

He had simply given Park the option: tell him what he needed to know by turning over the information on her university's servers, or I will extract the information myself... from your daughter's mouth.

He knew the man was furious, and rightfully so. But it had been a simple request: tell him how to get into the university's servers and where to find his daughter's work. He would even have hackers do it for him.

All he had needed was confirmation that the information was there and a plant, a person to get into the university and install an access point through which his hackers could work remotely.

Chung-Hee Park had not budged. At first, he claimed to know nothing of Seong's work. At first, he had denied knowing even what his daughter was working on.

Shortly after their last conversation, Chung-Hee Park had hired a group of men to come into his country, into *this* facility. He had received word from his contacts in South Korea that Park was sending a small team to retrieve his daughter. He apparently thought Dr. Yun was a fool.

He was sorely mistaken.

Let him try, Yun thought. It would be an unfortunate bump in the road — one that would pull his attention elsewhere temporarily, and force him to move faster than he wanted — but this was not the first obstacle he had faced in his career. He already had a plan in place to deal with it, in fact. Something quiet, something that would not cause any undue attention on his program.

You want to play games, we will play games, he thought.

SHANE WATCHED the Korean man's eyes as he spoke. He tried to read him, to understand what was truly going on in the man's mind. So far, he seemed saddened by all of it, perhaps a bit scared. What was he nervous about? What had he lost?

That much was clear to Shane. This was a man who was not trying to find something, adding something new to an existing collection.

He was trying to replace something that had been lost.

Had something been stolen from him? Shane glanced around the room. He was no art snob, but he had an eye for paintings and portraits now, thanks to his line of work. He could assess the quality and general price range of a work of art on most occasions. Nothing in the room told him this man was wealthy because of an art collection. The pieces he had scattered on the walls throughout the room seemed to be there not as a store of wealth, but simply as decoration for the room. He recognized one — a print of a Chinese artist that he knew was hanging in a museum in Shanghai.

No, not art. Perhaps it was something off-site. Cars, yachts, companies?

He raised an eyebrow. That would be an interesting grab — trying to wrest control of an entire corporation from someone who had hostilely taken over another. He wasn't sure he could even do that, or where he might start.

He shook his head slightly. *This isn't about business. This is personal.*

The other two men in the room also watched the North Korean man silently as he welcomed them and dove into a brief exchange of pleasantries. This, in spite of refuting, professing that he wanted to get started as soon as possible, the man was a victim of his own culture — this quick exchange of pleasantries was a requirement for his people. It was a sign of respect in both directions. They briefly commented on the weather, on the trip, on the food provided.

After about a minute, the man bowed his head once more and looked up at those in attendance.

"My name is Chung-Hee Park. And as you may have gathered, something of great personal importance has been taken from me."

Shane leaned forward ever so slightly, rocking on his heels.

"My daughter, Seong, 34 years old, was working toward her doctorate in genetic engineering."

Shane's mouth pulled sideways, to the left. "*She* was taken?" he shot out.

Everyone in the room looked at him. He hadn't meant to sound so harsh, so accusatory. Still, he had to know.

"Yes," Park said. "My daughter was kidnapped two days ago. I want —"

Shane held a hand up, copying the motion he had seen the Korean give him. "I'm going to stop you right there. I don't retrieve *people*. Never have, never will."

"If you would please give me the benefit of the doubt, Mr. Riley," Park insisted. "I believe I can persuade you to join my cause."

"I don't care what you believe," Riley snapped. "No people. *Ever.*"

The man seated to his left — the leader of the group of three that had joined the party — looked up and sidelong at Riley. "Who the hell is this guy?" he asked with a smirk.

"Mr. Riley is an artifact retrieval specialist," Park said. "His reputation led me to believe he would be a perfect addition to this mission."

"Like I said, I don't find people. That's not my game. Sorry, you're going to have to find someone else."

Everyone in the room paused, watching Shane's face as if they too were trying to discern the veracity of his claims. "Very well," the man said. "I will transfer the money to you this afternoon. I already have the information."

How the hell did he get that?

Park continued. "My men, Smith and Donovan, will escort you back home. I appreciate your willingness to comply and come for this conversation." Shane started forward, then stopped. *Just like that?* He had no reason to distrust the man, no reason to suspect he wasn't going to get his easy cash payout and be on his way if he said no, but still... it seemed a little too easy.

What am I missing?

He shook his head again, ignoring the smirk from the man seated to his left. He walked between the couch and the armchair, then veered over to where Smith and Donovan were seated on a couch along the wall. Their heads were rigid, facing forward, pretending as though they had not heard every word.

"Let's go, boys," he said to them. "Seems like this will be the best hourly rate I've ever earned."

Donovan stood up and moved toward the door, but Smith remained seated, his face impassive.

From behind him, he heard the older man begin speaking again, this time his voice a bit lower. And yet he heard it clearly, as if the man had turned and was speaking directly to the back of Shane's head. "My daughter was kidnapped just over 48 hours ago, while trying to send a message."

He wanted to offer a bit of condolence – he wasn't a monster – but he didn't want it to come out snarky, sarcastic. He meant well... he just wasn't the right person for the job. Instead, he said nothing.

"The message she was trying to send we were not able to intercept. But we know she was trying to contact someone, and we know who."

Shane squinted, stopping by Donovan's side at the front door.

"She was trying to contact your wife. Kate Riley."

9
SHANE

SHANE SPUN AROUND, anger flashing across his face. "My wife's dead, old man. She's been gone for over a year now. I thought you had a pretty good knack for intelligence gathering, finding my bank account information and doing some research on me and all, but you may have just overplayed your hand."

The man stood slowly. "On the contrary, Mr. Riley. I know your wife was murdered a year ago. I know they dumped her body offshore, near where you purchased your home. That's what you were doing when we picked you up, looking for her remains."

Nothing the man said was false. Nothing was a lie. Still, it stung as if he had stabbed him three times, opening fresh wounds on top of old ones.

He wondered what the other three men in the room besides Donovan and Smith thought. They were watching him, not the Korean man as he spoke. He couldn't read their faces, the light not quite reaching them well enough.

"What of it?"

"My daughter apparently did not know that your wife is no longer with us," the man continued. "I believe she was trying to get a message out to ask for help. I believe she has information that would have been important to your wife."

Shane's eyes narrowed further. His wife had been working for a nonprofit, studying genomic irregularities. She was researching the human genome to identify instances where DNA might lead to disease, hoping to find ways to prevent or treat these conditions.

It sounded like this man's daughter was in a similar line of work, and although he knew nothing about her, it didn't surprise him that she would have reached out to his wife for help. Kate was brilliant, capable of seeing patterns where no one else could. He didn't understand half of what she did – but no one else on the planet did, either. She was a rising star in the field, someone very capable of running her own firm one day.

That had been her plan, as well. She had always wanted to be a world-renowned researcher, not for the fame or fortune – there was hardly any of either in this line of work – but for the freedom to conduct the research she wanted. Unburdened by grant requirements, regulation, or the slow lockstep march of bureaucratic red tape. She wanted to usher in a new era of scientific exploration – to go boldly where no one had gone before.

He almost smiled as he remembered her quoting that exact line. She had been a huge Star Trek nerd her entire life, and Shane had reluctantly gotten into the original series and some of the movies with her. As campy as they were, he had to admit they were good storytellers.

And he took her word for it that most of the science checked out.

"You don't know what the message was?" Shane asked.

The man shook his head solemnly. "I only wish we had more information. As you can imagine, I want nothing more than to get my daughter back safely. However, it would behoove you all to know that while my heart is focused almost exclusively on my daughter's well-being, the safety of my country may also be on the line."

"What do you mean?" one of the men seated across from the couch asked.

"The South Korean government has been listening intently to news around the world of scientific development, related to the sort of studies your wife and my daughter were involved with. We received word that the North Korean government might have stumbled upon something groundbreaking as well."

Shane swallowed. He knew exactly where this was going, but he let the man continue.

"As you know, there is no more precarious location in the world than a location bordering North Korea. The government is not unstable, but they are belligerent, run by one crazed man. I don't need to rehash the details to you all, but I do need to reiterate the importance of wrapping this up as quickly as possible."

"I thought North Korea was decades behind the rest of the world in scientific research?" the other man asked.

Shane nodded. "That was my understanding, as well. I thought the fear with North Korea is that they were belligerent, with their fingers on the proverbial trigger. But whatever tech they have – whatever scientific research they've gotten their hands on – it's all been earned through thievery. Through stealing the work of other nations."

"For the most part, yes. North Korea is not known for conducting their own research – how could they? No one who plays by the rules will interact with them. But the intelligence community in South Korea has been eyeing a particular region very closely the last few years. I cannot get into the reasons why, but we believe there is something peculiar going on there. The sort of research we believe was started over 80 years ago."

Riley did the math. *World War II-era*. That could only mean one thing.

"Mr. Riley, I need your help. I know you want to avenge your wife's death; anyone would want that. I want that for you. I ask as a favor in return, find my daughter and bring her back to me safely. In doing so, I suspect you might find answers to the questions you've been searching for. I suspect you might find the reasons why your wife was taken and killed in the first place."

Shane let out a deep sigh. He already knew what his answer would be. He had decided the moment he had heard that his wife might have been involved in all of this. He looked at each of the six men in the room, briefly meeting their eyes. Then, with a heavy heart, he gave his answer.

"No. I won't help you."

10

SHANE

"I DON'T UNDERSTAND, MR. RILEY," the old man said.

Shane walked back a few paces toward the couch. Donovan and Smith were now both standing, still close to the door.

"Look, I feel for you. I'm sorry you lost your daughter. But I'm sure these fine folks can help you out. That's why you brought them here, isn't it?"

"Yes, but —"

"I work alone. You know that because you know everything else about me. I get that you're in the intelligence community, possibly South Korean government. You're a powerful man, so I'll let you put two and two together. There's only one of me, and that's the extent of my team, always. No matter what."

Chung-Hee Park did not seem to be fazed by Shane's outburst. "I *do* understand, Mr. Riley. And I ask that you understand where I'm coming from as well. I have invited you here because you are the best at retrieving things. You know where to look, you know how to go about finding things without getting caught. And, most importantly, you know how to bring them back home."

"Right on all counts."

"But *they* are here for a much different reason. They are here because they can get you into the country. They can sneak you across the border, gain access to places no outsiders are ever allowed into, and they can do it without being killed or captured."

Special Forces. At least he was right about that.

"Walking into North Korea alone is a death sentence," Shane said. "Walking in with more people than that is suicide."

"Not when you go with us," the leader of the mercenary group said.

"I'm sure, buddy," Shane snapped. "Doesn't matter, anyway. I work alone, and I don't retrieve people. How are you not getting this?"

"I would have thought that your wife's potential involvement would have convinced you," the Korean man said. "But I was prepared for such a rebuttal. I know you also respond to money, Mr. Riley. I ask, just this once – make an exception. I respect that you have rules, moral obligations to uphold. Just this once, forget them. Work with this team of contractors, and bring my daughter home."

Shane was sensing the punch line was coming quickly.

"For that, I will pay *each* of you a million dollars."

Shane's mouth dropped open – he couldn't help it. This was by far the biggest payout he had ever received.

"I am prepared to wire half of the money now – you are all trustworthy individuals, all people I know will not take the money and run. And if you do, fine. It will only set me back a bit of money, but I have already begun talking with additional teams to stand up to take your place. I believe you are all the best at what you do, and that's why I've called you first.

"But one group does not work without the other – these men cannot find my daughter, cannot bring her home safely to me. And you cannot get into the country, you cannot get past the North Korean army and their undercover spies working in and around their own nation. And I cannot let my daughter wait there for days on end. If you go in and fail, and I have to start over with a new team, I'm afraid it will be much too late for her."

Shane agreed with the last sentiment, at least. She would be dead, if she wasn't already. There was a very good chance whoever had taken her was already working on torturing her. He didn't even understand what it was she might know – what she had gotten involved with – but the North Koreans wouldn't care. No matter who it was, if they claimed loyalty to that disgusting nation run by crooks and criminals, there was no doubt in his mind that she was already being taken apart piece by piece.

Shane waited for the man to continue. When he didn't, he jumped in. "I appreciate your offer. It's a lot of money, more than I've made on any job, as I'm sure you well know." He flicked his eyes around to the other people in the room, knowing that they probably didn't know about him or his past. They, like him, had just been hired to do a job. Or, Park was *trying* to hire them to do a job. If they had any concerns, none of them had voiced any.

"Still, part of the reason you want me on the job is that you know you can trust me, because of my integrity. When I tell you I work alone, I mean it. I am willing to break one of my own rules and find your daughter, just this once. But I ain't doing it with anybody else in tow, slowing me down."

The man who had been sitting at Shane's left frowned and raised his voice. "Hey, I resent the —"

"I'll bet you're pretty damn good at what you do," Shane snapped, cutting him off. "But I'm better. I'm the only one on the planet who can get her back, and this guy knows it."

He turned to face Park. "You want the job done, you hire *me*. A million, not a penny more. I won't even ask you for reimbursable expenses."

The man smiled knowingly. "I always reimburse expenses."

"It's me, *alone*, or it doesn't get done."

Shane turned on a heel and marched toward Smith and Donovan, toward the front door. The old Korean man was already agreeing. "Yes, Mr. Riley. I will take you up on that offer. Bring my daughter back. But don't you want to hear the rest of details that I have? The information that I know? I was just going to explain —"

"Email me," Shane grumbled.

He had done enough *peopling* for the day, he'd had enough social interaction. He had never been introverted, but since the loss of his wife, he'd changed quite a bit. Growing up he had even been wildly extroverted, getting energy from being around people, from talking and laughing.

Now, not so much. There was very little laughing in his life these days. And he didn't need to be around other people to find his energy.

What he needed to find right now was a cold, dark corner that he could sit in. He took two quick strides to the door and opened it, eyeing Smith to make sure the man wouldn't try to stop him.

Then Shane Riley left Chung-Hee Park's apartment.

"YOU'RE ACTUALLY GOING to email that guy?"

Chung-Hee Park looked at Jonathan Evans as if he had just seen him for the first time. Evans, a tall black man from southern Georgia, did not look like the kind of person who would be conversing with a wealthy Korean politician. Though the world had changed for the better, racism and prejudice was certainly still around. Evans had not heard anything particularly egregious from this old guy's mouth so far, but the way he flicked his eyes over Evans body as he had collapsed on his chair made him think this man might have some reservations.

Maybe he didn't see my headshot before inviting me here, he thought.

"He wasn't kidding," the Korean man said. "He is the best at what he does."

"And *I'm* the best at what I do," Evans said. An ex-Army Ranger, Evans had retired from the military and gone immediately into private security paramilitary, working for Fortune 500 corporations, mostly overseas, ensuring that these companies could conduct their business without having to worry about 'issues.'

As part of the 75th, those issues had been explicitly defined by his supe-rior officers; they came from the top down. Private security was not much different – there was still a chain of command starting with the person hiring his company – but the rules were much looser. In private security, there was no waiting around for orders, no waiting for the bureaucratic buck to stop with any particular person.

There was the mission, the parameters, and that was it. Evans and the fire team he was currently with – preferred things that way. Things got done much faster, much more efficiently.

And he liked having a little say in the matter, as well.

Though the U.S. Army tried hard to get things right, there were times it had missed the mark. On more than one occasion, Evans and his Ranger squadron had ended up in some forgotten corner of the world, acting as a force multiplier for local military or militia, and things have gotten a bit confusing. The good guys started to look an awful lot like the bad guys, and vice versa.

With private security, the good guys were simply the guys who got paid by the company. They were the ones who prevented the bad guys from gaining access to places they weren't supposed to be in.

If this older gentleman wanted Evans to sneak himself and his team across the North Korean border, fine. He would do it, and none of his men would bat an eye. But it was risky, for sure. People who looked like Evans weren't exactly *welcome* in that country.

"Be that as it may," the Korean continued, "I meant what I said. You both need each other."

"You heard the man," Evans chuckled. "He works alone."

"Then he can work alone... in close proximity with you," the Korean said, matching Evans' grin. Though there was a smile on his face, Evans sensed resentment in the man's voice. Where before it seemed as though every word he spoke to Shane Riley was one of reverence, of respect, Evans felt nothing but disdain. He couldn't guarantee that it was because of the color of his skin, but he couldn't be sure it wasn't playing a role.

Whatever. He had learned to brush these things off long ago. Fighting about something as petty as skin color rarely helped anyone.

And a million dollars was a million dollars, no matter who was paying.

"So you still want us out there?"

"I want my daughter back."

Evans nodded. "Covert, then?"

"I don't know what Riley's reaction will be if he finds you and your men also hunting down her kidnappers," the man said. "My guess is that he will not be pleased. But he also is a man of character. He will find her, and if it comes to it, I believe he will take advantage of whatever help is available."

"I like to think I'm a man of character myself," Evans said.

"Very well."

His men – Sammy Lemieux from Québec, and Roger North from upstate New York – glanced at him. They could sense the tension in the room as well.

Evans gave a slight shake of his head. *Leave it.*

"You mentioned more information. The more you can give us, the better."

Park nodded. "I will send it securely to you and Mr. Riley. Separately, of course. She was taken 52 hours ago, in the middle of the night from her apartment. Local police have already contaminated the crime scene, so I doubt you will find anything useful there."

Evans smirked. Apparently police incompetence was not an exclusively small-town American problem.

"I mentioned the region my government has been watching. My best guess is that they took her there, a well-guarded and hidden research laboratory, we believe built in 1939. Originally intended to be a rural hospital supporting the numerous villages in the area, it was taken over by Nazi sympathizers soon after and turned into a government research facility."

"What exactly have they been researching?"

The man's expression changed to one of disgust. Evans read the answer clearly on his face, without Park having to speak it aloud. *You don't want to know.*

"Got it," Evans said. "We'll just let it be a surprise when we get there."

"When I say well-guarded, I mean it," the man continued. "Besides North Korean army personnel, you will likely find covert operatives throughout the region, possibly acting as villagers or even tourists. The North Korean government has always been on edge, but lately they have gotten quite suspicious of their own people, as well. For good reason – we have hundreds of operatives living and breathing on North Korean soil, hiding from the government there and also passing on information to us. It seems their esteemed leader is not quite as 'esteemed' as he used to be. There are chinks in the North Korean armor, and they are growing larger by the day."

"It's not going to be a problem," Evans said.

The man stared at Evans, as if waiting for an explanation. How could someone looking like him – tall, black, in many ways the antithesis of the stereotypical North Korean – sneak into a closed country and pull off a mission like this?

"It *won't* be a problem," Evans said again.

"Your reputation suggests that to be the case," the Korean said, putting on a smile that seemed more genuine now. "I *do* hope that is true. It will be worth it to you – as well as to me."

"And to your daughter," Evans said.

"Of course," the man said, standing. "We must not waste more time. Please give me a few minutes to forward you the information. I already know your secure mailbox address, and all I need from you is confirmation that my daughter will be returned safe, as well as what time you anticipate starting the mission."

Evans stood as well, shaking the man's hand. "I've already started, sir," he said, his mouth a thin smile. "As soon as I leave your apartment I'll make plans for transportation. I've got contacts in the region, guys I can trust. Everything we need I can get. My men will need a few hours to collect supplies, and I'll put a plan together while they work. As soon as we got what we need, we'll head out."

"I do wish you the best, friend."

Evans eyed the man as he wished him well, having a hard time discerning whether or not he was placating him. It seemed the Korean gentleman was genuine, as if trying to truly overcome the prejudices he must have grown up with. But his men were standing by the door already, and Evans shook it off. He nodded at each of them as he passed into the hallway. The door closed behind him, and true to his word, he began formulating a plan to get him and his men into North Korea.

But first, he had a stop to make.

12
SHANE

HE FOUND HIS COLD, dark corner after only a few minutes walk.

Shane Riley sat in the dusty bar nursing a ginger ale, trying to drink without letting the cubes hit his lip. He found a chair in the far corner, satisfied to sit with his back to the wall and watch the entrance. He wasn't particularly scared of anything, but it was an old habit that didn't seem to want to die. Nevertheless, he was somewhat of a people watcher and 'observer of the human condition,' as he used to joke with Kate.

The bartender was nice enough, a Korean gentleman who spoke decent English and smiled too much, but he had poured Shane's drink without fuss and accepted a bit of the cash Shane had nabbed from his bag. That bag was with him now, next to him on the booth seat.

Shane and his bag were the only other patrons in the joint. The bartender performed his stereotypical ritual of wiping down an empty counter with a dirty rag, even whistling along to the melody of the K-pop song blaring over the speakers above.

Shane amended his chosen preference for location. *Cold, dark... and quiet.* It wasn't that he hated music – though he did hate *this* music – it was that he was old enough now to prefer it to be completely silent most of the time, and on rare occasion just loud enough to be clearly audible.

Kate had been on Shane's mind more this day than any since she had passed away. The conversation with the old Korean guy had dredged up memories he had tried hard to suppress. Not forget completely, necessarily. He just wanted them to be like music – he wanted to recall them when he was ready – not be bombarded with them because someone else had decided to force the issue.

As if sensing this, the bartender turned the volume down a few notches, then nodded over at Shane.

He returned the gesture, thankful and appreciative. As he watched the man continue his cleaning regimen, the door opened.

The leader of the mercenary group he'd met in Chung-Hee Park's home stepped in. He spotted Shane immediately and began walking over.

Shane rolled his eyes, pulling the glass of ginger ale closer to him. The man was alone, no stooges in tow. Perhaps they were waiting outside, guarding the place. Shane didn't care.

He looked up as the man approached. Shane made no motion to shift position, or stand.

"Don't get up," the man said, his smirk returning.

Shane squinted up at him.

"What are you drinking?" The man turned to the bartender and raised his voice a bit. "I'll have what he's having."

He sat down across from Shane's bag, staring at him.

Shane didn't talk. He had wanted to be alone, not harassed by a mercenary trying to make friends.

"I thought you were more of a talker," the man said.

The bartender came over with another ginger ale and placed it in front of the mercenary. He took a sip, at first surprised, making a face back at Shane. "Not a drinker, eh?"

"Not on the job."

"You're on the clock? Since when?"

"Since about a year ago."

The man studied Shane for a long moment. "Is what Park said true?"

"Which part?" Shane asked.

"About your wife? About... her getting murdered?"

"You see me in here, huddled up in the back of a dingy bar, and you assume I want to talk about *that*? Or talk at all?"

Shane took a long sip of his drink, savoring the sharpness of the ginger. It was a good brand, one he didn't recognize. He was no connoisseur, but he had had his fair share of ginger ales and ginger beers.

"My men are going to take the job as well," the man said.

"I figured," Shane nodded.

"I thought you worked alone."

The bartender studied the two men from behind his perch, and Shane wondered what he was thinking. Did he assume they were hostile? Two military-trained men in a South Korean bar would definitely turn heads, if someone were to walk in.

"We ship out in a few hours," the man added. "Open invite for you to join us. Getting in is going to be tricky."

"Why do you care if I'm there?" Shane asked.

"The guy lost his daughter, man. The least we can do is help find her."

"The least we can do is absolutely nothing," Shane said.

The man looked like he was about to argue, about to snap back with some retort or another, but stopped himself. Shane, for his part, wasn't sure why he was acting so brazen. He truly did feel for the Korean man — and he had no grudge to hold against him. However, he was still hesitant to work with the other crew. He had his own way of doing things, and didn't want to risk anyone getting in the way.

"I'll think about it," he said finally.

13
EVANS

JONATHAN EVANS WATCHED the man across the table from him. He recognized that sadness in his eyes, knew that he had been through hell and had barely come out the other side. He realized that the man probably wished he had never come out at all.

Now, Shane Riley merely existed. There was no life, no love, no energy for solving a problem. It was just... existence. The fact that he wasn't talkative meant nothing — most men like him weren't. They held their cards close to their chests — Riley didn't know him from a bar of soap, nor did he owe him anything.

But their fates had been intertwined, and they would be working together to retrieve Park's daughter. Assuming, of course, Riley was even willing to play ball.

"What's your plan for getting into the country?" Riley asked suddenly, looking up from his own glass of ginger ale.

Evans smiled. "Well, I thought we'd just ask nicely."

No response.

"My guys are gearing up right now. We've got contacts around South Korea, a few here in Seoul. With any luck, we'll be fully outfitted in four or five hours and wheels up an hour after that."

Riley looked up and met his gaze. "Flying, then? Bold move."

"Shouldn't be. We'll fly low, bail out over the DZ. Just another Tuesday for us."

He didn't want to give Riley more information than necessary. While they had not agreed upon whether or not Riley would act as a member of Evans' team, or would just be a consultant, a contracted extra hand otherwise operating independently, he guessed the latter would be the case if it were up to Riley. Men like him didn't take orders from anyone — if he did, he would have stayed in the military.

It wasn't a disdain for authority, either. It was simply the fact that Riley had been around enough to know his own way in the world, to trust his own instincts. Evans admired that about some ex-soldiers. He knew it wasn't easy going civilian after a lifetime spent in the military. He had done it himself, but truth be told, his life didn't look anything like a civilian's.

He saw that in Riley, as well. The guy was a bit more rogue than Evans or his men — the kind of wild, adventurer type who retrieved artifacts or whatever for the highest bidder — but he wasn't naïve. Riley had most likely gotten himself into his fair share of scrapes — and out, as well.

"What's your call time?" Riley asked.

"Tell you what, Riley," Evans said. "Meet us at Incheon International at 2300, commercial deliveries. I'll have your name cleared for hangar access through the port entrance. If you want to do this, we'll take you on as part of the team."

"I have no interest in being part of your team."

"You've made that clear. But you remember what our mutual friend said. *We* can get you into the country, and that's the offer. I'll admit, I'm intrigued by how highly he spoke of you. If he's even remotely right, we *will* need your help once we're in. Something about this doesn't add up. It all seems a little convenient, a little too easy, doesn't it? For that reason, I want to be as ready as possible. Once we're in, you can do things however you want, as long as you stay out of my way. Let me get you into the country, and we can figure things out from there."

Evans waited, measuring the man's response. He figured saying something like 'figure things out from there' was the sort of phrase that someone like Riley would appreciate. Men like him didn't respond well to hard rules, plans, or wasting time worrying about logistics.

That was the military's game. Riley was no longer military.

But Evans knew that without any plan, their actions in North Korea would be doomed to failure. He had already started formulating the plan he and his men would follow, but he wanted Riley by his side; he wanted his help. If he needed to pretend there was no plan to get Riley on board, he would.

"Will you be there?" Evans asked.

Riley took a long draw from his ginger ale, then waved it at the bartender, who nodded and began pouring a new one from one of the guns on his rail.

He held it up for a moment, then set the glass back down on the table. He looked back at Evans, that same squint Evans had seen earlier on his face.

Evans waited, letting him do his thing. After a few more seconds, he raised his eyebrows, knocked on the table a few times, then stood up and smiled.

"Got it. Strong, silent type. Perfect." He stepped away from the table and turned back to Shane Riley. "We really could use your help, Riley. A million dollars ain't nothing, but I understand you're not motivated by cash alone. Just think about what Park said, all right? Think about your wife. You want answers? They're in North Korea. And we can help you get them."

14

SHANE

SHANE RILEY'S first move after leaving the bar was to wire a bit of cash to a local bank, pay the fee for the transfer and withdrawal, then stash the extra money in the pack Smith and Donovan had given him.

Next, he sought out a friend of a friend on the south side of town. The short, long-haired man owned and operated a pawn shop.

But it was the sort of pawn shop that sold weed whackers and musical instruments up front and more *interesting* items in the back.

After a minute of pleasantries, the man invited him into the back space through a locked door, and Shane whistled in surprise. An arsenal of weaponry spread out in front of him, covering three walls on pegboards that stretched from the ceiling down to two feet above the floor. Everything had a price tag near it, and Shane saw boxes of ammunition in every size imaginable filling cubbies below the pegboards.

Shane had felt naked the entire time he had been in South Korea, unarmed and wearing someone else's clothes. He'd ignored the clothes for now — they fit fine, and he'd never been one for particular brands or designs. Instead, he'd come here to fix the feeling of vulnerability he'd had. He purchased an old Glock 45 G5 hybrid that had been well-maintained, as well as a drop-leg holster that he could keep concealed under the loose-fitting clothes.

The weapon wasn't for the mission; it was for him.

He eyed a worn AK-47 hanging near the ceiling on the pegboard wall but decided against it. It didn't break down easily and would be hard to conceal in his small pack. He also purchased a couple of boxes of 9mm rounds, a concealed carry holster, and a combat knife that had a bit of rust on the tip but was otherwise sharp as a razor.

All these things he stuffed in the pack, paid the man, then left the pawn shop. He headed directly for the store across the street — a small tech shop, the kind dotting many busy alleyways and side-streets in any number of metropolitan areas around the world. The sort that had a pull-down chain-link gate in front of the door. He knew he couldn't expect to find the latest tech wizardry here, but it would certainly have something that would suit his needs. He had plenty of cash, so he walked in and asked the owner in English if he would accept US currency. He didn't want to visit an exchange house unless absolutely necessary.

Thankfully, the owner accepted, so he grabbed a small basket and walked around the store to shop for the odds and ends he needed.

Smith and Donovan had not given him a cell phone or any way to contact anyone, and he had not been able to go back to his bungalow first to retrieve his. It wouldn't have mattered much anyway – the only time he could use the internationally unlocked phone would have been here in South Korea. Once entering the country to the north, the phone would be as good as a brick. The North Korean Telecommunications network was – like everything else – owned and operated by the North Korean government. They had their own version of the Internet, but it was mostly Kim Jong Il fan pages and propa-ganda explaining how people who looked like Shane were pure evil.

He quickly found what he was looking for – a burner phone that had a card already installed in it. It was touchscreen, too – a far cry from the crappy old flip phone he was used to for missions like this. The touchscreen and rela-tively modern operating system would prove helpful, at least for the time he was in South Korea. He wouldn't have to buy a separate laptop or find an Internet café that would be closely monitoring his communications.

He wasn't necessarily afraid that the South Koreans were listening in to his every word, but just like back home and in the states with the NSA, one could never be too careful about discussing things openly on unsecured phone lines and Internet connections. The fact that he needed to make a call and pass along some sensitive information made him queasy, but there was no better alternative. He wasn't a techie sort of guy, but he had learned how to download and install a decent VPN app that would obfuscate his location by bouncing it around many networks.

The proprietor eyed him carefully as he perused the narrow rows of tech gear hanging from racks, which was an easy feat considering Shane stuck out like a sore thumb here. If the stereotypical Westerner was short, white, and loud, Shane was anything but stereotypical. He was white, but he was also

6'5". His head nearly touched the top of the door frame as he had entered the shop, and the small Korean man who owned the place never needed the wide, convex mirrors mounted in each corner of the store to keep an eye on him.

He grabbed a charger that fit the phone, picked up an extra data card, and swiped a USB stick off the rack. All of which he tossed in the small shopping basket and brought it to the front of the store. The man offered a small smile, and Shane returned an even larger one. He didn't need this man to think he was here to cause any trouble, but he also didn't want to come across as some selfish American jerk.

He hadn't opened his mouth yet to reveal that he was in fact from Australia, and the assumption in these parts of the world was that anyone who looked like him would be from America.

And being from America carried with it a load of baggage. He knew the stereotypes well; he had spent plenty of time in South Korea, as well as Japan, China, and Thailand. The different flavors of stereotypes changed a bit depending on where he was in the world, but they were generally all the same: Americans were seen as the arrogant, over-the-top saviors of the world, for better or worse. Many people in Eastern countries had a cautious appreciation for Americans, with a healthy bit of fear. American tourists often caused trouble — usually by not understanding customs and traditions of the countries they were in. While most visitors meant no harm, it was true that many of the locals were reluctant to share their lives with the outsiders for this reason.

Most of these countries had also experienced hundreds of years of purposeful indoctrination and jingoism, creating a curtain of agoraphobia that was just now beginning to lift.

Shane processed all of this and more as he stood at the counter with the big, stupid smile on his face, waiting for the man to count the bills.

He saw the proprietor thumbing through the cash, preparing to take a few bills from the stack, but Shane had already done the math as he had browsed.

"Should only need one," he said quickly in perfect Korean.

The man glanced up at him, wide-eyed, then nodded quickly. "Of course, of course." He handed back the stack.

He couldn't tell if the man was disappointed he wasn't able to rip him off or appreciative Shane didn't bash the man's head against his own counter because he'd tried, but he didn't care one way or another. This was how things went in the seedier parts of Seoul. The people here were exceptionally nice, very well-mannered, and normally accommodating to visitors. But in the lower-income districts — just like in every other major city in any country around the world — one had to be a bit more on the up-and-up. It was easy to get ripped off if someone didn't understand what was happening.

He thanked the man and grabbed his new toys, which the guy had put into a plastic shopping bag. Shane twisted a loose knot into the bag's handles and held it with a couple of fingers as he left the store. His next stop was to find another cool, dark place, preferably one with no one else around. He considered going back to the bar from before but didn't want to cause undue scrutiny from the sole bartender running the place.

The street was now dark, the sun having set far off to his left, casting huge shadows over the deep alleyway. Buildings rose on either side of him, low-rent apartments. A few shop owners were out, seated in plastic chairs or sweeping dirt and debris from the front steps, as if trying to change the fact that their shop was in the center of an old, grimy alleyway.

He found what he was looking for as he strolled north toward one of the busier intersections nearby. Sitting on the corner, with a door that opened to both streets, was a cafe.

The place was busier than the bar, but only a few patrons dotted the inside, each taking up a booth along the far wall. He gave the barista a slight nod, a twenty-something, rail-thin girl, but didn't order a drink. Instead, he found a high-top in the corner with no chairs around it. He walked over, smacked the plastic bag down on top, then began ripping it open.

He pulled the combat knife from his pack and used it to cut the impossibly strong plastic packaging away from the phone and the data card.

The phone had a bit of a charge — enough for a single call — but he plugged it into an outlet on the wall anyway. He wasn't sure how long he would be staying, but having a fully charged communication device was always a good plan to start with.

He waited for the phone to boot up, then began setting it up for internet access. The café had Wi-Fi, which he connected to and quickly downloaded a VPN app on the phone. He had an account with a few different providers, so he chose his favorite and logged in. It wasn't military-grade security, but it would at least make it more difficult to figure out where his call had originated from.

For the first time since leaving the bar, he stopped moving, allowing the gravity of the situation to hit him. The call he was about to place was not one he'd ever thought he'd make. But there was no other choice.

He let out a breath. The tech was ready to go, but was he?

EVANS GLANCED over the bags of gear his men had collected. Rayburn and Grudowski had a successful run, it seemed. They trio was seated in jumpseats at the back of a Xi'an Y-20 cargo plane flying over the Liaoning Province after having landed and taken off again in Dalian. The commercial flight was loaded to the brim with crates, only two humans — the pilot and copilot — on its manifest.

Flights like this formed the primary method of postal communication between China and North Korea. For Evans and his team, it was also a great way to hop into a restricted country from South Korea. South Korea to China, China to North Korea. After gathering the items they had wanted for the mission, Evans and the others had hauled ass to the airport in Seoul, where he had paid a pretty penny to get each of them hidden inside one of the large crates. The pilots had been paid off as well, as this very route was regularly used for smuggling. Usually weapons, ammunition, drugs, or some other paraphernalia the North Korean Army wanted to get their hands on.

It was a perfect ruse, too. The South Koreans didn't care – the airport workers were paid well for the task – and the Chinese didn't bother checking every postal flight in and out.

The North Koreans didn't care either — they didn't care what came into their country, as long as it wasn't an unauthorized human.

The plane had taken off and reached cruising altitude, and immediately Evans had opened his own crate, crawled out, and waited for his men to do the same. Now, they were gathered together near the back of the aircraft, huddled so they could hear their voices over the loud roar of the plane as it tumbled toward Dandong, gaining airspeed and altitude. They would fly over the Chinese city, heading northeast, toward their final destination — an area of rural plains and valleys near Kanggye, North Korea.

He looked down at the gear – plenty for four people – and had a moment of disappointment.

"Riley made his choice, I guess," he muttered.

One of his men heard. "Screw that guy; he would only slow us down."

"He might be abrasive, but if what Chung-Hee Park said about him is true, he would have been helpful to have along."

They had waited for an hour at the airport, watching as plane after plane took off and took to the skies. Shane Riley had never showed. The man was arrogant if he thought he had a better way into the country. There was no way a man who looked and talked like a Westerner could sneak into North Korea without being interrogated for hours on end. They would be turned away, at best.

He shuddered as he thought about the more likely scenario. *Interrogation would be the least of his worries,* he thought.

"Doesn't matter," Rayburn said. "We don't need him. We've got enough gear here to outfit a small army."

Evans shook his head. "No, Rayburn, we've got enough gear here to outfit four men fighting for two minutes against the North Korean Army." He chewed the inside of his lip. "But there aren't four of us, so some of this shit is completely useless. And this is all for worst-case scenario — the exact scenario I'm hoping to avoid."

The plan was simple, though it wouldn't be easy. Sneaking onto a cargo plane delivering mail was the easy part. Getting *off* on the other end – in North Korea – was the challenge. The North Koreans didn't take too kindly to outsiders sneaking in, especially if it was so obvious they were doing so in a covert way. For that reason, Evans' plan was to never make it to that final runway in the first place. The cargo plane was a perfect way to get *into* the country, but if they landed in North Korea while still inside of it, they were as good as dead.

So they would be ditching the plane halfway through their trip.

"This all looks good, boys," Evans continued. "We'll make sure it's split well, so carrying loadouts won't kill us. And we can leave Riley's here — consider it a gift for the Korean People's Army. But let's catch some sleep while we can."

They only had a few hours left in this second leg. They would wake up then, crawl back into the cramped crates, and hope the North Koreans hadn't gotten any more suspicious about Chinese mail since the last time Evans had done this.

16
MICHAELA

"THIS IS DR. EVERLY," Michaela said as she answered the phone.

As she spoke, Michaela Everly paced around the front room of her apartment, trying to remember where she had left the remote control. She wasn't clumsy, but she was certainly forgetful, absent-minded even, when it came to mundane, non-work-related things. She knew no more than thirty seconds had passed since she had set the remote control down, but she could not for the life of her remember where.

"Michaela," came the man's voice on the other end of the line.

She stopped pacing and let her eyes dart around the quaint living room. She hardly spent any time in the front room, opting instead to relax and unwind in her own bedroom at the back of the apartment space. She shared the apartment with no one but her cat, so she had little need for the massive TV and couch out here.

Not that she ever watched TV, anyway.

"Yeah," she said quickly, trying to refocus her attention. "Who is this?"

She thought she spotted the remote control on the stand next to the couch, but shook her head when she realized she had already checked there at least five times. It was just a tiny sculpture of a black cat, something a coworker had given her long ago.

Most of the people she worked with called her '*the* cat lady,' not '*a* cat lady.' Calling her *a* cat lady implied she was old and only had the companionship of hundreds of cats. Michaela wasn't old, and though she only had the companionship of a single cat, she loved the thing with every piece of her heart. She had grown up wanting to be a veterinarian, but found most of the day-to-day too broad for her interests. She had no interest in fixing someone's dog or mending the broken leg of a bird.

She wanted to help *cats*, and cats alone.

She had matured since then, of course, and hardly cared which particular animal someone had as a pet. Truth be told, she wasn't even that into cats. But she had once mentioned something of her upbringing and dream to be a 'cat doctor,' and her coworkers had taken it and run with it.

Hence the remote control-shaped black cat haunting her side table.

"Michaela, this is Shane Riley."

She stopped, her heart starting to race. She felt it beating, ready to explode. The very cat that had been the subject of her coworkers' teasing peeked its head out from inside her bedroom door.

"Shane?" she said, her voice a little shaky.

"Hey... how are you?"

She recognized the Australian drawl now that he had said more, but it wasn't his personality to ask her how she was. Not that he didn't care, just that he never bothered doing it before. He had always been more of a 'get-to-the-point' guy.

"I am... okay, I guess," she stammered. "Lost the remote control. Again."

"Check in the refrigerator," Shane said. She sensed a smile on his face on the other end. *"Kate used to do the same thing, and that's where it* always *was."*

Michaela knew the story. Kate was not forgetful, but Shane would often put things like car keys on top of leftovers in the fridge that Kate was supposed to remember for the next day.

"I don't think it's in the fridge, Shane."

There was a sigh. *"No, I don't suppose it will be. You still in Korea?"*

It was an odd question. After his wife had died, Michaela had heard exactly nothing from the guy. She and his wife had been best friends, working together at a genomics laboratory, both studying the intricacies of the human genome, trying to apply them to ways that might help future-proof human physiology.

It was groundbreaking work, but it was also *back*breaking. She and Kate were total workaholics — which was probably why Michaela was alone in a South Korean apartment with nothing but a cat and a lost remote control for company.

She confirmed. "I am. How are you, Shane?"

She had tried calling him a couple of times after Kate's funeral, but it eventually reached the point where she didn't even bother leaving a message. Shortly thereafter, Shane's phone line had been disconnected.

"Fine, I guess," he returned. *"I need... hey, can I ask a favor?"*

She knew Shane to be a bit abrupt, to the point. Nothing wrong with that – he was still polite and kind. But this was an odd way of speaking. She knew something was going on immediately.

"Of course, Shane. What's going on?"

"I'm actually in South Korea also," he said, his voice speeding up now. *"I've got... a situation. I think you might be able to help me out."*

She frowned. The only situation a man who did the kind of work Shane Riley did would need her help for was getting into *North* Korea. It was her turn to sigh. She knew this was what he was going to ask – there was little else she could offer someone who had Shane's experience. If he had gotten in trouble, she would be the last person he would call.

Funny how that worked. If *she* had gotten in similar trouble, he would be the *first* person she might call.

She could of course get him into the country. Whether or not it was a *good idea* was a different story altogether.

"What's going on?" she repeated.

"Wish I could tell you over the phone, but it's probably better we do this in person."

She nodded along, confirming her suspicions about why he had called from a number she didn't recognize. *He's on a burner.*

"Yeah, of course. Where are you now?"

He told her; she was not surprised to hear it was only a block away from her house. He knew he would be calling her eventually, she realized. But he had waited until the last minute. Why?

Was he hesitant about whatever it was he needed to do in North Korea? Or was he hesitant about meeting with *her?*

She bit her lip, wanting to see him again but knowing it was probably wiser to not get involved with his affairs at all. She had a knack not just for losing remote controls, but for getting in over her head with things she had no business in.

Shane Riley was *exactly* that sort of situation.

"You're close," she said. "Give me a minute to put the cat away and grab my phone. If I can... um, figure out where I left it."

"Michaela?"

She bit her lip harder. "Yeah?"

"You're holding your phone."

17

SHANE

SHANE SAW Michaela Everly before she spotted him. She was gorgeous, exactly how he remembered her: medium height, with long legs and short black hair that seemed to bob around her head like a little personal cloud, with petite features. For a scientist, she had a surprising knack for fashion, usually wearing trendy outfits and new designs. Whatever she wore, she wore well.

Best friends with his late wife, she was in many ways very similar to Kate. They both worked in the same field, which was how they had met in the first place, and both were *very* competitive.

Both women played it off as well, choosing to play the corporate glass ceiling game through subversion and strategy rather than overt action. Both women had had an 'aw shucks' attitude about them that tended to put their male colleagues at ease, leading to patronization but allowing them into inner circles of academic study previously kept closed to women in the field.

Kate and Michaela had eventually made their move, proving to their colleagues they had misjudged them. They weren't some ditzy academic wannabes who had gotten to where they were because of their looks and playful attitude; each of them was brilliant, calculating, and every bit as gifted as their male counterparts — if not more.

But in other ways, they were opposites of one another. Where Kate had been studious and diligent, Michaela tended toward effervescent and carefree. They had often butted heads over backing up their research discoveries with more data: Kate falling on the side of wanting more and more all the time, Michaela always opting for 'letting the results speak for themselves.'

Shane didn't understand half the crap the women had gotten themselves into — they were nerds, he was not, as he liked to remind them — but he knew the gist of what they had been doing at their workplace.

Studying the human genome was nothing new, nothing radical. But the revelations the two women had made, one after another, building on each other's success, was remarkable. Both had been renowned scientists in the field when Kate had been murdered.

It had been devastating not just for Shane, but for everyone in Kate's circle, especially Michaela. She had been so well-liked in the community, and though there was no small tinge of jealousy from her male coworkers, all of them openly admitted after Kate's death that she was a better scientist than them all.

Everyone but Michaela Everly.

Dr. Everly was every bit Kate's equal, and they both knew it. In fact, the loss to the community was nothing compared to the loss Dr. Everly felt at losing someone she could confide in. Kate had been one of the only people on the planet who could keep up with Dr. Everly, and she had told Shane as much.

"She was something special, Shane," Michaela had told him. "Something else. I'm so sorry."

Those were the last words she had spoken to Shane... up until a few minutes ago, when he had called her. Now she strode toward him down the block, her figure and walk unmistakable against the evening sky.

He sucked in a breath. This meeting represented more than passage into North Korea, more than just doing his job.

It meant more than just reconnecting with a close friend of Kate's for the first time since she had been killed.

As much as it pained him to admit it, it was going to be a struggle to stay focused. He wanted to ask her for her help, and then start his mission. But that was not going to be an easy thing to do.

All because of their shared past.

He was standing outside the café he had been in before, one location of many of the South Korean brand.

He fiddled with the lint in his pockets as she approached, suddenly feeling the weight of the pack on his back. He swallowed and cleared his throat a couple of times. He forced a smile, then let it disappear. He shook his head quickly, frustrated with how stupid he must look.

She walked close, her eyes wide, enchanting. She offered him a coy smile, the same one he had known for years.

He shook those feelings away. *Not now, Shane.*

Not ever.

She was in front of him now, coming in for a hug. He didn't want to return it, but he didn't *not* want to either.

What the hell, man? Why was he feeling so damned awkward? Why was he feeling like a 12-year-old at a middle-school dance?

Before he could stop it, she reached around his waist and pulled herself toward him. She ducked her head to the side as it landed on his chest. She squeezed, and he found himself squeezing back.

It... *did* feel good.

He thought he sensed a tremble and saw a glistening in her eyes as she pulled her face back and looked up into his. "Shane," she said quietly. "It really is good to see you."

18
MICHAELA

THEY SAT across from each other at a small table, this one in the center of the café. Shane had wanted to choose his usual spot – something tucked away in a dark corner – but Michaela had bounded across the rows of tables to find one smack-dab in the middle of the place.

She had done it on purpose, too.

He couldn't help but smile as she had offered him a seat facing away from the door. *At least she gave me that courtesy.*

He barely even shook his head as he nudged her into the chair and seated opposite, facing the door, as always.

"You haven't changed much," she said.

He cleared his throat again. "Neither have you."

"I suppose that's a good thing," she said, grabbing a small laminated menu from the center of the table. "I'm not getting any younger, so it's good to hear I'm not aging *too* fast."

"You're not aging at all," he said. He quickly shook his head as if to try to pull the words back out of the air and put them back in his mouth. Of course, that was impossible, and her eyes flicked upward and met his.

"Shane, we should probably just get everything out of the way before you tell me what it is you got yourself into."

"Get what out of the way?"

His fingers were clasped together, both hands laying on the center of the table where she had picked up the menu. She put one hand back down now, placing her open palm on his wrists. It was warm, and he felt it even through the long-sleeved shirt he was wearing.

There was nothing sensual about it, nothing inviting. It was just the warmth of empathy, of a shared bond. Nothing more, nothing less.

"How have you been?" she asked. "Are you back on your feet?"

He nodded once. "I'm working, if that's what you're asking."

She studied him for a long moment. "Sure, that's what I was asking, Shane."

"And you?" he asked. "You still working?"

He felt how stupid the question was as soon as it had escaped his lips. She flashed that coy smile again. "You know I am. Couldn't get away from it if I tried. And after Kate... there was some of her work to take over as well and... you know, I just sort of dug my heels in and got even more serious."

"You? Serious?"

She snorted, a laugh he knew well, one she claimed to be embarrassed by but never seemed to grow out of. "Touché," she said.

He felt looser now, comfortable. Michaela always pulled this out of him, somehow. Evans had called him the 'strong, silent type.' Hard to be that in front of Michaela, for whatever reason. He had been trained to push whatever feelings he had down deep, to focus on the mission, to focus on his team. But around her...

"Let's cut to the chase," she said. "I know you want to get into North Korea. Of course I can do that, and of course I will. But I'm not the *only* person you could have asked. Why me?"

Shane's head dropped.

"Because of Kate?"

Yes. But he didn't say it out loud.

"You don't have to tell me everything, Shane. But I need to know a little bit."

He gulped. "It's a job. Just like any other."

"*Just* like any other?"

He brought his head back up. Stared at her. Drilled into her eyes.

Those *eyes.*

"I miss you, Shane," she said suddenly, sniffing. "There, I said it, okay? I *miss* you, and I'm done being afraid of that. It's been a year; I've been mourning and grieving for a year, just like you have, and I'm not done yet, of course. But I'm done being afraid of how I feel about —"

"Stop..." Shane mumbled.

"I *won't* stop, Shane. I need to say this. If not for you, then certainly for me. It's cathartic, right? My therapist —"

"Damn your therapist."

She smiled again, her head falling to the side as she examined him. "My therapist said you would say that."

"I just need to get into North Korea. Do a job, come home. That's it."

"Yeah?" she asked. "And where is home these days, Shane?"

She had him there. *Dammit*, she had him. He couldn't say his bungalow was truly 'home.' It was a hellhole, falling apart a little more every day. Hell, for all he knew, one high tide from now until he got home might actually carry the whole damned thing away and deliver it to sea. Deliver it to...

"I've been trying to find her," he said suddenly. "I've been out on my boat... you know, in between jobs, and –"

"I think that's great, Shane," she said. "I think you *should* find her. Closure is great. So is talking it out, you see?"

"I'll take closure over talking any day."

He tried to keep his face passive but failed. There were tears in his eyes.

Her grip on his wrist tightened. "Shane, I owe you an apology for a lot of reasons. You know that, and you know I've tried. I'm going to keep trying, too. Until you get to the point where you can actually hear it. I hope that's okay."

Tears fell freely from his eyes now, and he felt every eye in the place looking at him. They weren't, of course, but he felt it anyway. He dropped his head again, not wanting anyone to see him this way.

"But it doesn't have to be today," she said. "Let's talk about North Korea."

19
EVANS

EVANS and his men trudged over the barren landscape, keeping their eyes on their perimeter as they moved. While all of them were well-trained and could move stealthily, they were also in a hurry. They also weren't small men, and their heavy boots crunched every other step or so. But Evans didn't feel like they needed be completely silent. They hadn't seen another living soul since leaving the airport in China. After landing, the plane's rear cargo door had been opened, and Evans waited for the bustling of airport and postal personnel to stop. He opened the lid and crawled out, waiting another minute to ensure they were alone. Finally, he and the other two men exited the back of the aircraft, which had been parked and abandoned inside a hangar.

They found an unoccupied airport security vehicle nearby, drove it to the single dirt road at the eastern edge of the airport, and then continued onward on foot.

Shane figured it was a bit less than a day's hike to their destination, and they had mapped out a route that would take them around any towns and villages.

Jonathan Evans felt a pang of nostalgia. He had been in North Korea before, but most of the time he had spent here was in the demilitarized zone in the south of the country, with a few stints into isolated regions around its eastern coast. Much of that time had been spent feigning subordination to the nation. While it was generally true that the rest of the world — the more *reasonable* portions of the world — did not support North Korea and its totalitarian regime, there had been pockets of pleasantness sprinkled throughout its 46-year history.

Every ten years or so tensions between North and South Korea would thaw just a bit, and emissaries from each nation would agree to meet for a certain amount of time to discuss trade, economic sanctions, and future plans. While most of these meetings were as useful to true humanitarian efforts as the English throne was to British governance, it at least allowed representatives from both nations into the other country without too much fear of losing their head in the process.

Evans had come across the border on two occasions, both times serving as a guard for South Korean ambassadors. He had mostly traveled with a convoy in a jeep, observing and scrutinizing everyone he saw or heard, careful to ensure no one got the slip on him or his men.

These were simple weekend missions, solely meant for show, but both times he couldn't help but notice that North Korea was, in many ways, just like South Korea.

And that's why the nostalgia had kicked in.

As they walked their line, heading toward the eastern ridge bordering their target location, Evans was struck once again by the realization he had before during his travels around the world.

As much as film and television wanted to make it seem otherwise, every place was similar in a lot of ways to every other place.

Sure, the Amazon rainforest differed from the Congo, and both places were unlike the Indo-Burma rainforest in many ways. And yet they were also the same. The same sorts of animals – predators, prey, insect, fish. The same sorts of plant life. The trees in each had different names, but there was continuity amongst them.

The bayous and swamps from his childhood looked a certain way, but they weren't too terribly different from the bayous and swamps in other places around the world. He enjoyed the feeling. It gave him a sense of 'place' had helped him feel at home no matter where he found himself in the world.

The villages and the people inhabiting them looked different, but at their core they were truly the same: each of them strived for survival, to exist in their culture free from oppression, free from starvation. They worked, they played, they lived.

The hills here reminded him of the rolling Appalachians back home, or even the foothills of the Afghan Hindu Kush Mountains. Sure, the names of the creatures and species were different, but they were all similar, each of them slotted into a particular role and group of Earthly life. These lush, verdant hills stretched as far as the eye could see, broken only by glowing yellow lights from towns and homes far in the distance.

It would take a few extra seconds for him to tell where on earth he was, if he didn't already know. Just because the government of this place hated outsiders and was fearful of letting its own people interact with the outside world didn't mean that its people were much different from the people in any other village in any other place on the planet.

He felt the soft crunch of stray leaves and bent grass under his boots as they marched in a line toward the ridge. The village they had dropped in on was behind them, and no one had been the wiser. They had not met with any interest at all, certainly not retaliation.

That was good – as long as they could stay under the radar, the longer they would be safe. He chewed on a quarter-sized piece of jerky as they walked, a luxury he had stowed deep within his pack. They were making good time – he was with good men – but he couldn't help but assume the worst.

Shane Riley had not come with them. Either the man was arrogant to the point of being insane, or he had other plans.

And while their way was not the *only* way non-citizens and military personnel could gain access into North Korea, it was the best way he knew.

Evans wasn't sure if their benefactor would turn down the million dollar payment if Riley did not fall in line and join Evans' group, but it was too late now — they were on the clock. Either Shane Riley was uninterested in helping out or he was in fact working a solo mission. Perhaps the old Korean had coerced him with talk of his wife, and didn't really care *how* she was returned to him.

Evans didn't fault Riley for his preferences, either. He had known men like him before – men who were not interested in working with others, for whatever reason. While Riley played the role of dispassionate, hardened soldier well, Evans had been able to read him easily.

The man was obviously hurt, still grieving from the loss of his wife. That much was clear from the background Chung-Hee Park had shared publicly. But he had seen something else – a fear, maybe – in the man's eyes. Shane Riley was not just mourning the loss of a loved one; he felt as though her death was his own fault.

The man told them he had two rules: he did not retrieve people, and he always worked alone.

He had told all of them point-blank what his hangups were, and their benefactor had pushed ahead notwithstanding.

Evans could excuse Riley for his cold demeanor; that attitude was not uncharacteristic of the types of people that filled the ranks of mercenary forces worldwide. Shane, in that case, was no different from Evans or his men

– they worked for a payday, and they didn't want to get involved in other people's business.

But he was still curious as to Riley's ultimate goal. Would he try to enter the country, try to find the man's daughter himself? If so, their paths might still collide.

As they marched toward the ridge, Evans began putting together a plan for just such an occasion.

20

SHANE

"SO, CAN YOU GET ME IN?"

Shane had ordered a tea, if only to have something to hold onto so his hands would stop shaking. He hated tea, and Michaela knew it. But when he'd ordered it, all she had offered was the same smile she always gave him.

Like she knew him better than he knew himself.

"Yes," she said. "I can."

"Same way as before?"

She sighed, and he knew before answering what the answer would be. Of course it was the same system – what else would it be?

Over a decade ago, the South and North Korean relations had thawed just enough to put together a rail system that ran from Seoul, South Korea, around Pyongyang, North Korea, then farther north all the way to a university south of Kanggye, Chagang. Originally meant for military and cargo transport between the two nations, and intending to serve as an easy way to get dignitaries into and out of each nation whenever the heads of state wanted to discuss matters, it had been also used at times for transferring citizens from one location to another. Border crossings were not common, but for some university researchers, scientists, and civilians with the proper credentials, crossing into North Korea was possible.

And Michaela had just such credentials.

"And you can get me on the train?" Shane asked.

She nodded, frowning. "Shouldn't be a problem, but it will be getting you *off* the train on the other side that poses more of an issue. Not to mention getting back out. That always proves to be the biggest challenge."

"Are things still pretty tense?"

She shrugged. "Who's to say? I have heard that the People's Army personnel in charge of guarding the depots are feeling more angsty lately, not having a major war to fight. They're jealous that the train is a sanctioned activity, and they can't extract money from it."

Shane nodded. "Sucks to be a pawn. I guess the best routes for extortion are coming in from China these days."

"That and the rest of the DMZ," she said. "We hear all the time that soldiers – both American and Korean – are making a pretty good income on the side sneaking people back and forth. And political tensions don't seem to have any bearing on it – when Kim Jong-Un is feeling threatened, he locks himself in one of his mansions, turns all eyes inward to keep himself protected, and pretty much ignores the rest of his country. When tensions are *not* stretched so thin, the soldiers themselves feel it, and they're a little less worried about getting caught smuggling."

Shane knew the gist of it. Everything, the world over, had gotten more expensive. Everything, it seemed, had gotten more difficult. *Any way to make a buck.* He didn't blame any of the perpetrators, either. Smuggling humans out of oppressive places was an age-old vocation. The very fact that it had to be done under cover of darkness — or risk certain death — proved why people tried to get out.

Smuggling people *into* places like that, on the other hand, was a bit more rare. Who actually wanted to go into a country like North Korea on purpose?

But because of the sheer number of people trying to get *out* of the country, there was a much higher chance of getting in without being noticed.

Getting out would be the problem, but that was a problem for the future.

JIN-TAK YEON MOVED COMPLETELY SILENTLY. Not even the bugs beneath his feet knew they were about to get squashed as each foot landed.

For years, he had trained with North Korea's elite forces. Not the regular People's Army or Navy — not any of the forces known to the outside world. He was part of the most elite of all – the Supreme Guard, a group of some unknown number of operatives – not even he knew the true size of the force – who operated individually and in small strike teams, similar to the Special Activities Division commandos working for the American CIA.

Only, his job was not intelligence gathering. Nor was it counterterrorism, or counterintelligence at all. The Supreme Guard had one job, and one job alone: to take out, swiftly and silently, the individual enemies of the North Korean government. Often these targets were enemies to the government itself, or to business interests of the government.

Sure, North Korea considered almost everyone else 'the enemy,' but Yeon's focus was on high-risk, high-reward targets. And while assassinations were part of the job, they were not his only task. There was an entire division of operatives that exclusively performed that sort of wet-work, operations to take out visiting foreign dignitaries – or even foreign nationals on their own soil.

Yeon's job was somewhere in between: if his government knew of a coup, an attempt to bring outsiders into the country who had military training and would otherwise be hard to pin down, he was dispatched. Now, he worked directly for a government research facility, providing something they called 'advanced defense and reconnaissance' for the station.

He had been hand-picked for this mission due to his past, and he approved. It was mostly an easy job, with few opportunities to risk his life — a life he preferred to keep as long as possible.

As he walked between the trees, a mere shadow against darker shadows, he kept his mission parameters in full focus in his mind.

Identify enemy combatants. Take them out silently. Cause confusion and chaos only as a last resort.

The mission was as simple as it ever was. *Find the enemy, kill the enemy.*

But his handler — the government official in charge at the research station — had still reminded Yeon about the necessary delicate nature of the job. The North Korean government frowned upon brutal military killings around civilians – the best way to keep civilians in line was to show strength, but to likewise not cause undue fear in the populace. Whatever he did, he needed to be careful to keep it away from the prying eyes of the local farmers and villagers.

He agreed with this assessment, as he knew many of the villagers in the area. Innocent people would jump to the wrong conclusions; they scared easily.

And he suspected the real reason he was to remain covert: this job, like so many others, could make someone high above him look *dirty*. The kind of job that could topple political careers, get the wrong people in the wrong kind of trouble, and generally did not look good for the country.

It didn't matter who it was, or what exactly was at stake – they had hired Yeon for a reason. He had accepted it without question. The pay was good, but this particular security detail interested him for a wholly separate reason.

A *personal* reason.

The message had been brief. *The outsiders trying to infiltrate this facility want to stop the research we are conducting. If they stop this research, there is no chance we will find the cure.*

There is no chance to finish our work before he dies.

Yeon remembered the tension in his jaw, stretching all the way to his throat and down into his stomach, as he had first read those words. That his handler and boss knew far more about his personal life than he would have liked was not the concern.

His concern was that his boss implied there *was* a cure. That there *was* a way to save his father's life.

He had known of the research facility prior to taking the job. He had grown up in the region, and as a boy, the Nazi-built station had been the subject of much speculation. There had long been reports of disappearances, of entire villages simply ceasing to exist. The region was fraught with legend and myth regarding the reasons why, as well. Everything from giant man-eating creatures to evil studies taking place inside. He had heard the stories since he was a child, knew that while most of them were fantastical, there was something eerie about the region.

After all, he had grown up just south of the place.

Most people from his village ignored the legends, but were still hesitant around it. They refused to farm the valleys immediately surrounding the base, and gave it a wide berth when traveling northward. It was ironic that his job had brought him back to this place, but now he could truly appreciate what they were doing here. His father was there, dying a slow and painful death.

Their work was going to save his life. *His* work was to prevent anyone from interfering.

A noise stopped him.

He crouched for a moment, trying to get even smaller still than his already slight stature provided. He waited, watching the darkness. He did not use night vision, since it interfered with his ability to feel completely at home in the woods.

Satisfied that he had only startled a bird, he continued forward. He could smell the Americans now, their scent trailing behind them like a disgusting plague. He would find them, one by one. He would root them out, stalk them.

And then he would kill them.

22

MICHAELA

MICHAELA HAD GIVEN Shane the breakdown of the rules before boarding the train. His only goal as they sat on the hard, un-upholstered seat inside the train was to blend in. There was no question he stood out in the train car. Every single person they had seen so far was Korean. Even Dr. Everly, born in San Francisco, had two Korean parents. She looked like she belonged here, and in a sense, she did.

The Doctor of Anthropological Sciences had submitted the last-minute proposal to her South Korean employer for a four-day visit to their sister lab in North Korea. The laboratory was one of the few bastions of rational thought that could be found in the isolated nation. While the North Korean government usually kept very close tabs on every visitor — professional researcher or tourist alike — that crossed its border, enough precedent had been set between the two universities that a bit of leeway was given to bringing along assistance and professional support.

Still, Michaela Everly had used many favors to get Shane Riley on board, especially considering he was an unknown name to both institutions — *and* because she no longer worked for the university. She couldn't exactly tell her new boss that she was bringing a trained assassin and professional mercenary into North Korea — the very look of the guy would earn him enough scrutiny. But she had worked up a good enough cover story that both sides of the train allowed it.

Thankfully, Shane had been prepared. He'd pulled out a fake passport, Australian-issued government ID, and other paperwork for a man who looked exactly like him but had a different name. He had smugly handed all the credentials to her, explaining that his work required 'special circum-stances.'

Michaela shouldn't have been surprised. She knew he was ex-military, and had gotten himself into a few scrapes. But Kate had rarely spoken of his work.

If it took using an illegal ID to get into North Korea to do something decent, well, she could live with that.

Michaela looked over at him, seeing the beginnings of sweat forming on his temples. It was warm in the train car, but she knew he was sweating for another reason. This was a high-risk play, one that could get both of them thrown in a North Korean prison.

Or worse.

He sat with his back rigid, eyes forward, not daring to make eye contact with any of the many train employees walking up and down the car, inspecting tickets and registrations.

He sported the fake ID, one that had already been approved for travel, and would be entering North Korea under the pseudonym *Jacob Wiley*.

She had initially scoffed at the similarity to his actual last name, but let it go. It wouldn't matter – the name would check out, and if anyone decided to investigate further, they would find that Jacob Wiley was an esteemed author in genetics research from the University of Melbourne, Australia. Shane already had the accent; the only thing he needed to do was pretend to be the world's foremost expert on gene sequence anomalies and their application to viral research.

She smiled at him as the car attendant left and the doors finally closed.

This was not the first time she had snuck someone into North Korea – in fact, it wasn't the first time she had snuck Shane Riley into North Korea. But it had been a few years ago, back when digital technology made it much more difficult to keep tabs on every person entering and exiting the nation. Database searches used to take days, not minutes. Facial recognition had been a pipe dream.

But now, things were different. They needed to be extra careful. One look at the wrong camera – one frown at the wrong guard – and this trip would be cut short.

If the North Koreans decided to get nosy, their lives could be in danger as well.

Even as the train started rolling, she swallowed, a slight shudder coming over her. With a career spent mostly in South Korea, the stories she had heard of the way North Koreans treated defectors and spies were no stranger to her. There were plenty of true stories of the regime's brutality and repression, of public executions, forced labor camps, the widespread surveillance and censorship.

The train picked up speed, departing from the station. The journey would take them several miles through the demilitarized zone, through no less than three checkpoints, where United States, South Korean, North Korean, and United Nations inspectors would board the train, double-check every passenger's identification and question their itinerary, then allow them to proceed. Meanwhile, their counterparts would check below decks, where any equipment or baggage was stored.

It was a slow, harrowing march northward, but it was a proven method — as long as someone had the proper credentials.

Or, in their case, as long as the North Koreans *believed* they had the proper credentials.

23
EVANS

WHILE THE EVER-PRESENT threat of North Korean military personnel weighed on his mind, Evans also knew this region should not be occupied by more than a few small, roaming patrols. North Korea was always at war, it seemed, but not within its own country. As long as they moved quickly and kept their heads down, they should be able to reach the checkpoint in time.

As if reconsidering this, Evans pulled his head up and glanced at the slope in front of him. Technically just a large hill, from this vantage point, it seemed to be no less than an entire mountain.

He let out a sigh, then pulled a clip of jerky from his pocket and placed it under his tongue.

He followed directly behind Grudowski, who kept a wide, sweeping arc with the barrel of his gun. Evans did the same, alternating so that there was never a section of terrain without someone's eyes on it. They had scared up a few small mammals and birds who had scattered by their approach but still had seen nothing larger than that.

They started up the hill shortly after, eventually having to boulder over a section. At the top, Evans allowed himself to be helped along by Grudowski, and both men sat on top of a large rock to rest while they waited for their other teammate Rayburn, who was pulling up the rear.

"Where the hell is he?" Grudowski asked.

"He was a scout, remember?" Evans said. He smiled from the corner of his mouth. "Cocky SOB, too. Likes to think he's some kind of Rambo. But he is a helluva tracker – probably just wanted to move a bit slower so he could check out our flank. If we don't hear from him in another minute, we can run down and check."

Grudowski glanced sidelong at him. "You mean *you* can run down and check."

Evans' smile grew. While he preferred to operate in less hostile territories, that was the nature of the job. He wasn't good at what he did because of diplomacy – he was good at what he did because he was ruthlessly efficient and didn't care much for navigating the myriad webs of politics that plagued these places.

A minute passed, and his partner raised his eyebrows. Evans rolled his eyes, then pulled himself up so he was standing on the rock now. He brushed off his pant legs as he spoke, keeping his voice low. "Time to check on our friend. But we both go – no sense splitting up now."

He got no argument from Grudowski, and together the two descended the same slope they had climbed a few minutes prior.

There was no sign of Rayburn.

They walked in a wide circle around their previous route, eventually coming to a point about half a click from their rest spot on the boulders. Ideally, Evans would have opted for a wider concentric arc around this one, covering more and more ground each time.

But they didn't have time for that. It was already impossibly dark out, and both men had donned their night vision goggles. Far from the old greenish-hued military glasses of yesteryear, these newer models sensed gradations in light so sensitively it could give them a digitized, colorized view of the world around them, even in near-pitch-blackness. It was almost like walking around in the middle of the day. Someone could still hide from them, but they couldn't just use the cover of darkness to do it.

But why would Rayburn hide from them? Evans didn't understand where the man could be. He swept his head left to right, suddenly feeling anxious.

"Where the hell is he?" Grudowski said from behind him.

Evans shrugged.

Rayburn was gone.

Evans was suddenly on high alert. This was not part of anyone's plan. If he had fallen, he would have cried out for help. If he was being chased, likewise, he would have shouted something. Sure, they didn't have comms, as they had planned to stay together and hadn't wanted to take the risk of having a signal get intercepted. The plan had been to move as one, quickly and quietly, never getting far enough apart for this to happen in the first place.

Evans had failed. He had not done his job, and now one of his men was gone.

Worse, he suspected he had been right about his luck all along – that it was going to wear out very soon. Standing below the boulders once more, giving one final sweep of the land they had covered extensively in the past hour and a half, he finally let the realization of the truth wash over him.

They were being hunted.

24

SHANE

THEY ARRIVED at the university in Kanggye about eight hours later. The train ran north-south, with only a few stops after the DMZ checkpoints for security. Riley had dozed off soon after leaving the last checkpoint, catching up on much-needed sleep. When the train began to slow into the final station, his eyes flicked open and regained his bearings.

Michaela was still by his side, smiling her mischievous grin. He frowned and cleared his throat, suddenly concerned about the state of his morning breath. He wished he had a toothbrush. A shower would be divine.

She stood up, and he followed suit, his knees and back creaking a bit as they groaned against the hard plastic seat he had been crammed into for far too long.

"Keep your head down and don't try to draw attention to yourself," Michaela said softly in English.

He yawned but nodded.

"And today's not really the best day to practice your Korean. Better just keep your mouth shut."

Shane knew his Korean was far from perfect, but his accent was even worse. Opening his mouth at all – in Korean or any other language he knew – would cause just the sort of scrutiny he was trying to avoid.

He knew his place here, deep in the heart of North Korea's Chagang state. This was Michaela's territory. Even still, she was an outsider as well. But familiar with the university and looking like a Korean, she could much more easily blend in with the citizens here. But for such a suspicious and paranoid society, even someone like her, with her flamboyant laughs and brilliant attitude, could easily draw attention.

A man boarded the train with two gun-wielding North Korean soldiers behind him. He barked an order and everyone sat back down. Shane and Michaela followed suit and waited impatiently as he checked – once again – everybody's ID and registration papers. Fortunately, they were toward the front of the car and only had to wait another five minutes before disembarking. They left the train without issue, and Shane found himself on a long concrete pier situated next to a squat building painted government beige, a color that seemed to be ubiquitous no matter the flavor or location of the government, no matter what country.

The part that was different about this university was that it was *small*. From what he could tell, the train had dropped them off on a platform connected to a single building — and that was it. There were no others in sight, and the single building he did see was only large enough to hold a dozen medium-sized rooms.

"You probably guessed, but this is all run by the state," Michaela explained as she briskly walked toward the far end of the building. "Opened in 2005, it's pretty new for universities. Even then, it's not really a *university* as much as a *government brainwashing facility.*"

Shane nodded, still not daring to speak in the midst of other North Koreans. There were a few glances in his direction, but most of them were from students and civilians probably interested in why such a large white man was bounding around their campus.

Michaela continued, her voice lowering. "They don't really allow *real* research here — it's basically a front for North Korean military research, like all other institutes of higher education. This one's got a speciality that happens to align with mine — genetic engineering — so they allow researchers in from outside, as long as we turn over all of our research to the university when we're finished."

Shane nodded again.

"I had to make up something to put down as my reason for coming," she said. "My boss will know it's bullshit, but he's pretty hands-off. Doesn't care, as long as I stay out of trouble."

Shane looked at her, squinting.

She smiled. "But we're *not* going to get into trouble, are we?"

They reached the end of the short building, and Michaela pulled the unlocked door open and yanked him inside. It was dark and cold in the room — an office that looked like it had not been occupied for years. Dust covered most of the tables and desks, and an old laptop sat in the corner of the room.

"Okay," she said to him. "You're in North Korea. What now?"

Shane smiled, chuckling at her direct, candid approach. He appreciated that she hadn't asked many questions, and he wanted to come clean. But he couldn't exactly say, '*Well, now it's time to find and extract some young woman from the regime's torture chamber, probably killing everybody guarding her.*'

On the other hand, she was not naive. She knew his past, his background. She knew what he had done for a living, so she had to figure he might be here for a similar reason. And if he had gone through all this trouble to reconnect with her, to ask for help, she would know it was important.

"Shopping," he said. "There's a shoe store in the region that I hear is *divine*."

Her smirked rose with her face as she rolled her eyes.

"First, I need a vehicle," Shane said. "Something inconspicuous."

Michaela nodded in the darkness.

"Actually, there are usually a couple of maintenance vehicles or work trucks they park right on the other side of the building."

Shane turned and pulled the door handle once again, stepping outside. Michaela followed behind him. He wanted to get moving as quickly as possible, especially since he had finally gotten some much-needed sleep.

He was ready to close this chapter of his life.

As they rounded the corner of the building, he saw the lot up ahead. Michaela picked up the pace, and Shane found himself following behind her, scanning the vehicles in view. None of them would be hard to steal – it was common practice to leave the keys on the seat or tucked into a pocket somewhere.

And though carjacking was a crime here, just like anywhere else, he really did not want to have to explain himself while in a North Korean prison.

But he wasn't worried about stealing *or* losing his head as he neared the lot. As he saw the cars and trucks spread before him, he knew the issue was going to be something else.

He reached the single row of cars, and his jaw dropped. He turned to Michaela, who was smiling up at him.

"See?" she asked. "Maintenance vehicles, free for the taking."

25
SHANE

"ARE WE... supposed to actually *fit* in that?" Shane asked. There was a smile on his face, but he wasn't feeling humorous.

Beside him, Michaela shrugged. "You said you needed a vehicle," she said. "This is a vehicle."

Shane's eyes widened as he approached the tiny, narrow truck. *If you can call it a truck.* "Is this *technically* a vehicle? Maybe. But it looks more like the kind of thing kids ride on in front of a grocery store entrance."

Michaela laughed. "Sorry, if you gave me more time, I could have called ahead and rented a Hummer."

The vehicle was all-electric, barely larger than a golf cart. An elongated bed stretched behind the vehicle, but still, it was barely eight feet long and had to be less than four feet wide. Shane walked around the truck, examining it from all sides and angles.

Four wheels, four windows, mirrors on both sides... What more could a guy want?

"They drive these around campus all the time," Michaela explained. "Groundskeepers, maintenance workers, even one of the deans has one they use to get from one building to another."

Shane smirked. "Campus? You mean this single building?"

Michaela shrugged.

"I guess Koreans really are smaller than Westerners," he quipped.

"But not every Westerner is a strapping 6'3" hulk like you," Michaela said, winking.

He stood for another moment in disbelief, not wanting to commit to the next couple of hours behind the wheel of this glorified golf cart.

Michaela urged him forward, her hand pressing against the small of his back. "Well, come on, what are you waiting for?" she asked, still giggling.

He pulled the driver-side door open and looked down. The seat seemed to be riding a mere six inches off the ground. Not only would he have to duck to get in, he would have to duck while driving, too. He crunched his knees up to his chest and grasped a meaty hand on the roof to swing himself inside. The steering wheel was millimeters from his chest, and with his head cocked to the side, his left ear pressed against the ceiling, he was able to get inside.

Not at all comfortably, but successfully.

Michaela walked around to the other side of the car and pulled open her door. Her thin frame and average height made getting inside far less of a chore. She planted herself in the passenger's seat, grabbed the handle above her head, then leaned back and stretched her legs, yawning while looking at Shane. "Spacious," she said.

Shane rolled his eyes, surprised that they were able to move freely. He found a lever to move his seat back. He pushed against the floorboards and got an extra half-inch, barely enough to get his knees down below the dashboard. His head was still smashed awkwardly to the side, but he was able to drop the top half of the seat back a bit as well, relieving that strain.

He pressed the ignition button on the dashboard and felt the truck hum to life, the engine noise barely louder than a whisper.

The university was situated southwest of their destination, and if Chung-Hee Park was correct in his assumption, their destination was surrounded on three sides by mountains. A small gap between two smaller hills allowed easy access from due south of the facility, and thus would provide the best – and least treacherous – way into the research lab. Plus, initial satellite imagery he'd sent to Shane suggested that only the immediate area around the base itself was guarded, not the hundred-mile-diameter circle of mountains surrounding it.

Shane knew that Evans' team would also be heading toward this location, but he had no plans to rendezvous with the other team.

I work alone.

His self-prescribed mantra nagged at him as he recognized the irony of having a passenger with him now.

I work alone. Usually.

He had to admit it was nice to have company — in a vehicle like this, they weren't exactly going to make great time. He had hoped to be at the doorstep of their destination in fewer than two hours, but as he pulled away from the back of the building and brought the truck up to full speed, watching the speedometer barely move, he realized they were going to be driving for a while.

EVANS WAS EXHAUSTED, and just when he was looking to stop and rest for a bit, they had run into this hurdle.

He had come into hostile territory, landed in the middle of nowhere, and worked tirelessly to get up the side of a mountain before daybreak — all in order to reach the rendezvous point on time.

And now he had lost a man doing so.

He berated himself for not being more attuned to their surroundings. He had assumed all along that their entrance into North Korea would be the challenge, that once inside they could largely operate unmolested.

He had expected to have to dodge the roving bands of North Korean soldiers, perhaps a few squads or small patrols. Thus, he had been on the lookout for vehicles — military paraphernalia — checkpoints and patrol stands dotting the main highways, which they had kept their distance from.

So he had never in a million years expected someone trained in the arts of stealth and assassination to be waiting for them the moment they landed.

Who the hell was it? And how the hell had they known where to look?

It was like they were running into enemy territory while the enemy knew full-well they were coming. It wasn't the stealth and surprise mission he'd expected. There was information he didn't have. He had told Shane Riley as much back at the bar.

None of this added up. There were still variables he didn't know, questions still unanswered.

But that didn't matter — he had rushed into situations far more dangerous than this, so he would keep moving, keep working. One of his men — a *good* man – was dead because of it, but Evans wouldn't crumple. If anything, it would make him stronger. Better. If they were going to be successful here, they needed that edge.

He thought again of Shane Riley. The man fancied himself a lone wolf, the kind of soldier who liked operating alone, who railed against authority and had the scars of someone who had been through too much to want to share it with anyone else.

Riley wore that pain on his sleeve, trying to hide it but doing it in an obvious way, as if proving to the world that he was beyond caring for himself and no longer willing to allow anyone else to get close. It was an act, one Riley might not even be aware he was putting on.

But Evans was no fool. He saw right through it. While the pain in Riley was likely very real, the manifestation of it was a ruse, a mask he wore. It was something that Riley chose to don, like putting on a shirt in the morning.

Evans knew the truth: fact was, Shane Riley *wanted* camaraderie, *wanted* companionship. He wanted someone to share his life with. He'd had it once, and that had been taken from him. Unlike many men Evans had known who were effective because of their drive toward defeating evil, Riley's drive was based on defeating evil because it had taken something so dear from him.

Riley had a personal vendetta.

Evans knew all this not because Chung-Hee Park had discussed a bit of Shane's past with him, but because he knew Shane was here in North Korea. He hadn't seen Riley yet, of course, but he suspected that Shane Riley would make good on his word to Park and find his own way into North Korea. He would be here soon, possibly even running into Evans at the rendezvous point they were now approaching, looking for Seong Park.

If all that turned out to be true, it meant Shane Riley was not the isolated, damaged man he claimed to be. Sure, he might be playing at it — taken to living alone and not having any friends — but it was all part of the act. The men Evans had known who *actually* preferred loneliness and isolation were the types of men who would balk at a mission such as this. They would never show their face in North Korea after making it a point to tell everyone around about their 'rules' for working alone.

No, those types would only show their face here for one reason: money. But Riley *had* money, and even if he were short currently, he had the means to get more. Instead, he had told them all in Park's apartment that he would not work with others, and that he would not retrieve people. He was a treasure hunter, a mercenary for hire who would track down any object around the world — the only exception: human cargo.

So if Shane Riley showed up here, it meant Evans was correct in his assumption.

Riley was a man still looking for closure, not a man who had already found it.

27

SHANE

THEY DROVE in silence for half an hour, both tired from the gentle bumping of the dirt road leading north through the hills, lost in their own thoughts.

There was a lot on Shane's mind. The beautiful woman next to him had flashed back into his life, after over a year of absence. He had assumed he would never see her again – she was one of the last ties back to his late wife – and they had a shared history he told himself he would rather forget.

But he had to admit that those memories weren't coming back as history he would like to forget, but instead as pleasantly nostalgic thoughts. He remembered the first time he had seen Dr. Michaela Everly — PhD student at the time — sitting next to the woman who would eventually become his wife.

Michaela and Kate were seated next to each other at a bar, nearly leaning on one another as they shared conversation. At first, he had assumed they were on a date. Seated alone at a booth waiting for a buddy to enjoy a beer with after a long day, Shane watched the two women with curiosity. Their backs were to him, but he could see the expressions on the sides of their faces as they interacted.

Whatever they were talking about was indecipherable from this distance, but it was obviously serious, and they were both into it. Their faces moved from impressed to quizzical to confused and back again, an endless cycle of back-and-forth, complete with hand gestures and drawing out diagrams of whatever they were describing with a finger on the bar top. They were completely ignored by other patrons and the bartender.

His friend arrived soon after, but Shane couldn't help but regularly glance over at the two women engaged in deep conversation at the bar. Eventually, his friend noticed.

His buddy had pushed him and urged him to walk over and talk to the women — something Shane had never felt comfortable doing. Nevertheless, he had a couple of rounds in him and was feeling looser than normal, so he obliged.

It went about as well as he had thought it might.

The woman on the right – Kate – saw him coming, frowning as he approached. But it was Michaela who spoke first. "We're not thirsty," she said quickly.

Shane stopped short, his palms up. "I'm just here for my friend," he said, trying to think on his feet.

"We're not thirsty for that, either," Michaela snapped.

Shane smiled, then reached out his hand. Michaela stared at it, but Kate, redirecting his hand into hers. She pulled him a half-step closer. "Tell your friend 'thanks but no thanks,'" Kate said. Her words were biting, but there was a playful smile on her face.

She released his hand then, and Michaela immediately dove back into their conversation once again. He had heard a few keywords, like *symbiotic* and *ribonucleic acid* – two words he remembered from grade-school science class, but certainly not the subject he expected to hear in a pub.

They were close to campus, however. He remembered thinking the women might be students there, perhaps graduate level. They looked about Shane's age, though they had done a much better job aging than he had.

He had turned to leave, feeling sheepish and embarrassed, his cheeks flushed red, when he heard Kate's voice call back to him. "But tell your friend if you guys want to switch places and try again, he might have better luck."

Shane stopped again, his back to the women, his cheeks growing even more red. But he couldn't help but smile.

The memory caused him to smile again, in the present.

"Penny for your thoughts?" Michaela asked, her voice catching him by surprise.

Shane snapped back, pulling the car gently to the right to work around a tractor moving slowly over the bumpy road.

"Penny for your thoughts?" Shane repeated. "I didn't think anyone actually said that."

"Something my dad used to say. I guess I always looked contemplative or something, so it was usually how he started a conversation with me."

"You did always have your head in the clouds," Shane said, smiling.

"*That* was Kate," Michaela responded. "I was always lost in my own thoughts, sure, but they were thoughts of DNA schema, chemical composites, and all the math that held it together. Kate was always more of a dreamer, always thinking up ways to push the boundaries."

"And you were the one who figured out how to do it," Shane added.

Michaela's warm smile reached her eyes. "She was pretty good at that herself," Michaela said. "But she was never one to take credit. She probably told you all sorts of things about how brilliant I was, how much of a genius everyone around her was, always holding back about how much she contributed to our work. *God*, I miss her."

Shane nodded, chewing his lip, unsure of where this conversation was heading.

"Sorry, I didn't mean to..."

Shane frowned, then shook his head. He cleared his throat. "No, it's fine. Actually, you asked what I was thinking about. I was just reminiscing. First time we met. The three of us – we were together all the time in the early days."

Michaela's smile widened. "True, but there was never a question in anyone's mind that it was going to be you and Kate. I think she had the hots for you from the moment she saw you."

Shane scoffed. "You mean when I awkwardly interrupted you at the bar?"

Michaela's eyes narrowed. "Two *gorgeous* young ladies like us always have to be on our guard. We eyed you the second you walked in. Had to make sure you weren't a predator."

"Did you ever figure it out?"

She tossed her head back and laughed loudly. After a moment, she spoke again. "We never used to go to the pub, you know," Michaela said.

"What?"

"Going to that pub was something we did on a whim. We were both heads-down in our work for months, and it felt like we never left the lab. It was her idea, I think. I'm *sure* it was, actually – I never would have suggested something like that – but we ended up there the same night you were there."

Shane nodded, the memory still fresh in his mind. "Wasn't something I did much of, either."

Michaela laughed. "Yeah, right. I know you. One of your favorite things to do is hide in the corner of some dank bar, nursing a beer."

"*Ginger* beer," Shane corrected.

"Fine. Ginger beer."

28
SHANE

"YOU KNOW, I wasn't supposed to be in that pub that night, either," Shane said. "I was meeting a friend from out of town, and he recommended that place. I don't even remember what it was called."

Michaela laughed again. "Neither do I. Seems like fate brought us together then."

Shane knew what she meant — that fate had brought him and Kate together. He gripped the steering wheel tighter as they trundled over the section of road rife with potholes and ruts. They were entering an area of the country that got a lot of rain, but only in the span of a month or two.

"What were you working on?" Shane asked suddenly.

"Generally?" Michaela asked.

Shane swallowed. "No, I mean when she…"

Michaela nodded, not talking for a moment. When she did, her voice was lower. "We didn't think there was anything conspiratorial or dangerous about it at the time," she began. "We were trying to sequence a section of the human genome that we thought was related to potential racial differences between human individuals."

"Racial differences?"

She nodded. "There's been a lot written about race, and how it's largely this construct we've invented to describe how to tell where someone came from, their ancestry, things like that. What foods they ate, how they lived. But it's just a construct — an invented label. For a while now, geneticists have known that there really isn't any particular DNA haplotype that can be used to pinpoint race. Haplotypes are probably helpful in determining population or ancestry similarities and differences, but not race."

"Until you and Kate came along?"

"Not necessarily us, that's just what we were working on."

Shane interrupted. "So you were trying to discover if there were real genetic differences between humans? Basically, trying to tie all of us to a common ancestry that allows for genetic variation within the species?"

"Succinctly put," Michaela said. "And exactly right. Basically, we wanted to sequence strands of DNA to determine racial profiles — down to a science. We know we're all the same species, right? That much is abundantly clear in our DNA already. But is the sort of thing that gives us blue eyes or green eyes just a genetic mutation — randomization — or is it something that could actually help to define a particular race? Assuming we could all agree on what that word meant, if we could tie race to a geographic area, could we use gene sequencing to determine which race people belong to, where they came from?"

"I'm sure that's rhetorical," Shane said.

She nodded. "It is, but it's also a hypothesis that's worth testing. What we don't want to do is tie race to a particular geography that exists today – that's wrongheaded and shallow. It's shortsighted, as well. Just because there are a lot of Jewish people that live in Israel today does not mean that historically all people with Jewish DNA markers — if those markers truly exist — are from that region, right? It might, or it might not mean that.

"We just wanted to see if there was a way to map the larger groups humans can be split into — haplogroups — then figure out if, during 70,000 years or so of our existence, differences in region and climate, as well as things like food intake, macronutrient nutrients, and mother situations forced differentiation between sequences within the genome, in the form of haplotype."

"Sounds like pretty important work," Shane said, "though not without some complexities."

"That's putting it mildly," she said. "There are a lot of people who don't want us to even do this kind of work for religious, political, or just moral reasons. They think somehow there's an ethical dilemma in searching the human genome for answers as to where we came from and how and why we split off from one another and formed groups."

"Well, there is a history of people doing this work for more nefarious purposes."

"Yep, right again. What we do is sometimes associated with eugenics, sure, even though we are not doing any experimentation whatsoever. We're not trying to change any DNA – we're just researching it, trying to unpack its mysteries. We have to be careful how we present the results though, because this work is the same sort of work that would have made Hitler even more successful."

"How so?"

"He was basically trying to prove that the Aryan people — another construct that doesn't really exist — were completely different – not even a different race, but a different species altogether. He wanted to paint the picture that they were better than human, and everyone else was worth eradicating. While our research was showing that not to be the case at all – people can and did misconstrue it in all sorts of ways. We were trying to just define what race means, from a genetic standpoint. Does it have any merit in the discussion of human haplogroups? Should it be relegated to a cultural and regional descriptor? Is it worth investigating further?"

"I see," Shane said. "And obviously there were people willing to go to great lengths to prevent you from continuing."

"Apparently so," Michaela said softly. "Once again, that's putting it mildly."

29
EVANS

EVANS AND GRUDOWSKI made it down the other side of the hill in less than an hour. A second hill blocked their view of the research station they assumed was waiting for them here, but they pressed on toward the hill anyway, trusting their intel and preparation. They covered the ground quickly, having determined that Rayburn was long gone.

It pained Evans to have to give up the search, but finding him was not the mission, and slowing down meant losing Seong Park. He had reluctantly ordered Grudowski forward once more, and together they reached the second hill.

At the bottom of this second rise, Evans called a halt as they met up with a winding dirt road. They waited there for fifteen minutes, trying to get a read on how busy the area might be. He knew there were a few villages dotting the plains and hills surrounding them, but no major cities. The road, however, was larger than he would have guessed — easily large enough for trucks and other vehicles.

He wondered if this was a main route to the government base they were looking for. Still, they didn't see a soul the entire time he and Grudowski waited. Finally satisfied they were safe to proceed, Evans led them along the side of the road, staying in the brushy undergrowth. If they saw or heard anything at all, his command was to immediately duck out of sight and stay hidden until whatever it was passed.

They walked like this for another half-hour, eventually cresting the rise of the second hill they had seen. They were now inside a crescent-shaped depression surrounded on three sides by mountains, heading due north. After reaching the top of the hill, Evans had Grudowski lay back while he strode up to get a sense of their surroundings.

The first thing Evans noticed was the sound of a vehicle, likely electric, whining as it began the sloping incline leading to his position from the south. He turned and squinted, trying to make out any of its features. It seemed *impossibly* small – and he wondered if it was in fact a vehicle or if his eyes were playing tricks on him. He ducked low, noticing that Grudowski had already hidden himself in the sticks and brushy bushes.

He continued watching the whitish blob as it came fully into view. It was a vehicle, though not one he recognized. He turned around, satisfied he was well-hidden behind the thick, low brush, and now examined the area to the north. He squinted again, letting everything come into focus.

There were blurs of brownish-tan that became rectangles, darker splotches of browns and blacks that became other detailed shapes. He saw people moving, milling about.

His heart sank as he realized what he was looking at — it wasn't the research station at all.

Evans crawled back to Grudowski. "There's a village down there," he said. "Pretty good size, too."

Grudowski frowned. "I thought you said there were no villages directly between our entry and rendezvous point?"

"That *is* what I said. You got the same intel I did. There wasn't supposed to be a village here. But that's what it is, just below us on the other side of the hill. Still, it's not a big city or anything, just big for what I would have expected around here. Maybe 500 people total? Houses, farms, tiny main strip this road leads to."

"What do we do?" Grudowski asked.

"I'm thinking about it," Evans said. "But we've got other company as well."

"The car?"

"*Barely* a car, from what I can tell." He poked his head up once more and looked south, at the car approaching. He eyed it for a few seconds before pulling his head back down. "But I do think I recognize the passengers... at least one of them, anyway."

The tiny vehicle — possibly related in some strange way to a truck — had just begun its taxing ascent up the hill. Evans watched it through a break in the brush and verified his suspicion. He *did* recognize the truck's driver. The large man was crunched awkwardly into the seat, knees clear up around the sides of the steering wheel, head to the side as it brushed against the roof of the car.

It did *not* look like a comfortable experience for him, and that brought Evans a little bit of joy.

He smiled, standing up. *Hello, Shane Riley.*

30
SHANE

"OVER THERE," Michaela said, pointing into the distance.

"I see. Looks like Jonathan Evans," Shane said.

"You know him?"

Shane chewed his lip. "Met him before." As he spoke, he pulled the car to the side of the road, flattening some small bushes and plants as he did. A soldier rose from a spot five feet from his window, taking him by surprise. He had been well-hidden, unlike Evans, who wore a goofy grin and was waving from the side of the road.

Shane brought the car to a halt and had the door open before it had even come to a complete stop. He got out, stretching. It felt good to be on his feet again. He secretly hoped one of the truck's tires had popped during their journey, rendering this an incapable vehicle to return in.

But knowing his luck, this was the North Korean version of a Toyota or something — a car destined to live forever, refusing to die even if he drove it off a cliff.

Evans ran over and shook his hand, still smiling.

Shane squinted at him. "Looks like you got here in one piece."

The grin disappeared. "Almost," he said. "I lost a man."

Shane couldn't hide his startled expression. He glanced around quickly, realizing that he had only seen two men – not three – pop up from the bushes. "Shit. What happened?"

"We were being followed," Evans said. "Seems we're okay now, though. We've been on high-alert since we lost Rayburn, but my guess is whoever it is, they're keeping far enough behind us we'll never know they're still there. They struck at night last time, picking off the guy at the back of the pack."

Shane nodded as he listened. He was sure Evans' small mercenary team was well-trained, but it was possible they hadn't been trained together. He knew Evans was American, but the other man with him now could have been from anywhere. European, if he had to guess. All three of them could have served for different countries, only joining Evans' paramilitary group recently.

Men like this, while well-trained individually, often suffered from leaning heavily on that individualized training. Each man thought he was invincible, each man trusted his own skills more than anyone else's. They likely weren't as cohesive as a team as they should be for that reason.

Shane eyed Evans as he spoke, trying to search the man's face for signs of grief or anything that might compromise his ability to continue on. He saw none, which was good. Evans had a job to do, and while he was down a man, he hadn't given up on the mission yet.

Shane found himself curious about why he cared. It wasn't like Evans was part of *his* team. "Sorry for your loss," Shane said.

Evans nodded. "Who's this?"

Michaela had walked over to join them, and everyone shared a brief introduction. The second mercenary introduced himself as Grudowski, but didn't offer any pleasantries.

Shane appreciated that — they were here to work. "Sitrep?"

Evans nodded quickly, as if appreciating the brisk change of topic. He motioned with a flick of his head. "Just behind me is a village, due north of here. Wasn't on the map, and it's likely sitting between us and our destination."

Shane frowned. "Village?"

"Pretty small, looks like mostly farmers and some infrastructure for community. Still, with its proximity to the research station and the fact that there's not supposed to be anyone here, I think it's best if we —"

"I'll go straight through," Shane said. "It's a village, not an army."

He saw a flash of anger come over Evans' face, but before the mercenary could respond, Michaela stepped up and grabbed his arm. "Shane, we should probably figure out —"

"I'm going through," Shane snapped. "I'll leave the truck here, but I'm walking. We can't afford to waste any more time."

"You're reckless, Riley," Evans said, his voice icy. "You're going to get us all killed."

Shane shrugged. "Didn't invite you."

"We'll go around," Evans said. "Circle the village, staying in the hills and work our way north. Hell, if we work together, we could even split my team to go with one of you, two and two. That'll give us line-of-sight the whole time."

Shane didn't acknowledge Evans' plan. "Going through the village."

He felt Michaela's hand on his arm. "Shane, let's just hear him —"

Shane shook off Michaela's hand. He turned and faced her. "You wanted to come along, but I told you before we're doing it my way. I'll admit, if there's something in that research station you understand, I'll need you by my side. We can't afford to kick trees and hide in bushes for another half-day trying to get around the village. If we cut straight through, we'll be at the research station in less than an hour. Assuming it's even there in the first place."

He sensed Evans' cool gaze on the side of his face, and he looked up to meet the man's eyes. "You going to be a problem for me? Or can we get on with it?"

Evans' jaw flexed a few times, but the man didn't speak. His mercenary counterpart stood to the side, watching the tense debate. His face was blank, and Shane couldn't get a read on whether or not Grudowski even had an opinion.

"I don't want anyone else getting killed," Evans said finally. "Riley, just come with us. We've got some of Rayburn's gear, and you're welcome to it."

"You look like mercenaries. Soldiers. Like outsiders. Especially you, Evans."

Evans raised an eyebrow, asking a silent question.

"I'm saying that *you're* the ones who are likely to get killed, not *me*. I'm unarmed, walking through a village with my friend. I don't look hostile, and I'm not. We won't look like anything but tourists."

"What if you run into trouble? How are you going to protect yourself?"

Evans' eyes flicked from Shane to Michaela, a silent question there.

How are you going to protect her?

Michaela spoke up. "Thanks for the offer," she said. "But I do have to stick with him. He's stubborn as an ass, but he's right. It's just a village. We'll take our chances, if that means we get to Seong Park sooner."

Evans stared at them for another few seconds, then finally turned to Grudowski. "Fine. Let's go. We'll head west, then turn back to the north and get around the village. If we're lucky, we can come in and flank the side of the research station. We'll be late to the party, but at least we'll be ready to fight if we need to be."

Shane felt the vulnerability of not having a weapon, but he knew he was right. He couldn't just march into a village armed to the teeth like these men.

That said, he couldn't just march up to a guarded research station unarmed, either. He needed a better plan of attack before he got to that point.

But Seong was waiting, and every second mattered. His first step was to get there, to see what needed to be seen.

Any plans could come later.

JIN-TAK

JIN-TAK WATCHED the rendezvous party through high-powered binoculars. He was at the top of one of the larger hills nestled at the base of the mountains on the west. He had climbed through the night after dispatching one of the mercenaries, hoping to get ahead of the group.

It helped that he knew their destination. He was intimately familiar with the region, having grown up right here, and he had worked for the research lab indirectly for the last year and a half. This mission was close to his heart – his father was suffering from a disease no one understood. The work being performed at the laboratory was crucial to his father's health, and it had been a circuitous and serendipitous twist of fate that he had ended up right back here, the first line of defense against anyone trying to topple or destroy the work being done.

He sat on his knees, elbows resting on a boulder that hid most of his body. He held the binoculars up again to his eyes, watching as the band dispersed. The two that had come in the small truck left the vehicle there, heading down the hill over the dirt road leading into the village. The other two – the remnants of the group that had whittled down from three – turned and began walking in his direction. They would pass just below him, likely trying to circle the village and reach the northern side of town in another half-day.

They wouldn't chance coming up this high on the mountain, knowing that he was out here, likely watching them.

It gave Jin-Tak options – he could come down the mountain a bit, once again ambushing this mercenary group before they reached their destination, or he could continue along the same path, moving faster over a wider arc to reach a spot just north of where they were headed. At that point, the two groups would converge again, and he could move in and take them all out at once.

Both were risky in their own way.

He was outnumbered, which didn't cause him any fear, but made him more wary of the situation. He could take out two, potentially three trained soldiers, but the men down below knew he was out here. They knew what he had done and were now going to be on high alert.

No, they would stick close to the village – close enough that they felt safe. Even if he maneuvered down the hill and waited for them, it would still be a battle against two prepared men, both of whom would be eager to seek revenge for their fallen brother.

And waiting north of town, assuming he could even get there in time, meant that the group of two would turn back into a group of four, making the odds even more out-of-favor.

No, Jin-Tak needed another plan. Something less obvious, something less direct.

It wasn't his time to attack. He had played his hand and reduced their numbers. But the cost was that he was now operating openly. The cost of that was that this group now knew there was an ever-present threat nearby. They wouldn't know it was just one man, but they would know to be vigilant.

He leaned back, putting the binoculars back in his pack and throwing it over a shoulder. He stood, pulling the strap of his rifle around and onto his back.

Worst case, if it came to it, he could take out all of them with a few rounds from the high-powered sniper rifle.

But that would interfere with the plan he had now.

While his bosses at the research station certainly would like to not have the threat of outsiders attacking their grounds, there was one thing he knew they wanted even more than that: leverage.

If he could get into a position where he could provide that to his superiors, it might help their cause. It might help his father.

Jin-Tak had seen that there were four people collected together at the top of the small rise leading into the village. Through the binoculars, he recognized two of the mercenaries, saw that a third man was another outsider, though not with the mercenary group.

It was the fourth that intrigued him the most. Smaller, thin, very obviously female. She didn't appear to be a mercenary or soldier, and neither she nor the man she had arrived with seemed to be armed. Neither of them even had so much as a fanny pack on their person.

That told Jin-Tak one thing: the woman, and perhaps the man as well, were not soldiers. They were not fighters.

Were they civilians?

That they had met up with the same mercenaries who had been trying to stop them also gave him a clue. They were not merely tourists, passing through. They were not outsiders who had somehow gotten lost. This village was so far off the beaten path there was no question that they had gotten here on purpose, planning their destination ahead of time.

They were headed for the research station, where scientific breakthroughs were being achieved every day. That might be key to fixing this situation.

And it told Jin-Tak Yeon exactly who this woman was.

Leverage.

SHANE WALKED JUST behind Michaela as they entered the village. The first houses, no more than mudbrick huts with grass roofs, stood off to the left. A few more were up ahead on the right side of the road, and a wide intersection with another dirt path cut diagonally just beyond these houses. He saw farmers working fields, and local villagers engrossed in their day-to-day activities. No one greeted them, and no one even seemed to notice they were there. He preferred it that way.

"What do we do if someone asks where we're from?" Michaela asked.

"We tell them," Shane said, shrugging. "Like I told Evans, we're not hostile. We're not here to hurt them. We can just say we are tourists, wanting to get a feel for what the *real* North Korea is like."

"And you plan on telling them this in English?" she asked.

Shane had to admit she had a point. He spoke almost no Korean, certainly not whatever dialect was spoken in this rural village high up in the mountains. He questioned if there were mountains in this area?

It was another reason he was glad to be with someone like Michaela. She spoke Korean fluently, having lived and worked here her entire life. While he had not planned on interacting with many locals, it was certainly a benefit to have someone who spoke the language well with him.

"But let's not talk to anyone, if we can help it," he said.

She slowed, allowing him to catch up so they were walking side-by-side. They passed a small store, and although the racks appeared to be empty, so far, no one even seemed to look in their direction. They made it halfway through the town, coming to a few two-story buildings that signified they were nearing the central town square, or whatever the North Korean equivalent was.

Shane slowed, noticing a group of small children playing up ahead. All of them were hunched in a circle, looking down at the dusty road. Whatever they were playing with was in the middle of the circle, invisible to Shane.

One of them broke off, then turned immediately and began running toward Shane and Michaela.

Shane cocked his head to the side. The kid was perhaps 12 years old, maybe a bit older, but it was hard to tell. He looked emaciated, his rib cage protruding under his skin. He was shirtless, wearing long pants that had been cut off at the shins. Bony and lanky, he sidled up toward them.

But it was not his weight or age that caught Shane's eye.

It was the kid's eye.

The young boy was missing an eye, wearing a patch of cloth that had been wrapped around his head, over his ears, covering the left socket. His right eye danced and widened as he saw the outsiders.

"He's coming over," Shane whispered. He pressed his arm back, pushing Michaela into the shadow cast by the building they were next to. He saw movement out of his right eye, saw two more people, adults this time, exiting a nearby building.

His heart rate rose. It wasn't as though he was afraid of a few school-children and two old villagers, but there was something about the way the kid was looking at them, bounding toward them, that gave him pause.

And then he realized it, at the same moment Michaela pointed it out.

"Them too," she whispered from behind him.

She had seen the two old villagers on the road. They too were wearing cloth bandages around their head, both covering their left eyes.

"What the hell..." Shane said under his breath.

The kid was there now, right in front of him. Looking up at his face. The kid stood there, silently staring up at Shane with one large eye. He looked over the kid's head, saw the kids in the circle behind him playing in the street. A mix of boys and girls it seemed, though it was hard to tell.

One thing was certain, however: each of the kids also had a similar patch or cloth over their left eye.

Shane backed up, pressing his back against the side of the mudbrick building.

"Where the hell are we?" he muttered.

"Shane, he's trying to talk." Michaela brushed by him and stood facing the child.

She spoke in a smattering of Korean words he didn't recognize.

The kid smiled and nodded excitedly, clearly happy to have someone who understood him.

Michaela asked him a few questions, the kid responded. Finally, she looked back up at Shane. "He says he wants us to meet his parents," she said.

Shane frowned. "Why? Are they important?"

She chuckled. "No, Shane. He assumes that we have money. He wants us to meet his parents so that we can give them money."

It was a cute, heartfelt effort, and at the same time, it saddened him. This village was different than all the other villages just like it around the world in name and location only. He had been born into a family that happened to live in a country of wealth. A country of surplus, that did not have a corrupt government placing impossible pressure on its people.

He wanted to reach out and hug the kid, to tell him it was going to be okay, that while he and Michaela didn't have any money for his parents, he was a smart kid and would do just fine.

He immediately realized it was a typical Western response to seeing poverty up close. In fact, he had no idea if the kid was smart or would be okay. He had no idea if the kid had access to a school and education. It was very likely he had been born into a family solely to help work the fields, to provide whatever it was they farmed for whatever dictator controlled this region.

It was very likely this kid might not make it to adulthood.

Shane swallowed, wishing he could disappear into the wall of the building.

"What did you tell him?" he asked Michaela.

She shrugged. "I just told him we're passing through."

The kid stared at them with his single wide eye for another few seconds, then just as quickly as he had arrived, he ran off and sprinted down the street. He disappeared into an alleyway between two buildings, and Michaela grabbed Shane's hand. "Let's keep moving," she said. "This isn't our mission. We're not here for them."

Shane looked at her. She seemed to know exactly what he was thinking, seemed to know precisely how he felt.

Perhaps she felt that as well? Perhaps she was struck by the abject poverty and starvation everywhere?

Or maybe she just knew Shane better than he thought.

He noticed the two old villagers watching the interaction. One of them lifted a finger and pointed in their direction. Shane nodded quickly. "Yeah, good call. Let's get through this weird place and back on track."

He didn't know what had happened here — what had caused all of these people – men, women, and children – to lose their left eye, but all of the answers his mind conjured were answers he wished he hadn't thought of.

The fact of the matter was he couldn't think of any natural way an entire village of people would lose their left eye.

Someone had done this to them. Someone had come to an oppressed village, seen its starving children and helpless inhabitants, and taken a piece of them away.

Shane wanted to recoil in horror as he passed the older couple, seeing more and more people now in the streets. He saw them watching from windows, saw them in the fields, turning to look as the obvious outsiders made their way through the street.

His heart rate rose by the second as every single person he saw, without exception, stared back at him with a single, right eye.

33
SHANE

AT THE FAR end of the village, just north of town, Shane and Michaela stopped to catch their breath. He still felt a sense of panic, his blood pressure high, as he tried to shake off what they had seen. It wasn't as terrifying as it was creepy, eerie even. As if a horrific entity had visited long ago, leaving the villagers in peace but marking each with a macabre sign. It felt biblical, sinister.

"So... are we going to talk about that?" he asked.

Having reached the northern part of town, they were surrounded by fields on both sides of the road. A gently sloping hill lay ahead of them, breaking the horizon. If the research station was down below, it would be hidden in the valley just a mile ahead. The road dipped down and disappeared, ending somewhere there. Between the end of it and the looming mountain beyond, Shane guessed that their destination would lie. Just out of sight, but they would check the spot nonetheless.

"Talk about what?" Michaela asked.

Shane gestured vaguely around them.

She forced a smile. "Yeah, just trying to lighten the mood a bit. That was... disturbing." Shrugging, she added, "It's an atrocity, for sure. But those people seemed... happy. Content, at least."

"Content? Michaela, they were all missing an *eye*."

"I noticed," she said calmly. "But I can't help but think whatever trauma these people have been through, they've gone through it together. And it's over now. It's in the past."

"Who the hell would do that?"

"Maybe there's some local cartel, some local regime that forces them to pay tribute like that, forces them to give their eyes to keep them all in line?"

"And that's a good thing?" Shane asked.

She shook her head, crossing her arms. "No, Shane, I'm not saying it's a *good* thing. I'm just trying to be an optimist. I'm trying to see the silver linings. It seems like these people are allowed to live here in peace – even after having their eyes ripped out of their head!"

She swallowed, taking a moment to compose herself. "And we don't know anything. How young they are when it happens," she explained. "I am obviously not trying to justify this sort of thing, but it's not like they are dragging people out of their homes."

Shane searched for the right words. Finally, he looked over at Michaela and shook his head.

"Have you ever seen anything like it?" she asked softly.

"I was about to ask you the same thing. You think there *is* some sort of cartel nearby? Some sort of regime that comes through and…" He couldn't finish the sentence. What kind of monstrous group could possibly enter a peaceful village like this and gouge out people's eyes? How could they possibly justify such action? What could these people have done to warrant such an egregious response?

"We need to get to this research base," he said. "If Seong is still there, she needs our help."

Michaela didn't argue. He felt the conflict in him, likely the same thing she was experiencing. People in this village needed help – they needed everything. From the boy who just wanted a bit of money for his parents to every other person they had seen clearly living in abject poverty – and terror – it was more than Shane could bear.

His mission was to find one person, and one person alone. There simply wasn't enough of him to go around. He couldn't help everyone.

He started forward again, following the road. Up ahead, he saw a car. It was white, facing them, small and narrow just like the one they had driven. As they approached, it became clear that it was their truck — exactly the same make and model as the one they had left at the top of the hill behind them.

Shane spun around quickly. He glanced through the streets and back to the hill on the other side. He wasn't sure if he had parked high enough on the hill to see their vehicle from here, or if his suspicion was correct.

"Shane, is that…" Michaela started.

"It is," he confirmed, approaching the vehicle. It was parked facing away from the town, sitting on the side of the road near a small hut about 20 feet away. A large pile of stones had been collected nearby, likely the beginnings of a stone fence or a sign planned for the future. Shane walked around the car, eventually coming to the passenger side door. He looked in and nodded. "It's definitely our ride. The driver's seat is still pushed back the exact same amount as I left it."

"Someone stole it?" Michaela asked.

Shane shrugged and was about to respond when he heard movement from behind the stone pile. He tried looking over his shoulder.

His instincts kicked in a half-second too late. The cold steel of a blunt object struck him on the side of the head, right on the temple.

He fell to the ground, his vision blurring. Dizzy, he glanced up. His eyes were playing tricks on him. There were four men, all making the same motion. All of them holding an object, raising it over their left shoulder, all of them stretching to their full height.

It was a strange choreographed dance, all of them acting as one. Then, his eyes adjusted and the four became two. He blinked a few times, forcing his eyes to focus harder. The two became one, and he realized it was a single man, holding a rifle like an axe, and once again he swung it down as hard as he could, hitting Shane in the stomach.

He doubled over in pain, retching. Just as quickly, he heard Michaela shout and begin to run toward him. He tried to work his mouth, tried to tell her to stay back. But the man who had attacked him lashed out with his right foot, kicking him in the head.

Shane's eyes closed then, and they didn't open again.

34
SHANE

SHANE OPENED his eyes but saw nothing. Darkness, interrupted only by a few orange patches of light flashing against his retinas.

He panicked. *They're taking my eye*, he thought. *This is what happened to all of the villagers, to that poor boy.* He forced his eyes to close again, distinctly feeling his lashes clasp together and part as he opened them once more. The orange rays were back, shifting as he moved his head. He forced his breath to steady, urged his mind to calm.

Still have both my eyes.

He felt weight on his head, the heat of his breath bouncing back at him, humidity rising instantly.

He was encased in some sort of sack, or more precisely, his head was covered by one.

He shook his head a bit, feeling the rough burlap scratch against his neck, then tried to move. His hands and feet were bound, and he was sandwiched between two sheets of metal, his feet pushing against one and his hands and back touching the other. He wiggled his knees, feeling the bump of metal there, but something softer on his left.

"Ouch."

He stopped. "Michaela?"

"It's me." He was relieved to hear her voice, but it didn't alleviate his worries about their situation.

"Where are we?"

"In the back of our truck," she said. "Apparently, it has less space than I thought."

Told you so. "Can you see?"

"They put a bag over my head," she said.

"Me too," Shane answered. "Did they... did they hurt you?"

"As far as I can tell, it was just one guy, a Korean man, but he was clearly a soldier. He hit you — knew what he was doing. I didn't get a good look at him; I was running around the truck when he kicked you. I was screaming, and before I knew it, he had overpowered me. He's impossibly strong. He knocked you out, then tied me up. He pressed me against the dirt next to the truck, next to you. I — I thought he was going to shoot us both."

"I guess we can thank him for not doing that," Shane said dryly.

"Where is he now?"

"I have no idea," she said. "You were only unconscious for a minute. We haven't gone anywhere yet – we're still just outside the village. I heard him talking. Just one voice, so he was on the phone."

"Has he said anything to you?" Shane asked.

"No. I overheard part of the conversation, though. Apparently, Seong Park's father was almost assassinated."

"Almost?"

"He seemed surprised too," she answered. "Then he mentioned us. Whoever he was talking to, he said he had us and would bring us in before the end of the day. He asked what the plan was."

"Get any clues as to what that plan might be?"

"Nope. He just said 'affirmative,' then hung up. I have no idea where he is now."

Just then, Shane heard the sound of an electric motor springing to life, followed by the slamming of a door. The tiny truck immediately began moving. Either the driver wanted to move slowly enough to keep his 'passengers' comfortable, or the electric truck simply was not powerful enough to move at high speed with cargo as heavy as them.

"I guess we found our driver," Shane said.

"Guess so."

"You think he's taking us to the base?" he asked.

There was a longer pause this time. Shane felt the truck shift, his weight falling to the left. He used his knees and hands to do his best to hold himself up, but failed and landed on Michaela's lap. He felt her push against him, urging him back onto his side of the truck.

"Well, it feels like we're heading that direction," she finally said.

Shane nodded, aware she wouldn't be able to see it. "I guess that saves us a little time," he said, attempting to make light of their dire situation.

They both lapsed into silence, the truck continuing its journey. It was a strange sensation, being moved without seeing where they were going or how fast. All they had were the feelings of acceleration, the vibrations of the vehicle, and the faint hum of the electric motor.

"Do you think they know who we are?" Shane asked, breaking the silence.

"I'm not sure," Michaela responded. "But they mentioned Seong Park's father's name — maybe that's why we're still alive. Maybe they know he sent us."

Her words hung in the air between them, a stark reminder of the perilous situation they were in. Even though they could not see each other, the tension was palpable. They were captives, blindfolded, and bound, on their way to an unknown fate. But they were also alive, which, given the circumstances, was something to hold on to.

"Michaela," Shane said, "no matter what happens..."

"Shane," she interrupted, "let's not go there. Not yet. We're still here. We're still together. And we're not giving up. We have to believe that we'll get out of this."

He wanted to argue, to tell her that there were things he needed to say, but he couldn't find the words. He felt her squeeze his hand, a wordless promise of solidarity.

"Yes," he agreed finally. "We'll get out of this."

35
SHANE

THE MINIATURE electric truck bounced over the road, heading towards the valley to the north of the village. In the back, Shane discovered, disappointingly, that the impacts seemed to be magnified. Every pothole they hit, every rut they traversed, jostled his insides, causing sharp pains to pulse through his body.

"I'm not getting any younger," he mumbled under his breath.

The truck was far too quiet for his words to be lost in the noise. Michaela heard him and responded instantly, "No one is."

The only solace he could take was in the fact that their bodies were so tightly packed together, the bumps weren't as bad as they could have been.

"At least we're in decent shape," Shane observed, "I can't imagine how this would feel if we were any skinnier, and didn't have our soft bodies to act as pillows."

She snorted in response. "Are you calling me fat, Shane?"

His mouth fell open in surprise, and he felt his cheeks flush, "I... no, I meant—"

"Shane, relax. We're tied down in the back of a truck after being assaulted by a kidnapper who's likely going to hand us over to people who want to kill us. I was just making a joke."

"I know," he replied quickly. "It's just..."

Just what? he asked himself. That she looked fantastic? That she hadn't aged a day since he last saw her? What could he possibly say to dig himself out of this hole?

Embarrassment quickly shifted to anger. He missed Kate, and this woman was a constant reminder of his late wife, the woman still waiting for him at the base of a hill whose name he couldn't remember.

"You okay?" Michaela asked, breaking his chain of thought.

He realized he had been silent for a good half minute. They were still bouncing over the rough road, and Shane sensed that they had taken a turn and begun descending. He pictured the valley they were heading into, the research station at the bottom. It seemed he had been at least somewhat right. Maybe this road spiraled around the interior of the valley, like a quarry or crater nestled within a larger valley.

"Yeah, I'm okay," he replied.

"Good," she said quickly, "Because there's one more thing."

He frowned under the burlap sack, "What is it?"

"I didn't get a chance to mention it before, but it's pretty important."

"Go on..."

"You said you were working for Seong Park's father, right? The wealthy politician?"

"Yes, the man who you said was almost assassinated."

"Right," she confirmed, "But what I heard — what the guy who kidnapped us *actually* said was, '*he was almost assassinated?*'"

"You already mentioned that," Shane interjected.

"No, I mean he *asked* that. In the form of a question."

Shane paused.

"And then he immediately asked if 'they' managed to stop it," she added.

"As in, prevent the assassination attempt?"

"Exactly, Shane. There's no other way to interpret it. Even translating the words from Korean to English one at a time, the intent was clear: the question he asked was, '*he was almost assassinated?*' followed by a slight pause, and then another question: '*it was successfully prevented by you?*'"

Shane felt as if he'd been punched in the gut. Michaela's revelation implied that the very man who had sent them on this mission had nearly been assassinated. It was peculiar, coincidental that it happened *now*, while this mission was taking place.

But being a politician and very wealthy South Korean, it was likely that Chung-Hee Park had numerous enemies.

But what was far from coincidental was that the man who had kidnapped them was conversing with someone who had apparently tried to *protect* Park. There had been an assassination attempt on the elder Park, and the man who was driving their truck now wanted to be sure that his superiors had *prevented* that attack.

And these were the very people Shane and Jonathan Evans would have to fight in order to find Park's daughter.

It was a strange triangle of relationships, one Shane couldn't possibly understand. But this information certainly muddied the waters.

It didn't add up. Shane reflected on Jonathan Evans' words in the bar, which felt like a week ago. *Something doesn't add up. It all seems a little convenient, a little too easy, doesn't it?* Evans had said.

Shane had ignored it then, not wanting to cause any more delay in finding Seong Park's daughter. If she truly was in danger, they needed to move quickly.

He had dismissed Jonathan's concerns as the musings of an overly paranoid mercenary. A man who had spent years seeing the worst in people and therefore assuming the worst in everyone around him.

Shane was far from naïve, but he had to agree that Jonathan might be onto something.

With this revelation, it seemed there was a *lot* more to this story than Chung-Hee Park had let on. Someone had kidnapped his daughter — that much might still be true. But was he somehow *collaborating* with the same people who had taken his daughter? Did he know something about what his daughter's research was trying to uncover?

And, most importantly of all: who was trying to gain the upper hand over whom? Who was trying to maintain the most leverage?

And why?

As the truck continued to navigate the bumpy road, Shane was left to ponder these questions. Their situation had grown more complex, with loyalties in question and motives uncertain. Yet, one thing was clear - they were in the thick of it, and finding the answers wouldn't be easy. But they had to, not just for their own survival, but for the truth that was dangling like a sword over their heads.

EVANS AND GRUDOWSKI flew down the side of the mountain. Thankfully, they were still nearly parallel with the height of the village, and it was no more than a steep hill they had to descend. The journey was difficult, however. Loose rocks and gravel covered the entire side of the hill, making their descent treacherous the faster they ran.

Grudowski had spotted the same white truck in which Shane Riley and Michaela Everly had arrived, driving down the village street, staying off the main road. The electric vehicle was surprisingly capable of navigating the bumpy fields behind the houses and buildings. Though moving slowly, its destination was clear.

Evans and Grudowski watched as the truck stopped at the far end of the town, facing the village, and waited. Initially, no one got out of the vehicle, but eventually, a thin, dark-skinned Korean man disembarked and hid behind a pile of rocks.

It was a trap.

Stopping on the hill, Evans initially watched with interest, then confusion, and finally fear. They owed no obligation to Shane Riley and his companion, but Evans was not a bad person. Riley was innocent and didn't deserve whatever the man behind the rocks was planning.

Dr. Michaela Everly *certainly* didn't.

Evans spurred his companion into action, making their way through the last mile of terrain at nearly full speed, without fear of being spotted by the enemy.

For all he knew, the man hiding behind the rocks who had jumped out of the vehicle was the only one pursuing them — the same assassin who had killed Rayburn early this morning. There was no way to be sure, but it didn't matter. They had a mission, and he needed to reach the destination before Shane and Michaela emerged from the northern side of the village.

As they reached the bottom of the hill, in line with the road and the truck parked by its side, Evans saw Shane and Michaela approaching the vehicle. He watched in horror as the man emerged from behind the rocks, struck Shane on the head, knocking him to the ground, and roughly grabbed Michaela, forcing her down as well.

He saw both of them get thrown into the back of the truck, flinching as Shane's head connected with the back window. The man put burlap sacks over their heads, then got into the driver's seat.

Evans knew in an instant two things were true: first, both Shane and Michaela were still alive and the man intended to keep it that way, and two, he was going to transport them elsewhere.

Maybe they would be tortured, interrogated. Perhaps the enemy just wanted to see the intruders' faces before killing them.

Either way, it bought Evans a bit of time. Not a lot, but some.

Hardly enough time to execute a solid plan — but he didn't have a choice.

"Head north, on my mark," Evans instructed Grudowski.

Grudowski snapped to attention and turned. They had been facing due east, aligned with the truck and the assassin, but Evans broke into a jog, then into a full-out run, covering the distance to the other side of the field, which disappeared over and down into another pothole-shaped valley ahead.

He hadn't had much time to study the region's topography, as most of their intelligence was merely speculative. He hadn't wanted to spend too much time studying a map of a place that might not even be the correct location. Instead, he had spent time devising a plan with Grudowski to enter the research station if and when they found it.

But Riley's kidnapping was not part of any plan.

Of course, he didn't want Riley to die. And while being tossed into the back of a tiny truck and delivered to enemy forces might be enough of an *I told you so,* Evans was certainly not above piling on just a bit to prove a point.

Once they reached the truck, assuming they weren't intercepted, Evans had a few choice words in mind for Mr. Riley. An *I told you so* simply wouldn't suffice. Riley had nearly gotten himself and an innocent civilian killed. Evans wasn't sure of Michaela Everly's role in all of this, but he assumed she was there to provide intelligence or support once they reached the research station.

Evans and Grudowski sprinted the entire last mile, pulling slightly to the west to remain mostly within a natural ditch on that side of the field, providing cover from the truck's view. Still, every hundred paces or so, Evans would dart up the side of the ditch and peek across the field to check their progress against the truck's.

To his surprise, they were a few hundred paces ahead. The truck was moving slowly, likely forced to crawl by the additional weight of its two additional passengers. He urged Grudowski to quicken their pace, and together they reached the edge of the shallow valley at the end of the field.

He paused, taking in the new terrain that had just come into view. They were standing on the edge of what looked like a crater, an almost perfectly circular indentation in the ground that hid whatever was inside from view unless one was standing precisely where Evans was now.

Just below him, about 20 yards straight down and 50 yards away, was the same dirt road. It was a steep hill, but it was nothing compared to what they had just descended. He was confident they could make it down in good time, long before the truck could reach them.

A plan was beginning to take shape in the back of his mind, but he kept his attention focused on the valley floor. Towards the back of the crater, about half a mile straight north from their current position, Evans spotted their target: a structure that resembled a prison, surrounded by a high chain-link fence, with one large H-shaped building beyond it, and four smaller structures at each corner of the fence.

"Looks like we found it," Grudowski said.

Evans nodded, though he didn't feel relieved. Instead, he felt a sense of dread. Whatever was here was clearly meant to be hidden. The valley appeared old, as if it had been dug out of the earth a hundred years ago. But it had obviously been dug out; the whole place was man-made, and the base had an aura of World War II-era fortifications and architecture.

He had no illusions about what they had stumbled upon.

This was a research facility that had been constructed by the Nazi regime, likely in the late 1930s.

He spotted four guards — two patrols of two men each, walking just inside the fence. One was in the southwest quadrant, and the other on the east side, heading north. There could have been more guards around the back of the building, but he didn't detect movement and Evans didn't have time for a full reconnaissance of the area.

His immediate task was something besides getting into the base — that would come later.

First, he had to rescue Shane Riley and impart a swift lesson about hubris.

"WAIT until he's almost on us," Evans instructed. Grudowski, lying next to him, nodded in acknowledgment.

The plan was simple: incapacitate the truck's tires first, with Evans subsequently taking a shot through the windshield at the assassin himself. The fragile state of the vehicle made it an easy target, but Evans remained wary of the driver. Any stray bullet aimed too high could easily miss and sail through the vehicle, puncturing the back wall and potentially hitting Shane or Dr. Everly.

Furthermore, their position was below the truck's level. They had sprinted down the second hill, crossed the road skirting the outside of the valley, and took cover again amidst the sparse vegetation on the other side. The valley floor was mostly barren, an open space punctuated by a few scattered trees. If they waited too long, the truck would wind around and approach the front entrance of the station from the north side. There, they'd likely be met by whatever guards remained, bringing unwanted attention to their presence.

If they continued down this road, any gunfire directed at the truck risked alerting the patrolling guards.

Evans tried to time it perfectly, so one set of guards would be approaching the northwest quadrant and about to turn south, while the other would have just moved past the southeast quadrant, heading north.

He knew that it was unlikely the two of them could open fire with their assault rifles without alerting the patrols, but it was a risk he was prepared to take—Shane's life depended on it.

The truck rounded the bend as predicted, right on schedule. Evans held up a clenched fist, signaling Grudowski to hold his position and await a signal. Finally, he hissed a quick "go!" and Grudowski opened fire.

The side of the truck erupted in a shower of sparks and bullet holes, most of which hit their intended targets. Both tires on the passenger side of the truck exploded, causing the vehicle to list to one side and face Evans' position. A moment later, the tires on the other side met a similar fate and the truck came to a complete stop.

Evans raised his own rifle, focusing on the driver's seat through his scope. His eyebrows furrowed in confusion.

Where the hell is he?

The seat was empty.

Grudowski stopped firing, knowing that any additional damage risked hitting Dr. Everly or Shane. He turned to look at Evans, seeking further instructions.

Evans cautiously approached the road and pulled himself onto it, still aiming towards the truck's front end. He half expected the bloody carcass of the driver to be sprawled out on the road, the driver side door open.

No luck. He shook his head in confusion as he saw the driver side door was still closed tight, nobody was on the ground.

Just then, he noticed movement out of the corner of his eye. Two of the guards had rounded the corner of the facility's perimeter fence and had immediately taken notice of the unusual scene. Their surprise attack was over.

He made eye contact with Grudowski, raising his eyebrows in a silent question. Grudowski responded with a nod.

At least we've got Riley and Michaela accounted for, Evans muttered to himself. He quickened his pace and jogged over to the side of the truck, finding the two occupants of the bed still bound with burlap sacks over their heads. One of them – the larger of the two – seemed to be fighting not against his restraints but against the size of the truck bed itself.

"Relax, buddy," Evans said. "I knew you couldn't handle going it alone. I figured you'd come back to me," He addressed the larger figure he believed to be Riley.

Riley spoke, but the words were muffled. The man's movements ceased, and the top of the burlap sack shifted in Evans' direction. He briefly considered keeping the burlap sack over Riley's head as punishment for his attempted escape, but quickly dismissed the idea. With enemy soldiers closing in, they needed all the help they could get.

Unlike Shane Riley, Jonathan Evans was not afraid to admit that.

Evans let out a deep sigh of relief, then quickly snapped back to alertness.

He gestured to Grudowski, indicating for him to keep a watch on the approaching guards while he checked on their charges.

As he climbed into the truck, he couldn't help but shake his head in disbelief. Why did these missions always have to be so damned complicated? Couldn't anything just go as planned for once? Regardless, they had a job to do, and despite the unexpected surprises, Evans and Grudowski were ready to see it through.

38

JIN-TAK

JIN-TAK OBSERVED the unfolding ambush with a measured curiosity. As he steered down the curved road leading to the base of the valley, the electric vehicle lurching at even the slightest provocation, he didn't reach for a handle but rather unlatched the door, pushing it open. The electric vehicle, reminiscent of a golf cart, did not surge and accelerate like a traditional motor engine would going downhill. Consequently, he was able to guide it smoothly downward, maintaining a consistent speed. He walked beside the vehicle, door ajar, hand on the steering wheel, ensuring it moved steadily onward.

Just moments before, he'd spotted a flurry of movement about a quarter-mile down the road. Two figures dashed down the hill, vaulting over the road to take cover behind the scrub brush lining the way. A moment later, one of the men reemerged and continued on, ending his journey on a small outcrop jutting from the hillside.

Jin-Tak's assumptions had been spot on – this pair of men was attempting an ambush, hoping to catch him and his passengers off guard as they neared the research station. Their strategy was sound. Any further down the hill, and the station guards might bear witness to their escapade and rush to Jin-Tak's aid. Equally, they couldn't afford to wait until the truck reached the front gate. Hence, they had to act now.

Or so they believed.

Jin-Tak kept his head low, tucked beneath the roof of the truck until they navigated a relatively straight stretch of road. The ambushers were still positioning themselves, and he was too distant for them to make out his figure in the cab. From their low vantage point, seeing him in the driver's seat would prove difficult.

Seizing the right moment, he quietly closed the door, maintaining his steady pace alongside the vehicle, staying crouched. Gradually, he veered off to the left, timing his uphill climb to coincide with the truck obscuring him from the view of the waiting men. He ran diagonally upward, eventually cresting the hill, where he laid down and waited. From this elevated position, he had a perfect view of the impending action, watching as the men sprang into action and began targeting the truck's tires.

Their maneuver was flawlessly executed; the truck even came to rest by the road's edge, its front end angled slightly downward, directly facing the group's leader. It seemed perfectly staged for the leader to deliver the coup de grâce, except the moment never arrived.

Jin-Tak watched with heightened interest, relishing the imagined expression on the man's face when he realized there was no driver in the truck.

Oh well, Jin-Tak mused internally, *this is where our paths diverge.* He raised his phone to his ear, dialing the number of his contact from the village outskirts. "Hello," he spoke rapidly in Korean, "There's a change of plans; I won't be escorting them all the way in."

"You were supposed to bring the doctor and her escort. Why this change?"

He paused, gripping the phone tighter. "No need for that anymore. They're coming to you."

"This wasn't the plan. You were supposed to bring her in. And her escort, alive if possible."

"The *plan* was to *prevent* anyone from accessing the station," Jin-Tak retorted. "That changed when *you* decided you would like to converse with this doctor."

"We were interested in the knowledge she might possess, but we know it is insignificant now. We cannot risk any of this information leaking. What's inside the base must remain confidential."

"Then why must *I* deliver them to the base? They are already coming to you."

"Just ensure they come. They must get there."

Jin-Tak frowned. There? "You're not at the base now?"

His gaze swept across his surroundings. At the far end, near the entrance on the north side of the station, he spotted an empty helipad. He knew what usually resided there - the ready-and-waiting helicopter. It was absent.

"We had to modify our strategies based on your inability to prevent these people from approaching. So we have taken matters into our own hands."

"Explain."

There was a pause. "You do not deserve an explanation. Suffice it to say, as long as they are delivered to the station, move away from it as quickly as possible afterward. If you value your father's life, you'll obey this command."

"And where is my father?" he asked.

"He is no longer in the station," came the reply.

Jin-Tak nodded and ended the call.

He knew what it meant — the leadership of this station was no longer present. They had disappeared, taking the chopper and flying safely away.

He let out a sigh. *That means whatever is going to happen at this place is not going to end well.*

From his vantage point, he watched the group down below regroup, apparently self-congratulating on their perceived successful operation. He knew better than to believe these foreigners would simply withdraw, assuming their mission was complete.

Already, guards from the base were rushing towards the scene, gearing up to engage. They'd likely be overpowered, but the outcome would remain the same: this group would be spurred on, their determination to penetrate the base and uncover its secrets redoubled.

Jin-Tak only knew a fraction of what was housed within the base; the rest was conjecture. He knew they were working on a cure for the strange illness that plagued his father, the very thing he had been contracted to safeguard. Answers were inside that base, answers he wouldn't uncover today, or any day, for that matter. If his father was no longer inside, Jin-Tak did not care about the information there. He did not care if this team reached the base or not.

If his superior's words were accurate, these Americans would be stepping into a trap by approaching the facility. And Jin-Tak intended to be well away from that trap when it eventually sprung.

Satisfied there was no more he could do, Jin-Tak rose to his feet, turning to face the mountain that loomed over the western side of the valley. He broke into a steady jog towards it, leaving the imminent chaos in his wake.

THE COARSE BURLAP sack that had been obscuring Shane's vision was abruptly yanked away, revealing a scene that was at once unexpected and yet somewhat familiar. "Hey, buddy," came the light, almost jovial greeting from Evans. His face was adorned with an idiotic grin, a clear mockery of the grim situation they found themselves in. Instead of responding in kind, Shane simply squinted up at him, still bound and laid out in the back of the truck.

"Don't thank me or anything," Evans added with a hint of sarcasm tingeing his voice.

"Okay," Shane responded, his tone as flat as the expression on his face.

Beside him, he felt the slight pressure of Michaela's knee nudging against him. She was speaking to Evans, her voice ringing out clearly despite the circumstances. "On behalf of both of us, I thank you. We were quite certain he intended to take us to that base situated at the valley's heart."

"... Which happens to be exactly where I was intending to go," Shane interjected, his voice terse.

A loud, roaring laughter burst from Evans, filling the tense air with its resonant echo. This comedic display came just as Grudowski began slicing through the tight bindings around Shane's wrists with a sharp knife. In a fluid motion, the same process was repeated at Shane's ankles and then on Michaela's wrists, liberating them from their bonds. In a few fleeting moments, they were all free. With newfound freedom, Shane swung his legs over the side of the truck and stood, feeling a symphony of protesting muscles and tendons popping and twisting in response to the sudden movement.

"Next time, I might just leave you in there," Evans quipped. "It seemed like a pretty comfortable ride to me. Though, I'm certain it was rather luxurious compared to the grim plans they might've had for you."

Despite the casual banter, Shane maintained his stern eye contact with Evans, finally giving him a quick nod of acknowledgement. "Appreciate the backup. Thank you, mate."

Evans' face lit up at this. "Oh, so we're mates now? That's perfect timing – seeing as a bunch of guys down there still want to kill us. They're getting into position as we speak."

Turning on his heels, Shane cast his gaze down the sweeping expanse of the valley. There, he could see two men – specks in the distance – closing in from about half a mile away. A second group of two were also approaching, but from a bit farther out.

"Four men? That's hardly an army," Shane commented, a note of mockery in his voice.

"I'm sure there will be more," Evans said with an ominous undertone. "And don't forget about the potential threats holed up in those towers. We haven't seen any movement yet, but they might just be lying in wait for us to get within striking distance."

Turning back to Evans, Shane asked, "What's the plan, then?"

A rifle was tossed his way from Grudowski. "Be nice to that piece. It belongs to our missing guy."

Shane nodded, his hands moving deftly to examine the weapon. It was a solid piece, hefty and cold in his hands.

"The plan is: let's take out these four hostiles as quickly as possible. The longer we wait up here, the more time we give that bastard who kidnapped you to get away."

"I was going to ask about him," Michaela chimed in. "Where is he? Did you manage to kill him?"

Shane watched Evans' face for his reaction. There was a flicker of annoyance, a brief cloud on his otherwise unflappable countenance. "No," Evans admitted quickly, a hint of frustration seeping into his voice. "The bastard got the drop on us, slipped away. The car was empty when we got there."

"I thought I heard movement just off the side of the car before we hit this road," Shane said, his tone apologetic. "I wish I could've been more useful, but I was... literally in the dark."

Evans waved off Shane's apology with a dismissive gesture. "No matter. Let's just deal with these guys first. Then we can turn back and comb through the woods. That's the second time now he's managed to evade us, and I don't intend to let there be a third."

With a nod of agreement, Shane moved towards the back of the truck, crouching low next to Grudowski. Michaela followed suit, positioning herself directly behind Shane. Her movements were careful, keeping the bulk of her body shielded from the enemy forces gathering in the distance below.

The sudden cracks of gunfire echoed around them, the harsh sounds bouncing off the surrounding landscape. They sounded far off, yet Shane knew that their aim would only become more deadly as the distance closed.

He returned fire, watching as the dirt sprayed up about 10 yards in front of the first group of men.

His primary goal, as Evans had instructed, was to neutralize these immediate threats. Yet, in the back of his mind, he was keenly aware that his mission wasn't as straightforward as simply eliminating their adversaries. His true target was that base nestled at the bottom of the valley. Despite the danger, he knew he had to get inside.

40

SHANE

"WE'VE GOT company on our six!" Grudowski hollered, his voice cutting through the noise of the skirmish.

Whipping his head around, Shane saw what Grudowski had drawn their attention to. Cresting the hill above the road they were on, three more guards had made their appearance, their weapons aimed unerringly at Shane's team.

Evans had already sprung into action, his rifle barking as he returned fire, Grudowski following close behind. Shane immediately grabbed Michaela Everly, instructing her to move to the back of the truck for cover.

Down below, the original group of four assailants was still intact. They had renewed their advance, edging closer to the base of the hill while returning fire at Shane's group. Now, Shane's team found itself in a pincer, wedged between two enemy forces, one four strong, the other three.

Although they held the high ground against the group of four, the situation was flipped against the three attackers above. The strategic advantage was rapidly slipping from their grasp.

"How the hell did they even get there?" Evans hollered, frustration straining his voice.

"No idea," Grudowski growled, his focus unerring as he continued firing. "These bastards are like gophers. Probably popping out of holes in the ground."

Amidst the confusion, a triumphant shout emerged from Evans as his shot found its mark, one of the men above taking the bullet and promptly dropping out of sight. "One down, two to go."

Breaking away from Michaela, who had hunkered down against the truck with her hands over her ears, Shane brought his newly-acquired rifle to bear on the four-man squad still pressing forward. He fired a swift round, satisfaction coursing through him as one bullet struck a man's boot, sending him sprawling. The threat wasn't neutralized entirely, but the man was effectively out of the fight. Redirecting his aim to the next man, his shot was interrupted as Grudowski's bullet clipped the man's shoulder, sending him down as well.

"Two down," Grudowski announced, tallying their small victories.

The firefight raged on, the team shuffling around the vehicle to avoid presenting an easy target for their adversaries. Shane prayed that they could divert the enemy's attention towards himself and his compatriots, sparing Michaela Everly. There was really no good place for her to hide except behind the truck, her side and feet exposed to the soldiers above.

Or soldier, as Shane belatedly noticed, the number whittling down as Evans landed another shot, reducing the total enemy forces to three. With patience, Shane waited for a clear shot, eventually taking down another assailant approaching from below. His teammate joined in, their combined fire causing a spray of red to burst from the man's throat, dropping him instantly.

Recognizing his predicament, the last man standing turned to flee back toward the base. However, swift justice found him as Grudowski and Evans teamed up to neutralize the last man up the hill, with Shane landing a hit on the back of the fleeing soldier. Eventually, the tumult of gunfire subsided, leaving seven enemy combatants motionless on the ground. Shane thought he heard a pained groan from one of them, but no movement suggested any imminent threat.

"Let's move," Evans ordered curtly. "We need to get off this road. Let's confirm those bastards are dead, then start looking for our elusive friend."

"Negative," Shane retorted, his voice steady and assertive.

All eyes swiveled to face him.

"What was that?"

"Sorry," Shane replied, his voice flat and firm. "I didn't think I would have to remind you *again* that I don't actually take orders from you."

Evans' face tightened into a deep frown, his jaw clenching as he visibly tried to control his rage. For a moment, there was only the sound of the wind whistling across the open terrain and their labored breathing.

"Well, then, Mr. Riley," Evans started, his voice cold and stern, "What do *you* propose we do?"

Shane took a moment, his gaze scanning the terrain. The deadly silence following the firefight felt eerie. He locked eyes with Michaela briefly, giving her a reassuring nod before he turned his attention back to Evans.

"We're too exposed here," Shane stated, the weight of their predicament clear in his voice. "We need to get to that base, regroup, and then we can plan our next move. We can't afford another ambush."

Evans studied him for a moment, his expression hard to read. Eventually, he gave a curt nod, "Agreed... we can't let our guard down. But that's why we need to keep moving, root these guys out, and —"

"No." Shane felt a slight sense of dismay. The last thing they needed was internal discord. He was well aware that their survival depended on their ability to work as a team, despite their differences. They had been forced into this position, together.

He was also well aware that *he* — Shane Riley — was the reason for the discord.

Still, I don't take orders from him.

"WHAT DO YOU MEAN, *NO?*" Evans asked, stepping forward until he was practically toe-to-toe with Shane.

Their feet were almost touching, Evans having to tilt his head up slightly to meet Shane's gaze. Shane's eyes narrowed in response. "What do you mean, 'what do I mean?'" Shane retorted, his tone sharp. "I'm telling you, Evans — I don't work for you, and I don't plan on starting anytime soon. You want to go chase after the psycho that kidnapped us, killed your man, fine. It's admirable, even. But *my* job is very simple: it's getting into that base and finding Seong Park."

"But if there's an assassin still out there trying to —"

"He's long gone, Evans. The guy's well-trained, as good as any of us; possibly better. Do I need to remind you how effective he is at working alone?" Shane interrupted.

Evans recoiled slightly, his body tensing as if bracing for a physical blow. Shane could see the man's surprise, but he stood his ground.

"Yeah? And how has working alone worked out for you so far?" Evans shot back, a hint of mockery in his voice.

"I *haven't* been alone," Shane corrected him. "This whole mission started going sideways once your team decided to join the party. Acting like a bunch of hired mercenaries playing babysitter."

"*Babysitter?* Shane, you're delusional. We've saved your ass twice now, and I'm sure we'll do it again. Look, I understand you're having a hard time out here, dealing with whatever this is. I get that, and I've been there. But don't think for a *second* that I'm abandoning the mission just because we need to turn around and deal with this threat. I can't afford to have someone sneaking around, picking off my men one by one."

"All the more reason to get into that base, find Seong, and get out," Shane argued. "We can't go looking around for ghosts when she's *right there.*"

"Shane, you're one man. How are you going to infiltrate a base that could be swarming with guards?"

"If we all go, it won't be just one man."

Evans' mouth tightened. "And I'm telling you right now, I'm *not* going. And that still doesn't address the problem of the guards. These seven guys won't be the entirety of their forces."

"Wouldn't we have seen more by now if they had more troops at their disposal?" Shane countered, "Seven guys just... marching to their deaths while the rest of their army hides inside? Seems a little suspicious, doesn't it?"

By this time, Michaela had joined Shane at his side, her hand finding purchase on his arm. The contact was comforting, grounding. Yet, he brushed it away, turning his full attention back to Evans. "I'm saying there's *not* going to be a welcoming party. We've already taken them out. We need to get inside. If Seong is still there, the only others left inside will be a skeleton crew, at best. But civilians, Evans. Just researchers, doctors, whatever the hell they staffed this place with. And they could be executing her right now for all we know. This place looks almost deserted."

Evans squeezed his eyes shut. "Shane, slow down and think this through," he pleaded. "From the beginning, I've said this doesn't add up. Doesn't it seem strange to you that there are *only* seven guards? If Seong is there, they would have more protection. Why would they just leave, their entire force reduced to seven men? *Especially* when they have a captive who's our primary objective?"

At this point, Shane met Michaela's eyes, and she looked back at him, then at Evans.

"What?" Evans inquired, picking up on their silent exchange.

Michaela hesitated, biting her lip nervously. "It's just... we have some new information. I don't know if we can trust it, but we overheard the assassin talking on the phone right after he kidnapped us."

Evans' eyes widened. "And?"

"And it means we need to get inside sooner, rather than later," Shane said.

"But it *also* means that you're right too, Jonathan," Michaela interjected, once again trying to mediate the escalating tension. "You're both hotheaded and stubborn — we can all see that. But you're both right. If Seong *is* in there, we need to find out soon. We can't risk leaving her there now that these people know we're here. If they were ever going to plan to kill her, it's going to be now that they know there's an enemy at the gates."

Evans swallowed, locking his gaze with hers, waiting for the other half of her explanation.

"But you're also right to say this isn't all straightforward. The parameters of this mission are more and more hazy the longer we're here. Seong's father..."

"What about him?"

"There was an assassination attempt on him today," she said.

Evans balked. "*What?* Chung-Hee Park? The guy who sent us here?" Evans asked, incredulous.

Shane simply nodded. "So it seems."

Michaela continued. "And it was foiled, thwarted."

Silence descended on the group, each of them processing the new information. Even Grudowski seemed confused, uneasy.

Finally, Evans broke the silence. "I suppose I'm supposed to ask *who* thwarted this assassination attempt?"

"The same person who tried to assassinate us, apparently. Whoever he's working for. They want Seong's father alive, at least for the time being," Shane revealed.

"But the people *in that facility* are the ones who took Seong Park. You're telling me *they* are the ones who *also* prevented an assassination attempt on her father?"

Michaela nodded.

Evans closed his eyes, shaking his head and chuckling bitterly. Despite their disagreements, Shane recognized the frustration and confusion mirrored in Evans. They were both soldiers, used to clear orders and well-defined objectives.

Yet here they were, thrust into a scenario where they felt like pawns in a much larger game.

No clear orders in sight.

This mission was becoming more complicated by the second, and they all felt the weight of the uncertainty. They'd charged into this situation without the full story. It felt as if they were being led to slaughter, and they needed to figure out how to change the game before it was too late.

42

SHANE

SHANE WATCHED Jonathan Evans pacing back and forth, a torrent of adrenaline coursing through his veins since their initial encounter with the North Korean soldiers. His anxiety was palpable, heightened by their yet-unrealized mission and the uncertainty of what lay inside the base. Evans' earlier decision reverberated in Shane's mind, his unshakable vow not to venture into the base until the lurking assassin was neutralized.

"So where does that leave us?" Evans queried. His voice carried a hint of sarcasm as he continued, "You can't *possibly* think venturing into an enemy base is a sound idea, especially with unknown entities still *outside* the base."

Shane nodded slowly, "I've never been known for my good ideas. But I *am* known for getting the job done."

"I got no idea who the hell you are," Grudowski said nonchalantly.

Both Shane and Evans glared at him.

Grudowski sighed and held his palms up. "Just to be fair."

"You might be right," Shane continued addressing Evans, "but I don't think it's wise to waste time trying to track down a professional assassin. He's more familiar with the area. I believe we should proceed to the base, try to get inside — at least one of us."

"Assuming you *do* go in," Evans interjected. "Where does that leave the rest of us? What's the plan, Shane?"

"See that tower?" Shane pointed to a tall, thin spire protruding from the top of the base. "That's a cell tower, not like the ones back home. This isn't just a Third World country; it's a country run by a paranoid totalitarian dictator.

That tower is only there because this complex serves some military benefit to him."

Evans tried to decipher Shane's point. "So... what are you implying?"

"No other towers are around; did you notice? That means this one's not part of a network — because our benevolent dictator isn't so keen on keeping his people connected. And the fact we heard the assassin on his *cellphone* means he was connected to *that* tower."

Michaela nodded along.

"So if we disable the tower, we could disrupt the guy's communication, as long as he's within the vicinity, but that's a radius of over twenty miles."

"A single central node," Evans said, nodding in understanding.

"Exactly," Shane said, not ignoring the good feeling it gave him of having Evans finally agree with him on something. "If we take out the tower, communication in and out of this region becomes challenging at best. If we're lucky, we'll neutralize the assassin's ability to work against us. He may still be out there, but if he hasn't attacked us yet, it means he's probably waiting for orders. We can get the upper hand by keeping it that way. We *need* to get in there, disable the communications array, and lock him out before he makes his move."

Evans, slightly amused by the plan, smiled. "I'll admit, it's a good plan. But you think it's as simple as that?"

Shane smiled back. "I've been doing this long enough to know *nothing* is as simple as that."

Evans' face told him everything. *Finally, a point we can completely agree on.*

Michaela approached Shane. "Let me understand. You want to enter that base, fight your way into the communications station – without knowing where it is — and then figure out how to shut down an entire cell tower?"

Shane shrugged. "I was hoping we could do it together?"

Evans shook his head.

"...But I'll do it alone if I have to."

"How will you know you're even in the right place?" Michaela asked.

Shane smiled. "I'll find something that resembles a cell tower control room — or something like that — then just blow everything up."

"We could assist with that part at least," Evans said. "We've got four grenades between me and Grudowski. We'll keep on, just in case. But if you can't figure out what to blow up with three grenades, you're more useless than you look."

Shane grinned. "I've never let a good grenade go to waste. I'll find *something* to blow up, trust me."

"Guys, this is insane," Michaela interjected. "You mentioned earlier you had line-of-sight radios that don't require connection with the cell tower?"

Evans nodded. "They don't, but getting a signal out once you're inside the station will be challenging. So we can set up a rendezvous point, as well as a plan of attack for out here. We'll give you... let's say half an hour, to find and neutralize the communications depot. If not, we'll assume the worst and storm in to provide support."

Shane nodded. "Seems like a good compromise. If I can't disable the communications within half an hour, it's likely because I've been pinned down. Having you storm in then will give us a second chance."

"Assuming our assassin stays away long enough for us to get in and cut him off," Grudowski chimed in.

"I agree with Shane on this one," Michaela said. "We're alive now because the assassin fled, likely to get new orders. He might still be maneuvering, trying to position himself for a flank attack. He'll expect us to enter the base, so he'll wait for that, then try to call it in."

"And he won't be able to," Grudowski said.

"That doesn't mean he'll abandon the mission," Shane said.

"Correct," Evans said sharply. "But we're going to attempt this. Michaela and Shane are right about Seong. If she's still in there, this is our last chance to rescue her. We can't afford to waste time."

"Alright then," Shane said, determination etching his features. "I'll take my chances with the front gate. You can monitor my progress from here, hiding behind these bushes. If there are more soldiers inside, you'll see them. If they emerge, I'll assess the situation from the front once I'm there. That's likely my quickest way in. Give me a radio I can bring to the gate. I'll update you then."

"Once you're inside, the radio will be useless," Evans said. "Those are thick walls, concrete and metal. I doubt you'll be able to get a signal out."

"Agreed, but at least I'll have it for a while. Plus," Shane continued, "this location offers a prime vantage point over the whole area. You, Evans, and Michaela can stay here and watch for our friend."

Evans and Grudowski nodded.

"Don't dawdle," Shane added. "We'll rendezvous at the north gate exactly thirty-five minutes after I go inside, got it? That's 30 minutes to locate and disable communications, and five minutes to run like hell and get back out. Once I take down their communications tower, they're going to notice pretty quickly. They'll either be here or they'll see it, but at that point, I'm exposed. I need you to follow quickly. Oh, and be prepared for another battle."

"Understood. Consider it done," Evans replied, his gaze steady and resolved.

Shane studied Evans' expression, finding nothing but sincerity there, and finally, the two men shook hands.

"Are you okay staying with the team?" Shane asked Michaela.

He hated leaving her, but it really was the best scenario. There was no need for her to risk entering the base just yet – let him take down the communications and get everyone inside focused on him. Once Evans stormed in, she could sneak down and locate Seong Park.

She shook her head. "No, but it makes the most sense."

"We'll take good care of you," Grudowski said, followed by a snicker of laughter.

Shane looked at Michaela. "Feel free to change your mind." And to Grudowski, "seems like you deserve a punch in the nuts. Care to partake?"

Grudowski spit on the ground, but Evans stepped in front of him. "She's safe with us, Riley," he said.

It wasn't a perfect plan, but it wasn't the worst he had ever come up with, either.

He just hoped it would work.

43
EVANS

GRUDOWSKI AND EVANS found positions with cover at their backs. They sat against a boulder and the truck respectively, each watching out in a different direction. They were on the lookout for movement, for more enemy soldiers.

For the assassin.

Michaela Everly sat next to Evans, who was watching the base itself. Shane had decided to take the direct route, unsurprisingly, and was making his way through the previous battlefield still littered with four bodies. He was currently near one of the guard towers on the southwest quadrant of the H-shaped facility.

No shots rang out, and Shane stepped out from underneath the turret. Evans could sense the trepidation in Michaela's body next to him. If the assassin was planning to attack, it would happen soon. Either he would come back to finish what he had started with Evans' team, follow Shane inside, or he would position himself to prevent Shane from getting inside the base altogether. He hoped none of those things happened, that Shane was right and the assassin had pulled back, waiting for orders.

That's what they were about to find out. Evans would never have risked one of his own men going into this place alone, but Shane had reiterated time and again that he was *not* one of Evans' men. He wanted to play lone operator, that was his business.

Evans would therefore use this operation as a test, a way to gather more data. If an army of men rushed out and killed Shane, it told Evans that what he feared most was true — that there were plenty more soldiers hiding inside.

But if Shane got inside successfully and was able to dismantle the communications tower attached to the roof of the station, it told him they were clear enough to get into the base themselves.

Either way, Evans felt anxious as he watched it unfold.

He felt Michaela tense next to him. The woman had a powerful energy, a warmth that seemed to radiate outward, consuming anyone close to her. It was no surprise that Shane was attracted to her.

She was gorgeous.

He wondered what the history was between this woman and Shane Riley. It was clear to everyone around – hell, probably even the assassin who had kidnapped them – that there *was* some deeper connection between the two.

"What's his deal?" he asked.

Dr. Everly turned her head to the side and looked at him, "His deal? What do you mean?"

"I mean, what's up with him? Why is he so... cagey?"

"You've never met a cagey soldier?" she asked.

He smiled. "I didn't say that. But every cagey soldier I've met had a past. What's his?"

"Broken, damaged, fragile — you pick."

"So you're not willing to share his story either?"

"It's not my story to share."

He shifted his jaw, nodding once. "Fair enough. Seems to me, though, some of *his* story is connected in some way to *your* story. Is your story a story you can share?"

Michaela watched him, and he did his best to hide the curiosity he was feeling. This woman was an enigma, attractive in all the best ways. There was no doubt she was whip smart, possibly brilliant. But he didn't even know what field of work she was in – was it related to the work being done at the station? Was that how she had gotten Shane Riley into the country and why she was here now?

It was obvious she was no trained operative – even without the weapon, the way she carried herself, the way she responded to the gunfire, told him she was a civilian.

"Sure, I'm an open book," she said. "But I hardly think this is the time. Don't you guys need to talk through... logistics or whatever?"

"Already did."

"When?"

"For the past decades of service, and then together as a team for about two years. Logistics, operations, tactics, strategy – all of it. We know what to do.

We just talked through the plan with Riley, and we're all on board. So, here we sit. Watching and waiting. Plenty of time for a good story."

Michaela smiled, a glint in her eye. "I never said it was a *good* story."

"Any story is better than Grudowski talking about how hot his daddy's new trophy wife is, or how often he gets gets the shits when he's deployed in foreign countries," Evans said.

"I heard that," Grudowski responded.

"I bet you did," Evans retorted.

"But my old man's new wife *is* quite the catch," Grudowski added.

Evans smiled. "See?"

Michaela shrugged. "Honestly, there's not much to tell. Shane was married. Kate is her name. I was his wife's best friend, her coworker. He met both of us at the same time. They hit it off, got married, and... the rest is history."

"Is it?"

Michaela paused for a long time, and Evans didn't fill the empty space.

"Shortly after we all met, I went away on a trip. Business, I don't even remember what I was doing. I was gone for three weeks? A month? When I came back, it was pretty much a done deal. They had fallen in love, got engaged, and were married two months after I returned."

"Short engagement."

Michaela shrugged again, turning and looking out over the horizon, above the mountain peaks. "I guess they both just knew what they wanted pretty quickly." She turned back to face Evans. "Besides, none of us were young. We were both postgraduate; Shane had spent his career with the military, and I think there was a sense of urgency for all of us. You know, if you're going to settle down..."

Evans squinted as the sun peaked out from behind a cloud and caught his eye. "Except you didn't settle down, did you? This girl Kate – and Shane – did instead."

He watched her face, keeping one eye on the base as Shane tiptoed around the next tower and began his approach to the northern gate where he would then attempt to enter the base. She pulled back, eyes darting down, a look of sadness on her face. What was that? Denial? Regret?

She didn't answer.

He shifted, pulling himself a bit away from her. He sensed the need to give her a bit more physical space. "Sorry, didn't mean to pry. Things are usually... quieter out here on assignment."

"No, it's okay. It's just — I know you didn't mean anything by it. Truth be told, I'm trying to figure things out as well. I haven't talked to Shane in over a year. Since..."

Evans didn't need to be filled in on the details. He remembered Shane telling Chung-Hee Park that his wife was dead; that Park had said she had been murdered. And the way Michaela was talking now, the way she was reminiscing and letting bottled-up emotions finally spill out, he could tell it was all more than she intended.

He could tell he had struck a nerve, harder than she had anticipated.

Shane had lost a wife, and this woman had lost her best friend.

He let out a long breath of air between two puffed cheeks. "I'm so sorry, Dr. Everly."

She nodded, accepting his sympathy. He didn't need to say anything more. He couldn't say anything more.

He had his own demons he was wrestling with, just like everyone else.

He only hoped they could stay inside him for a bit longer.

44
SHANE

SHANE HADN'T SEEN a soul since leaving Evans, Grudowski, and Dr. Everly behind. He crept around two of the ancient-looking guard turrets, seeing them for what they were now that he was closer. Each was falling apart, decayed, as if no maintenance had been done on them since they had been constructed. Portions of the edges crumbled, leaving chunks of concrete littering the ground around them. One such hole was big enough that Shane could see straight through into the interior.

It was dark inside, lifeless.

While Shane hoped he could find a similar lack of human defense inside the larger base, he knew that if he didn't find anyone inside, it meant he was highly unlikely to find Seong, either.

But he couldn't help but wonder why some guards had been left behind in that case. Why would whoever was in charge of this place totally evacuate the premises, leaving only a skeleton crew? Why not save the men and just leave altogether? Finding Seong would be like searching for a needle in a haystack; trying to chase her around the North Korean countryside would be damn near impossible.

But he was operating on assumptions and expectations. He needed eyes on. He needed to get inside, to see for himself what the situation was. If she was still in there, he would find her.

He reached the front gate and crouched beneath a concrete pillar holding up one side of the wrought-iron fence. The fence looked like the kind that slid sideways, allowing a vehicle access to the interior grounds. He was at the top section of the gate, which had been arranged north to south just at the base of the mountain. A meadow of overgrown grass stretched from the other side of this gate to what looked like the front doors of the base. They were about as ornate as he expected – nothing but plain slabs and rectangles to welcome him.

It looked every bit like the Nazi-era building he had expected.

No one fired at him or shouted, so he stood up, careful to take in his immediate surroundings to ensure he was in fact alone.

Finally satisfied, he reached up and pulled his body over the concrete rectangular pillar. He swung his feet around and over the fence, the gate, then pushed off the post and landed on the other side.

He was in.

He ran through the meadow, noticing the center of it had a circular concrete pad – *perhaps for a helicopter?* – And continued toward the front entrance.

Still, no one jumped out and started shooting at him. No one announced his arrival, he heard no sound of human life whatsoever.

He felt the chances of Seong's existence here diminishing, the window of opportunity closing fast. There's no way the people who had wanted her so badly would simply leave her here, alone.

He fell back against the left side of the first door he came to, holding the rifle Evans had given him up and ready. He waited for a few seconds, taking a few deep breaths. This was the riskiest move – moving into a dark, unknown space. He had no idea what to expect inside, other than knowing the general layout of the larger buildings.

But the building he was about to go into was massive – a sprawling complex, though only a single story aboveground, but he assumed one or two underground. The hallways and corridors were thick, wide enough that it would be possible to get lost inside if he wasn't careful.

He checked his rifle again out of habit, then said a quick prayer, openly hoping God was still listening. It seemed the man upstairs had forgotten this hellhole of a country, and he was once again reminded of the poor souls back in the village, all missing an eye.

He shook away the unnerving thought, focusing once again on the task at hand. He forced his mind clear, to do what it had been trained to do. Still, he felt out of his element – he had not been in active service for at least two years, and running into battle was not the career path he had chosen after leaving the military.

This is why I don't retrieve people, he reminded himself.

He stretched out his boot and pushed the door open with it. He pulled his shoulder around next, letting the heavy steel door, a windowless steel door, swing open. It hadn't been oiled in years, and a loud creak forced him to pause.

He took another two breaths, knowing that anyone waiting inside was now well aware of his impending presence. So, he did the only thing he knew how – he kicked the door as hard as he could, sending it flying open, then brought the gun up.

And that's when all hell broke loose.

BULLETS CLANGED against the steel door, the sound of rifle shots hitting him almost as hard as the impacts themselves. Thankfully, none of the bullets hit him, and he dove backward just as quickly as he had entered.

It was a good thing he did, too.

Just as he pulled to the left and pressed his back against the wall once more outside of the base, the door itself blew outward and sailed into the meadow. A shockwave brought with it dust and debris, and a significant amount of heat flashed against Shane's side.

A grenade.

Well, we found the welcoming party.

He pulled one of the grenades off of his belt given to him by Evans and yanked the pin out. He flicked it into the open door, followed by a second, this one directed farther to the right.

The consecutive concussive blasts were even louder now that there was no door to contain them, but he ignored the deafening roar and used the sudden chaos to get inside. He hoped the fragmentation grenades would offer enough force momentarily to daze his opponents — if they hadn't outright killed them. He needed a second, maybe two, to find cover.

If there was any.

Shane charged into the room full speed, aiming diagonally to the left. He found enough cover there to satisfy the immediate need. Not that it was much cover at all. An industrial-sized trashcan, circular and sitting on a rolling base, offered him the best option for protection. He dove and slid on his backside behind it, coming to rest between the trashcan and the far wall.

Just as he had reached it, he bumped the trashcan, which sent its sensitive casters into motion, and the whole thing began rolling away.

Dammit.

He pulled on the rim of the bin before it could get away, then let it come to rest once again, squeezing him between the wall and the terrible excuse for cover. Three rounds smacked into the trashcan, and Shane winced. He had no idea if the can was full or not. The thin rubber can itself would offer nothing in the way of protection, but if there were bags inside, it would at least slow or deflect the rounds.

At least, that was what he hoped.

He closed his eyes for a moment, trying to sense if any new holes had been opened up in his side. Finding and feeling none, he lifted his rifle up and sprayed bullets down the hallway. They were not intended to hit anyone, merely to cause them to duck. He immediately pulled his head out from around the side of the trashcan and then aimed properly.

Right after, two heads appeared, one bending around from the right side farther down, and one from the left, much closer to him. This man was hunched in the doorway, and Shane gladly took the opportunity to thank him for his less-than-ceremonious welcome. He planted a round right between this man's eyes, then threw himself backwards as the men farther down in the hall opened fire once more.

Shane had a single grenade left, but he was saving it for a rendezvous with the communications room.

But he had to find it first. He considered heading in the same direction, leaving the safety of his trusty trashcan, but what then? He didn't know this facility at all, and the hallway behind him was almost pitch black. They knew he was coming and had set up shop accordingly. He tried to keep track of how many rounds he had fired so far, but realized he hadn't been counting. He didn't have any extra ammunition within – Evans' team hadn't had any to spare.

That meant he had only the magazine in the rifle now. The man down the hallway fired again, two of the rounds smacking against the wall and zipping past his head, with one of them landing in the side of the trashcan once again.

He's getting better.

He wished he were facing an army of stormtroopers instead, much preferring going up against some untrained clones that couldn't shoot straight to save their lives.

He didn't have time to wait for the man to continue popping holes in the trashcan. He sucked in a few quick breaths, pulled his feet underneath him, then sprang upward and outward, aiming back toward the doorway. He stopped short, using the narrow entranceway as cover, pressing his back up against the wall. He hoped the man would assume he was heading outside once again, deciding to start the attack from a different position.

And that would be the man's downfall.

He waited a slow count of three seconds, then sprang back into the hallway, this time standing Rambo-style, feet shoulder-width apart, his rifle up and ready. The man was caught red-handed. He had been jogging down the hallway, gun at his side, useless, when Shane's barrel landed on him.

He fired a single shot, hitting the man in the chest. He staggered backward, trying to pull his weapon up.

Shane had already closed the distance. He swung the rifle around like a hammer, emulating the motion the assassin had used to take him out earlier. He heard a sickening crack as the butt of the stock connected with the man's skull, and the man fell to the floor.

He writhed once there, then fell silent. A bit of blood gurgled from his mouth and slid down his cheek.

"Dead enough for me," he mumbled.

He hadn't seen any more North Korean soldiers, but he knew they were probably waiting for him somewhere else in the facility. He needed to find his target – a way to access the communications tower sitting right above his head.

He had no idea how the North Koreans – or the Nazis who had built this place, for that matter – would have set up the communications depot inside the base. If he had to guess, he would assume it was somewhere deep inside, away from the extremities and appendages, relatively safe from outside attack.

"Okay, that means I'm heading..."

But the shape of this building was like a large "H". He was standing in the little center corridor that connected the two longer north-south wings. It could be in any one of the rooms dotting the halls around him, but he had an even better idea.

He saw a door off to his left. It was near where the trashcan had been that he had hidden behind when he first entered, and he examined the can now. The poor thing looked like it had seen better days, it was falling apart, its tough lid hanging down over itself, trash and papers spilling out of its mouth like it had just given up and died.

There was a sign next to the door as well, but it was in Korean and Shane didn't have any hope of reading it. Thankfully, he didn't need to. He saw what was inside easily.

Stairs.

46

SHANE

SHANE CAUTIOUSLY DESCENDED the stairs into the bowels of the facility. It was possible there were still more guards that had been left behind to watch the entrance, but it was just as likely there were hundreds more waiting for him downstairs.

It was *also* possible he had taken out the last of them already.

But why had they been here in the first place? He thought back to the sound of gunfire he'd heard. He was *sure* that's what it was, now. But who were they shooting at?

It still didn't make sense why the place seemed so deserted, so abandoned. He hadn't seen anyone who looked like a scientist, researcher, or even janitor. He thought of the trashcan that had met its demise upstairs. There had to have been a janitor here at some point.

He reached the landing between the first floor and the first subterranean floor, then turned and continued descending. He heard nothing, no shouts, no shots fired. Just an eerie silence.

The smell hit him first. Two steps to go before entering the first underground level, he stopped short. He reached a hand out and leaned against the side wall of the stairwell. The stench consumed all the air around.

Breathing in, he tasted it. He couldn't escape from it if he tried.

He considered turning around and heading back upstairs, but was afraid it would follow him up. His eyes were watering, his mouth gasping for fresh air. He knew the stench, though it was tinged with something sterile, like formaldehyde.

It was the smell of death.

Shane trudged forward, not content with leaving this place without seeing the truth of it. He wanted to know the full reality of what was happening here, why Seong Park had been taken here. If, in fact, she had been.

He walked out onto the hallway, once again noting the H-shaped layout. He was in a small, short hallway that went left to right, but he could see both sides of it led to other hallways he assumed were exactly the same layout as those above.

The good news was the stairs did not keep going. There seemed to be only one subterranean level after all, which meant his search would go that much quicker.

Unfortunately, there were no doors immediately around in this short hall-way. His prized communications station was not going to be accessible without a bit of snooping around. Which meant he was going to have to figure out where the smell was coming from, whether he liked it or not.

He opted not to hold his breath, knowing that he would eventually have to give out and breathe in a deep breath of the sour air, but also knowing that his nose would eventually get used to it. The human body was miraculous in that way, able to accept new sensations as normal only moments after they encountered them.

He pulled his hand away from the wall and stood upright once again. Taking a few short breaths to expedite the effect, he stepped into the narrow hallway and found that he had miscalculated.

The smell here was ten times worse. It hung in the air like a weighty humidity, as if he was swimming through it. The stench of death was unmistakable, the tinge of formaldehyde completely gone now. Whatever sterile, medical environment these people had tried to establish failed miserably.

Nevertheless, he forced his feet forward, forced his gun back up, prepared for anything. He chose left, mainly because he was left-handed. He turned into the longer hallway and stared down it. On each side of the corridor, all the way down to the end, were rows of doors. Individual rooms, like in a hospital wing.

He cautiously walked to the first one on his left. There was more Korean writing on a placard next to it, but otherwise, no markings told him what he was looking at. This could be a secret office facility or a state-of-the-art North Korean hospital. He simply had no frame of reference. He tried the door, finding it unlocked.

Shane nudged the door open. A light switch loomed on the wall next to him. He paused for a moment, then flicked it on. Light spilled into the hall-way, causing him to wince. Surprised that it had turned on, he lingered by the door for a moment, using his keen sense of hearing to determine if someone had been alerted to his presence.

Hearing no footsteps, he used the barrel of his rifle to push the door open further. He stepped inside, his eyes already adjusted to the dim light.

In an instant, he knew this wasn't a hospital room, at least not one he had ever seen. Yet, there were elements reminiscent of a medical laboratory - a computer terminal on a rolling cart in the corner, a long desk with cabinets above and below, and a canister bolted to the wall with a radioactive symbol above it.

On the opposite wall sat two chairs, the cheapest type found at any office supply store back home. They looked uncomfortable, but he presumed no one had ever sat in them.

However, it was the object in the middle of the room that truly captivated him. A doctor's office bed, the type he had encountered before - one whose back could adjust, complete with a roll of paper the doctor or nurse could stretch to cover the bed.

And on that bed lay a single patient.

The man, who looked to be in his mid-60s, was strapped down with thick leather straps across his chest, arms, legs, and feet. Though he was dead, a hole in the center of his forehead, his eyes were open.

Or, rather, his eye.

This man's lifeless face stared back at Shane with a gaping hole where his left eye should be. His single right eye stared up at the cold, concrete ceiling, and Shane imagined the missing eyeball in the left socket trying to do the same. He paused in the doorway, unsure of what to do next. This man was clearly one of the villagers he had encountered before.

After managing to evade losing his eye as a child, these people had come for it now, well into his adulthood. But why? What reason could there possibly be for these people - whoever they were - to want the left eyeballs of every inhabitant of a village?

Questions overwhelmed Shane, none of which had pleasant answers. Whatever the case, this man had been tortured, evident by the scrapes on his arms and bare legs. Methodical gashes marked his thighs, not accidental or caused by scraping against a thorn bush on his way here.

He couldn't afford to stay and examine the man and the room. He was on a deadline, still needed to find the communications room, still needed to disable the network and prevent any incoming and outgoing signals. And while he had killed a few of the soldiers left behind to guard the base, he wasn't sure if there would be more deeper in the facility.

Shane suddenly felt awkward, so he greeted the dead man. "Too bad you can't tell me what happened here."

Shane swallowed, attempting to mask his discomfort as he took one final look around the room. "Didn't think so. No matter – I'm going to check a few other rooms, then see about shutting this place down. Keep an eye out for me."

He winced at his inadvertent joke. *Thank God this guy can't hear me.* And then, *he probably didn't speak English anyway.* He turned and left the door standing open, but switched off the light as he exited. It felt inhumane to leave the man here, strapped to a table in the dark, but what else was he supposed to do? Leaving a light on was a clear indication of his presence, an invitation for the guards or the assassin to track him down.

Besides, he thought, *he's not going anywhere, anyway.*

He moved quickly to the next door in the line, sticking to the left side of the corridor, and opened it. Even before hitting the light switch, he could see in the shadows that this room had an identical layout. The same chairs, the same desk and cabinets, and the same daunting, rectangular doctor's bed stationed in the middle.

He flicked on the light quickly, then off again just as swiftly. In the momentary illumination, he spotted the bed's occupant: a woman. Like the man before her, she was around the same age and was missing her left eye.

She was also dead.

"What the bloody hell is this place?" he muttered under his breath, closing the door without speaking to the woman.

He continued on, checking two more rooms in quick succession. He didn't even step into these; he simply opened the door, turned on the light for a second or two, and then departed. Only one of these rooms had a person strapped to the doctor's bed, but he got the gist. Each room was effectively a clone of the others - a doctor's office, but one of a doctor who was sick, twisted, and willing to perform horrific experiments on innocent civilians.

Shane's mind flashed back to accounts he had read about Unit 731, the secret Japanese facility where numerous atrocities had been committed, all in the name of science. Inhumane acts like human vivisection, testing the human body's freezing point by subjecting the patient to ice cold water, and other horrendous acts, including rape, murder, and homicide.

This place felt the same; a den of inhumanity, hidden from the world's gaze.

Shane started to jog down the hallway, keeping his footsteps as quiet as possible. He hadn't seen another guard yet, but he expected more to be lurking somewhere. As he neared the end of the hallway, his heart sank. This level didn't share the H-shaped layout of the floor above. Instead, it had an extra feature: a hallway perpendicular to this one connecting two longer corridors. Another T-intersection, with one side bending back around to the east and the other heading farther into the subterranean complex.

Cold dread coursed through his veins. How large *was* this place? Would he be able to find the communications station or command center in time? With renewed determination, he pressed forward, ready to confront whatever horrors lay ahead.

47

SHANE

SHANE FELT COMPELLED to comb through the entire facility one door at a time, but he recognized the need for a more efficient strategy. He couldn't risk getting lost in these subterranean depths, yet the slow, methodical approach necessary to sketch an accurate map of this underground section wasn't a luxury he could afford.

He remained uncertain of where he might find the control or command center - if such a thing even existed here - but he held firm to the belief that it would be located near the facility's central hub.

So where is the center of this place? he wondered.

Opting for a course of action that increased his speed, he chose to get to the end of this current corridor and turn left, following that path wherever it might take him. Surprisingly, he encountered a staircase leading even deeper underground.

He descended the stairs two at a time and arrived at the bottom, turning left again. This presented him with another hallway, just as long as the ones above. He speculated that this corridor ran parallel to the sides of the larger "H" from above, but was situated in the middle of the space, two floors underground.

At least, that's what he thought.

He didn't want to admit it, but he was starting to lose track of where he was.

This new hallway was engulfed in total darkness, lacking even the red emergency lighting he had noticed marking the exits on the ground floor.

He didn't possess a mountable light for his rifle, but he did have his cell phone. Extracting it, he powered it on and waited for it to boot up. After about ten seconds, he activated the flashlight app, casting a beam of light into the murky corridor. It was a bit cumbersome juggling an assault rifle with both hands while also holding his phone, but he managed to balance it between his thumb and forefinger and position it to the side of his weapon.

The soft illumination revealed about twenty feet of the corridor ahead. He noticed that this section also had rooms lining it, but they appeared larger. The hallway itself was wider, and each door was heftier.

Instead of the sanitized feel of a doctor's office, this area felt more akin to a military bunker.

The doors to each room were substantial, entirely metal, and replaced traditional handles with brushed steel clasps, forged from a single piece of curved metal. Shane approached the first door and reached out, pulling at the clasp.

At first it seemed locked, but he quickly realized it was just far heavier than he had anticipated. He stowed his phone in his pocket, with the flashlight still active. The resulting glow, now a warm orange, was sufficient to light the immediate area around him.

With a firm grip on the door, he pulled again, the door responding with a loud, groaning protest. He paused, holding his breath, and listened. He could hear the distant drip of water somewhere deep within the facility, its sound echoing through the concrete and metal labyrinth. Otherwise, there was silence - no signs of life, no other sounds. He gave the door another pull, and it groaned again, softer this time. He dared to pull it open just enough to slip inside, the door resisting but finally yielding.

Once inside, he realized there was no light switch. He retrieved his phone again, wielding it like a torch in front of him as he stepped further into the room, gripping his rifle single-handedly in a style reminiscent of Rambo.

He squinted in the dim light, trying to decipher what he was seeing.

A shock of fear almost triggered a reflexive pull of the trigger as his brain grappled with a rush of incoming information, struggling to process the sight before his eyes. He nearly jumped into the top of the doorframe.

He managed to control his instincts despite being unable to fully comprehend what he was seeing.

He could see glints of reflections off glass surfaces, metallic and wooden rectangular structures - perhaps shelves - but he couldn't be sure. There was unquestionably glass present. And within that glass, housed in what he now realized were jars, were *eyeballs*.

Each jar was home to a single, solitary eyeball, the convex curvature of the jar enhancing the grotesque spectacle within.

The sight was almost unbelievable - floor to ceiling, jars filled with liquid and a single suspended eyeball at their center. These jars were meticulously arranged on shelves that lined the room, a horrifying spectacle of sterile preservation.

All of them, eerily, were gazing directly at him. A chill ran down his spine as he took in the scene, his mind grappling with the macabre reality.

He almost expected the eyeballs to blink, the surreal sight pushing the boundaries of his disbelief. He stood still, surrounded by the silent stare of countless eyes, all focused solely on him. It was an ominous sight, one that sent a wave of discomfort rippling through him.

Shane knew he had to continue his exploration. He was far from understanding the true nature of this facility, and as disturbing as this discovery was, it felt like he was only scratching the surface.

Clasping his phone tighter, casting its frail light against the glossy surfaces of the jars, he took a deep breath and stepped further into the room, ready to confront whatever further horrors this place had in store.

"OKAY, TIME TO MOVE," Evans said, glancing at Michaela Everly. Usually, he was skilled at reading people, but Everly was an enigma. Despite their earlier conversation while Shane Riley had entered the North Korean facility alone, he found it hard to decipher her true intentions. He didn't sense anything sinister about her, but he had a feeling that there was more to her than what he could perceive. It was clear that there was some emotional connection between her and Riley – a fact she had willingly shared with him. It was also apparent that Riley had experienced a great loss, and Everly was trying to help him recover, while also maintaining a safe distance from him.

Humans are complicated, he mused.

He and Grudowski were ready, and they set out immediately, positioning themselves to avoid being attacked from the sides or ambushed from the woods beyond the north entrance. Evans and Michaela Everly walked side by side in silence. He might not have known what was troubling the beautiful woman next to him, but he could sense that her thoughts were turbulent.

Just like his own.

It felt strange entering a North Korean Army facility, with hardly any resistance. There was still an unknown third party out there, capable of taking down Evans and Grudowski without their knowledge. They remained alert, of course, but it didn't alter the current situation.

Feels like we're walking into a trap.

They didn't need to voice their concern – their minds were synchronized, operating out of training and mutual respect, entrusting their lives to each other.

Their senses were on high alert, ready to pick up on the smallest movements or sounds.

As they reached the north entrance, both Evans and Grudowski noticed signs that Shane had encountered some resistance. They had heard the faint sound of gunfire, but that was expected. They assumed there would be guards inside, and Shane had assured them he could handle any threats.

They walked past an empty helicopter pad, and Evans noticed pockmarks on the ground and walls around the entrance. There had been a fight here — they had heard just the tail end of it — and just inside, Evans wondered what they might find upon entering.

Had Riley reached his destination, or had he been cut down somewhere up here? Was the communications tower and array offline? There would be no physical proof – no explosion, no signs of subterfuge. They didn't have any equipment to measure the strength of any signals coming in or out of the facility.

They had to operate on trust and hope. Not the ideal conditions for a mission, but it was all they had at the moment.

Michaela was equally silent as they neared the front steps leading to the facility. The entrance was long, flat, its old paint faded but not chipped, standing out starkly against the idyllic mountain landscape surrounding them. Evans spat to his left, the only sound in the vicinity. Even the birds had flown away after the firefight, leaving a haunting silence.

Or setting the stage for an ambush...

They reached the front door, and Evans stepped through. He quickly scanned the interior, then gave a brief nod. Grudowski entered, followed by Michaela.

Inside, the entrance was a scene of carnage. None of the bodies were Shane Riley's, which was a relief.

But the fact that there were quite a few guards here, and possibly more deeper in the facility, was concerning.

"Where are you, buddy?" Evans muttered to himself.

Just as Everly stepped in fully, a bullet whizzed past her head and embedded itself in the drywall between Evans and her. Grudowski let out a cry of surprise, but Evans was already moving. He pulled her down, pushing her flat to the ground and half lying on top of her. His rifle was aimed towards the door next to him. His gaze landed on the wide wound left in the concrete by the bullet, which had blown a six-inch hole in the drywall.

"Sniper," he identified.

"It's the same one from before," Grudowski said.

"We got lucky," Evans replied. "We might not stay lucky. We're trapped between the remaining guards and that sniper. We don't have the time to wait him out."

Everly, her face pale under the harsh fluorescent lighting, was quietly sobbing beneath his right arm. She had come within a hair's breadth of death, and the weight of that realization seemed to crash down on her all at once. Evans felt a pang of sympathy for the woman. They were soldiers, trained for this, prepared for the possibility of death lurking behind every corner. But she was a doctor, a healer. This was a world far removed from her own.

There was no time to console her, and there was no need to. She had known the stakes before coming along, and yet she had insisted. Her sobs subsided into the quiet echoes of the facility's labyrinthine corridors, replaced by a determination that Evans admired. She pulled herself out from underneath Evans and leaned back against the far wall, her face a mask of resolution.

Evans gave a nod of approval, shifting his body to get a better angle on the front door. Or, at least, the area where the door used to exist. He wanted to be ready in case someone attempted a surprise attack.

"Two options, boss," Grudowski said, breaking the tense silence. "We can try to get out there and find him, or we can keep moving forward through the facility. There's a chance we can track him from the inside."

Evans considered the options. Going after the sniper was risky, and it would split their already small team. They were in enemy territory, outnumbered and outgunned. Staying together was their best chance of survival. But pressing forward through the facility held its own risks. They would be moving deeper into the lion's den, the odds of encountering more enemy soldiers increasing with every step they took.

Making a quick decision, Evans replied, "We keep moving forward. We can't afford to split up or waste time chasing shadows. Let's go."

Everly, having regained her composure, nodded. The trio set off deeper into the facility, their senses heightened and their hearts racing, ready to face whatever lay ahead.

49
SHANE

SHANE FOUND himself in a silent staring contest with the eyeballs, each of them eerily staring back at him. He wanted to turn around and flee, to leave this place and never return. In all his years - and all the retrieval missions he had undertaken - he had never seen something as haunting as a room full of human eyeballs suspended in a mysterious liquid.

What was the liquid? Formaldehyde? He didn't know what kind of solution could preserve human eyeballs for such an extended period. He didn't have any information on how old these eyes were, or whether they were even technically alive. He suspected they were not alive but just preserved for whatever unscientific purpose. He speculated that these eyeballs were the same missing eyes that each of the villagers from nearby had been missing.

Of course, this realization didn't make him feel any better about the situation. He carefully stepped further into the room, half-expecting each of the eyes to develop a face and mouth to scream for help at his intrusion. Previously, he had been afraid of the unknown - what possible horrors might lurk down here? What remains of vivisection would he stumble upon? How many adversaries were waiting for him?

Now, knowing exactly what horrors awaited him in the depths of this facility, the reality was even more terrifying.

Who were these people? he wondered. *What kind of perverse experiments were they conducting?*

And how was Seong Park involved?

A shiver ran through him as he walked closer to one of the cases, behind which the enlarged orbs glared back at him, silent and unmoving.

Did one of these eyeballs belong to Seong? Was she watching him right now, through the walls of her liquid prison?

He gripped his rifle more tightly in his hands as he surveyed the room. As the only light was provided by his pocket-sized cell phone, he had to walk closely to each of the glass cases to see every corner of the room. He would have preferred to stay a few feet back, fully aware that none of these eyeballs could jump out and attack him, yet feeling the opposite nonetheless.

Shane finished his survey of the room and returned to the metal door, doing a final, full circle in the dim light cast from his pocket. This room wasn't a laboratory - it was a room intended for preservation. For safekeeping.

It was a library of eyes.

Whatever these people were working on, whatever experimentation they had engaged in, human eyes seemed to be their focus. However, this room was filled with intact eyeballs - as far as he could tell, none of these orbs had been dissected or sliced. They were whole, as if plucked from their human host and saved for a later date.

He needed to keep moving, to continue exploring this facility. As haunting as this room was, he needed to find out for sure what they were doing here. Any information might lead him to Seong. Though it seemed unlikely at this point, she might still be somewhere inside, waiting for him.

SHANE EXITED THE ROOM, leaving the door ajar, and ventured into the one adjacent. He was greeted by the sight of similar glass cases lining three of the walls, but the first case he approached on his left housed only a few jars, each containing an eyeball suspended in a viscous fluid.

But what held his attention was a slender table standing in the center of the room. Measuring about a foot wide and approximately six feet long, the table held a leather roll-up bag that had been unrolled and left splayed diagonally across the metallic surface. It contained various medical instruments - different sized scalpels, tweezers, forceps. The assortment was what one might find inside a surgeon's field bag.

Or perhaps, more grimly, a traveling torturer's kit.

Adjacent to the open bag was a trio of metal bowls, each smaller than the last, nested within each other. Beside those lay a pristine white cloth. It didn't take Shane long to understand that he was looking at a makeshift standing desk - a workstation. But unlike most desks that housed a computer and keyboard, this one was furnished with minimalist medical equipment. It was here that these individuals - presumably scientists - conducted their dissections. It was here where they would slice open a victim's eye, delve inside, and...

What then? Shane mused, baffled. He was still utterly clueless about the specific purpose of the research conducted in this facility. Clearly, whatever they were doing here pertained to the human eye, but that provided him precious little insight.

Overwhelmed with a sense of urgency, Shane left this room and pulled out his phone. He swiftly opened the next two doors, peering briefly inside each, and discovered that they shared similar layouts to the first two rooms - standing shelves protected by glass walls, perhaps a table or two in the middle of the space. It was now evident that he was within a wing dedicated to the study - not the extraction - of the eyeballs. He had stumbled upon a storage and research facility, a place where scientists could conduct experiments on victims, safely distanced from the shrieking, eyeless humans upstairs.

Though this realization provided him with information, it did little to quell his growing anxiety about the place.

Choosing to hasten his exploration, Shane skimmed through the next six rooms, bypassing every alternate one until he arrived at the end of the hallway. If the rest of the facility bore a chilling resemblance to a Nazi-era blueprint for sinister and terrifying structures, the room facing him was the antithesis. Instead of the usual stone and metal forming the walls and doorways, he was confronted with a wall made entirely of glass. Metal studs partitioned each pane at six-foot intervals, and holding his minuscule flashlight against the glass, he was able to illuminate a small portion of the space beyond.

This seemed to be the very room he had been searching for.

He spotted various pieces of computer equipment - most of it powered down, silent and dormant, but a few devices had front panels blinking rhythmically like rack-mounted equipment. There was still power being supplied to this area, albeit perhaps on standby, but he had discovered what he had come looking for.

Approaching the entrance to this larger room that stood guard at the end of the long corridor of eyeballs, he found it to be a double door. The first handle he tried proved unyielding, but the second one was unlocked.

He pulled it open, employing the butt of his rifle to hold the door open as he stepped inside. Unlike the traditional doors found elsewhere in the facility, this one was equipped with a hydraulic arm mounted near the top corner and threatened to shut on him as soon as he let go.

Shane snuck inside, letting the door close silently behind him, and immediately made his way towards the first rackmount cabinet he saw to his left. The rack was fully populated, but only three single spaced units bore illuminated power buttons. Shane was neither an engineer nor a computer expert; he simply hoped his subconscious would kick in and guide his actions. If he didn't find something in the next five minutes that suggested, *'turn me off to shut down the communications array,* he was prepared to simply start shooting each of these racks until there were no more glowing orange indicators.

That should do the trick, he thought. *Right?*

He meandered slowly around the wall-mounted racks and their occupants, not finding anything that particularly caught his attention. Each unit seemed akin to the kind of servers he would expect to find in a server room — at least, from what he had seen on TV.

He suddenly wished he had consulted with the others before undertaking this mission — perhaps one of them knew what the control system for a communications tower would look like.

He finished surveying the left wall and the far back wall and was just turning to inspect the dark wall to the right of the entrance when something attracted his attention. A persistent beeping sound filled the room, growing louder as he neared the row of desks, a gentle glow emanating from beneath one of them.

Getting warmer.

He approached and gave the computer mouse on the desk a wiggle. The screen remained dark.

He circled to the other side of the desk, where he thought the sound might be originating, and almost collided with a dark, rectangular monolith nearly waist high that had been set in the center of this room. It was pitch black, seemed to swallow light, which is why he hadn't noticed it before. Unlike the racks and other metallic surfaces in this room, this surface was matte and did not reflect any light, even after nearly bumping into it and holding his flashlight up over it.

He frowned in the darkness, running a hand over its smooth surface. It was clear that the top of this unit had been designed to function as a sort of desktop. But it was one unit, akin to a rack system that had been toppled onto its side. He hurriedly circled the six-foot-long desk and glanced at the other side, immediately noting more glowing indicators.

But rather than the typical orange power indicator he had seen — the same type of light that indicated that a surge protector was plugged in and operational — he spotted fainter, tiny blue lights.

He held the phone up, angling it to illuminate as much of the front of this strange device as possible. To his surprise, most of the buttons seemed to be labeled with English text, most of the words abbreviated. Near his phone hand, he noticed a label that read COMM DISP.

Communications Display?

Next to the label was a tiny, barely visible black circular button. He pressed it, and a small, elongated rectangle came to life.

"Ha!" he shouted. "I've done something useful!"

51
SHANE

SHANE USED the built-in trackpad next to the computer to navigate across the screen. As he feared, everything was in Korean.

Everything except for a single word.

English.

Feeling hope return, he moved the trackpad so the mouse hovered over the word, then he double-clicked. He was no computer expert — he didn't even own a laptop — but in that moment, he felt like the world's best hacker.

"Let there be... English," he muttered to himself.

Immediately, the words on the screen changed from Korean to English. He let out a *whoop* as he looked over the icons on the desktop. So far, it seemed like any other computer desktop. Not an operating system he recognized, but it wasn't too alien. He saw settings panels, a few shortcut buttons, and then, near the bottom left of the desktop, he saw what he was looking for.

Communications System Control.

He clicked this icon and a black screen appeared, green text displayed on it. He immediately felt the nostalgia, remembering playing with his grandfather's old IBM machine as a kid. He had never taken to computers, but he was familiar with what he was seeing now. While the communications system itself could be state-of-the-art, the control software for it was running on the most basic terminals. The mouse pointer had turned into a cursor, and navigating meant using arrow keys. He looked around, frantic, worried that he would need a Bluetooth keyboard someone had hidden away, or had died days ago.

Thankfully, just beneath the desk was a tray that slid out, revealing a modern-looking computer keyboard. He pressed the right arrow key a few times, satisfied to see the cursor move. In this way, he navigated around the screen, placing the cursor next to a word that said 'shutdown'. He pressed return.

A prompt displayed on the screen – *Would you like to continue?* – and he pressed return once more.

He held his breath, half expecting there to be a password prompt next. Instead, he was offered three choices:

Restart at 00:00:00. That would be midnight.

Restart at custom time.

Manual restart only.

He used the down arrow to select the third option. Then pressed return once more.

The entire screen went black. He waited, still holding his breath.

If this works...

He listened attentively to his surroundings, hoping no one was sneaking up on him. Feeling the tension now, he glanced up and let his eyes adjust to the dark hallway. He saw nothing, not that it meant he was alone. Two guards could be silently moving in and he would never know. He felt the rifle in his left hand, gripping the stock tightly.

The screen remained pitch black. He still heard a beeping sound, and it seemed some of the other computer components were powering down. A whirring sound seemed to be slowing, perhaps an onboard fan turning off.

He listened as different components around the room began to shut off.

Well, I'll be damned, he thought. *I guess I should be called Shane "Computer Wizard" Riley.*

More and more components shut down, and he realized that almost every machine in this room was somehow related to this *Communications System* – either internally or up above on the roof of the building, meant to broadcast the wider signal. He hoped he had done it correctly, but what else was there to do? What else was there to try?

He smiled, waiting.

Then his smile faded. *The beeping's still here...*

Shane decided enough was enough. He had an elegant solution to this problem. He pulled his rifle around and began firing through every computer component he could find.

Monitors, CPUs, rack-mounted gear blinking at him as if laughing at his incompetence.

He even put a few rounds through the mice and peripherals he could see.

He stopped; all went quiet in the room.

Beep.

He cursed under his breath. *You've got to be kidding me.*

He could have sworn this sound was one of the many that would have stopped upon shutting down the computer — and *certainly* upon shooting it — but then again, he knew he was not *actually* a computer genius. Everything he was doing here was just a best guess, 'failing forward' until the job was done.

He felt the urge to investigate further, just to see what the beeping sound was.

If it was another computer, somehow tucked away and hidden from the fury of his gun, it wouldn't hurt to turn it off manually using whatever switch he could find.

He walked over to the right side of the room, where the sound was loudest. Kneeling down, he saw a similar matte black rack, long and rectangular, about waist high. He crouched, pulling open the top drawers. Most were filled with a random assortment of computer devices – hard drives, wires and cables, other items he didn't recognize. One drawer had a laptop repair kit inside.

He chose to open the larger drawers beneath. Manuals – all in Korean – filled the one on the left. As he slid the center drawer open, however, he immediately knew he had found what he was looking for.

He sucked in another breath as the beeping filled the room. He looked down, seeing the lights flashing back at him. The illuminated device had been completely concealed in the closed drawer before, so the lights had not given him a clue as to its location.

But it didn't take a computer genius or trained operative this time to know what he was looking at.

A bomb.

This was one *just* like the ones he'd seen on TV. Wires splayed out neatly from a central control hub – some sort of receiver, judging by the thick, stubby antenna protruding from both top corners of the device. They wrapped around to the bottom of it, which he could tell was a large pack of plastic explosives.

An alarm clock was mounted to the top of the entire package, flashing a countdown timer.

1:27.

One minute and 27 seconds left.

"Aw, shit."

His mind raced. Maybe I can grab it and carry it out with me, he thought. He shook his head. *No, jostling it even a little might cause it to detonate on its own. Plus, what good would that do? The base would be secure and I would be nothing but a reddish mist in the wind.*

As much as he wanted to make sure Seong Park was safe, he *really* wanted to do it without blowing himself up.

There was no way he was going to get the bomb out in time. As he stood examining the explosive device, he pulled open the last drawer. This entire drawer was packed with more explosives. He swallowed. He looked up, doing a full circle in the room. He saw four other similarly shaped racks spaced around the room. He walked briskly over to the first one and pulled open the bottom center drawer.

More explosives.

Both drawers to the left and right were, as well.

"They've rigged the entire place to blow," he said to himself. They had set this up for his team to find, evacuating only the necessary VIPs and scientists working here, leaving low-level guards. Just enough people to make his team think the place was still occupied, so they would plow forward and recklessly end up down here.

Right next to the bomb.

He smacked his hand on the top of the rack, cursing. *It was a trap. It's been a trap the entire time. They wanted us to find this place. They wanted us to –*

He stopped.

Michaela. She's coming in.

He had to choke back bile as he stood, realizing that the rest of his team was about to make a grand entrance, enacting the *second* half of the plan they had made together.

"Got to get to them first," he said. He looked back across the room, walking over halfway to see where the countdown stood.

One minute, 10 seconds. Barely enough time for me to get out.

Assuming, of course, he could even *remember* how to get out.

He started running, gripping the rifle loosely, knowing that guards were no longer the biggest threat to his life here. If he met any resistance, he would do his best to aim and fire a few quick rounds, but he wasn't about to slow down.

52

SHANE

THE PATH forward appeared more obscure than before. Shane retraced his steps through the base, negotiating narrow corridors, and doing his best to maintain momentum despite his mounting uncertainty. His growing dread was that he would make a wrong turn, succumb to self-doubt, and veer off the correct route.

While his memory was not in any way photographic, and his sense of direction was questionable, he knew better than to question his instincts. He needed to trust his subconscious to guide him on the right path.

He almost halted to ponder the profoundness of that notion that wormed its way through his mind. *Stop doubting yourself.*

He surged forward, accelerating now, growing comfortable with the unknown. He had to assume there were no guards between him and the exit. He had dealt with the few remaining ones in the base, and now understood why no more were present.

They had all been evacuated.

After meddling in the communications tower in the control room and discovering the bomb, Shane no longer found the need to search every room. Those who had once operated this place were long gone, taking every scientist, researcher, and most guards with them.

He thought once again of the eyeballs in jars, shuddering as his feet pounded up a stairwell. Was this the right set of stairs? Was he still moving the right direction? He remembered coming into this place and doing a few switchbacks, turning completely around as he descended into the depth of the bunker.

Were the eyeballs watching him now as he ran past? Laughing at him as he tried in vain to outrace the literal ticking time bomb?

He swallowed, pushed the thoughts away. There were plenty of mysteries here they would have to leave unsolved. This place was going to crumble to ruin, concrete ceilings becoming dust covered debris on the floor, each layer collapsing down on the next until there was nothing left but a flat pile of rocks in a whole.

Seong Park was gone. Their reason for being here had vanished. At every juncture so far their mission had been undermined, their enemy always one step ahead. Where they believed they had snuck in undetected, it seemed they had been watched the entire time.

They had known Shane was coming.

Or, perhaps, it was an unfortunate coincidence that the research had concluded, and they had simply abandoned the place just before Shane and his group arrived.

At the top of the stairs, he hesitated, looking left and right. He thought he recognized the hallway. *Isn't this the same one I came down before?*

He shook his head quickly, refusing to admit he might be lost. *This is the right path*, he thought. *I just need to keep moving forward, complete the task.*

Memories of his late wife flooded his mind, reminding him of her work, her dedication. Was he projecting his own insecurities onto her? Sure, she had been a workaholic, but so had he. The difference was that she had been compelled to complete each project to the best of her ability every time.

In contrast, Shane was the kind of guy to do just enough to advance to the next step or level. Not that he didn't care – rather, he prioritized the long-term goal, the end game. He was willing to cut corners on things that seemed less important. She had never been that way.

He took a left turn, quickening his pace. His internal clock told him there was barely any time left. Just enough to escape the base, find Michaela and Evans, and tell them to stay back.

Rounding a corner, he found another set of stairs leading up. Korean signs were everywhere, but not a single word in English. As unsettling as the eyeballs in the jars had been, it was equally unsettling to Shane not to be able to decipher where the hell he was headed.

There were no reference points anymore, no recognizable doorways or landmarks. He slowed as he passed one door, peering inside to see if any horrifying experiments were on display.

Instead, he saw an office space, with a desk in the middle and two chairs in front of it. He didn't remember seeing it before.

Damn.

There was no time to backtrack or change course. He convinced himself that this was just a room he had bypassed earlier and hadn't bothered to inspect. He vaguely recalled the door being ajar, and from the opposite direction, he wouldn't have been able to see inside easily without pushing it open further.

Yes, that's got to be it. I've been here before. He took a breath. *I just needed to keep moving.*

He arrived at the final set of stairs and the last long corridor. Thankfully, there was only one direction to go now. He saw a door ahead and sensed that this was the one that led outside. It wasn't the main entrance he had used, so he assumed it was one of the doors at the end of the long H-shaped hallway on the north side of the base. Once outside, he could double back and alert his companions before they entered. He pictured the expansive field in front of the main entrance, the helipad, and the swaying grass at the base of the picturesque mountain.

He pushed forward, his legs beginning to protest.

Just a bit longer, old man. He urged himself to go faster, now sprinting full tilt towards the exit.

He desperately hoped the door could be unlocked from the inside. It had a bar across it, the kind that pressed inward and released the latch.

He was going to hit it at full speed, using his left shoulder. He crouched down, just a second before impact.

The door flew open, blinding him with the brilliant daylight outside. He blinked rapidly, trying to force his eyes to adjust.

Shane continued to run, distancing himself from the building while shouting Michaela's name.

There was no response, and he halted, finally turning around to get his bearings. He immediately recognized his surroundings, noting the mountain in the distance, gradually sloping down to meet the same ground on which he was now standing.

Except the secret Korean base he had just exited was standing between him and the mountain. That meant the mountain was on the wrong side of him.

He groaned as he completed a slow turn in a full circle.

No, he thought. *No, no, no...*

He saw the valley, the road winding down around the quarry he was now in. In the distance, he noticed the fallen guards who had attacked his team earlier.

It was all wrong. Everything was turned around.

He knew instantly what had happened. He *had* made a wrong turn somewhere. One of the confounding, maze-like corridors had led him astray. He had been so certain he was on the right path, refusing to entertain any other thoughts. He had been so sure he was going the right way, but...

He called her name again, hoping she was close, that they hadn't changed the plan and would be approaching from the south instead.

He checked his watch, pretending there was more time remaining. But his internal clock knew the answer.

Time had run out. There was certainly not enough time to navigate back through the facility – especially considering his disorientation – before the place would erupt and the corridors would fill with fire.

He braced himself for the explosion, wincing as the final seconds counted down.

Then he finally let his suppressed thoughts surface. The self-doubt he had pushed aside returned with a vengeance.

Go back in, you fool.

He tried to dismiss the thoughts. Two seconds remaining. He saw the door he had opened still standing wide, having hit it so hard that it caught on the wall and remained open.

He exhaled, cursing himself.

Then he darted back into the facility, just as time ran out.

53
EVANS

JONATHAN EVANS' team moved cautiously through the building. The upper floors seemed like office spaces, most of the rooms that were open were filled with filing cabinets, tables, and desks. They found a conference room, a break room, and what seemed to be a small cafeteria.

However, it was hard to tell due to the disheveled state everything had been left in, as well as the fact that North Korea did not seem to put as much interest in employee comfort as companies in America did. It was stark how barren the place was. There were no decorations whatsoever, save for portraits of the supreme leader hanging on every wall. There were no personal items in sight – if they existed, they had been hidden within desk drawers or elsewhere in the facility.

Evans shook his head as they passed yet another similar room. Working here would be like working in a racquetball court, albeit with less fun and exercise.

Dr. Michaela Everly had calmed down a bit, but he could tell the woman was on edge. They had been shot at, nearly killed, and the only thing attaching her to the real world outside was Shane Riley, whose status was currently unknown.

He had considered sending Grudowski ahead to check for the man, to see if there were any other guards and pave the way for him and Dr. Everly, but his team was small enough as it was. He did not want to risk sending any more men to their graves.

So they stuck together, a group of three, working through the facility, down long corridors, taking stock of what they could find.

What they found was of little help to them. Even though Dr. Everly understood and read Korean, any documents they found were either vague enough to be useless or nearly completely redacted, also proving useless.

The redacted files, at least, clued him into the nature of this facility: whatever it was, the government had deemed it important enough to keep it top-secret.

He knew they had deemed it important enough to guard it at all times. Why, then, had they also abruptly left, save for a small contingent of guards who had remained behind, guarding the exterior of the facility?

Everything in his professional training and experience told him that *he* was the reason.

He could only assume that the North Koreans had abandoned this facility upon discovering that he and his team were here. An unknown assailant had tried kidnapping Shane Riley and Michaela Everly back in the village, and they knew he was still at large, having escaped somewhere to the west. Evans assumed he was still out there somewhere, either waiting to attack or trying to communicate with his superior officers.

If that were the case, those in charge of this place would have known he was coming, and evacuated the facility prior to that. But it seemed improbable that an entire base like this, even staffed by a skeleton crew, could be evacuated so quickly, with so little forewarning. It made Evans question whether or not it had actually been evacuated because of him, or due to some unforeseen circumstance that had taken place.

There was no helicopter on the pad out front, so it was possible the last remaining people here – guards, researchers, scientists, or leaders and managers who had been staffing the facility – had left. But how many men could that have been? A dozen, max? The size of the helipad told him it was unlikely to have been more.

No, if he had to guess, he would guess that this place had been abandoned some number of hours or days prior to their arrival here. That would mean there was another reason they had left altogether. Another reason there was no longer anyone in the space.

As their walk-through of the mostly empty facility continued, Evans' suspicions seemed proven. Besides the guards they had seen upfront – men who had likely taken cover inside when Shane Riley had come knocking – they encountered no more hostile forces. It seemed everyone inside this place had been told to leave quite a while ago. The state of papers on desks was mildly disheveled – folders and documents were no longer neatly stacked, but placed on desks as if thrown there in a hurry. Still, the evacuation had not been executed in a panic – he didn't see papers strewn on floors, chairs overturned, there were no signs that fear had warranted a hasty escape.

Evans frowned, mulling over these thoughts as they descended down stairs that took them deeper into the base.

Where the hell is Shane Riley?

He questioned if the man had successfully disabled the communications array. That could explain why the fighting had stopped. However, it *didn't* explain why they were no longer being attacked.

These were all questions without answers, at least for the moment. Evans knew what they needed to do – they needed to keep moving, to keep exploring, descending.

He sensed the answers were here. Whatever had happened, they would stumble upon it, or they would find it by slowly peeling away the layers until the core truth was revealed.

Shane Riley was in here somewhere as well. Perhaps he had found something, and was currently investigating? Whatever it was, Evans wanted to know. He could sense it – they were close to the truth.

Michaela Everly now walked side-by-side with him, her head held high, as if feeling the same way.

They were going to get to the bottom of this, figuratively and literally, as they took each set of stairs downward.

54
EVANS

THEY REACHED A LOWER floor beneath the facility and continued their exploration. Somewhere on the floor above, Evans had decided to quicken their pace. Riley was missing, and they weren't finding answers.

Instead of dwelling on potential outcomes and inspecting every room they came across, Evans had made the decision to hasten their progress through the facility. They could always come back later and explore further; they had confirmed their suspicion that they were alone here.

They came across no guards. That provided them ample time to investigate later – right now, Evans wanted to reunite with Shane Riley and decipher what was happening here.

He still harbored a twinge of distrust for Riley; though he knew the man wouldn't betray them, he wasn't entirely sure about his intentions. Whether or not he would follow Evans' orders to inspect the facility or simply go his own way was yet to be seen. Sure, it had been Riley's idea to come here alone, but Evans almost felt like the man would oppose their plans just because he had consented to them.

He smiled to himself as they traversed the lowest level of the facility. He understood men like Shane Riley. They were always impulsive, quick to act, and slow to consider the consequences.

The kind of man who would rush into battle without discussing strategy or tactics.

The kind of man who often found himself in mortal peril.

There was certainly a need for men like Shane Riley, but not in leadership. Men like Shane got the job done, but they often ended a successful mission more battered than when they started.

"Churn and burn" seemed to be their motto. Men like Riley operated like ants – all on a mission for the greater good, yet unable to comprehend that they were individuals, not part of a hive mind. If one of them fell, another would promptly take their place.

At the surface, these men were perfect warriors – they didn't mind getting injured or killed in battle; they just wanted to fight, to win.

But to men like Evans, who had trained, fought, and bled alongside them – they were more than mere soldiers. They were people with dreams, interests, and beliefs. Each had hobbies and interests beyond the battlefield. Thus, he had always taken it personally when the higher-ups didn't understand why Evans pushed back. He didn't want to work with men like Shane Riley, not because they were bad soldiers, but because they were reckless ones. They didn't care about their own lives, so why should they care about their teammates'?

If all they cared about was defeating the enemy, well, they often accomplished that, but not without putting their own team at risk.

Evans preferred a more deliberate, tactical approach. He favored planning and thinking things through. There was always a time for action, but for every minute of action, he wanted to have spent five minutes training, planning, preparing.

So no, he couldn't trust Riley here, and hadn't since he met the man. Riley was a valuable asset, but best kept distant from his own men.

Far away from himself and Dr. Michaela Everly.

If Shane Riley wanted to endanger himself, there was nothing Evans could do but hope that he would at least neutralize some of the enemy in the process.

They still didn't know the purpose of this place or what research had been conducted here. It was clear, however, that it was partly a science lab. Some rooms on this level were open enough for them to peer inside. They found plenty of laboratory equipment, the kind reminiscent of his high school science class. He didn't recognize all the gear, and Everly didn't seem in the mood to explain.

He sensed she was still on high alert, bracing for a potential crisis. He hoped there wasn't a disaster waiting for them at the end of this hallway, but he tried to be prepared nonetheless.

Grudowski shouted to him as they advanced down the long corridor. He picked up the pace, now jogging towards a wide, open doorway at the end of the hall that led into a larger space. Even from the hallway, he could tell the room inside was wrecked.

Grudowski entered before him, and he heard a whistle from the man as they turned to survey the space.

Everything in sight was demolished; nothing had been spared from the devastation. Computers and devices — everything in sight — had been pierced by rounds fired from a high-powered rifle.

Was this Riley's handiwork? Had he gotten *so* frustrated that he couldn't figure out the communications system shutdown protocol that he'd simply destroyed all of it?

Evans chuckled again. It wasn't an *elegant* solution, but it was certainly an *effective* one. He didn't see a single computer or component that appeared operational. To his left, a bank of rack-mounted CPUs was still sparking, their connection to the facility's electrical system intact, but unable to establish a proper connection due to their damaged state.

They were all busy examining different aspects of the destruction when he heard footsteps and shouting. He frowned, looking up.

"Is that —"

He walked back to the door, joining Grudowski as they looked out along the corridor they had just navigated.

Running towards them, panting and breathless between shouts, was Shane Riley.

He was waving his hands, gesturing wildly.

"Get – get out!" He shouted.

THE MAN RUNNING towards Michaela Everly appeared deranged, with wild, insane eyes. She recognized Shane Riley, but he was breathless, exhausted.

It seemed as though he had run a marathon, and then another just for fun.

His arms flailed wildly, barely higher than his shoulders, and she knew instantly he was propelled by adrenaline alone, having long since exhausted his energy reserves.

"Get – get out!" he shouted. "You need to... you need to leave."

He stopped then, ten feet from the door to the destroyed computer room they were all standing inside, placing his hands on his knees to catch his breath.

He looked exasperated, but his head was down now, sweat falling to the floor.

"Shane, nice of you to –"

"Get... out."

The words were scratchy, barely above a whisper, but their sharpness cut Evans off. Michaela watched the exchange between the two men, once again noticing the growing tension. Only this time, it didn't seem as though Riley was angry with Evans. This wasn't a competition, it wasn't the same petty clash she had observed them engage in before.

Shane was scared of something.

Shane's head lifted, eyes locking onto hers. "There's a bomb... in that room."

Michaela's blood ran cold. Suddenly, she understood. He must have tried to stop them, must have ran upwards through the facility after discovering the bomb down here, trying to find her and Evans' team. To stop them, to save them.

Either he had taken a wrong turn or simply run out of time, ending up outside after she and the others had entered.

He had turned around then, no doubt already tired at that point, and run all the way back down to this location.

Evans and Grudowski were in motion, scouring the room for the afore-mentioned explosive device. She was impressed by the men's ability to act under pressure, to start searching for the bomb rather than running away from it.

She didn't feel compelled to get blown up, however. She moved swiftly, heading towards Shane in the hallway. She was certainly keen to put distance between herself and the bomb, but she also wanted to check on Shane.

"Are you okay?" she asked.

He ignored her. "It's going to blow.... only... seconds left."

He was still breathing heavily, panting raggedly as she reached him. She saw his back soaked with sweat, his hair falling over his forehead, plastered to his face with moisture.

"How do you know? Was it you who destroyed that room?"

He nodded. "We don't have time, we need to –"

"Found it!" Evans' man shouted.

Evans joined him and Michaela turned to watch as the two men hovered over something in the far corner of the room. Shane was silent next to her.

"There's a clock – a countdown timer," he continued. "But... it's off. At zero and just blinking."

"It means it's going to blow!" Shane snarled. "Any second now. That's why I –"

"No, it means you *did* it."

Michaela took a few steps back toward the room to better hear Evans' explanation.

"Shane, you destroyed this place, right? Probably couldn't figure out how to turn off the communications array up above, so you just started killing any blinking lights. Not a bad move, and it seems to have worked."

"What are you talking about?" Shane asked. He was standing now, still breathing heavily but not nearly in as bad shape as he had been a minute ago. He joined Michaela again, and together they approached the room.

Michaela felt uneasy walking towards an explosive that hadn't been deto-nated yet, but felt somewhat comforted standing next to Shane.

Not that he could protect her from it...

"This thing looks like it's hooked up to one of the computers down here," Evans said, pulling at the cable that ran from the back of the metallic box and into one of the racks of destroyed computer processors. "Usually, a terrorist would wire it up remotely, but the countdown timer would ensure the thing would go off. The goal is to make it tamper-proof – anyone messing with it gets blown up."

"That's not what this is?" Michaela asked.

Evans shook his head. "No, not at all. This device is much more sophisticated. It's essentially a microcomputer sitting on top of the trigger. It sends and receives communications signals – one hardwired into the array here that gets sent up to the tower above. That means it can be called in remotely. Likely from a cell phone."

"And you think Shane actually turned off the communications tower, rendering this thing useless?" Grudowski asked.

"I do. I've seen this before, this is no ordinary device. This wasn't meant to blow up at all costs, it was meant to detonate only if and when a specific cell signal reached it. Whoever set it up here wanted to level the place, but only on their signal."

"They wanted to kill us all, but only after they made sure we were inside."

"Yes, and only after making sure they extracted whatever they had inside here."

Next to her, Shane stirred. He shook his head, then let his head fall backwards, staring up at the ceiling. He took in a few long, deep breaths as the others watched him.

To say this man had been through hell and back was an understatement, but he was still breathing, still fighting.

"You saved our asses, Riley," Evans said. "Whoever set this thing up couldn't get a remote signal all the way down here. You took out the communications tower, which prevented them from sending it in. I'm not saying I want to hang out next to it for the next day or so, but for now, I think we're safe."

Shane didn't respond. Michaela walked over and saw what Evans and Grudowski were standing next to. Grudowski was in the corner of the room, watching but maintaining a respectful distance between himself and the bomb.

Everyone turned to look at Shane, and Michaela wondered what the man's response would be. Was he grateful? Relieved? Still terrified?

Finally, he smiled, still looking up at the ceiling as he breathed. His head fell back, locking eyes with Evans and then Michaela, as he spoke.

"Are you telling me I just *ran my ass off* running through this whole damn place... for no reason?"

56
SHANE

SHANE'S HEART rate had finally returned to normal. He was still shocked by the revelations down here, but for the moment they were alive, and his body functions seemed to appreciate that. He stood with his back against the wall of the long corridor, focusing on his breathing, while Evans and his man examined the communications room.

Michaela walked over and joined him. "A lot of excitement for one day," she said.

"Are you okay?"

She nodded, then looked away, back at the dark corridor.

"Nice try," Shane said. He smirked. "Kate used to do that. Did she learn that from you?"

"What?"

"That look. Trying to convince yourself you believe the words that just came out of your mouth."

She laughed. "Are you saying I'm lying to you?"

"You guys could have been sisters, you know," he said.

The words seemed to cut him as soon as they fell out of his mouth. He opened his mouth again to retract the statement, but Michaela was smiling up at him. "You know, she used to say that, too. We were so close. As competitive as we both were, I think there was so much more mutual respect than anything else. And eventually, love. I really did think of her like a sister."

This time, she flashed a look he had not seen before on his late wife's face. Confusion, mixed with regret. Sorrow, perhaps. In an instant, it was gone.

"Shane, we never got to... well, you know. We never got to discuss things after..."

"What's to discuss?" Shane answered. "She's gone, and nothing you or I can say can bring her back."

There was that look again. "No, but it's not about bringing her back. It's about making sure you're okay."

He suddenly felt anger. Who was this woman to suddenly barge into his life and pick at open threads?

"I'm fine," he snapped.

She paused. "Okay... well, *I'm* not. For me, then. We need to discuss things for me."

Shane wanted to roll his eyes, to try to make a joke or even just pretend he heard Evans calling his name. Instead, he stared down at Michaela Everly, the beautiful woman Kate had spent much of her career with. Early on, it seemed as though he could choose between the two women. He had been drawn to both; Kate for her exuberant, outgoing way, and Michaela for exactly the opposite reasons. The fact that the brilliant young woman had seemed to want nothing to do with Shane only made her more intriguing in his eyes.

As things had developed with Kate, his loyalty had gotten the best of him. He had completely forgotten about those initial sparks, consumed by the nurture and love Kate showed him. They became inseparable, and with Michaela traveling so often, rarely around Shane, his marriage to Kate had become inevitable.

And he wouldn't have changed it for the world. But now, watching this woman's face as it shifted in the deep shadows of the subterranean corridor, he couldn't help but ask himself those painful questions.

What could have been? Could something like this have worked between us?

And, inasmuch as he tried to push the thought away, the ultimate question: *if Michaela and I ended up together, would Kate still be alive now?*

He clenched his jaw, the telltale sign that Kate used to pick up on immediately. She would call him out on it, knowing he was stressed or deep in thought, wondering what was wrong and how she could help.

Apparently, Michaela knew his tell just as well. "What's going on in that mind of yours, Mr. Riley?"

She asked softly. He heard a commotion from the room; saw Evans' man begin walking in their direction. She ignored him.

"Nothing," he said quickly.

It was Michaela's turn to smirk. "Nothing," she mocked, deepening her voice and pretending as though she were a Neanderthal. "Typical testosterone speaking. Can't bear the thought of discussing your own emotional state, so you revert to pretending it doesn't exist."

Shane's eyebrows raised. "Wow, I didn't take you for a shrink. I thought your scientific expertise was relegated to much simpler matters, like genetic engineering and biology."

She laughed at this. "*Simple*, huh? Tell me then, why am I here? If you boys are so smart, and all of this science is so simple, why not just figure it all out for yourselves?"

Shane shook his head, sensing a subject change. "That's just it – I wanted you to find something here. I wanted you to be able to help. Instead, I just put you in more danger. Almost got you killed."

"I haven't found anything here, because we haven't looked. We rushed in, just as you did, hoping to find you and this communications room. Now –" she looked over at Evans and his men approaching them – "it seems like we've got time to investigate a little more closely. Some of these rooms have to be filled with research, documentation, or –"

"Or science experiments," Shane interjected.

The others had joined them once again, and Shane noticed Evans eyeing him curiously. He continued. "Yeah, as I was exploring around, trying to find this room, I happened across something... Weird."

"Weird in what way?" Evans asked.

Where to start, Shane thought. *How about: why was there a man strapped to a table upstairs?* "Those villagers – the ones Michaela and I ran through. They were all missing their eyes, right?"

Everyone nodded.

"Well... I think I found their eyes.

THE GROUP FOLLOWED Shane toward the stairs, stopping where Shane had found the room full of jars with human eyes inside. His skin crawled as he thought of it, not wanting to return there.

But for the necessity of continuing the mission – of finding out what was going on here – they needed to.

Plus, Shane's senses had returned, and apparently, he had no trouble navigating this facility again.

He almost laughed out loud as the reality hit. Only when he needed it most, when he thought a literal ticking time bomb was going to detonate if he didn't move quickly enough, was his subconscious unwilling to help. Now, it was as if his subconscious had produced and laid bare a perfectly accurate map of the entire space through the base he had traveled. He saw the H-shaped layout, saw the left side of it in his mind as they traversed upstairs and around corridors. He marched through the hallways confidently, knowing exactly where he was headed.

Outside the room, he stopped. Evans was right behind him, anxiously pressing into him, urging him forward.

"Actually," Shane said, turning to face them. "I'm going to wait out here. I think I've seen enough of this… whatever it is. But by all means, knock yourself out. There's no one in there. Not really, anyway."

He wasn't sure if single eyeballs floating in liquid counted as 'people' or not, but the disgusting thought of it once again forced his feet still. Unless there was a strong need, he was going to wait here.

Michaela had no such quandary. She burst forward, darting around Evans and Shane and pushing the door open. "Oh, my God," she said excitedly as she entered the room and began looking around. Her voice was one of awe, of wonder.

Like a kid in a candy store, Shane thought. And then, *gross*.

Shane waited while the others filed in and examined the space using flashlights. The room was lit, but each of them likely wanted to get a more visible view of exactly what was in the jars and figure out why.

Shane listened in as Evans and Michaela spoke from inside the room.

"Eyeballs," Michaela said. "Seems... weird."

"Shane's right," Evans said. "These must be the eyes of the villagers you two saw back there."

There was a pause, and Shane assumed Michaela was nodding or still examining one of the jars on the shelves. "Has to be," she said finally. "Still, it's strange that they would collect them. I mean, *why* remove them in the first place? It has to be related to the research they were doing here, but it will take weeks to dig through everything to figure it out."

"Not necessarily," Evans replied. "We just need to find wherever they were doing the actual research. It seems like the guys running this place left pretty quickly – they set their bomb and jetted. So I doubt they had enough time to completely purge this place, to wipe it clean of any information that might be helpful. They planned on the bomb doing that for them."

"True," Grudowski said. "I wonder if there's a laboratory room on this floor. Definitely somewhere in the building, I would guess. It will all be in Korean, but I understand enough — and she's fluent — so we can certainly read any medical reports or scientific papers we come across."

"Sounds like that's our next target, then," Evans said to Grudowski. Then, turning to Michaela, his voice softened. "What do you need, Dr. Everly?"

Shane bristled, then relaxed. He surprised himself by how much he cared for Michaela's next words. He could easily just walk into the room and be part of the conversation, and he found himself actually tensing when his subconscious got the sense that Evans might be making a move to protect her.

But he should be protecting her, Shane told himself. *That's his job. He's here to protect all of us.*

And yet, Shane couldn't shake the thought that Evans, during the time he and Michaela had been together without Shane around, was trying to do a bit more than just protecting her.

At the same time, Shane had to admit that he was woefully incompetent when it came to delicate social cues and romantic relationship building. For all he knew Evans could be gay and Shane would have no idea.

Still...

Shane stepped forward, turning and poking his head into the room. He saw Evans, facing the doorway, gripping his assault rifle. The man certainly was not off guard. He was prepared for anything. Apparently, he was prepared for Shane as well.

"Riley, glad you could join us," he said, smiling with a wink. "Michaela and I were just discussing what we might be able to do to figure out what was going on in this place."

"Seems like they were harvesting eyeballs," Shane said dryly.

Michaela snorted. "Yeah, I think we've got that much already. We were just trying to figure out where to go next. Did you happen to see any laboratories when you were poking around before? Anything that might clue us in as to what sort of research they were doing with these eyeballs – for the humans they took them from?"

Shane squinted. "Actually, yeah. There was a guy, strapped to a bed. Obviously some sort of prisoner or subject or something. Not your average medical patient, all comfy with pillows and stuff. He was just strapped to a table like they were about to dissect a frog."

"*Vivisect* is the word you're looking for," Grudowski said.

"Yeah, he was definitely alive... at one point." Shane shuddered again. "Anyway, he's here. I can show you where."

He turned and waited again in the hallway, hearing the footsteps from Evans and Michaela as they checked to see if there were any more soldiers around.

Once again, they began walking, following behind Shane, who took the lead. He still had his weapon as well, and made sure he was prepared for any potential threats as he led them to the door where he had found the unfortunate man strapped to the table.

There was a sense of dread slowly gnawing away at him, but he pushed forward anyway. This was not the time for second guessing. He wanted to finish the mission, to get himself and Michaela out of here safely. Then... he didn't know.

He felt confused, not just by the situation unfolding in front of him, the insanity of this place. He felt conflicted, his loyalty to Kate cracking for the first time. Just the smallest of fractures, but he knew where that led.

At the same time, he wasn't exactly feeling anything specific for Michaela. At least, he didn't think so. Why, then, had he tried so hard to ensure Evans wasn't encroaching on his territory. And why was he treating all of this like she *was* 'his territory?'

She was nothing to him but an old friend, a long-lost acquaintance. The tie connecting them had died a year ago, and was waiting for him at the bottom of the ocean. Why was he so tempted to ignore everything happening and grab Michaela's hand and run away? It was all he wanted to do, to go back to South Korea, to safety, with Michaela Everly in tow, and just... what?

He shook his head, trying to physically push away these thoughts. The last thing he needed was to be considering something like that while faced with a task so dangerously complex. He felt confident there were no guards still in the facility, but then again there was no way to be sure. He needed to be present, to be focused. He needed to resort to his training now. There was no thinking of home, no thinking of friends or acquaintances – or lovers – anymore.

He needed to keep his eyes on the target – on getting out of here safely, with Seong Park, and then back into a country that wouldn't simply kill him on sight.

58

SHANE

"IT DOESN'T MAKE SENSE," Michaela said. She was standing in front of the door Shane had found earlier, behind which waited the man strapped to the table.

So far, no one had gone inside. Shane wondered if they were all as conflicted as he had been — they couldn't afford to stop here, to search the place and see if there *were* any poor souls still alive inside. He doubted it, and even if they found people — it would surely slow them down.

Michaela continued. "I mean, I know this whole place doesn't make sense, but I mean specifically why they're keeping eyeballs in jars. We can assume they took them from those villagers we ran into, right?"

Shane and the others nodded.

"Still, why did they only take their *left* eye? That doesn't seem like torture to me — I mean, it certainly is gruesome, but it implies some sort of scientific reasoning. Why specifically the left eye?"

"Does going through the eye allow easy access to the brain?" Shane asked. "I mean, maybe they were trying to poke around inside their heads, and taking out the left eye was somehow the least invasive way of doing it."

Grudowski chuckled. "I'd hate to hear the reasoning behind that one," he said, making a joke of Shane's speculation.

"Maybe," Dr. Everly said, ignoring Grudowski. "We know ancient Egyptians used to go up through the nasal cavity in order to access the brain of subjects. This could be a similar — even more macabre — way of doing the same thing. But why the *left* eye? If it's the left eye every time, and we have plenty of data to suggest it is, it means they're targeting something specifically in the left hemisphere of the brain, perhaps directly in front of the hypothalamus or cerebellum."

She let her eyes fall, shaking her head in frustration.

Shane could see she was deep in thought, trying in vain to make sense of it all. He stepped forward, put a hand on her shoulder. "We've still got work to do," he said. "There might still be information here — files, computers, stuff we might be able to pick apart. You're the only one who can speak Korean well enough, and you're the only doctor."

"I never studied the human brain," she said. "Not like this."

"It's not about the brain," Shane replied. "It's about what they were doing to it. Maybe they injected something into the patients' eyes in order to study them. That caused swelling, and they had to extract the eyes and put them in jars."

"But why?" She asked, exasperated. "That doesn't make any sense."

"Let's find another room," Evans said. "Riley's right — we need to keep moving. We can't assume there are no more guards here, or that they won't send more soon. If Seong Park is somewhere in here, we need to get to her."

No one argued, but Michaela continued talking as they walked down the corridor. "I mean, it *would* be a good way to inject something directly into the brain," she hypothesized. "Removing an eye provides near direct access to the bottom of the brain, possibly even the brainstem, depending on how far back you go. I just don't understand what they were trying to do by going in that way. It seems like a rather permanent solution to a temporary problem."

"Unless it *wasn't* temporary," Evans said.

"What do you mean?" Michaela asked suddenly.

Evans shrugged. "I was just making a joke, really." Everyone stared at him, stopping once again as they waited for him to explain. He laughed. "Any of you ever worked on a car? My old man was a mechanic. Used to make that joke all the time; he used to say certain things were a 'permanent solution to a temporary problem,' like when a car owner would try their hand at fixing something by permanently mounting a piece of scrap metal somewhere.

"But he said it about other things in life, too."

Everyone continued staring, and Shane wondered where he was going with this.

"Think about it," Evans continued. "Say you've got a starter that needs to be repaired or replaced, and the starter is attached to the bottom of the engine, just off the engine block. Logic says you should go in from the bottom, putting the car on a lift so you've got room to access it. But so many amateurs won't bother with getting a lift or doing the job the right way — they'll just assume they can access it from the top.

"Of course, you *can* do that, but you end up having to take off all these other components, literally have to break down the engine from the wrong side just to access a single component. And then they end up breaking something in trying to get it off. So he used to say that was a 'permanent solution to a temporary problem,' because even the best mechanics had a hard time trying to put the engine back together the right way."

Shane squinted over at Evans in the dim light. "That's a terrible analogy," he said.

Evans laughed even harder. "Hey, I didn't say I was being serious. My old man was a bit of a kook anyway."

"But he's got a point," Michaela said, once again redirecting their attention. "I mean, say you wanted to do something to the human brain – you could put them under, full anesthesia, then drill open the skull and peel back the skin in order to access it."

"Gross," Grudowski muttered.

"Gross, *and* inefficient. If you're just trying to access a targeted region of the brain – and more specifically, you don't want to mess with anything else — it's extremely dangerous to go in from the top like that. You'd have to pull back individual layers of the brain. Not only do we not have a full understanding of the working relationships between different components of the brain, we know for a fact that cutting out even a small slice of brain tissue can have devastating effects down the road."

"More devastating than losing an eye?" Shane asked.

She nodded. "Absolutely. Depending on where the incision is made – and how deep it is – it could render the subject comatose, catatonic, or introduce a whole slew of issues that would take years to diagnose. If you didn't just kill them immediately."

"Okay," Evans said, "so we know these guys took out the eye because they were trying to gain access to some region of the brain found behind the left eye." Once again they all began to walk down the hallway.

Evans was targeting a door near the end of the corridor, one standing open a crack, when Shane spoke from behind him. "We *assume* that. It's a good assumption, but we can't rule out any other options. For all we know, these guys just have a thing for left eyeballs."

When Shane entered the room, Michaela was already inside. She was flipping through the pages of a binder amongst a stack of them on a desk in the corner.

Suddenly she gasped.

Shane whirled around and looked at her.

"No, Shane," she said. "It's not about the *eyes* at all. We were right – it's the brain they were after."

"How do you know?" Evans asked.

The group corralled around her in the corner as she held up the binder and showed them all an image. Shane didn't understand what he was looking at, but the look on Michaela's face told him it was bad news.

"They weren't just messing around with the brains of the patients," she explained. "They were *experimenting*. Specifically, injecting them with this."

"What is it?" Evans asked.

She pointed to the image, where Shane saw a few swirls and dots. It was all Greek to him.

"It's a disease."

Grudowski cursed, and Evans let out a breath.

"How bad?" Shane asked.

"It's a prion," she finally said, a note of dread in her voice.

"PRION?" Shane asked.

He stared at the model Michaela was showing in the binder. She flipped back and forth a few pages, displaying that each page had a similar model – the structure of a molecule, blurry in some places and clear in others. Each page showed a different set of circles within the molecule in full focus. Clearly, this was microscopic imagery, and the binder was full of printouts, likely explaining some component of this prion or another.

She nodded. "Yes, a prion. I would recognize this model anywhere. It's the same sort of thing that causes deadly infections, namely Creutzfeldt-Jakob disease."

"What's that?" Evans asked.

"Creutzfeldt-Jakob disease is a rare, degenerative, fatal brain disorder that affects about one in every one million people worldwide. It often leads to severe mental deterioration, involuntary movements, blindness, weakness of extremities, and coma. Classic CJD is sometimes confused with a variant, which is very similar to mad cow disease and some other prion-based diseases."

"Did they inject this thing – a prion – into these people's brains?" Riley asked.

He was pacing the floor now, examining the rest of the room. Like all the other rooms in this corridor, the walls were plain, made of concrete and unpainted. Unlike the others, however, this one seemed to be a library. Stacks of filing cabinets sat along one wall, facing a wall covered with shelves. Each of the shelves held binders like the one Michaela was holding, each labeled with Korean script, handwritten in permanent marker.

He wouldn't know where to start in a room like this – everything was in Korean. But Michaela Everly was versed in the language, and it seemed she had already made a breakthrough.

She frowned down at the binder, now holding it open for herself. "This binder is mostly just images of the actual prion. Whether it's something they were trying to find a cure for – literally a vector that could fight it – or this was the thing they injected into the brains, I don't know."

"Best guess?"

She let her head sway side to side as she considered. "Best guess, yes, this was something they injected into these people. Into the villagers nearby. Based on what we know of prion diseases, they are best transmitted through food, but even then it's a crapshoot. If you *really* wanted to infect the brain, to make sure it sticks, the best way to do it would be to insert prions directly into the brain."

"So these individuals were literally infecting the villagers with a prion?" Shane asked.

"Not a virus. Not a bacteria, either. There's no nucleic acid at all, actually. We used to think they were a virus, until we discovered that. But they're something different entirely, which makes them nasty little things. We don't really fully understand them, except that they are misfolded proteins. Literally mutations, not meant to be naturally present in the human body. As such, they're usually not considered infectious."

"So what kind of damage could they do?"

"They could kill you," she said. "Easily, too. Something like this, with no known cure, especially altered to be infectious and contagious, could easily spread and run rampant through an entire population. The fact that it *hasn't* already is telling."

"Telling in what way?" Evans asked. "Keep going — I think you may be onto something here."

"Well, we know how dangerous these things can be once they're inside a host, even in a well-controlled laboratory environment. But altered to become infectious? And let me just say – this place? Not even close to a proper laboratory environment. Dirty floors, no airlocks or biosafety suits in sight, and jars filled with eyeballs lining shelves? This place would make a safety inspector go crazy."

"This place isn't anywhere near a safety inspector's jurisdiction," Shane added.

"Exactly," Michaela said. "Which is why it's a miracle this thing hasn't gotten out and taken down half the North Korean countryside. If it leaked into a city..."

"Then why hasn't it?" Evans asked. "Have they not made it infectious yet?" His man stood nearby, examining the binders on the shelves as if browsing through stacks of a library. He seemed to ponder each one, and Shane wondered if the man did in fact read a little bit of Korean.

"That's just it," Michaela answered. "I *don't* understand it — what they were trying to do here. These guys clearly weren't thorough in their safety procedures. If this place was intended to be impossible to access by outsiders, there would be very obvious biosafety precautions signs all over the place, and we wouldn't be able to just march into a room full of research in the form of biological waste."

"Then maybe they aren't trying to inject the prion into these people," Shane said. "Maybe they're studying it, trying to find a cure. Maybe some of those villagers out there have something like this – Creutzfeldt-Jakob's disease, or whatever you called it – and this facility was designed to find a way to cure it."

"North Korea is not exactly known for its humanitarian efforts," Evans snapped. "Especially among the population of dirt farmers like those villagers."

Shane watched Michaela's face, examined her as she browsed through the binders. He ignored Grudowski, leaning against the wall and doing the same now, leafing through another binder. If anyone could figure out what was going on here, it was Michaela Everly. She was their only hope at figuring this place out. They could still find Seong Park, but without information about what was happening here, Shane would consider the mission only halfway fulfilled.

As he studied her face, Shane once again felt the pangs of regret. He wondered what could have been, what it might have been like between him and this brilliant woman.

It wasn't even a physical attraction – though he couldn't deny that was probably playing a role in his assessment as well. But she simply reminded him of better times, of simpler times.

She reminded him of Kate.

Was that allowed? Was it bad that his deceased wife's best friend reminded him of being married?

And was it bad that he longed for those feelings once again?

For longer than he could remember, Shane had been self-isolating. A recluse by design, he had spent the last year at least, after his wife died, detaching from the world he had known. He had reinvented himself, told himself he didn't need the things Kate used to provide. Told himself he didn't need to be attached to anyone.

Attachment only led to devastation. To despair.

No one liked those feelings, and Shane was no different. Michaela's face changed then, and she frowned. She bit her bottom lip as she flipped one more page, reading silently.

The text was all Korean, no images. Her frown deepened, then she looked up at the others. "I know what it is," she said.

Evans' man stopped browsing, turned, and faced them. He placed his hand in a pocket as he walked over. Evans and Shane were already looking at her, and she spoke softly.

"It's definitely a prion," she began. "But they're not trying to cure it here."

"They're not?" Shane asked.

She shook her head, solemn. "No. I think they *designed* it here."

THEY RUMMAGED through file cabinets and shelves, looking for clues like they had in previous rooms they'd entered. Michaela worked her way toward a computer in the corner. It appeared to be unlocked, and she scrolled through a strange operating system Shane didn't recognize.

"It's all in Korean, some sort of bundled OS that's proprietary to this place."

"How can you tell?" Evans asked, coming to stand by her side.

"Well, it looks similar to some of the government operating systems I've seen in South Korea. They use them on machines at universities and research facilities to keep everything tightly secured and safe." She said this with a smirk, and Shane couldn't help but move over to hear her explanation.

"Of course, in doing so, it ironically makes it *less* safe," she explained. "A normal operating system is developed by hundreds — if not thousands — of people, constantly being improved and having bugs fixed. Systems like this are often made by a couple of IT nerds, cobbled together from whatever open-source software they could find. After about a month or two, it starts to get bogged down with system resources and vulnerabilities are exposed."

"Sounds like you're speaking from experience," Evans noted. Shane couldn't help but notice the man's hand on Dr. Everly's shoulder, where it squeezed lightly. Michaela didn't brush it away. He swallowed, trying to ignore it and focus on the mission.

"Yeah," she said. "We constantly begged our group to get us normal PCs — off-the-shelf computers, with standard, commercial and professional operating systems. If they would spend their money hiring security professionals, our machines wouldn't have been constantly hacked and accessed. In fact, I have a feeling..."

She suddenly fell silent, glancing over at Shane.

"In fact, I have a feeling that Kate and I wouldn't have..."

She caught herself then, suddenly glancing back at Shane. He watched her, trying to gauge her state of mind.

"Go on," he urged.

"Well, I was just saying that Kate and I used to submit grant proposals for tech." She said this with a forced smile. "Can you imagine? The two of us writing grants for *technology*? We were so out of our element doing that. Both of us just wanted to work — to research — and neither of us felt like we could get anything done with computers that were constantly being hacked and exploited."

"Did any of those attacks ever lead to anything directly damaging?" Evans asked.

"Sure, I mean we have to assume so." She paused, looking back at the screen and then at Shane once more. "Actually, there was one time Kate got in trouble because of something she had saved to a folder that wasn't properly secured."

"I don't remember her telling me about that," Shane admitted.

"She was embarrassed by it, but it wasn't even her fault. She saved the file on the system we were told to use, but it wasn't password protected. And it's not like that was uncommon — we did that sort of thing all the time. I mean, we're using a computer on an intranet that wasn't supposed to be connected to the outside world at all."

"What happened?" Shane asked.

"Well, she just got reprimanded. Scolded by the director. I think he was jealous of how successful she was getting, and embarrassed that his computer system was subpar. Anyway, back to this — it's the same operating system, though clearly lifted and altered a bit from the internal one we used. That seems to be the North Korean way — what you can't make, steal."

"A fair assessment," Evans murmured, his voice soft.

Shane noticed Evans' man moving once again through the stacks of binders on shelves. He pulled out individual tomes, flipping through them quickly before moving onto the next. If Shane had to guess, it seemed as though the man was actually listening intently to what Michaela was explaining, rather than paying much attention to the binders he held.

"Point is," Michaela started, "I'm pretty sure I can navigate through and —"

She stopped herself short again, and Shane leaned forward, staring at the screen. It was all in Korean.

"Well, scratch that. I may have found something."

She clicked around for another half minute, before speaking again. "Yeah, hell, we just hit paydirt, boys."

Evans' hand finally moved away from her shoulder, and he crouched down by the screen. "What is it?" he asked hurriedly. "What did you find?"

"It's a list of treatments. Literally prescriptions for individual subjects. There are time and date stamps, medication descriptions, dosages, and success/failure ratios."

"Success/failure ratios?" Evans asked. His man had moved closer to them now, and Shane noticed his eyes peering over at the screen.

She nodded. "Yeah, basically a percentage of how effective a particular treatment was. Some of it will be guesswork, based on the doctors' and researchers' observations, but some of it is actually based on testable conclusions. And these seem to be pretty good numbers."

"Meaning they treated people here, and those treatments were successful?"

"Yeah," she said, distracted. She ran her finger down one of the columns in the center of the screen. "Except, these medication descriptions all match. They were all being treated with the exact same medication."

"Do you know *what* they were treated with? What the medication is?"

"It's not a word I recognize, which tells me it's probably an acronym. But the first word can probably best be translated to 'prion'."

Shane reeled, the realization striking him as if someone had punched him in the face. "So they *were* infecting people with a prion disease?"

She shook her head as she scrolled through the list, moving upward. She stopped at the top of the page and read a brief description. Finally, she pulled her hand away from the mouse and covered her mouth. "Yes," she whispered. "Yes, they actually did it. It says here they did infect these people with prions – most likely injecting them through the eye as we hypothesized earlier."

She sat back in the chair, blinking a few times.

"But they also figured out a cure. Either something they created here or something they found. But these treatments are for something that cured them."

"So they infected people with a life-altering disease," Evans summarized, "but then cured them with some sort of medication they made here in the lab?"

She nodded slowly. "Yes, that appears to be the case. Whatever they were doing here, it has something to do with this prion disease. But the reason this place is so tightly locked down, and was guarded so heavily, was because they were also producing a *treatment* for it."

61

SHANE

SHANE WATCHED as Grudowski moved around the computer station. "And all of this is on this intranet?" he asked.

Michaela nodded, looking up at him as if seeing him for the first time. "Yes — actually, the information I accessed is on..." She paused, looking around the computer station for something. She reached around to the back, where Shane noticed a USB thumb drive plugged into the back of the computer. "This. Though these facilities always want to have their own proprietary software, they don't have the money or time to produce proprietary hardware. As such, they always just resort to using whatever is on the market. In this case, standard USB drives."

She pulled out the USB drive with a flourish, showed it to the three men gathered around, then plugged it back into the computer.

Evans' man nodded, and Evans smiled at him. He turned and faced Michaela again. "These guys created a prion disease — or altered it in such a way as to produce some sort of negative side effects, I'm assuming?"

"Yes, that's my assumption as well. I haven't been able to figure out exactly what the side effects are, or what the actual prion disease was intending to accomplish, but I have a feeling it's no different than the latest wave of bespoke viruses created in labs around the world."

"Especially in places around the world hostile to the Western world," Shane quipped.

"Yes, but not necessarily. The United States has been cooking up viruses and dangerous bacteria for ages. For decades, they've been studying anthrax,

SARS, Zika, and more recently, COVID. They've been putting these little guys through their paces, trying to understand what all they can do."

"You mean, how governments might be able to turn them into weapons."

Her eyebrows raised, and Shane saw that she was neither confirming nor denying his statement.

Evans cut in. "*But* they also created a cure for this one, did they not?"

"Yes, I believe that's what this file said." She frowned as she looked down at the screen again. Shane saw what had her confused. The file she was looking at before was gone, likely having disappeared when she had unplugged the thumb drive. However, when she had plugged it back in, it had not reappeared on the screen.

He wondered if she needed to open it again, to navigate the peculiar operating system in order to find the USB drive and all of its contents.

"Anyway, best I can gather, they were doing something with the prion here in this lab. But they also wanted to make sure they had a cure for it as well. Very likely they treated all of those villagers back there with both the prion disease and its cure, as a way to study the effects of both the disease and the solution."

"I still don't understand why," Evans said.

Evans' man shifted to the side, moving behind Evans now. He seemed disinterested once again, slowly making his way toward the table in the center of the room that held another computer terminal. He played with the computer mouse for a moment, as if trying to see if this one was also unlocked like Michaela's was.

"I don't understand that, either," Michaela said. "The answer might be here somewhere. But we need to find Seong Park. We've got enough information now to at least understand what they were trying to do. Seong would understand this research — she would be able to help them, especially since this is all within her purview, what she was working on before her kidnapping."

"You know, I'm not convinced she *was* kidnapped," Evans said.

Shane glanced over at the tall soldier. "What are you talking about? Of course she was."

Evans frowned. "I'm not convinced. Yeah, her old man told us to go find her — told us that she had been kidnapped. But didn't you say back in the village that the guy working for the enemy was *also* working for Seong's father? We need to check and make sure this all checks out."

Shane chewed the inside of his lip, working his tongue over his teeth. He had to admit, it did seem a bit strange now. All of it. The fact that they were here, when the vast majority of the rest of the place had been evacuated. The fact that there was a bomb inside that had not gone off, as if it had been set hastily, relying solely on its connection to the communications tower above.

And yes, Evans was right — it was definitely strange that he and Michaela had almost been snatched in the village, almost taken out of the fight completely, by a man who seemed to be working for the very person who had sent them all here to find his daughter.

The pieces of the puzzle were all out on the table, but Shane could not yet see its resemblance to a full picture.

"We still need to act as though she *has* been kidnapped though," Michaela said. "Right?"

Evans nodded, but the frown remained on his face. "Yes, that's probably our best move. We should operate as though the mission parameters have not changed. We don't know if Seong Park's father is hostile, or if he is still on our side but lied a bit about his daughter's kidnapping. I don't like the implications of either, but all we can do now is be vigilant and continue moving forward."

EVANS LISTENED as Dr. Michaela Everly explained. He was quite enthralled by this woman — from her outward appearance to her ability to withstand enormous pressure. In the little time he had known her, he had realized she was an incredible asset to his team. Not just as a consultant, but as a personality who could help keep spirits high.

If only she were a soldier, he thought. Having a person on his team like her would have been an unbelievable asset in numerous sticky situations he had found himself in before. Her optimism, charm, and tenacity would have made many missions much more bearable.

And she certainly isn't hard to look at.

Evans forced himself to push these thoughts aside — these were thoughts for another time, conversations for another day. The truth was, she *wasn't* a soldier. She had nearly been taken down by enemy rounds outside, and he knew all too well the toll it could take on a civilian who was neither prepared nor anticipating such an attack.

But she was still alive, and therefore still incredibly useful. She had single-handedly been able to figure out what exactly was happening here, though they still didn't understand why.

She continued explaining as Evans and Shane Riley gathered around the computer station. "I just don't understand some of the nuance," she said. "Why create a disease that infects people in such a specific way?"

"What specific way is that?" Shane asked. "Does it have something to do with their eyes?"

"That's part of the nuance I don't understand yet," she answered. "No, I don't think it has anything to do with the eyeball specifically — that's just collateral damage. They just needed to get this thing into the brain, for whatever reason. My guess is since it's a prion disease that was delivered directly into one of the lobes inside the skull, it affects a person's mental state. That's just a hypothesis — it very likely could also affect their physical state as well, literally challenging their involuntary systems, or even making it hard to use certain muscle configurations."

"And they cooked up a solution to the thing, as well," Evans said. "Seems like the type of thing terrorists would be working on. Release a disease into the wild that's contagious, only to come out later and say, 'here's the cure. Pay us a bunch of money and we'll give it to you.'"

Michaela looked horrified, but Evans knew she wasn't naive. This was absolutely the way terrorist cells around the world thought and did business. They would cook up something in a lab — or, rather, hire an unscrupulous third-party firm to do the dirty work — then provide a solution to the very problems they created. Their target would have no choice but to comply or risk death.

Certain terrorist organizations preferred simple acts of terror instead — killing people in the name of some god or another. But the more modern versions of these organizations usually involved getting something in return for their deeds.

Money was common, but it was not the only form of currency accepted. Black-market weapons, illegal contraband, things that could be resold for a profit.

It seemed they were looking at the beginnings of a similar structure — they had found a prion disease, one that would be nearly impossible to understand before it infected many people.

Evans frowned. "One thing we *don't* know is whether or not it's contagious," he said. "If they were planning on releasing this to the population, or some population somewhere, we would have known by now. This would be killing people already, right?"

"Again, we don't know exactly what they were planning to do with it. That would be the obvious choice, but the fact that they've been so careful to not release it gives me pause. Usually, these types of things start tightly under wraps, but at this point, we haven't pieced all of it together yet."

She took a breath. "But if I had to guess... yes. These sorts of contagions are *extremely* transmittable. It's impossible to say how this one would be transmitted — obviously they are directly infecting patients by removing an eye and inserting it directly into the brain. But that could be a safeguard, meant to ensure the doctors and researchers here do not accidentally get contaminated with the prions. In the wild, who knows. This could be as dormant as a latent virus, or as hostile and aggressive as Zika. It could be transmissible through food, air, touch, or any number of vectors."

"So, if we assume it's contagious," Evans replied, "and we can assume it's extremely dangerous once it's infected, and we can assume these guys also cooked up a solution that renders the disease ineffective, the question remains: why? Why haven't they done anything with it, and why are they trying to do it in the first place? I don't think this is a terrorist organization — I think this is the North Korean government we're dealing with. Perhaps one and the same, depending on perspective, but a program like this is too specific, too granular. They're not just trying to incite fear. They were trying to accomplish something. They *are* trying to accomplish something."

Next to him, Shane shrugged. "It's impossible to say. But we've got some answers now. I think it's time to get the hell out of here, before they send in the cavalry and make sure that bomb downstairs goes off."

Everyone looked at him.

He shrugged. "Look, I'm no computer genius. For all we know, I just bought us twenty minutes."

"He's right," Evans said. "We can't justify staying here much longer. We need to find Seong and get out."

SHANE STOOD to the side while Michaela talked with Evans. He was so busy focusing on the computer screen, trying to decipher what the columns of data could possibly mean and what the people working here were intending to do with it, he almost didn't notice Grudowski slip behind his boss.

Shane frowned, watching as the mercenary picked up Evans' rifle he had set down and leaned against the desk. He examined it, as if inspecting it for cleanliness and checking its magazine.

But he wasn't doing either. Instead, he lifted the weapon up and held it over his head, then slammed it down as hard as he could, cracking it against the back of Evans' skull.

Shane's eyes widened and he cried out in surprise, but by the time he realized the betrayal, it was too late. Grudowski turned the rifle around and aimed it at Shane as Evans slipped to the floor, his body limp.

Michaela Everly almost tripped over the chair as she backed up in surprise. She turned, but Shane was focusing only on one thing.

The barrel of Evans' rifle was now pointed directly at him. His own rifle was still slung over his shoulder. Shane felt the rifle he was holding in his hand, gripping it tighter.

"Don't," Grudowski snarled. "It's not going to end well for you if you do."

Shane growled, his squint returning as he stared down the shorter, stockier man. "Seems like it's not going to end well for me either way, now is it?"

"What's happening?" Michaela asked. "What – what are you doing?"

Shane watched as Grudowski stepped a single pace away from both of them. Smartly, he didn't want to be in range if Michaela tried to reach him. But he held his rifle steady on Shane, knowing the man was the bigger threat than the doctor.

"I'm not here to kill you," Grudowski said. "That doesn't mean I *won't*, though, if given the choice or if forced."

"Then by all means, clue us in as to what *would* force you to do that?" Shane challenged.

Grudowski smiled, a sickly grin Shane had seen before but only in context of killing the guards outside. "First things first – drop the weapon."

Shane nodded, having already run this conversation to its inevitable conclusion in his mind. He had never been in a situation exactly like this, but he had been in enough – and knew enough stories – to know what came next.

Maintain the status quo.

Right now, Grudowski was working for someone besides Evans. *Someone* was paying him to do their bidding, and the status quo had shifted. Right now, he didn't need his boss getting in the way, and he didn't need Shane Riley and Michaela Everly arguing the point.

But they were still alive, which meant Grudowski still needed them for something.

Shane dropped the rifle and kicked it over without being asked. Grudowski's smile shifted suddenly to one of surprise and delight, but then turned evil once more. His deep, hollow eyes seemed to bore into Shane's.

"What now?" Shane asked. "You need us to ensure your safe passage or something? Get you out of the country? Then you kill us right before you get on the chopper?"

Grudowski seemed to consider this for a moment. "That's a good idea, actually. But, no, I've got different plans. And lucky for you, I was told there's no reason to kill you – you're pawns in this game apparently, so whether you live or die seems to be no one's concern. And just like pawns, if you *do* get in my way, however..."

Shane listened as Grudowski's voice trailed off. He glanced over at Michaela, who was standing shellshocked next to him. Her eyes welled with tears, but she was holding herself together for the moment. He wanted to reach out, to grab her arm and pull her closer. But any movement would be dangerous for both of them.

"What, then?"

"Same mission as before," Grudowski spat. "We need to get Seong Park out of here safely, back into South Korea. We do that, you two go free."

Shane risked pulling his hand up so he could rub his chin, thinking hard.

This had always been about Seong Park – why did the mission need to change now? Why was it –

Shane's eyes flicked to Michaela, then the computer, then back to Grudowski. "You have it, don't you?"

He sensed Michaela staring at him confused, but he kept his gaze on the soldier, drilling holes through him with his eyes. "You got the research. That's what you've been doing this whole time, isn't it."

Grudowski nodded slowly, then pulled his free hand down to his left pocket and pulled out a small thumb drive. "Very astute observation, Mr. Riley," Grudowski said. "Seong Park is still the *primary* mission. For you, anyway. But mine is a little different. I need to get this data back to my boss. The person *actually* giving the orders."

"And who is that? The old man from a few days ago? Seong Park's father?"

Grudowski stared, without nodding. He put the USB drive back into his pocket, then continued. "Get outside, take us back downstairs. If Seong Park is here, she'll be in one of those underground corridors. All those doors we walked past looked like cells. I'd bet my left nut she's in one of those rooms."

"How about betting your left *eye*?" Shane said.

No one laughed, and Shane was somewhat disappointed in that. He couldn't blame Michaela – she was terrified, and he had to admit it was probably an improper time for jokes. But what else was he supposed to do?

He couldn't let this guy simply give orders.

He needed to buy time.

"SO WE'RE JUST SUPPOSED to be running around here like idiots, looking for Seong Park?" Shane asked. "There's no one here. This place is deserted."

Shane thought back to the sound of gunfire he had heard upon entering the facility. It had come from down below, down where Grudowski thought Seong Park might be.

Are they still here?

He had assumed those guards — whoever had fired those shots — had left during his battle, or shortly after. But what if they were still here? What if they were still waiting, ready to attack?

"You don't know that!" Grudowski yelled. "And she *is* here. I have it on good authority."

"Good authority like her old man? The same guy that betrayed all of us? Lied to me and Evans? You trust *him*?"

Grudowski shook his head, still smiling. "You don't get it, do you, Riley? I had you pegged the minute you walked in the door. You even said it yourself — this is why you don't do people retrieval. It was part of your mantra, wasn't it? You think it's because you're some high and mighty guy, some paragon of moral standing. But it's because you have *no idea* how to read people. Because you have *no idea* what people are thinking. If you did, you would know that Seong's father was playing you all from the moment he grabbed you off that boat."

Shane frowned. "How do you know that? How did you know that's where they grabbed me? Seong's father didn't tell any of us that."

"You're naive, Riley," Grudowski said. "Those two men working for

Seong's father, Smith and Donovan? They're the ones who hired *me*. They're the ones who hired Evans and you, technically, but they handpicked me for the next phase of this mission. You think this is the end – that we are close to solving this and getting out of here. That's true, I hope, but it's also only the beginning."

Shane's mind raced. He tried to piece it all together, to figure out where he had gone wrong. This guy wasn't incorrect – Shane did have trouble reading into social cues and facial tics. Had he been so stupid as to have missed something obvious? Seong's father seemed desperate to find his daughter, distraught. Had he been playing them then, as well?

Was Seong Park really here, or was she in on this whole thing?

"The beginning of what?" Michaela asked.

Grudowski looked over, seemingly noticing her for the first time. "I don't know the details, that's above my pay grade. But it does have something to do with the prions we found. The research – that's why I needed to get it. That's what I'm here to do."

"You're working for a terrorist, Grudowski," Shane said. "You do realize that, don't you?"

"I'm working for someone who has long-term goals. And long-term goals – and the means to pay for them – means long-term employment for me."

"*Money?*" Shane spat. "You're doing this for money? Grudowski, people are going to die. People already have died. There are *far* better ways to make money, man."

At this, Grudowski laughed. "It really is just like you to be this naive. I've known men like you over the years. They always end up dead much quicker than me. Yes, you dolt. *Money.* You know, the thing that makes the world go round."

Shane's head fell. He stood still, motionless next to the computer and Dr. Everly. He wanted to get out, to see the sun once more and just stand there for a while and think. He wanted a break, to be free of all this.

He raised his eyes again and stared at Grudowski. "How did you know they found me on a boat?"

While he didn't have many cards to play, information like Grudowski's next words could prove useful to him. Could help maintain the status quo.

"*They* were on a boat, not *you*," Grudowski answered immediately. "*You* were diving, were you not?"

Shane cocked his head to the side, still staring. *Amazing. He does know the details.*

"What was it they told us? He's looking for his dead wife?"

Shane gritted his teeth, balled his fists. Next to him, he sensed Michaela tense. He sensed her looking at him as well, urging him to not do anything rash. Urging him to stay still, to not get them killed.

"Kate, was that her name?" Grudowski continued, now purposefully egging him on. "I hear she was hot. Like, blazing —"

Shane lunged forward, closing the distance between himself and the mercenary quicker than either of them thought possible. He gritted his teeth as he moved. "Say her name again, and it's the last thing you'll ever say." He noticed the mercenary's eyes widened slightly, taken by surprise at Shane's sudden speed and agility. Shane leapt into the air, trying to get to the side, to move sideways and provide as little a target as possible.

It didn't matter. The man reacted on impulse, firing a single shot that missed wide. He fired again, then a third time. One of them grazed Shane's wrist, but it did nothing but draw blood.

Shane felt nothing as he landed directly in front of the mercenary. He was still moving, punching with fists and kicking with legs and anything else that would move on his person. It was not a coordinated attack, not graceful in any way.

He pummeled Grudowski in rage, forcing the man backwards, the gun clattered sideways. It fell hard onto the concrete floor of the room, but neither man moved toward it.

It was a brawl now, the taller, leaner Shane against a shorter, thicker mercenary. Shane had been trained in hand-to-hand combat over years of service and training as a special forces officer.

But this mercenary was something else. It was as though the gun he had been holding was an impediment to his true power. Now freed of that burden, he landed blows on Shane that caused him to wince, cry out, and finally, be forced to heave for breath. Shane fell to the floor, on his hands and knees. It was over before it even started. Shane was no masochist — if he continued, this man would kill him with his bare hands.

"Stop!" Shane begged. He raised his hands above his head, just before the mercenary was about to land another blow. "Stop, you made your point."

"I warned you I would leave you here, dead."

"But you didn't!" Shane yelled. "You *wanted* to egg me on, you *wanted* to piss me off. If you wanted me dead, you would've just done it and then argued later that we put up a fight. Seong's father wouldn't care — we're not part of the mission. Getting his daughter back and getting that research is. So why are we still alive?"

The man stared down at Shane now, as if contemplating this question for the first time.

Why were they still alive?

JONATHAN EVANS FOUGHT against his natural inclination to open his eyes. He lay on the cold concrete floor of the room with the computers and folders inside. He heard voices, muffled at first but then growing clearer as his mind and body healed.

His own teammate had knocked him out — a man he thought he could trust. Now, he heard him explaining why he had done it, why he was going to do what he was going to do.

Money.

Evans gritted his teeth, trying as hard as possible not to jump up. He fought against the urge to push himself upward and try to attack Grudowski. He knew it was pointless — not only was he facing the wrong way, but his teammate had put space between himself and Evans' body on the floor, and he knew he was armed.

He didn't want to risk startling him and getting shot as he rose, and, for the moment, no one seemed to remember he was there. It was likely everyone assumed he was still knocked out, unconscious. He preferred to keep it that way. If there was any way he could glean information from the situation, figure out what made this guy tick and what his plans were, it might be enough to help save Michaela and Shane Riley.

He lay on the floor, feeling his left arm falling asleep but forcing himself to do nothing about it. Shane Riley argued back with the teammate, trying to extract logic from Grudowski's words. Riley didn't understand at first why he had waited until now, but that became clear after listening to Grudowski's explanations. Apparently, he was working for the same person Evans and

Riley had been working for. Only, Chung-Hee Park had doublecrossed them, handpicking Grudowski to run a counter-operation from within Jonathan Evans' own mission.

That alone was enough to make Evans' blood boil, but he fought down the rage and listened on. Apparently the old guy didn't trust anyone – not that Evans could fault him for that – but he had overreacted and offered even more money to his own teammate to ensure his daughter's safe return.

But Evans, like Shane Riley, wasn't convinced Seong Park *was* still here. This place had been prepped to blow, the entire facility about to crumble down in on itself. If the people running the show here had evacuated so quickly, wouldn't they have taken an asset like Seong Park with them? If she was the key to all of this, there was no way she would still be here.

Unless...

His mind worked over the repercussions. He tried to think like one of the North Korean government leaders in charge of this place. He tried to think like a researcher, one of the scientists performing the gruesome experiments and extractions on the villagers and subjects here.

He tried to think like Seong Park – he assumed she knew something of the research that had been done here, that she had been targeted for a reason.

The details were unclear, but the picture began forming in his mind.

If they thought she knew the key to unlocking some component of this prion research, they would certainly want to keep her alive.

His subconscious tugged at him. *Unless they had already extracted that information from her,* he realized. In that case, there was no use for her or any of the other subjects. They could effectively abandon this place for good, blowing it all up when they thought the American infiltration team was inside.

Two birds with one stone.

One gigantic, secret research station-sized stone.

If that were true, he reasoned, it meant Seong Park *might* actually still be here. The perpetrators would be long gone of course, but they now had a much clearer picture of what they were doing here. Dr. Michaela Everly had been able to pinpoint the prion disease and its treatment. He had been unconscious for some of the back-and forth, but he remembered her explanation before his teammate had smashed the rifle over his head.

Plus, Seong Park might know more. That would be a fantastic reason for Grudowski to have waited this long. He not only needed to make sure Seong Park was still here – he wanted to make sure the research was accessible. Retrieving his boss's daughter would not be enough, Evans knew. The man was shrewd, and wouldn't bat an eye at using his daughter as bait to get access to the research on the disease they were creating in this laboratory.

He almost shook his head, but stopped himself. *No, that doesn't track,* he thought. *Park loves his daughter and wouldn't knowingly put her in harm's way. So what happened? How did Seong Park get involved in all of this?*

He remembered Michaela overhearing their benefactor's name while hogtied in the back of the truck. Had Chung-Hee Park been trying to double-cross the people who'd hired the kidnapper, as well? Had he been trying to gain access to the research by allowing his daughter to visit this place? Perhaps it had started as a simple diplomatic mission – one that had ended horrendously for him and his daughter.

Or, perhaps, Seong Park had been studying a similar or adjacent topic, much like Dr. Michaela Everly had been. Perhaps she had been targeted, and there had been no previous connection to his boss.

It was all enough to make his head swim, so he relaxed and allowed his mind to wander.

It sounded like his teammate was finishing up, his words clipped, growing louder as he grew more frustrated with Shane Riley's combative stance.

"That's enough talk," Grudowski was saying. "You two, by the door. And just as a reminder, I don't *need* both of you from here on out. I'd prefer not to leave you dead, but to use you as leverage. Keep that in mind – open your mouth again or do something stupid, and I'll put a bullet in your back."

Evans heard Shane grumbling, but their footsteps indicated that he and Dr. Everly were doing as they had been told and moving toward the door.

There's no way he forgets me in here, Evans thought. *There's no way he'll just allow me to wake up and –*

"I almost forgot," his teammate said. "We can't just leave our buddy here, can we?"

Evans heard more footsteps, shuffling, and then he heard Michaela gasp.

"No!" Shane suddenly shouted. There were more footsteps, and then the sound of running. Evans opened his eyes then, involuntarily. He saw Riley running toward him – running toward Grudowski, who was standing just in front of Evans.

Shane's arms were out, flailing, no weapon in his hands. Michaela stood shocked by the door, her hand over her mouth.

Evans heard the gunshots before he realized what was happening. Grudowski was there; he had beaten Shane to him.

Two rounds, directly into Evans' back.

He lurched, convulsing on the floor as one round sailed through his side and the other landed next to his spine. The impact was intense, and he felt the bullet breaking through a rib and hit his lung. He tasted blood, then felt it spilling outward from his lips.

His eyes were wide in shock.

And that's when the pain reached him. He moved his mouth open and closed as he gasped for air.

But there was none. He heard Shane struggling with his teammate, but their voices and Michaela's shouting was fading.

His eyes closed again, and peace came over him.

Everything went black.

SHANE LUNGED FORWARD, nearly falling over but catching himself right at the last moment and breaking into a full sprint. He tried to close the distance, but there was no way he would make it in time.

Grudowski was hovering over Evans, gun ready. Shane had been a little slow on the uptake, not realizing what he was going to do until he had done it.

The two shots slammed into Evans' back just as Shane reached him. He pushed Grudowski backwards, hearing a satisfied crack as the mercenary sailed backwards into one of the bookcases. Binders and reports spilled out, landing at his feet. Shane kept moving, trying to drive him through the wall.

Grudowski was laughing, a maniacal cackle as he swung the rifle around. Only then did Shane realize his mistake.

He caught the side of the man's weapon with his temple and immediately saw stars. He stumbled to the side, and Grudowski backhanded him once again, a meaty fist smacking into his ear.

Shane worked his mouth open and closed as he forced himself to recover.

Shane backed away then, aiming for the far corner of the room. Grudowski was chasing him, menacingly stomping toward him as Evans lay heaving and dying on the floor. He stepped over Evans' legs and kept his rifle trained on Shane.

Shane's mind cleared for a split second, and he realized the predicament.

Grudowski was right – he didn't need Shane and Michaela. If he was in the man's shoes, he would choose the doctor over Shane, anyway. She was not only the smarter of the two, the one brought here specifically to understand what research was taking place, but she was unarmed and untrained in combat.

Shane's eyes widened as the man pointed the rifle at him. "I think you might be having trouble grasping the gravity of the situation," Grudowski snapped. He stood in the center of the room, his back to Evans and the computer station Michaela had been using earlier. Shane saw Michaela to his left, stepping inside the room once more, terror and grief plastered over her face.

"I meant it before when I said I didn't want to kill you. Are you *really* not going to give me that choice?"

For the first time since meeting this man, Shane felt dumbstruck. He had no words. He saw his life in front of his eyes now, saw Kate and heard the messages left on his phone, asking for him.

He saw her car, imagined her driving home to him, only to be intercepted by the murderers who had kidnapped her and killed her.

He saw the pictures of her dead body, the round, red circle in the center of her forehead. He saw her face, empty and devoid of life, but the look of sheer terror permanently etched across it.

This was how he had left her. This was his fault.

He couldn't control those thoughts any longer, they pummeled the inside of his mind like the same bullet that had taken her life... and now taken Evans'.

The mercenary took another step forward. "I would say you've forced my hand, but I'm actually a man of my word. I told our boss I *wouldn't* kill either of you, no matter what."

Shane's gaze shifted to Michaela, who was moving slowly along the wall. He didn't turn his head, didn't move at all.

What is he talking about?

"I was sincere earlier when I said I didn't care if you two died – I'm not here to take prisoners; it would be more convenient for me if I just left you all here like Evans. But I told our boss that *I* wouldn't be the one to do it. He understood battlefield casualties, collateral damage, all that. But it wouldn't be at my hand."

"Did you tell him that about Evans as well?" Shane said, his words venomous.

Grudowski shrugged. "Actually, yeah, I did. That's why I shot him in the back – it was a moment of confusion. I doubt our boss will ever come here to verify, but I'll sleep easy knowing I didn't just execute all three of you. My job is simple: get the data and get his daughter. I'm not here to keep any of you alive, nor am I here to kill you. That's that."

MICHAELA CREPT SLOWLY along the wall. She had moved inside the room once more, trying to avoid attention but also not wanting to leave Shane alone in there. She felt a strange sense of connection to him, especially now after a shared traumatic experience like this. She knew that was common in relationships – almost any person, thrown together with anyone else, would form an unbelievably strong bond after going through a terrifying and life-altering situation.

Her subconscious was supplying these thoughts, but she tried to turn her intellectual brain off for a moment. This was not the time to psychologically analyze herself or anyone else. This was not the time for digging into the human psyche. There was a very real threat in front of them now, and Michaela was not about to allow this guy to kill Shane without her fighting back.

Of course, she felt helpless. She was no soldier, and hardly knew the first thing about hand-to-hand combat.

She was also well aware that this would not be hand-to-hand combat. It would be a one-sided battle, served from the end of this mercenary's rifle barrel.

She tried to ignore Evans breathing slowly down by the computer station. The mercenary had shot him in the back twice, and while Michaela wanted more than anything to run over and check on the man, she knew her best option right now was to maintain the element of surprise.

If she *was* going to gain the upper hand at all, to allow Shane to come back into this fight, it would be by sneaking around behind the man standing in the center of the room.

She had one target in mind – Shane's rifle that he had dropped to the floor by the computer. She had been standing close to it before, but it had escaped her attention then. Not anymore. She worked her way against the wall, daring to step forward to move in front of the shallow desk-like piece of furniture bolted to the wall, careful not to make any noise. She only half-listened as Shane and the mercenary discussed.

She kept her eyes on the floor, as if that would help make her invisible. The mercenary was yelling now, shouting at Shane about this mission and something about keeping his word.

She didn't know this man, didn't know if he was just posturing or actually meant any of it. He'd already betrayed them, so why not do it again? Why not simply leave them all dead here and tell Seong Park's father they had fought back? Surely the man wouldn't *truly* care about any of their lives — so long as he got his daughter *and* the research.

Yet the man was armed and had not shot either of them yet. Evans was on the ground, and she saw a bit of blood pooling around his chest. He was lying on his stomach, head to the side away from her. She couldn't see if his eyes were opened or closed, but he was completely still, unmoving. She reached the weapon a few seconds later. She nearly kicked it with her foot, but stopped short. Shane was talking now, capturing the man's attention.

She bent down, knowing this was her best chance. She reached the rifle, feeling its cold steel in her bare hand. She picked it up, hoisted it. She swung around, aiming it directly at the man, placing her finger over the trigger. She slid her left hand farther out on the barrel, trying to make the grip comfortable. She looked down, noticing a small latch on the side.

A safety?

She moved her thumb over to it, preparing to turn it on... or off, she wasn't sure which.

"Drop it."

She nearly jumped out of her skin, but held the rifle. It shook in her hands. She glanced upward, noticing that Grudowski had turned and was facing her. She also noticed the rifle barrel he was holding had swung around.

"Ever felt the recoil of that gun?" he snapped. "It likes to rise quite a bit. Took me weeks at the range to really get the hang of it. It's got a kick, that's for sure. You might think your shoulder's nice and steady now, but I wouldn't bet on you from more than three feet away."

She knew he was trying to egg her on, to make her fumble so he could once again keep the advantage.

She wasn't going to let that happen. Her thumb hit the safety, and she flicked it. It clicked, and she steeled herself, padding the butt of the rifle with her shoulder, knowing that though he might not be telling the truth, there would absolutely be some kick.

But she was not going to falter. He swung the rifle back around to make sure Shane was in his place. She crept forward a step, but moved backward once again. Her back was pressed to the wall, her eyes looking over at him, pleading.

I can do this, she told herself.

"Just put the gun down; none of us have to get hurt."

She wondered if he even heard the words as they fell from his lips, or if he was just regurgitating what he heard in countless movies. Did he actually believe this? He had killed their friend in cold blood, betrayed all of them. He didn't care one way or another who got hurt. He just wanted to stay alive.

That sealed the deal. She lifted the rifle up, seeing his eyes widen. She aimed for the center of his chest, smart enough to know that going for a head-shot was risky with any firearm.

She pulled the trigger.

It didn't budge. It was stuck, locked.

Then the man smiled. He lifted his own rifle, but it wasn't pointed at her. He aimed for Shane, arching up just over his head. He fired a shot quickly, the sound deafening.

She screamed, and he turned the rifle back to her. Both she and Shane stood in the room, shell-shocked.

"Put. The rifle. Down."

She swallowed, then nodded as she let the rifle fall to the floor once more. Apparently, she had put the safety back *on.* It had been off when Shane was holding it, unsurprisingly, knowing the man would want to be ready for anything, not trusting anyone.

She should have known — should have guessed that. But it was too late now.

"Back to the door, both of you," Grudowski said. "Let this be a lesson to you."

Shane was moving toward her now, his side to the soldier standing in the center of the room. He didn't seem fazed by the man's threats, but she knew better than to think he wasn't taking them seriously. Shane reached her then, immediately grabbing her hand. She held it tightly, and he squeezed.

It was a small gesture, but it gave her immense strength. He tried to pull back, but she held tight. *No,* she thought. *We're in this together. Me and you. And we're going to see this through.*

He looked down at her, catching her eyes. They were wide, scared. But there was something else there, reassurance?

She nodded at him, as if trying to telepathically send thoughts to him.

It seemed he understood, at least a bit. He nodded back, and together, hand in hand, they left the room.

THEY SEARCHED the floor they were on first, working through the H-shaped layout quickly and methodically. No one spoke, no one offered suggestions. They simply worked together, Shane and Michaela taking turns inspecting each room they passed, at least the ones that were unlocked.

The first one they reached that was locked, their accompanying mercenary fired a round through the mechanism and kicked the door open. Inside was more of the same – shelves full of reports, filing cabinets stacked to the ceiling, desks, and tables lining the walls. Two armchairs sat in the center of the room, facing a large desk pulled out from one wall. It looked like the office of someone important, but the only pictures on the walls were of the current and prior North Korean dictators.

After that, they didn't bother unlocking the doors. Shane knew they all felt the same way – if Seong Park were still here, she would be downstairs in the rooms they had passed on their way to the communications space.

Closer to the bomb.

Though it hadn't detonated and seemed to be defunct, none of them wanted to be anywhere near it.

However, they didn't find any more subjects or patients — or anyone at all on the upper floor — besides the deceased individual they had found earlier. It seemed that, with the exception of ongoing operations, the subjects were kept prisoner on the bottom level of the base. That made sense to Shane, though he didn't like it.

They descended the staircase in single file, their mercenary companion behind them, rifle aimed directly at Shane's back the entire time. He felt a bit reassured that Grudowski had come clean and admitted that he was not there to kill them, but that reassurance didn't go far. He knew he wouldn't hesitate to shoot them in the back if needed.

Shane stopped behind Michaela at the first room. She tried the handle, and he watched as it turned in her grasp. It clicked open, but she held the door closed for a moment as she looked behind her. He was there, watching, nodding.

"It's okay," he whispered. "I'm right here."

He knew what she was feeling – he felt it as well. Trepidation, uneasiness. Whatever they were about to find in this room, it was going to give them answers. He was sure of it.

Their mercenary companion urged her to hurry up, and Shane helped her push the door open. It was heavier than all the doors upstairs, not one of those single-core, hollow doors they'd encountered earlier. It was solid metal, constructed undoubtedly to keep someone in or out.

Shane held his breath as they entered. There was no light, and Michaela didn't reach for one. Behind him, the mercenary turned on the light clipped to the end of his rifle and aimed into the room. Eyes stared back at them.

Shane jumped, pushing backward, but only bumped into their burly escort. The man shoved him off, keeping the rifle pointed toward the people in the room. They were people this time – not just eyeballs floating in vats.

Michaela let out a small gasp, and Shane couldn't help but stare.

Emaciated people stared back at him, their eyes coalescing into a point where Shane was standing. They were all staring at the door. Each of the people had only a single eye, their left removed. But unlike the villagers, these people wore no eye patches, bandages, or coverings of any kind. The sick, hollow openings were filled with congealed blood, pooled and viscous as they sat in the cavity.

And every single one of them was dead.

As the light danced around and collected the macabre scene into data Shane's mind could parse, he realized what he was looking at.

This was the scene of an execution.

Each of the people here had been shot, backs against the wall, seated on the floor. He saw what looked to be a family – a man, a woman, and a child in the woman's arms. They were all frail, thinner than any human Shane had ever seen in person.

He swallowed, suddenly feeling sick to his stomach. He closed his mouth with a fist, as if trying to hold back whatever was threatening to come up.

Each of the one-eyed victims had holes in their head, chest, neck, or face. It had not been a clean execution. It was not thorough or methodical. Some of

these people had been shot in places where death wouldn't have come immediately. They were all very dead now, but he saw one person sprawled face-
first on the floor near a central drain, their blood spilling out toward it.

"Jesus," Grudowski muttered. It seemed their captor was just as horrified
as Shane and Michaela. Still, none of the trio moved away from the door.
They stood halfway in the room, halfway out, as if straddling the line between
life and death itself.

What had happened here? Why had it been done?

He and Michaela had seen firsthand that people from this place – people
whose eyes had been removed – eventually made their way back into the
village. There, he assumed, they led a relatively normal life. At least whatever
a North Korean rural farming community could call normal.

But here... these people never had a chance. They had been tortured,
abused, their eyes gouged out, then left in a cell, only to be brutally executed
later.

Shane stood on the exact spot the murderers would have done it. He realized this was the place they were all looking at in death. It was where their
attacker had stood while firing into all these helpless people.

He coughed, then spat. There was a stench now that he hadn't noticed
before. This room was filled with death, and those who had died were beginning to decay. This was the smell he had smelled before — the reason for the
gunshots earlier, as well.

They killed these people right after I walked in.

Their bodies were fresh, but the stench of death set in quickly, he knew.
But he also knew this was not the first time it had happened — villagers had
been killed here before, left to rot, giving this place the stench of death.

"How – how long?" Michaela asked, unable to finish her question.

"A day, maybe two?" the mercenary offered.

Shane shook his head. He knew the truth — they had been too late. A day,
perhaps hours earlier, they might have been able to stop whoever had done
this.

Well, some of this.

For those who had been murdered earlier, there was nothing they could
do. But for some, Shane could have saved them. Like the man upstairs — how
long had he been kept alive?

Sure, there would have been an army of guards to fight through and no
shortage of employees and scientists working here trying to stop them, but
Shane knew he *would* have fought his way through. He *knew* he would have
been able to save at least some of these people.

These people... who had been executed just like his wife.

He gritted his teeth, balled his fists. Even now, unarmed and at the mercy of a man more than willing to kill them, Shane knew he would have fought alongside him to prevent this.

And then another thought struck him. If these people had been here a day ago, still alive, clinging to hope of rescue or release back into the village, why had they suddenly been killed? Why had it become so crucial to eliminate all of these subjects – prisoners – from the facility?

He didn't want to admit the answer, yet his subconscious wouldn't allow him to ignore it. He looked over at Michaela then, suddenly seeing her eyes on his. He knew then that she knew it, too. She was thinking the same thing.

It wasn't just that he was too late to save them. The people here – whoever they were – knew they were coming. They knew Shane was on his way and felt threatened. It was why they had abandoned the place so quickly. It was why they had left the bomb for him to find.

These people were now dead because of *him.*

A wave of guilt washed over him, a cold, nauseating torrent that threatened to knock him off his feet. He couldn't help but think that if he hadn't been so intent on finding the truth, on exposing what was happening here, these people might still be alive.

Next to him, Michaela let out a shaky breath. Her face was pale, her eyes wide and horrified as she stared at the carnage in front of them. They didn't need to speak to know they shared the same thoughts.

The mercenary turned to them, his face ashen under the harsh glare of the rifle's flashlight. "We need to get out of here," he said, his voice a harsh rasp.

"No," Shane said, his voice stronger than he felt. "We need to document this. We need to make sure people know what happened here."

Michaela nodded her agreement, pulling out her phone. Her hands were shaking, but she held the phone steady as she started to take pictures. Grudowski seemed like he was going to argue, but then he sighed and stepped back.

It was gruesome work, but it was necessary. They couldn't allow the horrors that occurred here to be forgotten. They had to expose the truth, to honor the memory of these people. And hopefully, in doing so, they could ensure that something like this never happened again.

The stench of death, the metallic tinge of blood, grew stronger as they moved deeper into the room. Shane had to fight back the urge to vomit more than once. But they pressed on, documenting every inch of the room.

When they finally finished, the three of them stood in silence, the only sound the faint hum of the generator outside. Shane knew their work here was far from over, but for now, they needed to rest, to process what they had seen.

As they exited the room, Shane cast one last glance over his shoulder at the victims, their empty gazes seeming to bore into his soul. He silently vowed to them that their deaths would not be in vain.

His heart heavy, Shane closed the door behind them, leaving the dead to their eternal rest. His mind was already working, planning their next move. He knew there were probably more rooms like this one, more victims to be found. But for now, they had done what they could. They had brought the truth to light.

And he was determined to make sure that light shone bright enough to expose the atrocities committed here for the whole world to see.

69
SHANE

SHANE CONTINUED DOWN THE HALL, once again trailing behind Michaela, Grudowski right behind him. Any hesitation was met with a slight bump to his back from the mercenary's rifle barrel. Shane was tired, exhausted, and not in the mood for snarky one-liners.

Under other circumstances, Shane would have normally spun around and smacked the guy across the face, or resorted to dirty jokes, but he was weary, frustrated, and beyond one-liners. He wanted to get out of here, with or without Seong Park.

He was reminded once again of his unofficial rule to never retrieve people.

This is why, he thought.

People were squishy, unpredictable. People couldn't be trusted, and their interests rarely aligned with his. Objects were far easier to grab — they didn't argue, didn't fight back, they fetched a price and that was that. Sure, he had to deal with people no matter what — people who paid him, people who wanted to stop him, people who tried to work with him. But generally, retrieving objects was a far safer bet than looking for other human beings.

Especially when an entire hostile government was trying to hide that person from them.

As they walked through, checking into the rooms along this lower corridor, Shane started to become desensitized to the gore and violence. Every room was full of people, all dead, all with their left eyes extracted. They had all suffered enough from the prion implantation and tests themselves, and yet they had all been so brutally murdered and left in these cold cells. It was an egregious waste, and Shane continued to feel the rage building inside of him as they marched on.

He was less affected by the sight of the dead villagers than he was by his growing need to exact revenge on those who had done it. He didn't know if he would ever be face-to-face with one of them, but he vowed then and there to do whatever he could to bring them to justice.

Michaela was sobbing, but she too had become desensitized enough to carry on. She moved forward purposefully, stopping before each door, taking a deep breath, and pushing it open. All of the doors had been left unlocked, not surprisingly.

They reached the last door on the left, the one right before the hallway split into a T intersection to head to the opposite side of the H-shaped layout. The communications room sprawled in front of them just across this hallway, and Shane could see the damage he had done to the place earlier in the dim overhead light.

He turned and faced Michaela, offering his hand. She placed hers in his, and he spoke. "You don't need to do this," he said. "You don't need to see anything else. I know it's been an entire hallway of this madness, but we can end it here."

"Keep it moving," Grudowski snarled from behind Shane.

"You can put one between my eyes or you can wait a *damn* second," Shane snapped back.

He turned back to Michaela, not even bothering to hear the soldier's clipped response. "You've done enough – you've figured out what they were doing here, how they did it. Just let me –"

She shook her head, silencing him. "No, Shane," she whispered. "We are in this together. For better or worse, now I need to know everything. I'm not going to wait in the hall – hell, I'm not even going to let you go first. I'm going to look into each of these rooms, one at a time, staring at these people and letting their faces become part of me. I won't ever forget them."

Shane felt tears beginning to form in his eyes as well.

He nodded, understanding exactly how she was feeling right now. He turned and faced the brute mercenary in the hallway. "Alright, asshole. Last door in this hallway. My assumption is there are more down the other hallway. But after that, I'm *done*. You can kill me or let me go, but I'm not your puppet after that."

Strangely, the mercenary didn't immediately argue with him. He swallowed, then nodded quickly. "Trust me, I want to get out of here as much as you do. Let's just look through these rooms in the interest of being thorough."

Shane nodded in return. He turned back to the door, where Michaela was already pushing the handle down and letting the door click open. As soon as it was open six inches, he thought he heard a sound.

A noise, coming from within the room.

Michaela stepped in first, but he couldn't see her face. She stopped, halted just inside the doorway. Her hair fell over her shoulders and around her neck, masking any clues that would have told Shane what she was thinking or feeling. He stepped in further, pressing the small of her back gently to usher her into the room.

Finally, he was able to see what it was that had caught her attention.

Just like the room upstairs where he found the old man, dead on the table, strapped down with only one eye, he saw her.

Seong Park.

She lay on the table, wearing nothing but a hospital gown with the bottom of it pulled up over her thighs. Her body looked cold, stiff. Yet even in death, Shane could tell she was beautiful. Her hair was long and straight, neatly laying to the side, some of it spilling over her right shoulder. The hospital gown's neck opening was far too large, and he saw some of her shoulder and collarbone peeking through.

Her face was pristine, peaceful, as if she were asleep.

Except for one thing.

"That's her," the mercenary said quietly as he too stepped into the room. "Except –"

"They did it. Those bastards." Michaela turned and pressed herself into Shane's arms. He reacted on impulse, wrapping his hands around her back and shoulders, pulling her in tight. He did not take his eyes off the table, off the young woman lying there.

They had killed her, but not before removing her left eye. Whatever they had been attempting here, even she had not been immune. She had not been able to escape the brutal trial they put everyone else through.

And though he couldn't see a bullet wound, they had killed her afterward, discarding her like a waste product. He saw where her arms and legs were strapped to the table, thick vinyl bindings wrapped underneath the metal and latched somewhere beneath. She had been helpless, forced down and bound.

He noticed her hospital gown pulled up high on one leg, questions nagging at him. He pushed them away, didn't want to even entertain thoughts like that.

Thoughts of what they may have done to her before removing her eye and murdering her in cold blood.

Michaela was crying openly, and even Grudowski seemed unable to comprehend what they were seeing. Shane wondered if this was the end for them, as well. Grudowski had ultimately failed his mission, and Michaela and Shane would be completely useless to him now. Would he just kill them here? Let them bleed out on the floor like he had with Evans, or put a bullet through their heads just like the others had with the villagers?

Shane looked over at the man, wondering if he might be able to attack him here, while he was emotionally compromised. He saw the gun in his hands, noticed his tight grip. It would be a struggle, but...

Seong Park gasped.

Her eye fluttered open, the other missing and covered in a bandage that wrapped diagonally around her head. She made a strange sound, like a cat mewling. But there was pain in it as well. Unmistakable pain.

Michaela sucked in a breath and pushed away from Shane, turning around just as Seong Park lifted her head.

She looked at the newcomers, confused, frightened, hurting. She gasped again, as if trying to catch her breath. She had been asleep – drugged? It was unclear, but it seemed as though she had just awoken from a coma.

She looked over at Shane, speaking a few words in Korean, then switching to perfect English.

"Who — who are you?" she asked, her voice weak but determined. The sight of her, alive yet so vulnerable, filled Shane with a surge of both relief and a renewed sense of purpose.

She was why they were here, and against all odds, their mission was not a total failure.

Not yet.

GRUDOWSKI CUT Seong Park's straps to free her body from the table, while Shane and Michaela took turns catching her up on who they were and why they were here.

Ten minutes had passed since they found the woman in the holding cell, and in that ten minutes, it seemed life had completely returned to her. Her skin was now vibrant, full of color, and though she was in severe pain from the post-traumatic stress injury of having her left eye removed, she seemed to be in relatively good spirits.

"The procedure was two days ago," she said, patting the side of her head next to the bandage on her eye. "They kept wanting information from me – information about the prion research I have been conducting."

"At your university?" Michaela asked.

She nodded. "Yes, I was conducting research on folded proteins, trying to perfect a method for determining what characteristics a subsequent infection caused by those prions might look like. It sounds mundane, but it's actually the holy grail of prion research."

Michaela's face lit up. "Oh, you don't have to convince me. I was working with... someone else about the same thing."

Shane noticed Michaela's eyes drift toward his as she said someone else, but he didn't dwell on it.

"We were making progress in genome sequencing, trying to determine how different racial groups might show different genomic sequences."

Seong Park frowned. "I thought there wasn't much overlap between race and DNA?"

"There's not – at least, not in the sense our society uses the term *race*. But nationality, certain physical characteristics and facial features common to subgroups of people, sure. Those things are genetic traits inherited from thousands of years of DNA overlap."

"But we've been able to identify certain sequences that carry forward certain traits. The research is still in its infancy, but we were making great strides."

Seong Park listened, then was silent for a moment. "Who were you working with?" she asked.

Michaela hesitated, chewing her lip. Shane moved in close to her, putting an arm around her shoulder and giving it a slight squeeze. Meanwhile, Grudowski was at the other side of the table, still holding his rifle out and pointing it at Shane.

Michaela swallowed, then answered. "Kate Riley. She was... his wife."

"Was?" Seong asked. "I am sorry. I knew she was married; I didn't realize you had split up."

Shane's eyes rose at this, and he stared at Seong, sitting on the table. "You knew her?"

A quick shake of her head told him otherwise. "I knew her name. Still do. Just as Dr. Everly has explained, she was at the forefront of research in the genetic realm. I was trying to contact her before... before they took me. I'm so sorry."

Michaela offered a comforting smile. "Don't worry about it. Yes, she was my closest friend and partner." She cleared her throat. "She's... no longer with us."

This seemed to take Seong by surprise more than anything else that had been revealed so far. Her mouth hung open. "I don't understand – how? The men and women at this facility mentioned her name; I heard it on more than one occasion. If I would have had to guess, I would have thought she was working with them."

Now, Shane and Michaela exchanged glances. He cleared his throat, even Grudowski looked over at him to pay attention. "She was killed," Shane said bluntly. "Murdered."

Shane didn't want to get into the details of his wife's murder, and thankfully, Seong Park didn't pry. She simply nodded along, understanding, then offered her thoughts.

"I've been stuck in here for over a week," she said. "Although it's hard to tell how long exactly. I was moved around the facility a few times, yet always locked to a table. They asked me questions for the first four days or so, trying to get information about what I'd learned from prion diseases."

"And what was that, may I ask?" Michaela asked.

"In time," Seong responded. "I think it will all make more sense if I go one step at a time, if that's all right."

"Of course."

"They threatened me, but I learned long ago that their words were just that – empty threats. They didn't hurt me. Not at first. I was terrified the first day, but I started to understand their tactics. They wanted me not just for my information, but because of who my father is."

She looked up at Shane then, as if wanting him to speak. "Chung-Hee Park," he said.

"Yes. He is a very important figure in Korea, as our family has ties to both nations. He's also a very skilled political player, and I believe they wanted *me* to ultimately get to *him*. I was hoping your wife — Kate — could help me before that."

"As we mentioned before, he's the reason we are here," Shane said.

Grudowski nodded as well. "He sent us here to find you."

"Yes, I believe that," she said, smiling slightly. "But I also know my father. His true colors. While he would do anything to get his only child back safe, he would never pass up an opportunity to exert some influence for possible political or monetary gain."

"What are you saying?"

"I don't know exactly," she said, "but I know his company funded a lot of my research. He has his fingers in almost every industry imaginable, and he is very good at putting two disparate pieces of seemingly unrelated information together to produce something he can sell."

"So, you think he wanted to send us here to discover what they were doing in this facility?" Grudowski asked.

She nodded. "I believe so, yes. Even you told me he was playing a game, correct? That Mr. Riley and Dr. Everly believed you were all on the same side for this mission?"

Her words were even, measured, but Shane couldn't help but sense there was a bit of vitriol behind them.

Grudowski tensed. "That's correct," he said. "I don't need to justify myself to anyone. I made a deal, and I will honor that deal. You're all still alive, are you not?"

Shane gripped the edge of the chair he had pulled over for Seong, but she had remained seated on the cold metal table.

"What happened after that?" Michaela asked.

"Well, they got anxious, I guess. Something changed, as if a switch had been flipped. They were decent before, manipulative and threatening, but decent. It's hard to explain, but I got the sense that they wanted me to be scared, but that they weren't going to actually do anything to me."

Shane tried not to look at the bandage covering Seong's missing eye.

"Obviously, they did. The fourth or fifth day – I can't be sure – they yanked me off of the table, threw me in a wheelchair and strapped me to it. Then they wheeled me to another room down the hall and did this."

She pointed to her eye and bit her bottom lip, her nose turning upward in a snarl.

"Did they say why? Clue you in at all as to what they were trying to do?" Shane asked.

"Not really, no. But based on my research, I have a feeling it has something to do with prions. The fact that they have been removing a subject's left eye, specifically, tells me that they are then injecting something into the brainstem directly. It suggests they are attempting to plant some sort of laboratory-produced infection."

"So you saw the other patients?" The mercenary asked.

She shook her head. "No, but I heard them screaming. And when I was first brought here, I had a bag over my head. Once we got inside the building, however, they removed it and I could see everything. Upstairs, in one of the hallways, there was a door... open. I could see inside. I could see it clearly, and I know exactly what it was."

She spoke as though she were about to reveal something unbelievable, but Shane beat her to it. "It's okay, we know. I saw the room full of eyeballs as well. They're from villagers nearby. Michaela and I got a brief tour."

Seong looked horrified. "Innocent women and children, too?"

SEONG PARK LOOKED around at the group in disbelief. Shane Riley, the man she had been speaking with, nodded solemnly.

"Yes," he said. "Whole groups of children and their parents — men and women. All of them had a bandage over their eye, or some sort of patch covering. Some of them didn't. All of them were missing their left eye."

"And it was strange," the woman sitting next to Shane Riley, Dr. Michaela Everly, added. "It was like they were *protective* of their village — they didn't attack us or anything, and they weren't outwardly hostile, but it seemed that they knew we were trying to find this place, and they didn't want us to. They followed us throughout the village, keeping an eye on us — er, watching us — the entire time."

"They followed you all the way here?" Seong asked.

"Well, I bet they would have. But we got... intercepted by someone else."

She frowned, waiting for Shane Riley to continue. Instead, he just shrugged. "That's a story for another day. Point is, this place has been experimenting on those people from the village, and if I had to guess, they're all totally fine with it."

Next to him, Michaela Everly shifted, her face a mask of confusion. "I don't know," she said then. "It's like... it's like they weren't *happy* that everyone from the village was experimented on, but it was sort of like they *knew* it was the only way."

"The only way to what?" the soldier behind Seong asked. Seong turned and looked at him. He was shorter than Shane Riley, a bit thicker, but it looked as though he had spent years in the gym to earn that body type. "I didn't get the chance to interact with them," he added. "You think they're somehow *involved* with this? Beyond being kidnapped and experimented on against their will?"

Dr. Everly shifted again. "I can't help but think that's the case. It's like they were all told they would have a safe and prosperous life if they just complied. That payment for being protected was an eye."

"An eye for an eye," Shane whispered. "Biblical."

"I've never seen anything like it. Or heard of anything like it. Maybe there's an arrangement with the government? Perhaps the village is left alone, their farms along the countryside and the valley their source of food and revenue, and they are allowed to prosper here. In exchange, the North Korean government – whoever was running this place – keeps anyone else – people like us – away."

Seong nodded along. "As macabre as it sounds, it does make a sort of logical sense." She stood up now, feeling that her legs were finally ready to support her own weight once more, and took a few steps around the room. The mercenary standing behind the table made a clicking sound with his mouth, then checked his watch. She sensed he was about to hurry her along, to keep them all moving, but he didn't voice any concern.

"What happened after they took your eye?" Shane asked her.

Now that she was standing, she saw how tall he actually was. He was built and fit as well, though not squat at all like the mercenary guarding them. He seemed leaner, but she could tell he was just as strong. "I honestly don't remember," she said softly. "They put me under for the surgery, thank God. I woke up hours later, I'm sure. I had enough drugs in me to control most of the pain, but it made me terribly drowsy. I drifted off again, and I may have slept for a day. When I woke up, I was parched, thirstier than I'd ever been. Hungry, too."

"Did they feed you?" Dr. Everly asked.

She nodded. "Not exactly a five-star restaurant, but yes. They never wanted to kill me, just experiment on me for whatever reason."

She noticed Shane glancing between them. "Well, about that..." he said. "We found something downstairs. Down the end of this hallway. Turns out they might not have wanted to keep you alive after all."

Her eyes widened. "Really? But why? If I was valuable to them, then –" she cut herself off. Suddenly, she understood. "My father."

The word came out cold, harder than she had intended, but as she continued, she realized the truth her subconscious had been trying to offer. "He's ruthless. I've always known it, but I never thought it would come to this. When they kidnapped me, they wanted information about my research. I never gave that to them, but I have no doubt they would have enhanced their interrogation methods soon enough. But you said my father sent you. It wouldn't surprise me in the least if he's the reason they did this. At least, the reason they wanted to stop the research immediately and get away."

Facing her, Shane swallowed, then nodded. "I was afraid of the same thing. I think your old man wanted to get you back, but he played his hand too quickly. Or at least allowed someone on the inside to see it. They must have gotten spooked when they found out, so they killed the remaining survivors and fled. Everyone, except you."

The reality of it hit her like a physical presence. She stepped backward, feeling the cold edge of the table in her hand. "Yes, that has to be it. They were going to try to extract information from me, perhaps using me as leverage against him. But he forced them into action. Because of him, they had no choice but to change their plan."

SHANE LISTENED as Seong Park spoke. He agreed with her assessment – he had suspected as much earlier. Seong's father wanted not just to get his daughter back safely, but to take any political advantage possible. Men like him dealt in information, and he would have likely killed everyone here on his own to save his daughter and to get access to whatever they were studying if it had come to it.

Instead, he had somehow tipped his hand and given the North Koreans enough clues to discover that he had sent Shane and Evans here. That was the first domino that had caused the others to fall, and though they had Seong Park with them, they were still in danger. There was a bomb in the facility, and Shane wanted to finish debriefing anywhere else but here.

"We should move," Grudowski said. "I'd feel a lot safer having this discussion outside."

Shane nodded, for the first time today agreeing with the man. "You and me both," he said. "Let's get upstairs and find an exit. Once we're outside, it'll be easy to see where we are and which way the village is."

The mercenary smirked. "Why? Your sense of direction not what it used to be?"

Shane squinted, cocking his head to the side as he remembered his escapade trying to get out the northern exit of the facility earlier.

They all moved toward the door, but Shane stopped when he reached the hallway. Michaela looked at him curiously, but he shook his head. *Not now.*

He was working on a plan, one he wasn't sure he would get the chance to enact, but one he needed nonetheless. He couldn't help it – he needed to feel like they had the upper hand once again, or at least feel like he could maintain the status quo. Though the mercenary had said he was willing to keep him and Dr. Everly alive, he now had Seong Park, alive and well.

Shane's own life would be far less important now in the mercenary's eyes.

Grudowski was in the hallway now, waiting for Shane to exit. He did, then turned right and walked up the hallway toward the stairs. The last thing he needed was for this man to discover that Shane might still be working against him and get suspicious. Shane needed to act the part, to pretend everything was fine.

He didn't know if Grudowski would still turn around and kill them once they got outside, but he couldn't take that chance. He also refused to purposefully put Seong Park and Dr. Everly in danger.

They walked the length of the hallway in line, Michaela and Seong side-by-side. Michaela helped the smaller woman with an arm around her waist, though she was quickly regaining her strength. If the pain from the medication's waning had any effect on her, she didn't show it. Shane respected that about her, and hoped he would be able to get her out of this place alive.

No one spoke for the time, everyone lost in their own thoughts. Shane tried to assume what those thoughts might be – Grudowski had one thing on his mind, and was thus the simplest to figure out. If the man were going to kill them, there was a good chance he would have done it already. But that didn't mean Shane and Dr. Everly were off the hook. At any moment, he could put a bullet through their backs and leave them here to die, like he had Jonathan Evans.

While he seemed to be a simple grunt — nothing but a soldier interested in making a buck — Shane knew better than to underestimate Grudowski. Perhaps all of the pandering and posturing earlier was just that: a way to throw Shane off the scent.

Perhaps the mission was, in fact, to kill him and Dr. Everly and leave them to die in the facility. It would be a far cleaner mission, in some respects.

For that reason, Shane kept his ears focused behind him, doing his best to interpret every small noise the mercenary made. If he heard the slightest indication of Grudowski's rifle shifting, or any other quick movements from the man, Shane would duck and roll, preparing to fight.

None of that happened, but the more he thought about it as they walked, the more convinced he was that there was *no way* this mercenary had a good plan to bring him, Dr. Everly, *and* Seong Park back to South Korea safely.

There was no way one man could control three others, even if two were untrained civilians.

And Grudowski would know that.

No, Shane knew almost without a doubt this man was going to kill them after all. He had only waited because he had needed them – he needed their help to find Seong Park, needed Michaela's help to discuss details with her, and needed Shane in case they ran into extra trouble on their way down to find her.

Shane felt the anxiety rising. Fists clenched, his muscles tight. He found himself moving quickly into fight or flight mode, still unconvinced which of the two was the right option. It was very likely he could get away, push himself in front of the other women and up the stairs, where he could easily hide in the depths of the facility. But what good would that do? He would leave Michaela exposed. This man probably wouldn't kill Seong Park, but he certainly would use the other woman as leverage.

Plus, that left the bomb. Though its signal from the communications tower seemed to be severed, Shane didn't trust it. It was still a bomb, a trigger for any number of other explosive devices planted around this place. And by the rushed way they had all evacuated the place — and killed the remaining villagers — he trusted its integrity even less. An accidental shift in the wind might be enough to set it off.

He had no idea, but he didn't want to take the chance. Any extra moment down here with that thing was too long.

That left one option. *Fight*.

He didn't have a clear picture of the mercenary's position behind him, as they had walked the entirety of the hall. Had Grudowski fallen behind? Was he still only a few feet away? These things mattered, since Shane would be attacking unarmed. He had no doubt he could hold his own in a fistfight, so he needed to make sure that's what it came to.

That meant he needed to disarm his attacker, and there was only one way to do that.

He needed to let the man get closer.

He wondered if Grudowski was currently thinking the same thing – that it was finally time to get rid of Shane Riley and Dr. Michaela Everly.

Shane turned around, slowly, his arms raised, trying to feign ignorance about the situation.

But Grudowski was one step ahead. The mercenary's smirk returned, and lengthened into a full smile as he spoke. He was standing about 5 feet away from Shane, his rifle pointed directly at Shane's chest.

"Good guess."

73

SHANE

GRUDOWSKI FIRED, but Shane was already in motion. The shots erupted like tiny missiles on the ceiling, dislodging chunks of concrete that sprayed down on his head.

Shane had reached up and out, clipping the barrel of the rifle just before Grudowski fired. The man still held the rifle, but Shane wasn't finished.

While Grudowski was focusing on getting off a clean shot, Shane barreled toward him, aiming his solid body down toward the shorter man's chest. He wrapped him in a bear hug, a perfect on-the-numbers tackle, and together they flew backwards.

Michaela screamed, but Shane was focusing only on one thing.

He had to get the weapon out of the man's hands.

That part turned out to be easy – Grudowski tossed the rifle to the side to free his own hands.

That's when Shane realized his mistake. He suddenly remembered how powerful the man's fists were, how well-trained he was in hand-to-hand combat.

Shit.

The old adage flowed through his mind. *Fool me once...*

Grudowski's fists went to work immediately. Shane felt his temple rocked by a punch, eliciting stars and immediate dizziness. He reeled backwards, only to be somehow met by another blow that landed behind him, as if the man had reached behind his back and punched him in the spleen.

That one hurt even worse.

Shane did his best to parry the blows. He lifted his arms and covered his face, ducking and dodging as he anticipated where the blows would land.

He got about half right.

Already beaten and only taking more damage, he tried to croak out instructions.

"Run – run!" he stuttered to the two women.

There was no response, and he dared a look from behind his protective elbow in front of his eyes and saw that Michaela and Seong Park were gone. "Get out – get help!"

He wasn't sure who they would call for help, but the women were smart — they would figure it out. The last thing he wanted was for this man to beat him to a pulp, grab his weapon, then chase after Michaela and Seong.

But there was little Shane could do. He tried getting in a few blows – powerful in their own right, but far short of useful – but Grudowski wouldn't let up.

He felt as though the man had been holding pent-up rage for years, looking for a target and finding one in the form of Shane Riley.

Two blows landed to his midsection, but Shane had been flexing his abdomen and they bounced off relatively harmlessly. He used the momentary respite to bring his arms down and send a few punches toward the man's face.

One of them landed alongside Grudowski's jaw, and Shane heard – and felt – a crack. It was too loud to have been just Shane's hand, and he felt a bit of satisfaction knowing that he had finally injured this brute.

But the pain he was feeling on his right hand was *exquisite*. He winced, feeling tears stinging the sides of his eyes, but still he carried on. He followed with an uppercut with his left, aiming for the soft part under the man's chin, but Grudowski was prepared. He ducked his head and Shane's left hand now smashed against his chin.

This time the *crack* was all Shane's.

With two busted hands, Shane roared in agony, opting now to use his elbow as his main striking appendage. He swung his entire torso around, connecting the point of his elbow with a spot near the man's temple, which sent him stumbling backward a few steps. Shane followed that up with another tackle, but Grudowski wriggled free before he could bring him to the ground once more. That likely would have been for the better, as Shane did not want to end up beneath Grudowski throwing punches onto his face.

Shane's hands were screaming in pain, but Grudowski was turning around to prepare for another standoff.

Shane sized up the situation in an instant. Michaela and Seong Park were gone, hopefully heading upward and out of the base to get away. That was fine, as long as they were free he didn't mind dying down here, holding back this assailant.

Though he would prefer not to die. He looked around quickly, noticing the rifle between him and Grudowski. They locked eyes, and Shane knew then that Grudowski was well aware of the situation.

Grudowski had about three extra feet on Shane – if they both started now, Grudowski would get to the rifle far quicker.

And Shane could no longer hold his own in a fistfight. His hands were broken, his face bloodied, and as much as he wanted to smash this guy's head in, he had to admit he was a far better fighter than he was.

He did the only thing he could. He dove to the right, twisted around, and shot toward the stairs.

He heard the man's footsteps behind him, heard him groaning as he reached down to grab the assault rifle that had clattered to the floor.

But Shane was at the stairwell then. The first shots rang out, all wide, and Shane was twisting around the first set of stairs.

Grudowski had given him a brief head start while he picked up the weapon, but now it would be a race through the mazelike tunnels of the research facility.

It was the only advantage Shane had now. He was still faster than this guy — longer legs meant longer strides.

And he had a *very* good reason to stay in front of him.

He sailed upward, aiming for the top floor of the facility. He wanted to get out of the base, to find Seong and Michaela.

But he had one more thing to do first.

SHANE'S LEGS carried him through the facility faster than he could have imagined. He wasted no time listening for Grudowski behind him, assuming the man would be climbing the stairs now to chase after him. He knew his footfalls would tell the mercenary exactly where he was headed, but he didn't care. He knew he could move faster, and that was the only edge available to him.

So he took it.

He didn't see Everly or Park on his way through the base, either. That was good news. It meant they too were running, hoping to stay out in front of Grudowski. Seong Park was the missing piece to all of this, the thing that had kept them alive so far.

It was the *only* thing that had kept them alive.

The mercenary would have simply killed Shane and Dr. Everly when he had shot Evans, leaving them all to die if not for the promise of finding Seong Park downstairs.

And once they had done just that, the man had waited until they were all neatly stacked in a line in front of him — in front of his gun — and was about to kill them. For the first time that day, it seemed Shane's gut had not led him astray. His instinct had pulled him in the right direction, telling him the man was about to attack, that he needed to go on the offensive before he tried to kill him and Dr. Everly.

It had worked — barely. But it was enough, and now Shane was free for the moment. More than anything, he wanted to find Michaela Everly and

Seong Park once more, to reconnect with them and guide them out of the station.

Thanks to his meandering earlier, he was now quite familiar with the layout, and confident that he knew his way around pretty well. He could get them out safely, try to navigate back to the village toward the road they had come in on, and eventually into the peace and safety of the South Korean nation.

But he still had a plan, and against his better judgment, he couldn't ignore it. There was one more thing he needed to do, and he reached the top level of stairs, breathing heavily once more, as he darted forward and out onto the long corridor.

He flew past the rooms they had checked in before, some of them still standing open, revealing either empty offices with desks and tables, or the macabre scene of eyeballs floating in gels inside test tubes on shelves.

All of this he ignored.

His target was further ahead – the room on the right side of the hallway near the offshoot that would lead to the main entrance on the north side. Satisfied he had not gotten turned around again, he raced toward the doorway and almost kicked it open before catching himself.

He didn't need to move stealthily, but he still needed to move carefully. While he thought he knew what would be behind this door, he didn't want to take any chances. He was unarmed, and had loudly announced his presence on this hallway. He rounded into the room, stopping short before entering. He frowned.

He stood still, staring at Jonathan Evans, now seated on the same chair Michaela Everly had been sitting at before, when they had first discovered the prion disease and its treatment. Evans was holding a pistol in his lap, pointed directly at Shane.

Shane squinted. "Evans?"

Evans nodded. "You alone?"

Shane's eyes didn't move from Evans' face. He nodded, then answered aloud. "Yes. But... what is this? What the hell?"

Evans summoned him into the room — Shane, unarmed, couldn't exactly decline — and he stepped forward a few paces. Evans waited, looking as unsure as Shane felt, then spoke again. "Shut the door behind you," Evans instructed.

Shane did as he was told, keeping his hands where Evans could see them. The last thing he needed was to get shot by the very man he was here to save.

He shook his head, cursing to himself. How had he made such a mistake? How had he not seen the signs?

And how was Evans even alive?

"Body armor," Evans said, as if reading Shane's thoughts. "Not as protective in the back, and it still hurt like hell. One of the bullets punctured, causing me to start bleeding pretty bad. I think's just short of the bone, though I'll be bruised for months."

As he spoke longer sentences, Shane heard the wheezing and shakiness in his voice. The man was in pain. Shane wondered if there was pain medication somewhere onsite. He had to assume there was, but had Evans actually found some, then returned here? There was no way he would come back here if he had — which meant he likely hadn't left the room yet.

"What is this? What's going on?" Shane asked.

Evans finally lowered the pistol and set it on the desk, letting out a breath. "Just disaster preparedness, Riley," Evans said, his voice low. He spat. "That *bastard* worked with me for years. I thought I could trust him."

"So it wasn't just all for show?" Shane asked. "You weren't in on it, either? The fact that Grudowski was playing us?"

The man smiled and shook his head, in disbelief. "No, and I have to admit it wasn't much of a ruse. I should've caught it. It's not like he's trained in subterfuge and espionage – he's just a grunt."

Shane nodded as he listened, agreeing with the finer points of Evans' speech.

"Where is he, anyway? And Dr. Everly? Is she okay?" Evans' eyes got frantic for a moment, and Shane saw him sit up straighter in the chair, then wince in pain as he hunched over once more.

"They're fine – well, for now," Shane said. "We need to go. Grudowski is still after them – after *us*. I got away, buying them some time, but just barely."

Evans nodded. "Yeah, that's going to be the trick. I hate to ask, but –"

Shane was beside him in an instant, lifting his arm and putting it over his shoulder. He didn't have a choice now – he had made his choice downstairs. He was going to get Evans out of this place, dead or alive. The man deserved more than just to become a forgotten corpse amongst others.

He deserved more than betrayal, backstabbing.

And he deserved more from Shane.

"You know, I never pegged you as the sappy buddy-cop type," Evans joked. "And yet you came all the way back for little ol' me?"

Shane's squint returned in full force. "Keep thinking I'm doing it for you, pal," Shane snapped. He tried to make his voice sound cold and hard, but it failed.

Evans laughed, eliciting a slight groan at the end. "Hurts like a demon, but

I've been through worse. Let me start walking a little bit, I might be able to loosen it up."

Shane didn't argue – the last thing he needed was to have another full grown man hanging off of him the next time he had to face Grudowski. He listened now, wondering where the man was. If he was coming here to check on Evans – to finish what he had started – Shane would have heard him by now.

That meant only one thing: he was going after Seong and Michaela.

Once again, Evans seemed to read his thoughts. "We need to get out ASAP, don't we?" he asked. "He's going after the girls."

Shane nodded. "Yeah, and that bomb is still down there."

"About that..." Evans trailed off.

Shane stopped at the doorway once more, then pulled back a bit to look at Evans' face. He tried to read the man's expression, but it was inscrutable.

"Walk and talk, soldier. Let's get you outside," Shane said, urging Evans to move.

"Can't argue with that," Evans agreed. "Anyway, I have a feeling we're going to need to hustle a *bit* faster than we initially thought."

"WHAT ABOUT THIS BOMB?" Shane asked. "I thought it was unstable, but didn't I disable it before?"

Evans shook his head as Shane dragged him down the hallway. They were aiming for the northern entrance – the one they had all come in from, and the one they were closest to now. Shane already saw remnants of the firefights that had taken place there, the short-lived battles he and the others had gone through. He saw pieces of furniture – the trashcan he had hidden behind, and tons of empty shell cartridges scattered on the floor from the assault rifles firing.

He even spotted two massive holes in one wall – a new feature he hadn't noticed before.

"No," Evans answered. "You did well – you disabled the communications tower by destroying the computers connected to it. That shut down their connection to the bomb. But it was only temporary. If someone came back to check their work, they'll be in direct contact, and they won't need the communications tower to relay the message."

Shane rolled his eyes. "You've got to be kidding me. So what does that mean? You're telling me at any moment they can –"

He felt it beneath his feet before he realized what was happening. A deep, hearty growl from the depths of the base startled him, causing him to nearly drop Jonathan Evans. Instead, the soldier he was carrying seemed to pull him forward now.

"They just detonated it!" Evans yelled. "Time to move, Riley."

Together, the men stumbled forward over the debris and dead guards.

The explosion was growing in intensity by the split second, and though they were only 15 feet away from the front door, Shane wondered how quickly this place would go up.

Or down, for that matter.

His feet were unsteady now, the floor literally leaning to the side as the detonation consumed the floors beneath them. He imagined concrete pillars running vertically throughout the H-shaped facility cracking and falling, steel girders no longer able to hold the weight.

They were running now, awkwardly arm in arm, both men helping the other equally. Evans was screaming, either in pain or in frustration or just sheer adrenaline, but Shane was silent as he pushed forward. Sweat dotted his brow, and he nearly fell, his knees buckling as a section of floor fell away.

He jumped over it, landing on the side of his foot. He felt his ankle roll and crack, still aware that his hands had been decimated by the mercenary's blows. Everything on him hurt. Every bone seemed to have at least a bruise or three.

Still, he pressed on, aided now by Evans. Both men worked in tandem, holding each other up as the floor twisted, turned, and eventually buckled. A deafening roar was growing by the second, the shrieking wails of failing walls and ceilings and floors flying upward from down below.

Shane raced forward, aiming for the gaping maw where the front door to the facility used to live. There was a sudden shift, and the ceiling above the doorway collapsed, bringing down a massive block of concrete that completely covered the space.

Without hesitation the men changed direction slightly, now heading toward the twisted metal and glass wall next to the doorway. They both turned inward, using their shoulders as leverage to push through the remaining aluminum and glass. Pieces of it shattered, some of it catching in Shane's side, but he ignored the new pain and focused still on getting free.

They were outside now, on the large pavilion spanning the entrance. But they were not safe yet – not by a long shot. They were still well within the confines of the H-shaped layout, and he knew that the integrity of the ground beneath them was going to be compromised by the collapsing facility and its subterranean levels.

He also got an answer to a question he had earlier – he saw pieces of the above-ground sections of the facility collapsing – the far reaches of the H-shaped layout of the building. The perpetrators *had* planted more than one bomb – while he had found the main detonator and timer, he had correctly assumed that the North Koreans had left more than just a single explosive device.

They had rigged everything up in tandem – likely planting the explosives in the facility long ago, in preparation for something like this.

Shane and Evans continued hobbling through the courtyard, onto the grassy field where the helicopter pad sat. They were aiming for the fence they had come in from, where they would then turn left, follow the fence and perimeter of the place, and maintain a safe distance from the crumbling complex.

The ground began settling, even as Shane heard and felt the results of the detonations. Pebbles and small pieces of debris pelted the back of his neck, tiny pinpricks as they jogged. Evans was no longer screaming, his voice just a low groan, his teeth gritted as he fought through the pain of his bullet wounds. Shane thought he saw fresh blood dripping from the makeshift bandage he had tied around his torso, but he couldn't stop to render aid.

Neither man spoke as they reached the fence, finally stopping to catch their breath. Hands on his knees, Shane turned and watched as the entirety of the building collapsed in a huge cloud of dust. It was like a mushroom cloud of concrete and dirt, propelled upward by both the blast and the pressure wave caused by thousands of tons of concrete collapsing inward on itself.

It was an incredible sight, horrifying and terrible, yet freeing all at the same time. They had narrowly escaped death, and Shane was grateful for that.

And Evans was alive, standing next to him and catching his breath. That was a win.

An even bigger win would be if Grudowski had been trapped inside when the place went down. Could he be so lucky?

He wanted to wish it into existence, but at the moment all he could think about was the safety of Michaela and Seong Park.

MICHAELA EVERLY HEARD THE RUMBLING, and her feet pushed her forward faster without her overtly acknowledging what they were doing. She subconsciously knew what was going on, and it was only a second later before her conscious mind picked up on it.

"The bomb!" she shouted. "It's blowing up... they detonated it somehow."

Thankfully, Seong Park didn't stop and ask for clarification – she didn't need any. The younger woman ran in front of Michaela, already knowing her way through the facility, or at least following clues that would lead them out.

Michaela didn't offer her any help – from her memory, she knew they were in a long straightaway that would lead to an exit. She had seen the doors on the very tips of the H-shaped building as they had passed to find the north entrance, and now all she wanted to do was get out.

It didn't matter where they ended up.

Grudowski was still behind them, the mercenary moving a bit slower through the place but no less menacingly. He had fired a few potshots toward them, to keep them unquestionably aware of his presence, but it wasn't until they had reached this long section of straightaway on the south side of the building before he had a good shot.

Before now.

She heard the man whistling, an absolutely terrifying sound against the backdrop of the low rumbling of the explosion. She thought she felt the ground wavering beneath her feet, thought she felt it undulating...

Seong Park slowed down, and Michaela nearly bumped into her. She pushed her hand out and placed it on the woman's back. "We can't stop, Seong, we can't slow down. Not yet. Let's get outside first."

That seemed to give Seong Park strength, and the woman burst forward with a newfound speed that led her to the door. She had no idea if it was unlocked, but Seong pressed the bar with both hands and Michaela heard a click.

She saw a blinding white light as the door cracked open.

Michaela said a quick prayer of thanks as Seong Park burst through the opening door, just as three rounds pinged into the wall directly next to her. She instinctively ducked away but forced herself to keep moving forward. She flew through the door as well, not bothering to turn around and close it. It was on a hydraulic arm, and would slowly shut on its own. There was no way to lock it from outside, so it would be suicide to stand and wait for the mercenary to barge through as well.

Besides that, the base was collapsing, and she wanted to get as far away from it as possible.

She was glad they had made it in time – at first, she and Seong Park had gotten lost on the lower levels, purposefully at first. She wanted to make it as difficult as possible for Grudowski to find them, so she had Seong move silently with her as they crept through some of the darker corridors on one of the mid-subterranean levels. For a few minutes, they had hidden in silence in one of the rooms where they had found the bodies.

They had waited for signs the soldier was following them, all the while trying to push back the sensation that all of the single-eyed corpses lining the walls in this room were staring at them. Next to her, Seong Park had sobbed quietly. Michaela didn't offer any words of encouragement – she needed to keep quiet – but she knew there was also nothing she could do. She understood the woman's reaction to this place, to this room.

She had felt the same way earlier.

After they left that room, they ran to another one down the hall, closer to the stairs. Michaela thought she had heard the sound of footsteps then, so she had pushed them into another room, this one smaller, no larger than a closet. They waited there for another half-minute, but Michaela eventually knew it was time to leave. If they had calculated correctly, Grudowski would assume they had moved upward and out of the facility, trying to put physical distance between themselves and the man. Hopefully, he wouldn't assume they were just hiding down here.

It was a chance they needed to take – they needed to get out and find Shane, see if he had made it away from the mercenary. Michaela didn't want to consider the alternative: that Shane Riley had succumbed to the mercenary's blows, and was now either dead or dying on the floor downstairs.

Once leaving the closet, they crept up the stairs quickly until they'd reached the top level. There, they waited again in silence until Michaela felt confident they were alone.

That had been their mistake.

If only they'd traversed the corridor when they first reached it, they would have been outside already. But by waiting, they had inadvertently synced their arrival with that of Grudowski, who was coming up the far set of stairs.

They had been halfway down the hall when he began running toward them.

Their mad dash ended with them in broad daylight, running over the flat field situated at the bottom of the quarry-like valley to the south of the facility. To her right, she saw mounds laying in the grass – the dead guards Grudowski, Shane, and Evans had killed earlier that day. Up above, she saw their vehicle, where the standoff between the two sets of guards above and below had taken place.

But she continued running straight. There was a lone tree at the far side of this valley, due south, and she was hoping it would provide enough cover for them to start climbing the steep ridge on the other side of it to get to the road. Anywhere else along this ridge and the mercenary would have a clear shot of both of them.

It wasn't a great plan, but it was the plan she had.

She heard the door opening, the mercenary barreling through it and allowing it to pound against the collapsing facility's outer wall. She dared a look over her shoulder and saw Grudowski running, fighting against the ground as it buckled beneath his feet.

It was incredible, like watching an earthquake in slow motion. But that earthquake sped up, and eventually he fell to the ground.

Michaela stopped then, turning to watch as the building finished collapsing behind him. He got to one knee, then back on his feet, then started running again, only to fall once more.

She didn't watch the rest – the building was in shambles, almost completely destroyed, and Grudowski was stumbling. There was a good chance he would be pulled under as well, to become one of the many corpses beneath the dirt.

Right now, getting to that tree was her sole goal. Seong was now ahead of her by about 15 paces, and obviously running for the tree as well. Michaela was working through the plan in her mind – envisioning their route up the ridge toward the road that would lead back to the village.

And that's when she saw them.

Seong noticed them as well. She slowed, then halted, just 20 feet in front of the tree. Both women looked up, looking at the ridge that Michaela hoped would be their salvation.

Only the ridge wasn't empty anymore.

Faces dotted the ridge, all with one eye, the other missing completely or covered with a bandage.

Those faces were attached to the bodies of the villagers, who had crept up silently onto the ridge, watching as the facility that had taken their eye from them vanished into the ground.

She wondered what they were doing, whether they were here to somehow pay tribute to this place or for another purpose. They must've started coming this direction a while ago, so there was no way they could have known the facility would be detonated, would be destroyed.

That's when she noticed their weapons.

They weren't looking at the facility, watching it as it collapsed into the ground. They weren't looking over her head at Grudowski, either.

They were all staring at *her*. At Seong Park.

In their hands, sticks and rocks and even knives and longer blades. A hodgepodge of whatever weapons they could find in their rural, poverty-stricken existence.

Each of them was staring down at the two women approaching the ridge, and Michaela couldn't help but interpret the look she was getting from each of them.

They were not happy.

MICHAELA

THE VILLAGERS BEGAN their descent down the ridge. It was a steep slope, about twenty feet high, filled with loose rock and dirt. Yet the villagers traversed it as if it were a paved city sidewalk. Michaela watched in horror as the one-eyed North Korean farmers and villagers moved menacingly towards her, weapons clutched in their hands.

A sense of dread crept over her as she realized their intent seemed to be to close the distance for an imminent attack.

But why? What had she done to invite this behavior?

She surmised that her mere presence here likely had instigated the villagers' disdain. She and Shane had passed through the small town of thatched-roof huts and stone buildings as foreigners, outsiders.

She didn't look Korean, because she wasn't. And Shane would have stuck out even more to these people, and she got the impression these people had gathered their forces and were marching toward the facility in response.

The sight of another Korean among them, Seong Park, seemed to have little effect. The villagers advanced down the ridge, encircling Seong and Michaela. The tree they had hoped would serve as a protector now seemed destined to mark their final resting place.

Silent as shadows, the villagers focused their attention on her, faces filled with a potent mix of anger and confusion. Michaela knew little about rural North Korean life, but she recognized this universal reaction to strangers: suspicion and hostility, often escalating to violence.

They treated anyone they didn't know as hostile, as outsiders that needed to be killed.

Or punished.

She wondered if that was it, then. All of these people were missing an eye – were they going to try to take hers? Would they force her to give up her left eye in order to satisfy some strange religious belief?

Perhaps this village, set in such close proximity to the terrifying research lab to the north, had bought into an old myth, fabricated to keep these people tame, to keep them from acting out?

She knew the facility lying in ruins behind her had been here for decades. Built sometime in the World War II era, perhaps this place had been performing its research for almost 100 years. That would certainly be long enough to establish enough myth and fear around the place that generations of villagers would pass down to their children that this was simply the way of life here.

The more she thought about it, the more it made sense. She was witnessing a symbiotic relationship. The research facility needed subjects – they needed to remove the left eye of these people in order to inject the prion disease into them for further testing – and these people needed protection, likely from their own government.

By working together, offering the villagers as test subjects, and receiving protection in return, both of their needs would be met.

And she had to admit, besides the last-minute murdering of the remaining test subjects in the base, the vast majority of the villagers were living a full life, albeit with one less eye. It seemed the people running this facility were studying the effects of the prion disease on these people, but then giving them the cure when those tests had been completed.

It wasn't exactly humanitarian, and she wasn't under any illusion that those people were going to be up for a Nobel Peace Prize anytime soon, but it wasn't a completely one-sided affair.

And maybe that's why these villagers were so zealous about protecting their local eye-removing laboratory. Perhaps they not only had deep-seated religious beliefs but knew that in the long term, their sacrifice was paid back with protection and a relatively safe life.

And Michaela, Shane Riley, and the others had come here to ruin that.

The results of their excursion were lying behind her now, nothing but rubble.

A male villager, easily in his late 70s, approached. He held one of the few blades she had seen – a long, sickle-like curved knife she assumed was some sort of butcher's utensil. He didn't look like the stereotypical butcher, however. He was shirtless, thin and frail, and she saw his sinewy muscles on inch-thick arms. He looked emaciated, though it was likely a combination of living a hard, farming life and being nearly an octogenarian.

He spoke quickly, in a strange dialect of Korean. "You are not welcome here," he said.

She understood the Korean, nodding just as quickly as he spoke. "Yes, I'm starting to see that. But whatever this was, we didn't –"

"You have brought down pain on our family. On our people."

Michaela watched in awe as he spoke. The human in her couldn't help but be amazed by the fact that she was conversing with someone so far removed from what her world was like. These people thought of themselves as family, as one body.

It seemed she had been right about her assumption – that these people believed outsiders were the enemy.

"We are not here to hurt you," she said.

The man frowned deeply. "You have *already* hurt us," he said. "This place and the people there were *our* protection. They watched over us. Now they are gone, returned to the dirt."

The Korean was clipped, though the dialect had a slight lilt to it, common in many rural communities around the world. It was the same language she knew well, but his voice would place him far away from any modern cities.

"Those people *hurt* you," she tried. "They took your *eyes*. Women and children as well. How can they justify this?"

"The sickness does not spread after we give our eyes," he said, as if this was a perfectly acceptable explanation.

"The sickness? What are you talking about? The prion disease?"

The man nodded. "The sickness takes us, unless we sacrifice. It is a small sacrifice to make us whole again, to let us live a long life. For that reason, we are happy for our children to know our ways, to experience this wholeness with us."

So that's it. The disease – the prion infection – was something that threatened this population of people. Why? Did the researchers here purposefully allow it into this community? Did they spread it somehow amongst these villagers, promising that they would be okay only if they allowed themselves to be experimented on?

"But we are not here to hurt you," Michaela said again, reiterating.

Next to her, Seong Park nodded, smiling at the man as if trying to lower his defenses.

Michaela paused, smiling, then spoke again. We came to find out what this place was – and to find her."

Michaela felt bad potentially outing Seong like that, but she felt she had no other choice. She needed a bargaining chip, and if she could convince this man and his villagers that Seong Park was the sole reason they had come, perhaps he would let them leave in peace.

"She is also an outsider," he said. "But she has made the sacrifice." He lifted a bony finger up and pointed at her missing eye. "She is healed, made whole now. The sickness cannot claim her."

"Can it claim me?" Michaela asked. The scientist in her was curious now, she wanted to know what these people knew. What they believed this sickness would do.

He nodded solemnly, his eyes falling to the ground. "We must take you, to prevent you from spreading the sickness. No one who comes to our village may leave if they are from the outside. Unless they make the sacrifice."

Michaela's face fell. She was horrified. They would *take* her? How would they —

"Remove her clothes," the man said suddenly, turning his head to the men and women gathered around them. "She must become the sacrifice she has not made."

"No! Don't remove my —" Michaela tried to argue, but hands were on her arms and sides already, tugging and pulling at her clothing. "Stop it! We can explain why —"

They ripped her sleeves, pulled her shirt up almost over her bra. She pulled it back down quickly, but they were starting in on her pants, trying to unbuckle her belt.

If you're just going to kill me, why do I have to be naked first? she thought.

She was about to voice these concerns aloud, but next to her, Seong watched, horrified, as even more hands held her back. The villagers had surrounded her as well, pulling her toward them and away from Michaela.

She was screaming, but Michaela couldn't hear anything.

No, wait. It was her own voice she was hearing. She screamed again, the terror reddening her vision as she felt a blade picking at the skin on her exposed side. It danced over her torso, and onto her back, where it found more fabric. It tickled, but she shivered. She felt it ripping, cutting through the outer layer as the hands moved over her body, trying to tear the clothes from her.

Their hands were rough, not trying to be gentle. She looked at Seong Park and saw the woman trying to plead with those holding her, but it was no use. The villagers' shouts and cries turned into whooping cries of victory, as if this was some prize prey they had captured and brought to camp for roasting.

Rocks began pummeling her; she felt one hit the back of her head. She saw stars, saw the sun fading from her vision.

She began to cry, unable to hold back the tears as she screamed and cursed the villagers. They continued working over her, her pant leg now torn, revealing her calf. Her boots had been removed, and she was laying backwards, cradled by more hands and arms.

She stopped fighting, realizing that it was hopeless. Every time she moved, something struck her back, something dug into her flesh, something hit her.

She forced her eyes closed then, hoping it would be quick.

GUNSHOTS RANG OUT, and Shane snapped his eyes in that direction. He and Evans were walking side-by-side still, Evans with his arm around Shane's shoulder to help support his weight. The man seemed to be doing okay, the blood once more stanched, but moving more slowly to keep it that way.

At the sound of the gunfire, Shane began moving quickly, eliciting a slight cry of pain from Evans. But he knew the man didn't care - he wanted to get back to Michaela and Seong Park as much as Shane did.

"See anything?" Evans asked.

Shane shook his head, not replying. They were walking around the tip of the H, near the southern side of the base. The facility had completely collapsed in on itself, leaving mounds of concrete, twisted metal, and debris. Piles of rocks spilled outward, leaving huge ten-foot-tall piles making it impossible to see what lay on the other side.

They hustled over as the sound of more gunfire out through the air. Shane surveyed the field then, saw the lumps where he and Evans' team had killed the guards before their arrival at the facility's doorstep. He saw the truck up there, saw the road leading back to the edge of the quarry and down to the village.

And he saw the villagers.

Their skin, dark against the bright sunlight, undulated and danced as they moved. They were holding objects, some long and pointed and others dull and round. Shane couldn't see what they were doing, but he did notice that they were apparently angered by the gunshots.

He saw why, now. A few villagers were clutching their sides or their legs, one of whom was on their knees. He watched as more gunfire rang out, separating a few villagers from the rest of the pack as they moved toward the sound as well.

He turned his head to the left, trying to see the cause of the gunfire.

There.

He saw their old friend Grudowski standing about a hundred feet away, firing wildly into the crowd. He was backing away slowly, trying to keep distance between himself and the now progressing villagers.

A few of the younger villagers – all teenage boys, it seemed – ran toward the mercenary. He fired at the first one, who fell to the ground with a dull thud.

Shane was pulling Evans along much more quickly now, and they neared the site of the exchange. He tried to cut the distance in half, putting equal space between the mercenary and the crowd of villagers, as he wasn't sure which side to focus on first.

Grudowski cut down another villager, but dropped the rifle to his side and began backing away more quickly as he realized the three villagers heading for him were speeding up.

Surprisingly, Grudowski then stopped, dropping to a knee. Apparently deciding that the remaining three young villagers were an easy enough target, he popped another magazine into the bottom of his rifle and started firing again.

The third and final villager fell at his feet only a few seconds later.

He stood up, turning his head and glancing over at Shane.

Grudowski yelled something to Shane, but he couldn't make out the words over the sound of the screaming villagers still congregated by the tree to his right. The mercenary charged forward then, holding his rifle up and shooting a few rounds into the air.

Finally, this seemed to make the villagers stop whatever it was they were doing.

Shane made his choice then – the mercenary was heading that direction, so he and Evans would as well. He still hadn't seen Michaela or Seong, but there was something nagging at the back of his mind. He felt uneasy, his stomach rising in his throat, but he kept moving forward, kept pushing toward the throng of North Korean villagers.

Shane and Evans reached the outskirts of the crowd at about the same time as Grudowski. Grudowski wasted no time — he plucked one of the smaller stragglers from the back of the group – a man likely in his 50s or 60s, and shot him point blank.

This once again got the villagers' attention. Whatever they had been doing, they stopped completely and turned to face the newcomers now. Some dropped rocks that they had been holding.

Shane ignored the mercenary, pushing through the people now to try to get to the center. His hands hurt as his broken knuckles impacted arms and bodies, but he didn't slow. He would use fists again if he had to, regardless of the damage it was doing to his hands.

He reached the center of the circle and gasped.

His voice caught in his throat, and he felt unable to breathe.

He saw Michaela then, lying on the ground, bloodied and broken, eyes closed, half of her shirt and a pant leg ripped away. Seong was nearby, being held by two villagers.

He clenched his jaw, trying to work it free as he attempted to analyze what the hell had happened here.

SHANE

SHANE WAS SCREAMING. "What happened here? What the *hell* happened?"

He was frantic, his mind racing. Even as he screamed, shouting obscenities at anyone who looked his way, he knew *full well* exactly what had happened here.

They had attacked her.

They had *killed* her.

Shane was going to tear off the heads of each of these people, with nothing but his hands.

With his bare, broken, hands.

He no longer felt the pain, no longer felt sidelined by the rush of blood to his extremities caused by the trauma of punching relentlessly.

He tore through the crowd, lifting entire human beings and tossing them aside as if they were rag dolls. They might as well have been for as little as they weighed and how fueled by adrenaline Shane was.

Evans was next to him, trying to calm him down. "It's okay... she's still – she's still alive."

Shane realized he was trying to look through tears, his entire world blurry. He hadn't noticed that Michaela had tried sitting up, had pushed off with her elbow and was now working upward. Evans started forward, but Seong Park beat him there. The smaller woman lifted Michaela up gently, cradling her in an arm.

The two villagers who had been holding her stepped backward, pressing themselves into the crowd, trying to disappear.

It wouldn't matter. Shane would kill them all. One at a time, each of these men and women – even the teenage boys – would die.

Why had they done this? *How* could they have done this?

He saw their weapons, their sharpened sticks for spears, rocks for blunt weapons, and even some small blades, likely converted kitchen knives and shop implements. These people had nothing – no money to their name, living as subsistence farmers in a region far removed from even a moderately-sized city. To think that they had gathered here for one purpose – to kill an unsuspecting outsider – made his blood boil.

What would have happened if Grudowski had not fired at them and stopped their progress? Shane knew there was a chance that his gunfire could have accidentally hit Michaela or Seong Park as well, but he remembered how thick the throng of villagers had been, how well protected from the gunfire Michaela and Seong had been.

But not protected from the crowd itself. It felt biblical, as if watching a scene from 2,000 years ago. Men mostly, but even women coming out to stone the sinner.

What had she done? What sin had she committed to constitute such an act of violence?

And who the hell were these people to assume they had the right to enact this form of justice?

Shane watched one of the younger villagers – a boy who couldn't be older than 13 or 14 – as he came and crouched near Shane's right side, holding a rock in his right hand.

He snarled loudly at the kid, squinting through barely open eyes.

The intensity of it scared even Shane. The kid jumped backwards, drifting into a small group that had separated from the main crowd of villagers.

Shane pulled Michaela gently to her feet, Seong helping Evans with his own injury. They all needed medical care, but Shane's only goal was getting Michaela away from these people. Her head fell onto his shoulder, and he embraced her, lifting her and carrying her along. She wrapped her legs around his for support, her hands gripping the small of his back tightly. He felt nothing as he pushed through the people, felt nothing as they began clucking at him in their native tongue, felt nothing as he heard Evans trying to reason with him.

"...they don't mean it, Riley, this is just part of their –"

Evans voice was cut short as the sound of a rock striking flesh cut him off. "What in the name of St. –" even the man's obscenity was cut short as a stick then swung around and caught Evans on the side of his head. It wasn't a heavy blow, but Shane understood what was going on.

"They're attacking again," Seong Park said. Her voice was barely above a whisper, but it was as if she was speaking directly into Shane's ear. He heard it clearly, nodded once in understanding, then sped up, holding Michaela the entire time.

Seong was helping Evans along, but the man was doing fine on his own, using a meaty left fist to clock villagers as they rushed him. Sticks and rocks tumbled away, useless against the much more powerful soldier. He roared in anger and triumph as he took out a tall, thin man with a swipe of his left foot. The villager screamed in agony as he landed on a twisted wrist.

And then they were free. They punched through the outer layer of villagers and continued moving through the open field.

Shane felt eyes on him, and turned left. He set Michaela down, readying himself for another attack, this one from Grudowski.

Grudowski had been standing apart from the villagers, working his way toward Shane's group. He had his rifle out, but he was still pointing it at the group of villagers while he watched Shane. He fired a few rounds into one of the younger ones, a woman holding a small rock she had been preparing to throw directly at Shane.

She fell, screaming, then went silent. Another round took out a teenager.

Shane couldn't help but feel the horror at dozens of rural farmers and villagers meeting their demise at the hands of a Western-made, high-powered rifle. If he hadn't seen the entirety of the scene play out, Grudowski's actions would look like an insufferable injustice.

Instead, he was reminded that the mercenary was just the *first* of the many people he had vowed to remove from the face of the planet today.

But killing the villagers was now a lower priority to him. Evans and Seong were standing close, hovering around Michaela as she pulled herself up from the ground. Shane's eyes were on Grudowski, but he focused on Michaela. It seemed she was okay — more rattled than injured. She was making noise, her head rocking side to side, but otherwise able to stand on her own.

He moved over, using his wide frame to block her from view, turning to face Grudowski head-on.

For a moment, all was still. The villagers had stopped their useless onslaught against his group, now scared of the angry weapon in Grudowski's hands.

Shane had not forgotten about his and Grudowski's standoff, and it seemed everyone else in the world was also anxiously awaiting their next move.

80

SHANE

GRUDOWSKI LOOKED OVER AT SHANE. They locked eyes. Grudowski's smile returned, the sly grin that told Shane the man's plan had not changed.

"Well, I see you found our friend," he said. "Welcome back to the land of the living, Evans. For now."

Shane snarled an unintelligible response, but Evans just shook his head, stepping up next to Shane. "I'm a little bit harder to kill than that, Grudowski," he said.

Shane kicked himself for not stopping to find a weapon while he was running through the base. They were sitting ducks again — Grudowski the only one of them armed.

The dust and debris from the facility's implosion had finally begun to settle, revealing a beautiful, blue sky. He looked up at it, noticing the sun beginning to descend toward the opposite side of the valley, trying to calculate how long he had been here.

How much time had passed since he had come into this valley to die.

Their situation had not changed substantially. Sure, Grudowski had been busy keeping the violent villagers at bay, but he knew the man was carrying at least two more full magazines. It wouldn't take that many rounds to totally neutralize that threat.

His group was largely unarmed. Evans had a sidearm, but Shane knew how long that would last against Grudowski's assault rifle, and the man was too injured to draw it, aim, and fire before Grudowski could react.

Shane thought for a moment. *If we can distract him, I might be able to get off a shot.* He wondered if his bruised and broken hands could even handle that.

"Evans," Grudowski said suddenly. "Toss your pistol over here."

So much for that idea.

"Like hell I'm going to do that," Evans said. "Why don't we just slow down, figure out exactly –"

A single shot rang out, Grudowski jerking the rifle upward and firing directly above Evans' head. "Next one *won't* miss, and I don't need to remind you all about the status quo here. Seong Park stays alive until the very end. It's *you three* who die first. So: any volunteers?"

"Jesus, Grudowski. Fine." Evans yanked the pistol out from behind him, groaning with the exertion, cradling it between his thumb and forefinger. He held it up so Grudowski would see it wasn't a threat, then he tossed it lightly.

It landed about halfway between them, maybe six feet away.

Grudowski shook his head, his smile fading. "Neat trick," he said. "You think that's funny or what?"

Evans just shrugged, and Shane noticed him wince in pain as he did. "I'm not here to make it easier for you."

"You already *have*, Evans. You're well-trained, a good leader, too. But you slipped up – all that training and leadership ability means that once you begin to trust someone, it's *real hard* to lose that trust."

"Well, consider it gone."

"The thing about trust is that it's very subjective. Anyone want to take a guess as to what's *not* subjective at all?"

Shane knew Grudowski was trying to get them riled up, to get them angry before he killed them all. And he had their attention. Shane's group stood still, silent, waiting for Grudowski's next words.

Even the villagers seemed interested in what Grudowski was saying. They had all congealed together into a singular mass, their bodies pressed tightly together as they shivered in fear. They were a fickle bunch, apparently. Able to go from trying to kill another human being with their bare hands with sticks and stones to shaking in fear at the sight of a person trying to do the same to them.

If Shane's own life wasn't on the line, he would've laughed. Thankfully, no one offered a response.

"I get it," Grudowski said. "No one wants to play ball. No one wants to give me any more ammunition. Well, I'll tell you the answer anyway. Here's what's *not* subjective: money. Untraceable, cold, hard cash. *Lots* of it. And this is just the beginning. *That's* what real trust is really built on, Evans. Money.

Take note — though I'm sure you're not going to need notes where you're going."

"You gonna kill me then?" Evans asked. "Aim for the head this time, if you can. Finish what you started."

There was a brief pause while Grudowski seemed to consider his options. The brute looked back at him as if he were speaking Greek. Then, with a simple shrug, he lifted the rifle and pointed it the 12 or so feet toward Evans. "Yeah. That's exactly what I'm going to do."

Shane involuntarily shut his eyes, he heard the snap. The pull of the trigger, followed by the blast from the rifle. A shriek from one of the women standing next to him, cries and shouts of surprise from the villagers.

In an instant, he assessed the damage to his person. There was none, of course. As he'd expected, Grudowski had killed Evans first. Likely making good on his promise, not wanting to waste more time with useless speeches.

Shane waited a few more seconds, opening his eyes but looking down at the ground. He wanted to be ready to attack, to run toward Grudowski and draw his fire toward himself. He had taken two steps forward, but had stopped when he realized there had been no other gunshots.

Grudowski's rifle was silent, after only a single shot.

Shane looked up.

Behind him, Evans shouted something, but Shane couldn't focus on the man's words. He continued forward, running once more, knowing then that his plan was useless.

Because Grudowski was already dead.

The man's head had simply ceased to exist, disappeared in a cloud of haze and mist. Reddish droplets sprinkled down to the grassy field, larger patches of blood catching dried strands of grass and causing them to sink down.

The man's body joined his blood. He fell forward, his knees locked in place and his entire frame slamming downward. Shane felt the thud, now only a few feet away. He didn't reach a hand out, didn't try to stop the man's fall. It would've been useless, and he didn't care to help the man down anyway.

Even without his head, Shane wouldn't have wanted to help.

"What the *hell* was that?" he heard Evans asking. Shane just stared, looking down at the body on the ground, the man's rifle lying next to him.

There was running, footsteps behind him, and Dr. Everly and Jonathan Evans came over. Seong Park followed behind, moving slower. The villagers were frantic now, their shouts and cries rising in volume, then subsiding as they realized no more shots had been fired.

Everyone was looking around.
Everyone was trying to find the gunman.

81
JIN-TAK

JIN-TAK YEON ASSESSED the scene in an instant. The moment he fired, he felt confident it was the right move. Far up above, 400 yards away, he watched as down in the valley the villagers attacked the two women. He knew one was Dr. Michaela Everly, and he assumed the other was Seong Park. He had never met her in person, but he had seen pictures and knew all too well that her father was behind most of the reason for this mishap.

And a mishap it was.

Jin-Tak had considered firing into the crowd of villagers earlier, but even though he was a highly capable sniper, and winds were nil, he didn't want to risk hitting either of the women. Nor did he feel comfortable attacking the villagers.

They were doing what they always did. These people believed in something so powerful he couldn't fault them for their barbaric tendencies toward outsiders. Sure, the two women they had started attacking were innocent, but the villagers did not know any better. It would be like screaming at a toddler for an outburst — they were just doing what was appropriate for a group that had been oppressed and misled for generations.

So he had sat and watched, horrified and stunned into inactivity. Eventually, he saw Shane Riley and the leader of the mercenary group he had come with round the corner of the building that had recently collapsed.

He knew now what had happened.

He understood how — and why — he had been betrayed.

It didn't make anything right — that would be up to him — but at least the full picture was becoming clearer now.

As he watched, Shane Riley and the other man stumbled toward the group, ignoring a third mercenary standing a ways off from the group of villagers attacking Michaela Everly and Seong Park. He watched as Riley ran forward and began peeling villagers off the pile to get to the women, to save them. Even from here, Jin-Tak thought he could hear the man's shouts and cries as he pulled one enraged villager after another away.

And then the mercenary standing apart from the group began to fire his weapon. The villagers stopped their attack, some of them trying to make a break for the mercenary and attack him.

All who ran toward the man were cut down. Brutally, efficiently, and – Jin-Tak had to guess – unceremoniously. This man didn't care for the villagers, why would he? He simply wanted to complete the mission.

And that's when things began to click into place for Jin-Tak Yeon. He knew what role he had played in all of this – both knowingly and unknowingly. Now, he was beginning to understand the others' roles as well. Shane Riley, Michaela Everly.

And this new factor — the mercenary who clearly was not part of either team. Whatever loyalties he'd had upon coming here, he had abandoned inside the facility.

So Jin-Tak had made his choice. As the battle dissipated, the villagers separated briefly, just long enough for the women, Shane Riley, and Jonathan Evans to escape. They reconvened into a tight group of people, but stood silent watching the mercenary who still pointed a gun menacingly at them. Eventually, the man had turned and pointed the rifle at Riley's group instead.

Jin-Tak couldn't hear their words, couldn't hear the exchange, but he could see their expressions through his scope. He could see the heated argument, even the sly grin the mercenary wore as he threatened them.

That had been the final straw. Jin-Tak knew all about strategy and tactics, all about status quo and rules of engagement. He knew about warfare, espionage, surprise.

There was a very small chance he was wrong, and his actions now would simply make matters worse.

But that was an infinitesimally small chance.

His confidence only grew as he lined up the shot, his finger depressing the trigger. The gun lurched beneath him, racking through his prone body, and a small cloud of dirt picked up. But he was focused only on the round.

Only one shot.

There was a military precision, a keen interest in wondering if his shot would hit the mark, that flowed through him.

But there was also a somewhat personal interest. An *emotional* interest.

He was doing this for his father. A father he knew now was gone, dead. A father who had been taken from him, lied to just as these villagers had been lied to, and told to work or risk death.

He knew all of it was a façade – that his father had died the moment they had ripped him from his family's home. Jin-Tak's entire life had been spent training, preparing for this moment, earning the skills and experience he would need to find the enemies who had taken his father from him.

But he had never expected those people to be the same ones who had employed him. He had been led astray, had been sold the very lies everyone else around him seemed to believe. He had been told one thing, only to discover another, over and over and over again throughout his military career. Finally, mere days ago, he began understanding the clues that surrounded him. And only now did he understand their meaning.

Satisfied his shot was true, he considered packing up his rifle and beginning his journey down the ridge. Instead he stayed for a moment, watching.

The mercenary was now missing most of his head, just a corpse of a man still standing. Eventually he fell, rigid and straight, leaning forward diagonally until gravity won out and he slammed onto the floor of the field.

Only then did Jin-Tak start to move. Only then did he carefully inspect his tool, take it apart, pack it away, and pull out the much more mobile field weapon – the assault rifle he had been carrying on his back.

Only then did he stand and begin descending the ridge toward the group of villagers and the shocked group of people standing next to them.

82
SHANE

SHANE WATCHED the man descend into the wide valley and start walking in their direction. He moved quickly, smoothly. The man did not seem frantic, upset, surprised. He carried an assault rifle slung over one shoulder, and Shane saw a longer zipped bag on his back. Likely where he stowed his longer rifle, the one he'd used to shoot Grudowski.

Shane frowned into the sunlight as he stared on. Michaela was by his side, her hand in his. He didn't shift, didn't move. He let it hang there, frozen in place just as he felt frozen in time. The only thing moving was the man — the shooter, no doubt.

The guy was a good shot, too. The lack of wind in the valley and the easy daylight would have proven no challenge for a professional sniper — but only for a professional. Shane assumed this man must be military trained. Good conditions or not, it was a long shot, and he had made it flawlessly.

And just in time, too.

Shane swallowed, finally removing his hand from Michaela's. He stepped forward, toward the dead mercenary. He picked up his pace, noticing the sniper moving toward him quicker now as well.

He crouched, grabbing Grudowski's weapon and hoisting it. He checked the magazine quickly, his eyes never leaving the newcomer's face, never moving them away from the man approaching. Finally, he pulled the rifle up to his shoulder and aimed down the sights.

"Go ahead and stop there," he shouted.

The man halted, raising his hands above his head, not reaching for the assault rifle he carried on a shoulder. Still, if this were some sort of trick,

Shane knew the distance would be in the other man's favor, not his. Shane might be able to get off a few bursts, but this man could easily start running farther away, sidestepping all of them to find an approach with enough distance between them for Shane's rifle to become useless.

Then they would once again be sitting ducks.

Shane's squint deepened, his brow furrowed as he considered the angles. No, this didn't seem like a trap. The guy was trained, obviously. Which meant he knew very well he was changing the status quo by approaching them. He would know Shane knew how to handle his own weapon, and he would know that by coming closer he was putting his own life at risk.

Plus, he had taken off the head of the biggest threat around. The mercenary lay dead on the ground behind Shane, while the group of villagers had moved off to the side, corralling again by the tree he had first seen Michaela and Seong run toward. If they were going to continue their attack, Shane didn't see how they would be much of a threat. He was armed, they knew it, and they seemed to lose interest in killing them after he and Evans had rescued Seong and Michaela from the fray.

He noted their presence, forcing himself to keep an eye on them, but he wasn't sensing any threat from them anymore.

The only potential threat, was directly in front of him.

The man's face came into view now, his darkened skin revealing its features.

Shane gasped. He inadvertently stepped back, clutching the rifle tighter. "What do you want?" Shane asked.

He immediately cursed himself. *What a stupid thing to say.* This man obviously didn't want to kill them or he would have done it already. And it's not like he would tell them the truth anyway, if he had come here for nefarious purposes.

"I want to tell you the truth," the man said.

Shane's eyebrows flicked upward briefly. *Well, that's a good start.*

Michaela joined him, positioning herself directly behind him. He wanted to tell her to stay back, but realized once more how exposed they all were. It didn't matter where they stood – they were all still very much in the line of fire if this man chose to attack again.

"Okay, tell me the truth then."

The man stepped one foot forward and raised his own eyebrow, then stared hard at Shane. "May I?"

Shane motioned with the rifle, shrugging, but kept it pointed at the sniper. The man walked a few paces forward, positioning himself right within Shane's sweet spot before stopping again.

He's definitely trained, Shane thought. *And he's keenly aware of where he's standing.*

He wasn't sure if that gave him hope that this guy was telling the truth, or caused him trepidation that the guy wasn't at all scared for his own life.

"Sorry to bring the place down on your head," the man said.

"You didn't," Shane snapped. "The assholes that built this place had it rigged to explode. That communications tower that used to be on top was set to receive the signal. But I took down the whole array – at least, I thought I did."

The man nodded slowly. "You did, but it was unnecessary..."

"For a while, it seemed to work. There was a countdown timer. Not only did we make it out in time, but whatever I did shut off the tower from receiving the signal."

The man smiled. "You did, and again, I apologize. The communications array was unnecessary because I sent the signal myself. *Locally.* I was close enough that it got through without needing to bounce from the tower."

Shane's grip on the rifle tightened.

"As I said, I'm sorry. I didn't know you were inside. It wasn't my goal to kill you – or her."

Shane swallowed. "Do you know who she is?"

"Seong Park," the man answered without hesitation. "Genetic engineer and scientist. She was crucial to their plans. At least, what she knew was."

"Seemed like she was more of a prisoner than someone they enlisted to help," Shane said.

The man nodded again, taking another step forward. Shane tensed, but the man's posture seemed to change, as if deflating. "My name is Jin-Tak Yeon. I've made mistakes. Some assumptions I should not have made. Namely, that my interests were aligned with the people here." As he spoke, he motioned over his head at the pile of rubble in the distance. "This facility has been here for a long time. My entire life, in fact."

"Since the Nazi era, I presume," Shane said.

"Yes, but I meant the research they were conducting here – they've been doing it since before I was born."

"You were working with them, obviously. You kidnapped us and were going to bring us to them. That's how you know everything that's going on?"

"I was working with them. I have been for a long time. But no, I know of this place because it has been a part of my life forever. I was born here. In the same village these people are from."

SHANE HEARD Michaela gasp next to him. She stepped forward. "You – you were born here? You're one of these... villagers?"

A quick expression of shame or regret crossed Jin-Tak's face, but the trained soldier shook it off quickly. He nodded once. "Their village is a shell of what it used to be. These people are hardly the people I grew up with. But yes, I was born there. They recruited me, eight years old, trained me, then sent me to the Army for even more training. I served, then came back and discovered that they had taken my whole family. My brother and sister, my mother, all dead. My father, they said, was sick."

"Sick how?"

Jin-Tak shook his head. "A disease... it doesn't matter. They made it up. All of it; I know now it was all lies. At the time, I was angry. They told me my family died from the strange element that seems to plague our people. Elders in the village even talked about times before the sickness, before there was any hope. They would always speak highly of the people at the facility. Said their ways were crude but effective. That if we submitted, they would heal us."

Shane nodded slowly. "They used your father as bait. To solidify you to their cause."

His reply was solemn. "Exactly. I believed he was here, somewhere inside this facility. Of course, they never showed me. Just pictures, showed me him suffering, of the work they were doing and the results that made me believe they were making progress."

"The prion disease," Michaela said suddenly. "The cure they were working on – I thought it was real."

Jin-Tak nodded again. "It's real, but the disease was manufactured here. They used my village and my family and friends as lab rats. Forced us to give them our bodies to make progress toward their goals. They took our eyes."

"Not yours, though."

"Not mine. I had another journey, another destiny. As I said, they chose me at a young age. I was angry but smart. They honed that, turned me into a killer. They needed me to be able to see, to be able to... work."

"I see," Shane said. "So you served, learned how to be a soldier, a sniper, learned English, then came back to do their bidding. You've been protecting them for all these years."

He nodded. "I was misled. Made mistakes. But I've made my last mistake with them. I brought this place to the ground because they abandoned it. They were going to continue their research elsewhere. I figured if I detonated the explosives they planted, whatever research they left here would be gone."

"But they already left before you did it," Shane said. "This place was a ghost town. They killed the rest of the subjects, murdered them point blank then hightailed it out of here. They left her behind, too."

"They did," Jin-Tak said. The look of regret had returned. His arms fell to his sides, and he sighed deeply. "I believe they will try to continue their work. They've been working on a disease that affects only a subset of the population. They've developed a cure that works, but it's not perfect yet. I believe they will continue working on it somewhere else."

"Where?" Shane asked.

His head swung side to side. "That I do not know. But I can find out. I will find out. It is my calling now, my vocation. I was helping them, protecting them. Now I will make it my life's work to root them out wherever they might be."

Shane considered this for a long moment, chewing the inside of his lip as he squinted at the North Korean soldier. For the first time he saw how tired the man seemed. A weary look in his eyes, as if he had lived a thousand lives, all of them hard. "I can help, but –"

The man held up a hand. "This isn't your fight. You've done enough. You need to get her back home, too. She has more work to do."

Seong stepped over and greeted the man in Korean, then changed to English for Shane and Evans' sake. "He's right, Mr. Riley," Seong said. "I understand why I was brought here – they used me to get to my father. But he's right in that there is more work to be done. I tried to warn your wife, because she was doing the exact sort of work they wanted from me. They wanted to get what she knew, to help their cause. Or..."

She didn't finish the sentence.

"Or kill her," Shane said.

No one spoke for a moment. Park's eyes fell. She nodded. "This man will find them, and I will make sure their research never sees the light of day. They may think they are close to achieving their goals, but I assure you — they are missing a key component. I can find that, because I know where to look."

Shane knew she was referring to something in the human genome — something he couldn't understand.

"And I can help with that," Michaela said. "But we do need to get out of the country and back to South Korea first."

Shane glanced from one to the other, before the man spoke again. "I can help you," the man said. "I have connections for that, if you can trust me."

JONATHAN EVANS SAT QUIETLY in the back of the transport vehicle. The truck bounced over ruts, like traversing a battle-torn field. Every small bump lurched him sideways, reigniting the pain from his gunshot wound.

But he had been patched up well, hours ago at the tiny field clinic Jin-Tak had taken them to. They all rode in the same truck Shane and Michaela had been kidnapped in — a hilarious sight, since the tires had been shot out earlier. Thankfully, those tires were rubber-core tires, and could not reach high speeds anyway. Still, they bounded over the potholes and ruts in the road extra slowly. Jin-Tak drove, with Shane Riley in the front seat. Evans, Michaela, and Seong bunched their knees up and smashed together in the truck's bed. The going had been slow, Jin-Tak driving carefully so as not to reopen Evans' coagulating wound.

Once at the small hospital, a kind North Korean nurse who didn't ask questions helped Jin-Tak patch him up.

It turned out that most North Korean civilians didn't ask questions. While they got strange looks due to their obviously foreign appearance, none of the people they interacted with in the hospital or afterwards so much as raised questions about what they were doing in North Korea.

Evans knew why. No one wanted to cause undue scrutiny, or bring down attention from the People's Army on their shoulders, no one dared to meddle. As it turned out, fear was Evans' and his group's best asset, the ally he didn't think they would have.

Their luck had continued after leaving the clinic an hour later. Jin-Tak

Yeon had found a convoy of army trucks – three in all, led and trailed by two smaller jeeps, passing through the region just south of Miyeon. He apparently had some clout with those in power in the North Korean government, and another 15 minutes passed before they were all bundled into the back of one of the trucks.

Evans didn't know what Yeon had said, but judging by the zip ties he and the others were wearing, he assumed Yeon had convinced the Army personnel he was extraditing prisoners from North Korea. Whatever he had told them, it seemed to work. Yeon sat across from him now, unflinching.

The one time he tried to ask Jin-Tak Yeon a question, a North Korean soldier yelled for him to keep his mouth shut. It didn't bode well that they had put their trust in a man who had kidnapped them, hunted them, and killed two of their teammates — but they felt they'd had no other choice.

Besides, they weren't dead yet. Evans assumed there was at least a *chance* Yeon would come through for them after all.

But he couldn't help letting his mind race with thoughts of how they might escape, should the need arise. He kept his guard up, focusing on the three men in the back of the truck who could potentially betray them. The two soldiers, obviously, would follow whatever orders they got from anyone they deemed superior or higher ranking than they were.

But Yeon was the unknown.

He had already killed two of Evans' men – one back on the ridge before reaching the North Korean facility, the other more recently. Evans knew Yeon was capable, a man who certainly could kill him. Evans was in no shape to fight, and Yeon would certainly make short work of him.

But he trusted Riley. He hadn't before, but Riley had come back for him, had made things right. That was more than enough in Evans' book – that sort of thing was a characteristic ingrained into him from childhood. That Shane Riley was literally a world apart from him in so many ways, yet had come back, risking his own life along the way, just to save a man who should have already been dead, told him everything.

And he knew Shane could fight. If Jin-Tak tried anything back here, he was positive Shane had a plan already. He was positive the ex-soldier had worked out enough ways to kill the people in the back of the truck; he would have options to spare.

He knew that because it was what he was doing now. He looked up, catching Shane's eyes. The special forces operative had not taken kindly to the idea of having his hands bound, either. But he, Jin-Tak, and Evans had all shared a knowing glance before marching down to the convoy. Zip ties were hardly enough to keep a full-grown adult — much less a trained soldier — at bay. By holding the wrists together tightly, separating the elbows, and then slamming them down onto the top of their thighs, the zip ties would break easily on the first try.

Evans remembered his own training years ago, the practice he had done proving just this. He had taught other men as well, working out ways to break free from all sorts of bonds, including zip ties like these.

But being able to break zip ties wasn't the point. They were all acting, pretending to be prisoners of Jin-Tak Yeon as he extradited them from North Korea. The journey would take over six hours, only if they stayed on highways and major thoroughfares. Yeon had assured them they wouldn't be stopping at any bases or checkpoints along the way, as these convoys were usually regular supply caravans sent down to the DMZ.

The truth of that lay at Evans' feet. Dozens of smaller boxes and crates had been arranged on the floor of the truck. Straps had been thrown over the tops of the piles, collecting them and holding them together for the bumpy ride. The seats had been left open, and the six soldiers inside this truck had all moved, save for the two guarding them now, split between the other two trucks and jeeps.

So far, Yeon's word had held. But Evans kept an eye on each of the men just in case. They reached a long stretch of highway and the trucks and jeeps accelerated. The engine noise rose in volume, loud enough for Seong and Michaela to talk quietly. They were seated next to one another, next to Jin-Tak Yeon, and his head blocked their faces from view of the other guards.

Evans couldn't hear what they were saying, obviously, but he knew they would be discussing what they had learned about the facility they had just escaped from. They would be talking about the prion disease, its cure, and all the villagers they had left behind.

Jin-Tak Yeon's people. His family and friends, people who had raised him. Evans shuddered as he considered all that he had learned while standing on the field next to the group of crazed villagers. When Jin-Tak had appeared, they had all fallen away, once again docile and harmless. At the time, he had assumed it had been Yeon's sniper rifle they had been scared of, but now he knew the truth.

They *recognized* him, knew him. They had trusted him. Perhaps that was enough for Evans to trust him now. He had saved their hides once already – twice considering Grudowski's betrayal and Yeon's assassination of him — and he was ostensibly trying to do it again. His story checked out, and Evans believed Jin-Tak's words — that he wanted nothing more than to find those responsible for enslaving his village and people.

He took solace in all of those facts.

He let out a deep sigh, for the first time in over 24 hours feeling a bit of relief. Their mission was done – their job successful. Sure, they still needed to get out of the country, but every mile they marched on, he felt confident they would do just that.

TRUE TO HIS WORD, Jin-Tak Yeon led the group towards the demilitarized zone that separated the contentious North and South Korea. There they passed through a minor North Korean checkpoint, an inconspicuous, flat building, set against the vast expanse of the desolate terrain. The checkpoint was embodied by a single, unassuming building, guarded by a handful of watchful soldiers whose steely gazes scanned the horizon in anticipation of some elusive adversary.

Stretching across a menacing crevasse that acted as a natural, hostile separator between the two countries was a drawbridge, the only pathway out of the North Korean territory.

The convoy leader hopped out of the jeep, heading towards the building that housed the checkpoint controls. In the meantime, Jin-Tak was busy orchestrating the exodus of the Westerners from the confines of the truck. His movements were quick, driven by an unspoken urgency that Shane immediately picked up on as he climbed down from the vehicle.

Breaking the tense silence, Yeon leaned in, whispering quickly, "The people I worked for... they'll know about what happened by now. They'll know I'm the culprit. I suspect we have less than an hour before they broadcast the alert and the entire army is on my tail."

Shane matched his tone. "Sounds like we better keep moving."

Shane, despite the inconvenience of having his hands bound in front of him, turned and offered his shoulder to assist Michaela down from the truck. He felt the mild irritation of the restraints, but the trust he'd grown to have in

Yeon kept him from snapping the bonds. For now, he'd continue playing the prisoner as long as Yeon played the captor.

Their plan was to slip into South Korea under the guise of captives discovered in the university by Jin-Tak Yeon. Since Jin-Tak was military but connected to a shadowy part of the government that generally drew no questions, they'd managed to evade heavy scrutiny on their journey so far. Shane guessed that lack of scrutiny would continue.

One of the soldiers turned to assist Seong Park out of the truck, before quickly reverting back to his watchful silence, eyes locked on the distant horizon. In this country, it wasn't the fear of the dictator that gripped people; it was the fear of his power, his ability to do whatever he wanted, whenever he wanted. Shane understood that here, one didn't do anything to draw attention to oneself.

It was a rule he was forcing himself to follow.

Shane met Yeon's gaze, giving a quick nod as he fell in line with Evans, Michaela, and Seong. With a gentle push of his rifle, Yeon nudged Shane forward, and the small group began their trek towards the drawbridge.

Every step brought them closer to the border, and to their freedom.

"I UNDERSTAND NOW," she said.

Shane Riley looked across the small table at Michaela Everly. He had always been fond of his late wife's best friend, he had always enjoyed being around her. Her smarts, beauty, her effortless humor. It made Shane want to be a better man.

Kate had had that same effect on him, and looking at Michaela now only made him miss his wife even more.

But there was something different in the air now, something unspoken. He wasn't sure what to call it, how best to phrase it.

He got the sense that it might be better left unsaid.

He played with his mug, savoring the deep, rich chai. He still wasn't much of a tea drinker, but he had to admit, this was good. It was less tea and more spiced hot water.

They had met in the same coffee shop they had been at before, in South Korea near Michaela's house. After escaping North Korea, they had parted ways with Seong Park and others.

Seong would confront her father, putting a plan together to make him answer for his sins. At the same time, she didn't want to hurt him. After all, the man was her father. He had made mistakes, misjudged. It had almost gotten his only daughter killed, and it was the very reason she wanted to confront him.

They had seen how conflicted the young woman was upon leaving her at the train depot just north of town. They had offered to bring her into the fold, to give her a place to stay and get back on her feet. But Seong was strong-willed and capable, more than ready to begin the next chapter of her life. She told them she would be reaching out to a friend of a friend, somebody who had worked for the military of South Korea and was politically opposed to her father.

If she needed muscle, he would be the man to call.

She would also continue researching the prion disease the North Korean government had created. The perpetrators were still at large, but she knew what to look for. She was convinced she could find where they were headed next, where they would regroup. None of them believed they had defeated the North Korean researchers. They would build the program back up again somewhere else, working faster to bring the project to a close.

Jin-Tak swore to Seong Park and the rest that he would be on the trail as well, still having connections to many of the people he had previously worked for. With luck, he would be able to maintain the illusion that he was still working for them, that he had simply been duped by Jonathan Evans and his team.

For his part, Evans had wanted to help others and Seong Park, but he understood that their current mission was over. Their job in North Korea was done. They had taken him to a hospital in Seoul, where he had been patched up, his wounds cleaned even better than what they had done at the small field clinic. He was currently on his way back to the states, needing some time to regroup as well. He had lost a man and he had been betrayed by another, and Shane knew he would be licking his wounds for a while.

Men like Evans took things like this hard – he was a good man, committed and loyal to his team and friends. It wouldn't be easy to compartmentalize their deaths and move on, but he knew Evans would pull through.

As he played with the mug in front of him, Michaela continued.

"I mean, I understand your rule."

"My rule?"

"You don't retrieve people."

He forced a smile but was only able to raise one side of his mouth. "That's just one rule. I also work alone."

"You broke *two* rules on one mission, Shane," Michaela said, smirking. "Is that a record for you?"

"I always heard rules were meant to be broken," he said.

"They're good rules. As I said, I understand them now. You don't retrieve people. You work alone. Anything else besides that gets a little..."

"Complicated."

"Complicated," she confirmed.

"Where did those rules come from, anyway?" she asked. "I'm assuming there's no merit badge for Retrieval Specialist that teaches you all this stuff."

"I wish," Shane said. "It would sure make things a lot easier." He took a sip of tea. "It was a decision I made when I first started doing this. Just seemed like it made sense."

She looked at him then, scrutinizing him where before she had simply been listening and paying attention. He paused, waiting for her next question. "Where were you when you made that call?" she asked.

"Switzerland, actually. My very first time out in the field as an *official* retrieval specialist."

"Official?"

"Well, as official as it could be. It was my first job, or – I guess I should say, I was *trying* to land my first gig. Big art auction type thing, full of rich fancy people. I figured they'd be the type to hire somebody to acquire something for them without getting their hands dirty."

"I see. Did you get the job?" she asked.

He shook his head, smiling. "No, didn't. I had to make a pretty quick exit from the premises, if I recall."

"If you recall..." Michaela said mischievously. "Something tells me you *recall* just fine."

Shane smiled then, more genuinely this time. He pictured the narrow escape from the top of the resort's hotel, the lunge off the edge of the infinity pool situated at the edge of the cliff. The hastily donned BASE jumping suit that miraculously did what it had been designed to do and deposited him safely at the bottom of the valley.

"International Man of Mystery: Shane Riley. Retrieval Specialist. Kinda rolls off the tongue, doesn't it?"

"It does not."

He took the mug of chai and lifted it to his lips, taking a deep sip. When he set it back down, Michaela was leaning forward, her chin resting on her clasped hands.

"I've got another mission for you, Shane," she said.

He arched an eyebrow.

"I know you said you don't retrieve people, but..."

"Michaela, if this is about me and you..."

She stopped. He didn't say more, and neither did she. For a few excruciating seconds, it looked as if she was going to cry. She reached out suddenly and grabbed his hand that he had let rest on the table.

It was warm, soft.

Comfortable.

"Michaela, I –"

"I *love* you, Shane. I'm sorry... I don't think I've always loved you, and I would *never* do this to Kate on purpose. But I just need to say it. I just need to come clean or I'm going to kick myself for the rest of my life."

"I..."

"I don't need you to say anything," she said. "Really. I just know that when you leave here, you're going to try to disappear. You're going to fall off the face of the earth again, and I know damn well I may never see you again, Shane. So regardless of how *you* feel, I need you to know how *I* feel."

There was a question in her words, an inflection. He stared at her, then let his eyes fall down to his mug.

When he looked back up, tears moistened the corners of her eyes, one collecting and rolling down her cheek. Her voice was a mere whisper. "Can you just... can you just promise me something?"

He raised his eyebrows even higher.

"Can you just come back for me? When you're done with whatever it is you need to do, can you promise me you'll find me? Promise me that no matter where I am in the world, you'll find me when you're ready."

"Michaela —" he started, then stopped himself. He was choked up, trying to hold back tears himself. "Michaela, I came out here for *closure*. I came out here to understand my wife's death. To find peace."

He had a feeling she knew where he was going with this, but it didn't matter. He needed to say it.

"But I didn't find that, at all. I'm no more at peace than I was a week ago. I just – I just can't understand any of this right now, so..."

"Don't say it."

"No."

Their eyes met once again as the barista walked by, noticed their emotional state, then kept moving.

Shane continued. "No, I can't promise you that. I wish I could..., at least, I *think* I wish that. But I just can't. Michaela, you're a huge part of my life. The closest person I've got. But you're also the closest remaining thing I have to Kate. I hear you, I truly do – it's just that I can't make a promise like that. And I don't expect you to understand, I just –"

"I do understand."

Her words were short, clipped, and she was biting back sobs. Still, she had forced herself through them. When she'd finished, she nodded once, then stood up.

"Michaela, let's just –"

She pushed her chair back and stepped away from the table. She turned around, facing the doorway to the small coffee shop.

As he sat, his mouth hanging open, his own tears now flowing freely, he watched as Dr. Michaela Everly walked out of his life.

###

Enjoyed this one?
Keep the fun going with Shane Riley Adventures, Book #2!

AFTERWORD

If you liked this book (or even if you hated it...) write a review or rate it. You might not think it makes a difference, but it does.

Besides *actual* currency (money), the currency of today's writing world is *reviews*. Reviews, good or bad, tell other people that an author is worth reading.

As an "indie" author, I need all the help I can get. I'm hoping that since you made it this far into my book, you have some sort of opinion on it.

Would you mind sharing that opinion? It only takes a second.

Nick Thacker

Six Assassins Thrillers

Primary Target (Book 1)

Subtle Target (Book 2)

Unstable Target (Book 3)

Captive Target (Book 4)

Vendetta Target (Book 5)

Final Target (Book 6)

Mason Dixon Thrillers

Mark for Blood (Book 1)

Death Mark (Book 2)

Mark My Words (Book 3)

Harvey Bennett Mysteries

The Enigma Strain (Book 1)

The Amazon Code (Book 2)

The Ice Chasm (Book 3)

The Jefferson Legacy (Book 4)

The Paradise Key (Book 5)

The Atlantis Artifact (Book 6)

The Book of Bones (Book 7)

The Cain Conspiracy (Book 8)

The Mendel Paradox (Book 9)

The Minoan Manifest (Book 10)

The Napoleon Job (Book 11)

The Embers of Siwa (Book 12)

The Epsilon Event (Book 13)

The Cerberus Protocol (Book 14)

The Russian Betrayal (Book 15)

Harvey Bennett Mysteries - Books 1-3

Harvey Bennett Mysteries - Books 4-6

Harvey Bennett Mysteries - Books 7-9

Harvey Bennett Prequels

The Icarus Effect (written with MP MacDougall)

The Severed Pines (written with Jim Heskett)

The Lethal Bones (written with Jim Heskett)

Gareth Red Thrillers

Seeing Red

Chasing Red (written with Kevin Ikenberry)

The Lucid

The Lucid: Episode One (written with Kevin Tumlinson)

The Lucid: Episode Two (written with Kevin Tumlinson)

The Lucid: Episode Three (written with Kevin Tumlinson

Standalone Thrillers

The Atlantis Stone

The Depths

Relics: A Post-Apocalyptic Technothriller

Killer Thrillers (3-Book Box Set)

Short Stories

I, Sergeant

Instinct

The Gray Picture of Dorian

Uncanny Divide (written with Kevin Tumlinson and Will Flora)

Nick Thacker is a thriller author from Texas who lives in Hawaii and Colorado. In his free time, he enjoys reading in a hammock on the beach, skiing, drinking whiskey, and hanging out with his beautiful wife, two dogs, and two daughters.

For more information and a list of Nick's other work, visit Nick online:
www.nickthacker.com